the Coldest War

Tor Books by Ian Tregillis

Bitter Seeds
The Coldest War

the coldest war

**VOLUME TWO
OF THE
MILKWEED
TRIPTYCH**

Ian Tregillis

TOR®

A Tom Doherty Associates Book
New York

Tregillis (signature)

THE COLDEST WAR

Copyright © 2012 by Ian Tregillis

All rights reserved.

A Tor Book
Published by Tom Doherty Associates, LLC
175 Fifth Avenue
New York, NY 10010

www.tor-forge.com

Tor® is a registered trademark of Tom Doherty Associates, LLC.

ISBN 978-0-7653-2151-0

First Edition: July 2012

Printed in the United States of America

0 9 8 7 6 5 4 3 2 1

For Melinda, confidant and co-conspirator

Acknowledgments

The Milkweed books would still be nothing more than an idea in the back of my head if not for my friends and colleagues in the New Mexico Critical Mass Workshop: Daniel Abraham, Terry England, Ty Franck, Ed Khmara, Emily Mah, George R. R. Martin, Vic Milán, Melinda M. Snodgrass, Jan Stirling, S. M. Stirling, Sage Walker, and Walter Jon Williams.

Thanks also to Michael Cassutt, for sharing his knowledge of the Soviet space program; S. C. Butler and Char Peery, Ph.D., for critical reading; Felix Dorsch, Andrew Miller, Leonid Korogodski, B. K. Dunn, and Ed Khmara (again) for translations; Michael Prevett, for smart questions; Eliani Torres, for copyediting.

My marvelous agent, Kay McCauley, championed this project (and me) from the beginning. Thank you, Kay.

Last but certainly not least, heartfelt thanks to my editor, Claire Eddy, whose diligence and compassion have been nothing short of inspirational.

Mankind is a rope tied between beast and superman—a rope over an abyss.

—Friedrich Nietzsche

Live with your century but do not be its creature.

—Friedrich Schiller

Thou shalt not suffer a witch to live.

—Exodus 22:18 (KJV)

the Coldest War

prologue

24 April 1963
Forest of Dean, Gloucestershire, England

Warlocks do not age gracefully.

Viktor Sokolov had drawn this conclusion after meeting several warlocks. Now he watched a fourth man from afar, and what he saw supported his conclusion. Age and ruin lay heavy over the figure who emerged from the dilapidated cottage in the distant clearing. The old man hobbled toward a hand pump, an empty pail hanging from the crook of his shriveled arm. Viktor adjusted the focus on his binoculars.

No. Not gracefully at all. Viktor had met one fellow whose skin was riddled by pockmarks; yet another had burn scars across half his face. The least disfigured had lost an ear, and the eye on that side was a sunken, rheumy marble. These men had paid a steep price for the wicked knowledge they carried. Paid it willingly.

This new fellow fit the pattern. But Viktor wouldn't know for certain if he had found the right person until he could get a closer look at the old man's hands. Better to do that in private. He slid the binoculars back into the leather case at his waist, careful not to rustle the mound of bluebells that concealed him.

The clearing was quiet except for the squeaking of rusted metal as the old man labored at the pump, a narrow pipe caked in flaking blue paint. But that noise felt muted somehow, as though suffocated by a thick silence. Viktor hadn't heard or seen a single bird in the hours he'd lain here; even sunrise had come and gone without a peep of birdsong. A breeze drifted across his hiding spot in the underbrush, carrying with it the earthy scents of the forest and the latrine stink of the old man's privy. But the breeze dissipated, as though reluctant to linger among the gnarled oaks.

The old man hobbled back to the cottage. His palsied gait sent water slopping over the brim of the pail. It muddied the path between the cottage and the well.

Wooden shingles rattled when the man slammed the door. Viktor didn't need binoculars to see how the roof sagged. This had likely thrown the doorframe out of true; the single window had probably been stuck closed for years. Sprigs of purple wildflowers poked out of gaps in the shingles here and there, alongside bunches of green and yellow moss.

Raindrops pattered through the trees. Just a sprinkle at first, but it swelled into a persistent drizzle. The cold English rain didn't bother Viktor. He was a patient man.

Another hour passed while Viktor, unconcerned by inclement weather, convinced himself that he and the old man were alone. Satisfied their meeting would be undisturbed; he decided it was time to introduce himself. A dull ache throbbed through his arms and neck; the joints in his knees cracked as he unlimbered himself from his blind.

He strode to the cottage with rainwater trickling through his hair and down his collar. The cottage rattled again when Viktor knocked on the door, three quick raps with his fist. The man inside responded with a startled oath. Like the others, he guarded his solitude jealously, and discouraged visitors.

The creak of a wooden chair and shambling footsteps sounded from within. The door groaned open a moment later.

"Sod off," said the old man. His voice carried an unpleasant rasp, as though the soft tissues of his throat had been damaged by years of abuse. He made to slam the door again, but Viktor caught it and held it open.

"Mr. Shapley?" he said in his best Midlands accent. He offered his free hand, but the old man ignored the gesture.

"This is private property. Go away."

"I will in a moment. But first, are you Mr. Shapley?"

"Yes. Now piss off." Shapley tried the door again.

Viktor said, "Not yet," then forced his way in.

Shapley backed away, bumping against an aluminum washbasin. "Who are you?"

Viktor shut the door behind him. It was dark inside the cottage, with mustard-colored light leaking through the dingy window. He crossed the room and grabbed the old man's arm. He towered over Shapley, inspecting first his good hand, followed by the crippled hand.

"What are you doing? Let me go." The old man struggled feebly.

A network of fine white scars crisscrossed the palm of the crippled hand. That clinched it: This man *was* a warlock. Viktor's informant, whoever he or she was, had been right again.

"Excellent," said Viktor. He relinquished his hold on the other man.

"Look," said Shapley. "If you've come from Whitehall, I'm not—"

"Shhh," said Viktor, with a finger to his lips. "Stand still, please."

And then he opened that locked compartment in his mind, and called upon the battery at his waist. A subtle alteration to the voltages in his brain pulled a trickle of current along the subcutaneous electrical pathways embedded along his back, neck, and skull. It energized that potential the Nazis had called the *Willenskräfte:* sheer, undiluted human willpower. A supreme ability with which the Third Reich could have conquered the world.

And they would have, too, if not for the warlocks.

Viktor dematerialized. He reached into Shapley's chest. Shapley screamed. But by then Viktor had his fingers wrapped around the old man's heart. He massaged it gently, confounding the muscle's natural rhythm until Shapley's nervous system panicked itself into fibrillation. The wide-eyed warlock flailed at Viktor, trying to push him away, but his blows passed harmlessly through Viktor's ghost body. Only Viktor's fingertips, locked around the old man's failing heart, had any substance.

They stood in that awkward posture until Viktor felt the final spasms of cardiac arrest. Then he released the warlock, rematerialized, and cleaned his hand on the kerchief in his jacket pocket. The floorboards gave a hollow thump when Shapley collapsed at Viktor's feet.

It would have been much simpler just to shoot the man from a distance. But that would have left evidence. Viktor would take care to ensure there was enough left of Shapley's remains on which to perform a proper autopsy; in the unlikely event that somebody took an interest in the old man's death, they would find that the poor fellow had died of natural causes.

Viktor stepped over the dead man and inspected the cottage. The single room had been crudely divided into two spaces via a wool blanket hung on a clothesline. Pulling the blanket aside revealed a cot and bed stand strewn with a handful of personal items. A watch, a comb, a few coins. A kerosene lamp hung from a nail in the far wall. A squat, cast-iron wood-burning stove occupied one corner of the cottage, alongside the washbasin. The only other pieces of furniture were the chair and table in the center of the room, and the rough-hewn bookcase propped against one wall.

The dead man had owned few books, but he had used them extensively: a dog-eared natural history of the Lake District; a few heavily annotated treatises on Old and Middle English; and Shirer's *Rise and Fall of the Third Reich*. Most of that was pristine, though the sections covering 1940 to 1942 were scribbled with extensive marginalia.

A lacquered mahogany case not much larger than a deck of playing cards caught his attention. Even under a thick layer of dust, it was still the finest thing in this sad little hovel. Viktor opened it. Inside the case, a six-pointed bronze star rested on a bed of crimson velvet. The 1939–1942 Star. An inscription inside the lid stated,

FOR EXEMPLARY SERVICE AND VALOR IN THE DEFENCE OF THE
UNITED KINGDOM OF GREAT BRITAIN AND NORTHERN IRELAND.

Which was probably true as far as it went, Viktor mused, if a bit misleading. Most of these medals had gone to the few handfuls of pilots who had weathered the disastrous Battle of Britain, or the minuscule number of soldiers who had survived the tragedy at Dunkirk. . . . Britain had indulged in a bit of historical revisionism in the decades since the war. It had distorted the narrative, adopted a fiction that assuaged its wounded national pride and gave meaning to its incomprehensible—and improbable—survival.

Shapley had been no soldier, no sailor, no pilot. He'd probably never handled a gun in his life. He and his colleagues had wielded something much more potent. Much more dangerous.

Any evidence of which was conspicuously absent from Shapley's belongings. Viktor glanced around the room again, then turned his attention to where the old man had fallen. One of the gaps between the floorboards was slightly wider than the rest, perhaps just wide enough for a finger. He dragged the dead warlock aside, then opened the hatch.

The compartment under the floor contained several leather-bound journals along with one yellowed, wire-bound sheaf of paper. These were the warlock's personal notebooks, and his lexicon: the record of that chthonic language with which warlocks could summon demons and subvert the natural order of things.

Viktor set the journals and the lexicon on the table. Next, he took the kerosene lamp and arranged Shapely's body as though the old man had suffered a heart attack while lighting it. The key thing was that the death looked natural. Then he embraced his *сила воли,* his "will-power," again. But he invoked a different manifestation this time, choosing heat rather than insubstantiality. Tongues of fire erupted from the floor next to the lamp, near Shapley's body. Viktor shaped the flames with his mind, sculpting the inevitable conclusion that any investigators would draw.

The cold English rain sizzled and steamed on Viktor Sokolov as he began the long walk back to his car.

24 April 1963
East Ham, London, England

Children called him Junkman. But he had been a god once.

They called him Junkman because of his tatty clothing, his shabby auto, his scruffy beard. But most of all, they called him Junkman because of his cart, piled high with odds and ends, broken radios and other electronic bric-a-brac. He hoarded junk. And that was the definition of a Junkman.

He never spoke. Not that any of the children had ever heard, not even the oldest ones. He couldn't, they said. His throat had been cut by Hitler himself, or Mussolini, or Stalin, or de Gaulle, they said. This they knew with great certainty, the kind of certainty that can be found only on the playground, sworn upon with crossed hearts and spit and the threat of dire retribution. But common wisdom held that if Junkman could speak, it would be with a French accent, like many of the refugees who had crossed the Channel to escape the Red Army in the closing days of the war.

They were wrong. His English was excellent. Flawless, without a hint of accent. He had been proud of this, once.

He spent most of his time secluded in his tiny flat. None of the children knew what he did in there, though one boy had found the courage—on a solemn dare—to follow him all the way across the council estate to his building and his floor. He caught a glimpse of Junkman's home as the man slipped inside with his clattering cart. The flat was filled, said the intrepid scout, with junk. Piles and piles of it, some almost reaching to the ceiling.

Sometimes their parents paid Junkman to repair their radios and televisions. He was good at it. Their appliances would disappear into his lightless den for a day or three, and emerge working not quite good as new. Repairing things was how he paid for food and his tatty clothing and his dingy flat.

Sometimes Junkman ventured out with a newspaper tucked under his arm. Sometimes he'd be gone all day, returning in the evening—or sometimes even the next day—the boot of his auto filled with more scrap. When this happened, the children followed him down the long service road from the car park as he wheeled his new prizes back to his flat. The *skreep-skreep-skreep* of his cart called to them like the Pied Piper's flute.

"Junk man!" they jeered. "Garbage man!" they called. "Junk man, garbage man, rubbish bin man!"

For the most part, they threw only taunts and jeers at him. But the children remembered the winter a few years earlier, an especially cold season when snow had lasted on the ground for weeks at a time. (But not nearly so cold as the hellish winter that had broken the Nazis, said their parents.) That winter somebody had taken the idea of punctuating their insults with snowballs. And so, on this particular day, they armed themselves with clods of earth made muddy by intermittent spring rains.

Junkman struggled to direct his cart across the slippery pavement. And still he never spoke, not even when the mud splattered against his cart and knocked down a spool of wire. This emboldened the children. They aimed for Junkman, whooping with glee as they unleashed mud and scorn.

Until one boy hit Junkman square in the forehead. It knocked him down, shook off his trilby hat and tousled his wig. A *wig*! Peals of laughter.

Junkman scrambled to regain his hat. He ran his fingers over his head and his ridiculous hairpiece, again and again, delicately, as though worried his skull had been cracked. And then, after apparently reassuring himself that his head was still attached, he stomped over to the boy who'd made that throw.

The children fell silent. They'd never taken a close look at Junkman before. They had never seen his eyes: the palest blue, colder than icicles. Junkman had always kept them downcast.

Junkman lifted the boy by the collar of his coat, lifted him clear off the ground. First, he shook the boy, and that was frightening enough. Junkman was sure to kill them all, they thought. But then he pulled the boy close and whispered in his ear. Nobody heard what he said, but the boy lost the flush on his cheeks, and trembled when Junkman set him down again.

Nobody followed Junkman back to his flat that day. The others crowded around the crying boy. He was, after all, the only child in the entire council estate ever to hear Junkman's voice. "What did he say?" they demanded. "What did he tell you?"

" 'You'll burn,' " he sobbed. "He said, 'You'll all burn.' "

But worse than what Junkman said was how he said it.

He called himself Richard, a self-taught electrician from Woking. But he had been Reinhardt, the Aryan salamander, once.

He lived in a vast, soulless council estate. One of countless housing projects that had sprung up throughout London in the years after the war, when much of the city still lay flattened by the Luftwaffe.

Reinhardt wiped the mud from his face as best he could, though it was wet and sloppy. It stung his eyes. He manhandled his cart into the lift, one eye clenched shut and the other barely slitted open. He breathed a sigh of relief when he made it to his flat and bolted the door behind him.

He tossed his coat on a crate of electrical valves, stepped on a cockroach before kicking his galoshes into a corner behind the soldering equipment, flung his hat across the room to where it landed on the flat's only empty chair, and then carefully peeled off his sodden hairpiece. He never ventured outside without one, and after living secretly for so many years, the thought of leaving his wires exposed to the world gave him a frisson of anxiety. As did the possibility those miserable whelps outside had caused damage.

The wires had frayed over the years. The cloth insulation wasn't suited to decades in the field. But of course, that had never been the intent; if things had gone the way they were meant to, Reinhardt and the others would have had ample access to replacements and upgrades. He inspected the wires daily, wrapping them with new electrical tape as needed. But he would never be able to fix damage to the sockets where the wires entered his skull. It was hard enough to *see* the sockets, sifting through his hair while holding a mirror in the bathroom. If the children had damaged those, Reinhardt's dream of recovering his godhood would be permanently extinguished.

To think he might have endured so many humiliations, countless degradations, only to have his goal rendered unreachable by a single child . . . Another unwelcome reminder of how far he had fallen. Of how vulnerable he had become. How *mundane*. But the wires and sockets were undamaged.

Reinhardt breathed a deeper sigh of relief; it ended with a shudder and a sob. He struggled to compose himself, to draw upon an emotional Willenskräfte, while secretly glad Doctor von Westarp wasn't there to observe his weakness.

There had been a time when he could have—*would* have—torched the little monsters outside with a single thought. Back when he had been the pinnacle of German science and technology, something more than a man. Terrible miracles had been his specialty.

Dinner was a bowl of white rice with tomato and, as a treat to himself, the rest of a bockwurst he'd been saving in the icebox. It lifted his spirits, reminded him of home. In the earliest years of his exile, when London still carried fresh scars from the Blitz, German food couldn't be found for any price. That was changing, but slowly.

After dinner, he sorted through the odds and ends he'd brought home. He'd been gone for two days, and assaulted by the little bastards who infested this place when he returned, but it was worth it. The Royal Air Force had decommissioned an outpost down near Newchurch, one of the original Chain Home stations dating from the war. It was one of the last to be replaced with a more modern and sophisticated radar post that could peer deeper into Socialist Europe. Such posts would provide a futile first warning if a wave of Ilyushin bombers and their MiG escorts started heading for Britain.

The decommissioned radar station had meant a wealth of electronic equipment practically free for the taking, pence on the pound. The sensitive equipment had been carted away long before any civilians set foot on the premises. But Reinhardt didn't care about any of that—it would have been the high-frequency circuitry, microwave generators, and other esoteric things. What Reinhardt sought was also esoteric, but wouldn't be found in a newspaper advertisement.

He'd snatched up condensers, valves, inductors, relays, and more.

An excellent haul, even better than the estate sale of the deceased ham radio enthusiast. He'd even found a few gauges, which would serve him well when he re-created the Reichsbehörde battery-circuit design.

When. Not if.

Reverse engineering the damn thing was a painful process. He had learned, through trial and error, how to induce hallucinations, indigestion, convulsions. . . .

He mused to himself, bitterly, that he had collected nearly enough equipment to build his own radar outpost. How ironic. Radar was touted as one of the great technological innovations of the last war, but Reinhardt himself was the greatest of all. Yet in all the years since the war had ended, he had failed to recapture the Götterelektron.

Then again, Herr Doktor von Westarp had enjoyed the resources of the Third Reich at his disposal. The IG Farben conglomerate had assigned teams of chemists, metallurgists, and engineers to the devices that had fueled Reinhardt's feats of superhuman willpower.

But Reinhardt did not have IG Farben at his disposal. It didn't even exist any longer.

They had always called them "batteries," but that was misleading. They held a charge, yes, but Reinhardt had deduced over the years that they also contained specialized circuitry tailored to deliver the Götterelektron in precisely the correct manner.

The accumulated detritus of his quest had transformed his flat into a cave. Most of it he had purchased or scavenged, but some came from the work he did repairing televisions and radios. It was demeaning work, but even gods had to eat. Sometimes he lied, claiming the device was beyond repair, and then kept the parts.

Reinhardt stored his journals in a hollow behind the gurgling radiator. When he had first come to England, he'd had no training in electronics, nor in the scientific method, for that matter. He'd been raised by one of the greatest minds of the century, but he'd never bothered to pay any attention to how Doctor von Westarp worked. And for that, he cursed himself frequently.

The journals contained hundreds of circuit diagrams accompanied by lengthy annotations describing Reinhardt's experiences with each.

But none of those circuits had elicited anything like the tingle of the Götterelektron. Reinhardt retrieved the latest journal, opened it to a new page, then settled down at his workbench (a discarded wooden door laid across two sawhorses).

Hours passed.

It was some time after midnight when Reinhardt, bleary-eyed and exhausted, abandoned his efforts for the evening. He brushed his teeth. Then he brushed them a second time, and his tongue, too, trying vainly to scrub the odd taste from his mouth.

A metallic tang.

Reinhardt had all but forgotten it: the copper taste, that harmless but annoying side effect of godhood.

He tossed his toothbrush in the sink and rushed back to the bench, where the evening's final experiment still stood. He worked backwards through everything he had done, searching for the combination that had coated his tongue with the taste of metal. Beads of sweat ran down his forehead, stung his eyes with salt as he trembled with the exertion of calling up his Willenskräfte. Nothing happened.

But then—

—a blue corona engulfed his outstretched hand, just for an instant—

—and died.

Strive as he might, he couldn't call it back. But it had *happened*. He had *felt* the Götterelektron coursing into his mind, fueling his willpower. He tasted copper, and smelled smoke.

Smoke?

Reinhardt thought at first he had inadvertently started his flat on fire owing to rustiness and a lack of finesse. But no. A faulty condenser had shorted out. Reinhardt realized that as it had died, its electrical characteristics had changed in some random, unpredictable way. Changed in a way that had, just for a moment, returned his power to him.

Children called him Junkman. But he had been a god, once.

And would be again.

one

1 May 1963
Arzamas-16, Nizhny Novgorod Oblast, USSR

Gretel laid a fingertip on Klaus's arm.

"Wait," she whispered.

Several seconds passed while she consulted some private time line that existed only in her head. He recognized the look on her face: she was remembering the future, peering a few seconds ahead.

Then she said, "Now, brother."

Klaus pulled the merest trickle of current from his stolen battery, just enough of the Götterelektron to dematerialize his hand. It was a gamble, one Gretel had assured him would work. But he'd practiced for weeks.

His hand ghosted through ferro-concrete. He wrapped his fingers around one of the bolts that sealed the vault. Klaus concentrated, focusing his Willenskräfte like a scalpel, and pulled a finger's width of steel through the wall. Gretel caught the slug before it clattered to the floor and gave them away.

They repeated the process twice. Klaus severed all three bolts, and the alarm circuit, in fifteen seconds. But the damage to the door was strictly internal; a passing guard would see nothing but pristine, unblemished steel.

It would have been easier for Klaus to walk straight through the wall with his sister in tow. But that would have tripped sensors and triggered their captors' fail-safes before he was halfway through. The entire facility, this secret city the locals called Sarov, bristled with antennae and circuitry attuned to the telltale whisper of the Götterelektron. Unauthorized expression of the Willenskräfte instantly triggered the electromagnetic equivalent of a shaped charge. The British had developed a crude precursor to this technology back during the war; they'd called their devices "pixies," and they had a range of a few hundred meters. The Soviet fail-safes could knock out a battery at six kilometers. Klaus knew the specs because he'd helped them test the system. He'd had no choice.

Gretel never worried about the fail-safes. Klaus stood on the cusp of fifty (according to his best estimate; he and his sister had been war orphans) and yet he still didn't know how or when Gretel called upon the Götterelektron to see the future. He suspected she relied upon batteries far less than she let their captors believe, and not when they thought she was using them. It had been that way back home in Germany, too.

They eased the vault door closed after slipping inside. Klaus groped for the light switch. Sickly yellow light cascaded from the naked bulb overhead, chasing shadows past rows of cabinets and shelves. A musty smell permeated the vault; their footsteps kicked up swirls of dust. The Soviets still referred to this place, almost reverently, as ALPHA. But they came here rarely these days.

The cabinets contained papers the Soviets had obtained during their lightning-fast occupation of the old REGP, the Reichsbehörde für die Erweiterung Germanischen Potenzials; the shelves held physical artifacts from Doctor von Westarp's farm, where the Reichsbehörde had lived and died.

Gretel and Klaus sought the batteries their captors had confiscated at the end of the war. He had managed, after months of preparation, to sneak a single battery past the Soviets' stringent inventory controls. But if his sister had foreseen things correctly (of which, of course, he had no doubt), they would need every millivolt they could muster on their long trek to the Paris Wall.

The rechargeable lithium-ion packs had been cutting-edge technology, decades ahead of their time in 1939. But they were blocky, bulky things, and hopelessly outdated compared to the sleek modules the Soviets had developed. Gretel's prescience aside, it was difficult to believe the Reichsbehörde batteries had retained any charge after twenty-two years. Klaus wiped away the layer of dust and grime coating the gauges. The batteries were degraded but still serviceable. If the gauges could be trusted.

Although Klaus had suffered tremendous misgivings about Doctor von Westarp's research, and had lost his unswerving faith in the Götterelektrongruppe long before the Communists' master stroke, he now felt a frisson of relief and pride. German engineering. A reminder of those golden days when the world had been so much simpler, their shared destiny so much grander. Even degraded, these old batteries represented a wealth of power and opportunity. More than Klaus had known in decades.

They also found a few of the old double harnesses. Klaus and Gretel stripped to the waist. It was awkward, but they both managed to don two harnesses, one in front and one in back. When they had finished, they both carried four batteries beneath their clothes. It was very uncomfortable.

"Let's go," he said, taking her hand.

But Gretel said, "Wait. We need something else, too." She led him down one aisle and up another, to a shelf holding a pair of jars filled with sepia-colored solution. Beside them lay an empty rucksack.

"What are those for?"

The corner of Gretel's mouth quirked up in a private little smile. "Don't worry. I've packed for you, too."

Something in the way she said it dislodged a forgotten moment from the recesses of Klaus's memory. It was the day of their capture, minutes before. He'd been away, and had rushed back to the farm to retrieve

Gretel before the Communists overran the facility. He'd taken her hand, preparing to pull her through the wall, desperate to get back to the truck and drive ahead of the advancing Red Army:

"Wait," she said. She pointed at the rucksack. "We'll need that."

The sack clattered like ceramic or glass when he lifted it. "Don't worry," she said. "I've packed for you, too."*

Klaus took one of the jars. A pallid, shriveled mass floated in the murk. The jar had a wide opening, and the lid had been sealed and re-sealed with wax. The yellowed label listed a set of dates and other annotations printed in Cyrillic, in a variety of hands and a variety of inks. The jar had last been studied six years ago. It was dusty.

He blew away some of the dust, then lifted the jar to the light, trying to peer inside. The contents settled against the glass like a dead fish.

Klaus frowned. "Is this . . . is this Heike's *brain*?"

"Part of it."

Heike. The invisible woman. Another of Doctor von Westarp's children, one of that small handful to survive the procedures and learn how to embrace the Willenskräfte. They had grown up together, lived together, trained together back at the Reichsbehörde. Until poor, fragile Heike had spent a long afternoon in private conversation with Gretel, and killed herself the next day.

The doctor didn't mourn his dead daughter. He dissected her. It was, after all, a perfect opportunity to study the physiological effects of channeling the Götterelektron. Since Heike had done that via the electrodes in her skull—like Klaus, Gretel, Reinhardt, and the others—the doctor had paid particular attention to her brain.

Gretel took the jar from his hands. She crumpled the label and tossed it aside, then picked at the wax with her fingernails. It flaked away in long clumps. Klaus caught a strong whiff of formaldehyde when she cracked the seal.

"Why . . ." Klaus trailed off. He tried again. "How will Heike's *brain* help us to escape?"

"It won't," said Gretel, as though explaining something obvious. She dumped out the contents. Formaldehyde and brain matter splattered on the floor. And then she added: "But we need a jar."

"What? I don't—"

Comprehension dawned, and something icy slithered down Klaus's spine. It became an oily nausea when it reached his gut. He put a hand over his mouth and swallowed. *Oh my God.*

Back during the war he had seen Gretel do strange things. Inexplicable things. Terrible things. Perhaps none more so than what she had done to Heike. Now he understood the why of it, but that only made things worse: Heike's suicide was a tiny cog in a vast machine. Gretel had prepared their escape long before they were captured. She had caused an innocent woman to kill herself, just to ensure one perfectly normal jar would be there twenty years later, exactly when and where they needed it. The sheer callousness rivaled anything ever done at the Reichsbehörde or Arzamas. But the *scope* of Gretel's machinations . . . It was a wonder Klaus's blood didn't crystallize in his veins.

Gretel was weaving cause and effect across decades. The farm had fallen because Gretel wanted it to happen. Why? It had gnawed at him since before their arrival at Arzamas. He'd asked, of course, but Gretel never answered his questions. Just smiled as she weaved her plans.

And here he was. A ghost along for the ride.

Klaus sighed. He feared this insight into his sister, but he hated Arzamas more. "What now?"

"Now you go to the bathroom."

Gott. *This is getting worse and worse.* "In the jar?"

Gretel frowned. Her braids—long raven-black locks streaked with gray—danced past her shoulders as she shook her head. She'd always worn her hair long, except in the early days here, when the Soviets had shaved their heads.

"No. You *go,*" she said, pushing him toward the vault door, "to the *bathroom.*" Another nudge toward the door, and this time she put the glassware in his hand. It was slippery. "Clean this. Leave it on the sink."

He started to talk, to ensure he understood what she said, but she interrupted him. "Go. And don't linger."

Klaus ran the water as quietly as possible, so that he could listen for footsteps in the corridor. He half suspected that part of Gretel's escape plan involved him getting caught outside the dormitory after curfew.

The jar made his hands stink, and a layer of gunk had accumulated around the rim. He scrubbed it away as best he could with a towel. Working quickly, he managed to get the jar looking like it was mostly clean. And then, because the incriminating towel stank of formaldehyde (like his hands), he hid it behind one of the toilets. He balanced the jar on the narrow ledge of the sink, where a water-stained wall joined rust-stained ceramic.

When he returned to the vault, Gretel was slipping something into her blouse. "All done, brother? Time to go." She led him into the corridor.

Before it became a secret city, Arzamas-16 had been known as Sarov: a dozen churches built around the Sarova monastery, home of St. Seraphim. Everything was closed by order of the state when Sarov became a research facility. It grew quickly.

But inside and out, the architecture here was unlike most Soviet towns of comparable size: most of Arzamas-16 had been built by POW labor from Axis troops captured during the Red Army's sweep across Europe in the final months of the war. Arzamas-16 had a distinctly European, distinctly *German,* feel. It could have been a Thuringian village. The early days had been profoundly disorienting, when Klaus had watched the buildings going up and felt he was witnessing the destruction of the Reichsbehörde in reverse.

Arzamas-16 was a large and heavily guarded facility, ringed with walls, fences, and aggressive perimeter defenses. Including the fail-safes. This building, number three, sat near the center of town. Klaus suppressed the urge to keep looking over his shoulder while his sister led him toward the guard station.

Gretel pulled him to a stop at the base of a stairwell. They backed up a few stairs, until they perched in the shadows around the corner from the guard desk.

Klaus whispered, "The patrols—"

"There won't be any tonight." Gretel put a finger to her lips.

As Klaus's breathing slowed, he started to make out sounds from around the corner. He recognized the sound of liquid sloshing inside glass. It reminded him of poor Heike, and her ignominious end. Nothing happened for several minutes.

Then footsteps echoed up the corridor. Klaus braced for a fight he hoped to avoid. At best, he'd get a few seconds of complete insubstantiality before tripping the fail-safes, barely enough time for him and Gretel to escape through the wall.

A voice said, "What the hell are you doing?"

Another answered, "Drink with me, Sacha."

"Are you drunk?"

"I am *not* drunk. I am celebrating! It is, as I say this to you, not twenty minutes after midnight. Do you know what that makes today?"

The sound of glass on metal, like a bottle pulled across a desk. "Where did you get this?" That was Sacha's voice again. Klaus didn't know the guards by name, but he might have recognized their faces.

"It makes today," continued the first guard, "International Workers' Day. And so I am celebrating my hardworking brothers and sisters. To them!" A moment later, the sound of smacked lips.

"You're disgraceful, Kostya. Have you done the rounds, or must I do your job for you?"

Gretel patted Klaus on the knee when he tensed. *Trust me,* she mouthed.

"Disgraceful? I am a patriot, I'll have you know."

"You would drink jet fuel, if you could find it. What is that?"

"I distilled it myself." Again, the sound of a bottle being pushed across the desk. "One drink. To the workers."

A gasp. "I'm not putting that thing to my lips. Don't you ever brush your teeth? Your breath smells like shit."

"Suit yourself, Sacha."

"Not getting shot for dereliction of duty, that's what suits me."

"They don't shoot people here. They give them to the troops. Comrade Lysenko's special troops. For practice."

"I'd rather be shot."

"I'll drink to that."

A minute passed. Then: "One of us has to do the rounds. I suppose that's me, since you're hell-bent on getting shit-faced."

"No, no, I'll do the rounds. It's my service to the great Soviet Union." A wooden chair squeaked across pitted concrete. "But first I must piss.

Patriotism is the only drink that stays in your blood. Vodka comes back out again. Watch the boards while I'm out."

The other guard—Sacha—sighed. "I'll watch."

Kostya's unsteady footsteps sounded louder and louder until he appeared around the corner. Klaus held his breath because he and Gretel were sitting in shadow but still easily visible to anybody who looked in their direction. His sloe-eyed sister watched the guard with something akin to dark amusement playing across her face. The guard shuffled past them without a glance.

From the direction of the bathroom, Klaus heard banging, flushing, belching, and running water.

Kostya shuffled past them again a few minutes later, jar in hand. He waved it triumphantly overhead. "Good news, Sacha!" he announced, disappearing around the corner. "I found this in the bathroom. *Now* you can have a drink with me."

Klaus turned to stare at his sister. She winked.

From the guard station, Sascha's voice said, "You found a jar in the bathroom? It's probably a sample jar. I'll bet somebody pissed in it."

"Nonsense. Look. Clean."

"Did *you* piss in it?"

"One drink. On Workers' Day."

Glass clinked against glass as somebody, probably Kostya, poured into the jar.

"Not so much. I don't want to go blind."

All Klaus could think of was formaldehyde and poor Heike's brain; the thought of imbibing from that jar nauseated him.

"To the Great Soviet." More clinking of glass.

Several moments passed in silence. And then Sacha said, "This isn't half bad."

After that there was more pouring, more toasts, and more clinking. Time passed. Gretel nudged Klaus with her elbow at one point, jerking him back to alertness. "You were going to snore," she whispered.

Klaus asked, "Do we rush them? They're both drunk."

Gretel rolled her eyes, but didn't say anything.

Not long after that, Sacha said (sounding more relaxed than he had before), "You smell like a wet dog, but you make a fine drink."

"Thank you."

"Is this really your own?"

"Yes." Kostya sounded blurry, subdued.

"How?"

Klaus understood the question. This was the most sensitive facility in the entire Soviet Union: an empire that stretched from the Atlantic to the Pacific. Even the guards were subject to scrutiny here. Klaus imagined the guards' quarters were searched almost as frequently as his own. So how did Kostya manage to distill his own vodka?

"I do it where they never look."

"They look everywhere."

"No." Kostya paused, possibly for another sip. He smacked his lips. "They never search the fail-safe chamber. Nobody likes to go down there . . ."

Klaus filled in the rest: . . . *because it's full of high explosives.*

The Götterelektron was the key to the superhuman feats of Doctor von Westarp's children, and their Soviet successors. But it was also their Achilles' heel. The circuitry was susceptible to a suitably crafted electromagnetic pulse. The British had designed their pixies after reverse engineering Gretel's battery, and used them with middling success during an ill-fated raid on the Reichsbehörde. Later, when the tide of war turned against the Reich, the Communists had unveiled a more potent version of the same technology.

The Arzamas fail-safe devices dwarfed the original pixies, but they worked on the same principle. They used chemical explosives to crush an electromagnet, blanketing the facility with a crippling EMP.

The bottom line being that nobody in his right mind willingly spent time near the fail-safes. An unannounced drill, a malfunction, even an escape attempt might come at any time. Death would be quick, and it would be certain.

Nobody searched the fail-safe chambers.

Sacha said, "Genius. To you."

"To me." *Clink.*

"Maintenance . . . they do that, time to time. What then? Pay them in vodka?"

"Some I could. Others would take my vodka and still sell me out. Pigs." Kostya spat. "Come. I'll show you."

Sascha belched before responding. "Into the chamber? Not going down there."

"It's safe. I've done it many times."

"You're a drunken madman." It sounded as though Sacha was making an effort not to slur his words. "I am smarter and more responsible."

"Then we'll disarm the fail-safe before we go down."

"Yes. That's a much better idea."

And then, after some discussion of whether they'd take the remainder of the bottle with them, they stumbled off to visit Kostya's still.

Gretel stood, stretched. "Well," she said. "Off we go."

Incredible, thought Klaus.

After half an hour of sneaking, hiding, dodging, and sprinting—each move dictated by the time line in Gretel's head—they stole a car. And, because the fail-safes had been disarmed, there was nothing to stop Klaus from dematerializing the car and everything in it when they reached the perimeter.

They escaped Arzamas-16 without incident, just two more ghosts in the gulag.

3 May 1963
Belgravia, London, England

Candlelight flickered through crystal wineglasses, glinted on true silverware, shimmered on fine tablecloths. The restaurant hummed with the murmur of genteel conversation punctuated by the occasional *clink* of fine china or *pop* of a wine cork.

Lady Gwendolyn Beauclerk said, "You're hopeless, William. You won't stop until you've found your way into a pauper's grave. I'm quite convinced."

Lord William Edward Guthrie Beauclerk, younger brother to the Thirteenth Duke of Aelred, squeezed his wife's hand. She laughed again.

"Pauper's grave? Never, my dear. I've left very specific instructions to be carried out on the event of my death."

"Have you?" Gwendolyn took another sip of the Chilean red. William hadn't tasted it, but the unanimous consensus at the table was that France's collectivized wineries would never produce anything approaching the South American wines.

"Oh, yes."

"You haven't mentioned this to me," said Will's brother, Aubrey.

Gwendolyn cocked her head. Her gown, royal blue silk, matched her eyes. Eyes that shone in the familiar way that meant, *I'm listening.*

Will paused to savor a last morsel of breaded veal. "When the time comes, darling, and I have departed from this mortal coil," said Will, "you and Aubrey shall bring my remains to the Tower Bridge. And there, from the highest parapet, you'll toss my body in the Thames."

Aubrey's face betrayed a flash of anger. "William!"

Viola Beauclerk, his horsey-faced wife, tittered behind an upraised hand. She stifled herself when the sommelier returned with another bottle to refill their glasses.

Will gently laid one hand over his unused glass. The sommelier acknowledged the gesture with a nod, sparing only the briefest glance at the stump of Will's missing finger. He whisked the glass away, looked doubly abashed: the glass ought to have been removed at the start of the meal, and he ought not to have noticed the injury. Such things were unimportant to Will, but the sommelier worked at the fringes of a social set where such lapses bordered on inexcusable.

Aubrey frowned. He waited for the sommelier to pass out of earshot before saying, "Must you talk so common at the table?"

"I'm merely reporting the facts of the matter, Your Grace." Will gestured at Gwendolyn. "You wouldn't ask me to keep secrets from my better half, would you? After all, this affects her as much as it does you. You'll be the ones carrying my body." Will patted his stomach, where the beginnings of a paunch were just visible beneath his vest. "You agreed it should be so."

"I have most certainly done nothing of the sort," said Aubrey. A quick, vocal disavowal fueled by the concern that somebody might overhear the conversation and somehow believe it to be the truth. *Poor Aubrey,* thought Will. *Even as a child, you were humorless. I can't resist winding you up, and you know it.*

Aubrey would never be capable of leaving Will's dark years entirely in the past. He'd spent too much time worrying about being seen with his younger brother, which at one time would have been social suicide. Will had come close to scuttling Aubrey's political career on more than one occasion. To this day, a sheen of anxiety—fear of embarrassment, of damaging publicity—settled over Aubrey whenever he and Will were together in public.

Will shook his head. "Oh, indeed you have. You ought to take more care when signing documents for the foundation." He winked at Gwendolyn and his sister-in-law. "An unscrupulous fellow could take advantage."

The flush of indignation crept up through the folds of fat at Aubrey's collar to his face. Quietly, he said, "It's your job to prevent exactly that sort of thing."

"Yes, it is. And you should be thankful that I am ever vigilant. Still, some things cannot be helped," said Will. He turned to Viola. "The arrangements for your husband's funeral are nothing short of scandalous. Still, it will be his final wish and by honoring it we shall honor him. Though I can't begin to speculate how we'll find so many Morris dancers on short notice."

Viola tittered again, the guilty laugh of the mildly scandalized.

Gwendolyn didn't enjoy baiting Aubrey as much as Will did. She said, "Well, then, at least it won't be a dour occasion. Let the Communists have their gray little lives." She shook her head. "Terrible."

"That's a rather unfair stereotype," said Aubrey, clearly pleased at the chance to change the subject. "They're just like us, truthfully."

Will read the subtle cues that told him Aubrey's attitude had riled her a bit. He settled back to watch. It was an old argument, but he never tired of it. Gwendolyn had no equal in verbal contretemps.

"Just like us? Forgive my ignorance, Your Grace, but I was unaware that the Kremlin had instituted a House of Lords," said Gwendolyn. "Or have you collectivized the estate at Bestwood?"

Touché, Will thought, and covered his mouth to hide a smile. *Step lightly, brother.*

Aubrey sidestepped the barb. "A fair point. I meant simply that the people of the Soviet Union have the same wants and needs as the rest of us. Their leaders may have different ideas about how to provide these things, but in the end we're all the same people."

"We're free to move about within the UK as we see fit. I quite suspect you'd find it a different matter if you tried to drive from Poland to Portugal. What was it Mr. Churchill once said? About the iron curtain that had been drawn around Europe?"

"Churchill was a good man for his time," said Viola, joining the discussion to support her husband. "The man we needed during the war. Nobody denies that bringing us through those years was nothing if not miraculous." Under the table, Gwendolyn squeezed Will's hand. Unaware that she had raked an old wound, Viola plunged ahead, parroting things she had heard from her husband: "But that was a different time. He had an outmoded, adversarial view of socialism. It's fortunate we're not tied to that yoke any longer."

"Well said, dear," said Aubrey. To Gwendolyn, he said, "I do agree that our cousins across the Channel are not so enlightened as we in certain areas. Which is precisely why I've sponsored several measures over the years aimed at fostering greater openness and cultural exchange between our peoples. We stand to benefit as much as they."

("Surely you mean 'comrades across the Channel,'" said Gwendolyn, sotto voce.)

"Aubrey has been pushing for such reforms since before the notion of détente was in vogue," Viola said.

"Détente? Is that what we're calling it?" said Gwendolyn. "The African situation strikes me as something of a stalemate. They support a revolution, or a workers' revolt, and we counter it by supporting the opposition."

Viola ignored her. "In fact, he was advocating for change long before the Great Famine of '42."

Aubrey shook his head. "Dreadful, that."

Gwendolyn squeezed Will's hand again. This time her soothing touch lingered, and Aubrey's disdain for open displays of affection be

damned. The Great European Famine was the result of an exception-
ally harsh winter. An unnatural winter. Will had been part of the team
of warlocks tasked with creating that brutal weather. He'd been cut
loose before the effort succeeded (more honestly, it had succeeded because he'd been tossed out), but not before he'd done wicked things for
Crown and Country. Magical acts bought with blood.

Talk of the famine dredged up haunting memories, rekindled a long-
smoldering guilt. Raked a wound that was always fresh, always tender.
Sometimes, late at night when the memories attacked, Will couldn't meet
his own eyes in the mirror.

But of course, Viola and even Aubrey were unaware of such things.
There were men in Whitehall who would be quite displeased if they
knew how completely Will had confided in his future wife during his
long recuperation and reintroduction to civilized society. But they could
go hang. Each and every one of them.

"I'd also submit," said Gwendolyn, "that the Japanese don't share your
views of détente."

The Greater East Asia Co-Prosperity Sphere scraped against the
eastern reaches of the Soviet Union like flint on steel. Border skirmishes
flared where the sparks fell.

Viola shook her head knowingly. "Well, now, you simply can't reason with those people. They're not like us, you know. Brutal. Warlike.
They lack the civilizing influence of a Christian faith. Twenty years of
fighting!" She shuddered. "And what they did in Manchuria . . ."

"Speaking of cultural exchanges," said Aubrey, nudging the conversation in a direction less upsetting to his wife, "I spoke to Ambassador Fedotov today. He'll be hosting a reception next week." He raised his eyebrows,
looking earnestly at both Will and Gwen. "You're available, I hope?" His
smile was of the type wielded by only the wealthiest men, and only to
their peers. "I give you my word the gathering won't be too terribly dour."

"Of course," said Will. "It would be a pleasure."

"Excellent. Fedotov said he looked forward to meeting you again."

Gwendolyn turned to Will. "You know the ambassador?"

Will shrugged. "We've crossed paths." Tipping his head at Aubrey,
he said, "Via the foundation. Queer little fellow, the ambassador."

"I find him rather charming," said Viola.

As servers cleared away their dinner plates, Gwendolyn said to her husband, "You haven't told me about this."

Will shouldered more guilt. Not for deeds of the past, but for secrets kept in the here and now. She deserved better.

"Meeting the ambassador? It truly wasn't notable, darling. He had occasion to visit the foundation recently. It was the day of our whist tournament with Lord and Lady Albemarle, in fact. I was leaving, and in something of a state—you'll remember I was a bit tardy—"

"Yes. I remember." Gwendolyn didn't roll her eyes, instead letting the tone of her voice carry the effect.

"—and happened to encounter Aubrey and the ambassador as they came through the foundation. We exchanged niceties, that was that, and then I was out the door and somewhat manic about it."

Gwendolyn sat silently, watching Will for several moments. "Hmmm. Fascinating."

"Oh, if you haven't had a chance to enjoy his company," Viola said, "then you *must* attend. Do come. You'll find him delightful, Gwendolyn."

Gwendolyn smiled, just thinly enough that Viola wouldn't notice she was gritting her teeth. "I'm sure I will. I look forward to it."

Dessert was crème brûlée served with a raspberry reduction and bitter Rhodesian coffee. Will declined the coffee, ordering instead a strong Indian tea with lemon. Conversation turned to more mundane and less charged topics: race riots in the United States (disgraceful); another disruption in train service to the Midlands (disgraceful); Buckingham Palace's first color television (decadent).

The evening ended as they frequently did, with Will and Aubrey discussing foundation business at one end of the table while Gwendolyn and Viola chatted. The North Atlantic Cross-Cultural Foundation was a small, private, nongovernmental organization chartered with fostering improved relations between the United Kingdom and the Union of Soviet Socialist Republics. Aubrey had created the foundation via permanent endowment in 1942, just in time for it to take a leading role in dealing with the flood of refugees streaming across the Channel. The flow of refugees came to an abrupt halt the following spring when the

Iron Curtain slammed shut. But the foundation remained, and quickly became the place where, publicly, the British and Soviet empires intersected. Will liked to joke that he was both a lion tamer and a bear keeper. As the head of the foundation, Will worked closely with members of the Soviet diplomatic mission, their British counterparts, various members of Parliament, and occasionally the Foreign Secretary himself.

On the ride home, the London night cast dark shadows across Gwendolyn's face, interspersed with pale reflections from streetlamps shining on the white stucco houses of Belgrave Square. The interplay of light and shadow turned her blond hair white; it spun the faint dusting of gray at her temples to silver. She sighed, and tucked an errant lock behind her ear. She noticed Will watching her.

"What is it?" she asked.

"I might ask you the same," he said, smiling. She sighed a second time. "Out with it, now. Your burdens are my own, and vice versa. We had something about that in our vows, as I recall."

"Oh, Will. I'm sorry. It's just . . ." Her voice dropped to a whisper, so that their driver wouldn't hear her. "Your brother's wife is a vapid cow."

Will's laughter, loud and barking, startled the driver. In the rearview, his eyes briefly checked on the couple before turning back to Lyall Street. Will took Gwendolyn's hand, and he felt her tension begin to melt away as he stroked his thumb along the inside of her wrist.

"You know, there was a time when Aubrey wanted nothing more for me than to settle down with somebody like Viola."

"You'd have gone mad."

"Back then? I nearly did," he said, squeezing her hand and feeling grateful as ever that she had entered his life.

4 May 1963
Walworth, London, England

A garden shed in springtime: mud, mildew, spiders, and the stink of compost. Squalid solitude. Blessed solitude.

Raybould Marsh, formerly Lieutenant-Commander Marsh of Her

Majesty's Royal Navy, and formerly of MI6, sat on a wobbly stool he'd nicked from a pub. He inspected tomato plants for bruises and fungus. He'd been taking them outside for longer periods each day and longer into the evening, acclimating them to the insult of cooler temperatures before permanently transplanting them into the garden. Done gradually enough, the transition wouldn't shock the plants.

People, thought Marsh, were much the same. Change things slowly enough, for long enough, and before you knew it, the world was warped beyond recognition.

He had expanded the shed soon after the war with materials scavenged from a disassembled Anderson shelter. The addition featured a low, sloping roof of translucent plastic, once smooth and white, now cracked and dirty by weather and age. Marsh's workbench sagged under paper sacks of potting soil, fertilizer, piles of planters. His cot stuck halfway under the bench, covered with rumpled sheets and a thin, water-stained, army-surplus blanket. A handmade bookcase, crammed with volumes of Kipling and Haggard, formed a makeshift headboard. A few old photographs had been pinned to the shelves, their edges yellowed and curled.

The clatter of a broken dish echoed from the house. Liv, his wife, raised her voice in shrill alarm. Marsh reached behind the plants and clicked on the wireless.

He didn't particularly care for the news or the state of the world, but it did drown out the noise. Running electrical mains to the shed had been something of a job, but necessary for preserving his sanity. Sometimes, when the clamor from the house became too much, he'd tune the radio between stations as a white noise generator.

The small of Marsh's back twinged when he leaned over to inspect another plant. Pain flared in his knee, too. The problem in his knee was an old one, something he'd had even as a young man. It came and went over the years. The pain in his back was a souvenir of age.

The odor of hot earth wafted through the shed. As the valves in the wireless heated up, they scorched away the fine layer of dust that had settled through the grille. Static became an ethereal warble laced with the suggestion of human voices. The amplifiers stabilized, and the voices became a Russian choir. Most stations on the Continent sounded like this when they weren't spreading the latest propaganda from Moscow. Sometimes, when he could stomach it, he listened to those broadcasts. They reminded him of desperate days from long ago. Days spent studying maps, conferring with warlocks, hoping to entice the Soviets to finish off the Third Reich.

Marsh gave the tuner dial a few flicks of his thumb. It landed on something loud and discordant—modern music played by a group out of Liverpool. Another flick brought him to a BBC station playing more familiar music. Marsh recognized the Benny Goodman recording, and remembered when it had been new. The big band hour was popular among people old enough to remember life before the war.

He listened to the remainder of the program while mending a leaky hose with bit of inner tube cut from a bicycle tire. The hose was a motley thing, riddled with patches down its length, but Marsh had kept it working long past its useful life. They might have scraped together enough money to afford the extravagance of a new hose, but Marsh never suggested this to Liv. A new hose would have meant fewer excuses to spend time in the shed. Meant cutting off another avenue of escape.

They'd purchased the bicycle for their newborn son, John, in happy anticipation of the day he'd be old enough to use it. It still leaned behind the shed, unused, rusting into nothing.

Vera Lynn sang wistfully of bluebirds and white cliffs. Liv used to sing the same song, better than Lynn herself. But she hadn't sung in the house since John was born.

Marsh made to change the station again, but the song ended before he could get his hands free, and then it was the top of the hour and time for the news. That morning's moon shot was the lead story. Three cosmonauts had departed the space station; in a few days' time, they would become the first men to see the far side of the moon with their own eyes. Von Braun was sure to receive the Order of Lenin upon their safe return. Predictably, President Nixon had sent effusive congratulations to Khrushchev on behalf of the American people. In the Near East, the Royal Navy had stationed the carrier HMS *Ocean* into the Persian Gulf, near British Petroleum's Abadan refinery in southern Iran, in response to increased Soviet activity along the borders of the Azerbaijan and Turkmen SSR. Elsewhere, scattered and confusing reports had trickled in to the BBC bureau in Cape Town, including rumors of abandoned villages in the Tanganyika Territory. Closer to home, foresters investigated a recent fire that had burned acres of woodland in Gloucestershire.

Outside, the kitchen door creaked and slammed. Marsh sighed. He flicked off the wireless.

Liv barged in a few moments later, rattling the tools hung behind the door. She stank of antiseptic and watered-down perfume. Marsh saw the bags beneath her eyes, darker than usual, and decided not to mention it. John had had one of his bad nights.

The wrinkles in the hollows of her cheeks creased into the edges of a frown. "Were you planning to spend the entire day out here?"

"I'm nearly finished."

Liv pursed her lips. "Nearly finished," she muttered. "You always say that."

"The sooner I get these in the ground, the sooner we can have a decent salad again." Marsh cringed inwardly as soon as the words passed his lips.

"Decent," she said. "As opposed to the indecent meals that I prepare the rest of the year."

Marsh wondered, as he sometimes did, about the passage of time. The years had transformed Liv's freckles, once so endearing and erotic, into age spots that repulsed him. How had things gone so terribly wrong? Time was a cruel alchemist.

"Don't, Liv. You know what I meant." She carried her handbag, he noticed. And she'd done her lips. Liv hadn't bothered in years, but she'd begun again recently. It meant she'd come home late, smelling of another man's aftershave and not respecting Marsh enough to hide it. "Where are you going?" he asked.

"Out," she said. Somehow, the plants didn't shrivel and blacken before the naked contempt in her voice. But Liv never missed her mark, never missed a chance to make him feel useless. Emasculated.

She flung something across the cramped shed. A ring of keys clattered on his workbench, knocking a large chip from a terra-cotta planter.

"Feed your son." Over her shoulder as she walked away, she added, "It's your turn."

He waited in the shed until he heard the screeching of the garden gate. It banged shut behind Liv; he made a mental note to oil the hinges and replace the spring. Her heels clicked on the pavement outside, and then faded into the general low-level thrum of the neighborhood.

Marsh considered finishing with the tomatoes before going inside, but rejected the idea. John had to eat.

The house was quiet, but for the simmering of a pot Liv had pre-pared: barley soup with peas, carrots, and a bit of beef. Marsh filled a bowl, grabbed a towel, and went upstairs. The stairs creaked. John launched into a new round of keening.

John's room was down a short hallway from the bedroom his parents ostensibly shared. Marsh fished out the key ring with one hand while balancing the bowl in the other. Four keys hung from the ring. John paused when Marsh scratched the first key into the first lock. Marsh noticed a puddle beneath the door when he worked his way to the final and lowest lock.

He braced himself before turning the last bolt. Sometimes John ran, blind and mindless. But his son didn't rush the door. Shards of crockery splintered beneath the soles of Marsh's work boots when he entered. John had flung a bowl of soup across the room.

The room stank. The door behind Marsh was splattered with brown stains. John had flung other things at Liv, too. No wonder she'd left for the day.

Marsh turned on the light. Every wall had been covered with calico, and stuffed with carpet scraps, horsehair, and newspaper. Homemade soundproofing, the best Marsh could manage. In places, where the in-sulation was torn, he could glimpse the original robin's egg blue walls. The paint was a holdover from those last giddy days, when they'd done up the nursery in the final weeks of Liv's pregnancy. Before they'd taken John home from the hospital; before they'd discovered something wrong with their son.

That was the doctors' term. Wrong. Because they didn't know what else to call it.

Everything he'd done, everything they'd endured, all for naught. Ruined by a fluke of fate.

Yellowing placards lined the walls near the ceiling, displaying the letters of the alphabet. Those were leftovers from the period before they realized the extent of the problem, when Liv had thought she might be able to homeschool their son.

John himself huddled in his usual corner, naked. They'd given up trying to clothe him after he'd grown large enough to overpower Liv. He clenched his knees to his chest, rocking sideways and knocking his head against the wall with a steady, monotonous rhythm. That was another reason for the padding. John could do that for hours, even days, unless somebody moved him.

"It's me, son," said Marsh. "Your father."

Sometimes—on good days—John paused in his rocking, ever so briefly, when Marsh entered. A token acknowledgment, a hint of connection. But not today. John kept batting his head against the wall without interruption. Marsh had recently replaced the padding there.

"I brought something to eat."

Pat, pat, pat, pat, pat.

Marsh hunkered down next to John, cross-legged, ignoring the protests from his knee. John's rocking wafted the scent of his unwashed body at his father; he smelled faintly of sour milk. It took two people to bathe him, but Marsh and Liv rarely stayed in the same room together.

"I see you gave your mum some trouble today. You shouldn't be so difficult to her."

Pat, pat, pat, pat.

"She loves you as much as I do."

Pat, pat, pat.

Marsh sighed. "Let's get some food in you, son." He laid his hand on John's shoulder.

John rolled his head toward Marsh, turning a pair of colorless eyes at him. It always unnerved Marsh when he did that, just as much as it cut him with slivers of irrational hope. He knew those eyes were sightless, equally devoid of function as of warmth.

John sniffed the air. He leaned toward Marsh, snuffling with a machine gun burst of quick, sharp inhalations. Marsh held his free hand toward John's face, so that his son could get the scent. Then he did the same with the soup.

John's mouth fell open. But before Marsh could get the spoon in, his son began to wail: a single, unbroken note that lasted as long as the air in his lungs.

He did it again. And again. And again.

two

Modern London wasn't a patch on its former self. The smells, the sounds, the architecture . . . little remained of the city Klaus remembered.

He'd been here once before, briefly, on a rescue mission after Gretel had handed herself to a British agent. From time to time during the long years at Arzamas-16, his thoughts had drifted back to London. Britain had survived the war; to Klaus, that made it a shining place.

He was a different man now. More enlightened. No longer the devoted, unquestioning tool he'd been a lifetime ago. But London had changed even more than he.

He remembered a place somber yet grand, a temple built of granite and brick and marble. Gothic buildings, baroque buildings, and others for which he lacked the vocabulary. Statues, monuments, and memorials. They had struck him as a decadent obsession with the past; an omen of Britain's inevitable downfall. What a naïf he'd been.

But what he saw as their train entered London shocked him. And the deeper they delved into the heart of the city, the more it saddened him.

Bits and pieces of the old city remained. Sometimes entire streets, but those were rare. Often the remnants were sandwiched between newer and utterly uninspired constructions. It was as though the city's character, its personality, had been scrubbed away. The Blitz had destroyed the city's soul—shattered it, charred it, tossed its ashes to the wind—and the hole had been patched with a cheap prosthetic. Functional but soulless.

"It's so different," he whispered.

"Nothing lasts forever," said Gretel from the seat beside him, concentrating on her newspaper. The chill, his constant companion since their final night at Arzamas, tingled at the unscratchable spot between his shoulder blades. As it often did when she spoke. The Luftwaffe's domination of the skies over Britain had unfolded largely because of her advice. She clicked the biro she'd snatched from a passing businessman and circled something in blue ink. She'd been scouring classified ads since they arrived in the country. Klaus hadn't known what classifieds were until she'd explained the idea to him.

It wasn't just the buildings that had changed. He'd been immersed in half a dozen languages since crossing the border. Predominantly French, but also Dutch, Italian, Spanish, Portuguese, something he guessed was Basque . . . even some German. The languages of those who had found a way across the Channel before the Iron Curtain slammed shut.

Klaus had never perfected his English. He took comfort in knowing it didn't matter any longer.

Gretel and he had kept strictly to English since their midnight embarkation at Calais. Britain's border policy wasn't what it had been, no longer welcoming with open arms the huddled masses from the sliver of supposedly free Europe wedged between Paris and the coast. Draconian measures on both sides of the Channel had throttled the flow of refugees and immigrants to less than a trickle. Those without papers had little chance of staying in England. But Gretel, of course, had seen a way.

Ireland and Canada sounded like better destinations, but she had shrugged off the suggestions.

The screech of wheels on track reverberated through the train as it slowed to enter Waterloo Station. Klaus slid forward in his seat. He checked his fedora again. He didn't have a wig, so he'd have to make do with a hat and ill-fitting clothes to hide his wires. During his first trip to London, he'd worn a wig and a counterfeit naval officer's uniform. He yearned for that disguise now. Strutting around in public with exposed wires contradicted a lifetime of training.

Gretel didn't bother to hide her wires. They were twined, as always, through her braids. She had worn them that way back at the Reichsbehörde, too. Even then, the affectation had seemed overly young for her.

They filed off the train into a muggy heat on the platform. But it wasn't crowded, which made it bearable. At one end of the platform, a man with a roller brush and a putty knife scraped down placards announcing a lecture sponsored by a group of British Socialists. The speaker was a member of Parliament. The advertisements appeared to have been printed crudely and slapped up quickly.

Klaus said, "Where now?"

They had nothing but the clothes on their backs, the few remaining batteries concealed beneath, and the money Klaus had pulled out of a cash register at the port. "We need to find a place to stay."

"That's easy." She looked up at him. "You shouldn't worry so much, brother."

"We'll also need money. We can't keep—" He paused, lowering his voice. "—stealing."

"Pfff." She waved away the concern with a petite hand.

"Well, then? What does your plan say? What do we do?"

Gretel folded the paper in thirds, then took his arm. "I'm in the mood for a rummage sale," she said.

The taxi smelled of perfume from a previous passenger. It was a boxy, black hackney cab with suicide doors, like the only other London taxi Klaus had ridden in his life. That ride had ended with him killing the driver. He hoped this would be different.

Their driver was very young, and olive skinned, but not with the gypsy look of Klaus and Gretel. A Spaniard, judging from his accent, perhaps a refugee from the purges after "spontaneous" workers' uprisings had deposed Franco and put the puppet Juan de Borbón on the throne.

Their route took them past a swath of green space. A park. It surprised Klaus to see something so vibrant and colorful in the middle of the sterile urban jungle. The taxi stopped at a traffic light. Cross traffic thrummed past the windscreen; a stream of pedestrians filled the zebra crossing. Klaus watched the park.

A man and woman held hands while they strolled around the edges of a duck pond. Farther inside, a crying boy watched an adult—his father?—try to dislodge a shredded red kite from the boughs of an oak tree. Somebody else stood at an easel, painting a scene from the park.

The light changed; the taxi pulled away. But Klaus held tightly to those glimpses. There was something odd, something unusual, about the entire thing.

They pulled to a stop at a church. Their driver flipped a lever; the meter stopped with a *ding*. He put his arm across the front seat, craned his neck, and said something to Gretel. She handed him money. His face cracked into a smile when he counted the bills.

She'd given him the last of their money, but Klaus was too preoccupied to object. He had figured out what struck him as odd about the scene in the park: no guards.

The people in the park weren't the subjects in a vast experiment, weren't training for combat, weren't prisoners of war. They were doing things—painting, feeding ducks, flying kites—merely because they wanted to. It was a revelation, a color-blind man's first glimpse of a rainbow. He had never truly understood what freedom meant. Now he did. It made him want to grieve for himself.

Gretel interrupted his ruminations. "Coming?" She'd already exited the taxi. The driver glared at him. Klaus climbed out. The cab sped away, leaving them standing on the pavement in a cloud of exhaust.

They stood on a neatly trimmed lawn. The adjoining cemetery wasn't so well tended; irregular rows of crooked, cracked, and weather-stained gravestones dotted the grass inside a low, wrought iron fence. A few graves had fresh flowers upon them. Rows of folding metal tables had been arranged on the church lawn. The tables contained all manner of odds and ends: lamps, books, old radios, salt and pepper shakers, jigsaw puzzles, candy dishes, wooden toys, half-used tubes of wrapping paper, clothing, and shelves and boxes of the same. People milled in the aisles between the tables. Browsing, haggling, chatting about the weather. It was difficult to distinguish the vendors from the customers.

Klaus looked at Gretel. "What are we looking for?"

"You'll know when you find it." She shooed him away. "Go have fun. I'll be nearby." She wandered off into the sparse crowd.

He didn't move. There he was, recently escaped after two decades in captivity, on his first day in a free country, and what was he doing? Perusing a church fund-raiser without a penny to his name. Why? Because Gretel wanted it that way.

Still, without her, he never would have escaped.

Without her, he wouldn't have been captured in the first place.

Over by the cemetery, Gretel kicked off her shoes. She hiked up her dress, hopped the fence, and strolled barefoot through the graves.

Klaus sighed. He went up and down the aisles, studying the assembled goods for something significant. Reich memorabilia, perhaps? A photograph? Another piece of Heike? Nothing leapt out at him. It was all junk.

He turned the corner at the end of an aisle and almost bumped into another shopper.

"Pardon me," said Klaus, making to move aside.

But the other fellow didn't move. His eyes widened. An icy blue gaze bored into Klaus, sharp as twinned icicles. . . . Klaus looked closer.

The stranger's scraggly beard hid his face. But when Klaus noticed the trilby hat, the long hair, and the high collar, he knew what lay beneath.

"Son of a bitch," said Klaus. He took a half step backwards, dumbfounded.

The other man stared at him just as intensely.

Several moments passed while they gaped at each other, motionless like stones inside a stream of penny-ante commerce. Other shoppers stepped around the two men.

Klaus recovered first. "What are *you* doing here?"

"What the hell are *you* doing here?"

"I thought you were dead," said Klaus.

"I thought *you* were dead," said Reinhardt. "I thought I was the last of us."

"Hello, Reinhardt," said Gretel.

Reinhardt took one look at her and rolled his eyes. "I should have known."

"Lovely to see you again." She carried a handful of golden and lavender lilies. "These are for you."

Raised voices caught Klaus's attention. Over by the church, a gray-haired lady spoke urgently with the vicar. She pointed at the cemetery, then at Gretel. The vicar looked upset.

Klaus said, "Maybe we should have this reunion somewhere else."

Reinhardt saw the matron and the vicar walking in their direction. "I can't believe this," he muttered. "Twenty years I've been living here. Twenty years. Quiet, unnoticed. You two show up, and inside two minutes, you've blown my goddamn cover. Why don't you go rot in hell?"

Gretel twirled a finger through one braid, pointedly tugging on a wire. "I think you've missed us. And I think you'll want to hear what we have to say."

Reinhardt mulled this over. He looked from Gretel to Klaus to the vicar, and back to Gretel's wire.

"I have a car. Follow me."

Reinhardt lived in a shithole.

It was a large, ugly housing development, gray and blocky. If anything, it reminded Klaus of Soviet architecture. Sarov was a rarity; much of the Union looked like this, and probably for the same reasons. Quickly built and utilitarian, with no attention to aesthetics.

A group of children playing football in a field adjacent to the car park stopped to stare as they pulled up. When Klaus and Gretel emerged from Reinhardt's car—a battered 1938 Vauxhall—one of the children called to the others, "Lookee this! Junkman got hisself some mates!"

The children took up a chant. "Junkman! Rubbish bin man!" Gretel seemed amused by this; she rewarded the kids with her little smile. She still carried the flowers.

"Ignore them," said Reinhardt. He set off at a quick pace down the pavement, head low.

Klaus caught up to him. "Junkman? *That's* your cover?"

Reinhardt muttered something that Klaus didn't hear.

"What, Reinhardt?"

The other man wheeled on him. In a harsh whisper, he said, "Never call me that! I'm Richard now."

"Oh, yes. Richard the Junkman." Klaus couldn't resist.

"Eat. Shit."

Behind them, Gretel sighed. "Poor Junkman."

"Both of you."

Reinhardt set off again, leading the siblings toward the lift. The lift had a mildewy smell, like damp carpet that never had a chance to air out properly.

When they got to Reinhardt's flat, it took no imagination to understand how he'd gained his nickname. Piles of junk filled the place almost to the ceiling in places; mostly electronics, from the look of it. It was dim, too; Reinhardt's collection obscured most of the windows. Insects scuttled in the shadows. A musty scent tickled his nose, though not so bad as that in the lift.

Reinhardt locked the door. He tossed his hat onto the back of a chair (the only chair, it seemed) and peeled off his wig. His wires, Klaus noticed, were badly frayed.

Gretel headed straight to the kitchen. She rummaged through Reinhardt's cabinets.

"Hey! Hands off my things, you crazy bitch." Reinhardt took the chair.

Klaus looked around the flat again, and then at Reinhardt's wires. "What happened to you?"

"Oh, no. No, no, no," said Reinhardt, slipping into German. "Skip the bullshit. After all these years, you assholes show up on my doorstep expecting me to take it in stride? Expecting a happy reunion? Mere coincidence?" He pointed at Gretel. "It hasn't been so long that I've forgotten there's no such thing with her. So what the hell are you doing here, and what the fuck do you want from me?"

Similar questions had been nagging at Klaus. Reinhardt had expressed their essence.

"Yes," said Klaus. He turned to stare at Gretel, who had found an empty milk bottle. "Why *are* we here, Gretel?"

"Wait—you don't know either?" Reinhardt laughed. "Have you ever done anything she didn't tell you to do? They made a mistake when they put Kammler on a leash. It should have been you, lapdog."

Klaus struggled to find a response. He failed. Reinhardt's barbs had struck true. They hit the bull's-eye of a target Klaus hadn't known existed. It deflated his anger as quickly as a burst balloon. Reinhardt's ridicule filled him with shame. Damn him, but the man was right.

"Kammler's dead," said Gretel conversationally, while filling the bottle at the sink.

Reinhardt said, "I can't believe you expect me to—wait, what happened to Kammler?"

"Spalcke shot him," she said. She set the churchyard lilies in the milk bottle. While arranging them, she added, "As per his orders, one must assume. So that the Communists couldn't take Kammler alive, to study him." Gretel took a step back, cocked her head, then altered the flower arrangement. She made a little *hmph* sound of satisfaction. Carrying the makeshift vase to Reinhardt's table, she concluded, "But they did study his corpse."

Reinhardt raised an eyebrow and looked at Klaus. "We heard about it later," Klaus said.

"Heard about it?" Reinhardt narrowed his eyes. He glared at Gretel warily. "And how exactly did that happen?" He turned back to Klaus. "What happened to *you*? Let's start there."

Klaus remembered the last time he'd seen Reinhardt. They had been traveling together during the most hellish winter on record. People had gone mad that winter, driven insane by the preternatural weather while their children spoke in tongues. Word came that the Red Army had crossed Poland and was plunging deep into the Reich, which had been rendered defenseless by the malevolent cold. Their rivalry had simmered over as they debated what to do: Should they return to the REGP and defend Doctor von Westarp's legacy from the Communists? Or should they race to Berlin and confront the invaders head-on?

Reinhardt, ever the glory hound, had insisted upon the latter. Klaus chose instead to return to the farm, hoping to find Gretel and escape west before the Reichsbehörde fell. But the Soviets were there, pixies at the ready.

And so they had spent two decades as war prisoners and test subjects, the foundation of an immense research program in a secret city in the depths of the Soviet Union.

Reinhardt smirked as Klaus wrapped up his summary. "I told you going to the farm was a mistake. Captured, eh?" He stared at Gretel, who had perched on a stack of crates. Quietly, he mused, "Now, I wonder why she let that happen. Seems to me she might have warned you."

Klaus's former comrade in arms was a self-aggrandizing braggart, a narcissist, and, among other things, a necrophiliac. Still, the man had a point. How unsettling.

"So you've escaped after all this time," Reinhardt continued. "Why now, I wonder?"

A cold tingle leached into Klaus's spine, his gut. Questions like these forced him to confront unpleasant truths about his own foolishness. He changed the subject.

"How did you end up here?"

Reinhardt fell quiet. At last he said, "I engaged the Soviets northeast of Berlin. An armored column. I fought them alone, fought them to a standstill! I melted their tanks, incinerated their troops, reduced their artillery to slag. And when they shot at me, I laughed. It was glorious. I was magnificent! Finally, I had become the instrument the doctor had intended." He fell silent again. "But there were more Communists than batteries. Many more."

Klaus said, "I warned you about that."

"I had to retreat while I still had the Götterelektron."

"I'm sure it was a glorious retreat, too," Klaus said. "Or were you running for your life?"

Reinhardt made a crude gesture. "I returned to the farm for more batteries, but it had already fallen. It was obvious that you and the other cowards had rolled over the moment the Red Army arrived."

Klaus crossed his arms. "They had *pixies*. Dozens of them. There was nothing we could do."

"I spent my last battery staying ahead of the advanced forces. I crossed the Pyrenees on foot, and made it out of Spain about a year later. Canada was my destination. They had an open-door policy for former Schutzstaffel, like us. Too terrified of the Red Menace to turn away a potential ally, I suppose. This dirty, dinky island was supposed to be just a stop along the way . . . but I ran out of cash."

"Poor Junkman," Gretel repeated.

Reinhardt jumped out of his chair. "I swear to God, if you say that one more time, I'll strangle you on the spot."

"No, you won't." Klaus leapt between them, seized his Willenskräfte, and put a fingertip through Reinhardt's sternum. A warning.

Reinhardt staggered backwards, looking dumbfounded. "My God," he whispered. "My God." He fell into his chair, still staring at Klaus in his ghost form. A shaking hand touched his scalp. "You have batteries?"

"Of course," said Gretel.

"My God . . . I thought, I, I thought you were like me. . . ." Reinhardt shook his head, as if dazed. "How many?"

Klaus became substantial again. "We left Arzamas with eight," he said. He unbuttoned his shirt and peered at the gauge on his harness. Defusing Reinhardt's threat hadn't taken much charge, but the old battery had seen better days. They all had. "We have a few left."

Reinhardt's pale eyes shone with a strange reverence when he saw Klaus's harness. Almost unconsciously, his hand went up to touch the battery. The reverence became hunger. Lust. "Give them to me."

And then Klaus knew, knew beyond any possibility of doubt, why they had come here. Why Gretel had engineered this reunion. He saw the piles of electronics, heard the desperation in the other man's voice, and knew.

Gretel had come here to make Reinhardt dance.

"We need them," Klaus said.

Reinhardt leapt from his chair again. "Do you even realize what you have? Have you forgotten the meaning of that harness? How can you appreciate what you've never missed? Without those batteries, you, and me, and her—" Reinhardt jabbed a finger toward Gretel. "—are *nothing*. But with them, we are gods."

The passage of time had transformed this once-fearsome weapon of the Reich into a desperate, pitiable man. If Klaus didn't loathe Reinhardt so much, he might have felt sorry for the fellow. Maybe he did anyway. "We're not gods, Reinhardt. We never were."

"Please," said Reinhardt, his voice barely a whisper. "Just one." He stared through the one unobstructed window, down to where the children played. Klaus could imagine what he had in mind. It was sickening.

"We can give you more than that," said Gretel.

The two men looked at her. She leaned back on the crate, legs kicked forward, stretching. The hem of her stolen skirt revealed her ankles, bony as always but now dark-veined with age. With two fingers she reached into her blouse and produced a folded piece of dark blue paper.

Reinhardt whispered, "Is that what I think it is?"

Gretel unfolded the paper and held it up for them both to see. It was a blueprint, a jumble of spidery white lines. One of the secrets of the old Reichsbehörde, rendered as cobwebs on cobalt.

"Annotated in the doctor's own hand," she said.

"Now I understand." Reinhardt stepped forward, hand outstretched. His old swagger had returned. "You want me to build replacements for you." He wiggled his fingers.

"No." Gretel tore the battery blueprint in half.

"What are you doing?" Reinhardt clutched his head in dismay. "God damn you mongrel whore! I *need* that!"

"Now, now," said Gretel, wagging a finger at Reinhardt. "Don't be greedy." She tore the blueprint again, oblivious of his cries of rage and despair. He fell to his knees. A neighbor pounded on the adjoining wall.

"Relax," she said. "Have you forgotten how in the past I delivered your heart's darkest desire?"

Klaus thought back to poor dead Heike. He shuddered.

"But this you'll get in pieces," she continued, fluttering the blueprint scraps. "In the meantime . . . I need two favors. Little things. You might even enjoy them. Each errand will earn a piece of the blueprint in the post."

Reinhardt stared up at her. "I hate you."

She stood. "Where do you keep your stationery? I need a pen, paper, postage stamps, and a pair of envelopes." Gretel gestured at the piles of discarded equipment crowding the flat. "And, Reinhardt? You'll need a camera."

10 May 1963
Walworth, London, England

Another," said Marsh.

He rapped his knuckles on the bar. Once, twice. The boards were damp with liquor he'd spilled; his fingers came back smelling of whiskey. Circlets of condensation riddled the bar. Like the rings of a tree telling the story of winters and summers and floods and fires, these rings spoke of a long afternoon.

"You been here all day, mate. Why don't you get along now?" The proprietor was a short, pale man with tattoos on the knuckles of his left hand.

Marsh fixed him with an angry stare. Partially to make a point, and partially to focus on something while the room swayed. "Another," he managed.

The barman shrugged. "Your funeral, mate." He refilled the shot glass. While drawing another pint, he said, "If I came 'ome that pissed, the missus would cut me bollocks off."

"Liv wouldn't notice. Not today." Marsh tossed back the shot. He squeezed his eyes shut, shook his head. Speaking past the fire in his throat, he added, "We have an agreement."

"You're a lucky man, then."

"Lucky." Marsh spat, wiped his hand across his mouth.

"Oy! I'll have none o' that in here!"

A few of the closer patrons paused in their conversations and domino games to stare at the barman and his unruly patron. The black-and-white television in the corner shouted a shaving cream jingle into the silence.

One by one, they shook their heads and returned to their own lives. The regulars recognized Marsh, though nobody knew his name. And vice versa. He knew what they saw when they bothered to notice him: a graying man with the craggy face of an unsuccessful boxer, with dirt under his nails and holes in his denim coveralls, well into the pudgy years of late middle age. A pathetic fellow even by the standards of a low-class establishment in a down-on-its-luck neighborhood like this.

The barman shook his head at somebody behind Marsh, made a placating gesture. He pulled a towel from beneath the bar and cleaned the spot where Marsh had spat. In a more moderate tone, he said, "You're havin' a bad day, I respect that. But pull that again and you'll be out on the street with that shot glass up your arse."

An odd thought flickered through Marsh's head, tempered by anger and alcohol and memory. The barman was shorter than he; garroting him wouldn't be hard. He knew from experience that taller men made for longer, more dangerous, less silent kills. But Marsh didn't have a garrote. And he'd prefer to keep drinking.

He shrugged off the threat. "I've been thrown out of better places. Got tossed from Sunday service once."

Marsh gulped at his beer, changed the subject. "It's my daughter's birthday." John's older sister would turn twenty-three a little bit before midnight.

"That's something good. Why don't you go home, then, and spend it with her?"

"The worms ate her long ago. She died in the war."

"Oh." The barman shook his head. "Sorry to hear it, mate."

Marsh ignored that. "Maybe it was rats. Could've been rats that ate her up. We never buried her proper. No body. Too much rubble. Just a casket. An empty casket." He pulled on his pint. Foam from his lips spattered the bar as he said, "It was so small."

Quietly, the barman said, "Blitz?"

Marsh grunted.

The barman sighed in sympathy. "Bloody Jerries."

He drifted away, down the bar to deal with a few of the other regulars here at this early hour of the afternoon.

Bubbles streamed up through the amber depths of Marsh's glass, like tongues of smoke billowing up into a still evening sky. Williton had been reduced to a sea of smoking debris by the time he and Liv arrived. Worst of all, he remembered the smell: the sharp scent of cordite lay over the ruined village like a fog, mingling with the baby smells from Agnes's blanket.

From somewhere far away, he heard Liv saying, "What if she's cold?" And from somewhere even farther away, he heard, "Leave 'im alone. He's grieving."

Marsh shook his head, shook off the memory. Now the telly shouted the BBC news at quarter past. Cracking his knuckles against his jaw, Marsh turned on his stool to get a glimpse of the screen.

A kerosene lamp had been identified as the cause of the recent fire in the Forest of Dean. The rumors of abandoned villages in Tanganyika had proved false, but now similar reports were coming out of British-held India near the Nepalese border. The Eighth Cruiser Squadron was soon to join the HMS *Ocean* in the Persian Gulf. Radio receivers at Jodrell Bank in the U.K. and Parkes, in Australia, reported the space station had fallen silent. Urgent transmissions from the cosmonauts returning from their orbit of the moon suggested they had received no communications from the station since emerging from the moon's shadow a day ago. Moscow denied any problems.

Closer to home, news of the day concerned a sweeping new trade agreement between the United Kingdom and the Union of Soviet Socialist Republics. His Grace, the Duke of Aelred, was credited with brilliantly shepherding the initiative through a period of increased tensions between the two nations. Up flashed an old clip of Aubrey Beauclerk shaking hands with a member of the Soviet diplomatic mission. The duke was thought to be a likely successor to the Foreign Secretary, if the BBC could be believed.

Then the image changed to a clip of the duke's brother.

"Turn it off," said Marsh.

The younger Beauclerk, long a political outsider and burdened with what was delicately referred to as a "murky" past, had in recent years become one of the duke's closest advisers. Lord William Beauclerk had played a major role in hammering out the new agreement; the commentary predicted a bright future for the duke's brother, complete with twee metaphors about sunlight after the storm.

William fucking Beauclerk. It wasn't fair.

"I said, turn it off!" Marsh hurled his pint glass at the television. He missed. It shattered against the wooden cabinet, splashing the screen and those closest with the dregs of his beer. The room erupted with shouts of anger and alarm.

"Oy!" the barman yelled. "That tears it!"

Somebody tried to grab Marsh's arm; his knuckles connected with what felt like a jaw when he threw a punch. But dizziness and rage made it a wild, uncoordinated swing, little more than a glancing blow. The hand on his forearm tightened its grip.

Marsh jumped from his stool, reflexively thinking to use it as a weapon to break the hold on him. But when he wheeled to face the man holding his arm, a punch landed solidly on his cheekbone, just beneath the eye. The sting of torn skin; the thrower wore a wedding ring.

Somebody else grabbed Marsh in a wristlock and slammed his head to the bar hard enough to rattle glasses. Marsh struggled, but half-heartedly. The barman stood in the corner, telephone receiver to his ear, glaring at him.

He knew that look, and it took the fight out of him. He'd lose his job if he got tossed in the clink again.

Marsh wrested free of the man holding him. Every eye in the room watched him warily. The pub was silent as he plucked the towel from the bar, gathered his hat from the hooks behind the door, and stepped outside. The murmur of conversation—mostly "tsk, tsk" and "shameful drunk"—resumed as he slammed the door.

The pub shared a doorstep with a shoe repair service. Marsh sat there, trying to staunch the flow of blood with the towel, waiting for the police. It stung; the towel had whiskey on it. The sunlight left him feeling cold. A white-haired lady hurried down the street with a grocer's sack. Marsh scowled at her; she crossed the street.

Blood still trickled from the gash along his cheekbone when a black Ford Corsair rolled to a stop in front of the pub. The police radio squawked something incomprehensible; the driver responded into a handset while his partner emerged from the car. Marsh suppressed a sigh of relief.

The copper looked at Marsh, then nodded toward the pub. "They throw you out?"

"I threw myself out."

"Throw anything else while you were at it?"

"Yeah. A pint glass. A punch or two."

"Caught one, too, I see," said Constable Lorimer. He brushed off a spot next to Marsh before sitting down. "Why do you keep doing this?"

Marsh said nothing. His sense of loss, his rage at the world for what his life had become—these were private indignities. Only one person in the world could even begin to understand how he felt, but she had stopped caring about his ills a long time ago.

The constable said, "Dad used to talk about you, back in the war. Said you were 'right clever for a Sassenach tosser.' " He pronounced the last part in the style of his father's Scottish brogue. Marsh had fought alongside James Lorimer and had been present when he died. His children had grown up in London raised by a Welsh mother, and so inherited different accents than their father's.

"But you don't seem all that clever to me."

Marsh glared at the young Lorimer. Cotton threads from the towel tugged at the spots of blood crusted on his face when he turned his head. The towel smelled of blood and booze. As did Marsh. "Sorry to disappoint."

The copper shook his head. "Look, Mr. Marsh. My point is that this can't continue, and you're smart enough to know that. Any more of this, and I'll have to write you up good and proper, toss you in jail at Her Majesty's pleasure. You knew my dad, and I've let you slide on account of it. I keep it up, they'll have my arse in a sling," he concluded, with a slight nod toward the car and his partner.

He stood. Marsh followed, gritting his teeth against the ache in his knee as he climbed to his feet. It took Marsh an extra moment to steady himself.

"I ought to haul you down to the station house."

"But you won't."

The young Lorimer waved an admonishing finger an inch from Marsh's nose. "I will, if there's a next time, Mr. Marsh. You've exhausted my surplus of charity."

Marsh inspected the towel. It was ruined.

"And have somebody take a look at that cut, eh?"

"I'll take care of it once I'm home," said Marsh.

"Need a ride?"

Marsh shook his head. "Better not. Liv wouldn't like seeing me escorted by the coppers."

"Straight home," said the constable, climbing back in the car.

Marsh acknowledged this with a little salute. He set off at a slow walk. After the coppers disappeared up the street, he balled up the towel and threw it at the boards covering the shattered window of a derelict storefront. It hit the door with a weak thump, unraveled, and fluttered to the ground.

Home was fifteen or sixteen streets away. Marsh took his time. He remembered running this same route in the other direction, during the blackout, before dawn on the morning his daughter was born.

Doing that today would get a man mugged. Or worse. Smart folks didn't walk these streets after dark. Back then, the neighborhood hadn't been marred with graffiti and broken windows. The smell of rubbish didn't permeate the streets on hot days. It would have been a good place to raise a daughter. But the economic burden of rebuilding great swaths of London had meant that other parts of the city had been victims of benign neglect.

Cheap rents had attracted an endless progression of immigrants and refugees. But few of their shops and restaurants had persisted for long. Marsh had never set foot in any of them. Couldn't afford it.

Marsh wished it were late at night, perhaps even raining, rather than a bright springtime afternoon. Hooligans drew their courage from the shadows and ill weather. He knew; he'd been one of them, long, long ago.

He cracked his knuckles again. His rage and self-hatred needed an outlet. An excuse to boil over. *An attempted mugging. No copper would fault a man for defending himself. . . .*

But he made it home without incident, after filing the idea away for further thought. The yowling from upstairs, like an endless screech of fingernails on slate, greeted him before he opened the front door.

Liv didn't say anything about his bloodied face when he entered. The look on her face shamed him more than any words could. Even his cock-ups were beneath her contempt now. She took it for granted he was a washed-up failure of a man.

So did he.

When did it happen? Could he remember the moment when the last glimmer of love went out of Liv's eyes? When the world snuffed that final fading ember of affection like a candle, to replace its feeble glow with cold shadows and foul vapors?

No. There was no such single moment. History provided no comfort in what-if, no solace in if-only. The twists and turns were too complex to chart. The corruption of his family life, the perversion of his dream, grew from the long slow grind of years. Gretel killed their daughter, but the failed attempt to begin anew had killed their marriage.

Marsh trudged to the garden shed, the drink in his veins too dilute to provide comforting numbness against the yowling from his broken son.

11 May 1963
Soviet Embassy, London, England

What the world had lost in fine vintages when the Soviet Empire col-lectivized the French wineries, it had more than regained in the form of Caspian Sea caviars. Will, whose lips hadn't touched a drop of wine in decades, found this a perfectly acceptable trade. And the Gruyère de Comté was excellent. He mentioned this to Gwendolyn.

"You see, dear? The wineries were a dreadful mistake, but they acknowledge it. They haven't done the same with the dairies."

She nibbled on a toast point topped with salty black roe. While dab-bing at her lips, and with her mouth hidden behind a serviette, she said, "William, you daft, daft darling. Cheese doesn't grow in the ground. I'll wager it merits little interest from Lysenko and those academic still-births he calls colleagues."

Her choice of words caught Will, as it so often did, unawares. He tossed back the last of his tonic water to suppress the laughter that escaped him. Too late; his outburst turned heads and collected attention.

Ambassador Fedotov weaved through the room to join them. Behind him, past a swirl of diaphanous curtains, Aubrey and one of his politburo counterparts chatted on the balcony overlooking the horseshoe drive. Next to the cold fireplace, the Foreign Secretary and his wife (*what is that woman's name again? Gwendolyn will know*) listened to the Party General Secretary of the Republic of Belgium as he outlined his plan to introduce mandatory Russian language instruction in schools across the Republic. Under an immense cut-crystal chandelier (Will called it decadent; Gwendolyn called it shamefully czarist), two members of the House of Lords debated the merits of cricket with a member of the ambassador's staff. HRH the Prince of Wales discussed an oil painting (mostly blacks and reds, depicting a group of noble farmers in a noble moment of noble uprising) with the embassy's gray-lipped cultural attaché, Cherkashin.

The string quartet returned from their break. They struck up another piece by one of the modern Soviet composers, all of whom were indistinguishable to Will. He thought it more suited to marching than dancing.

The ambassador took Gwendolyn's hand. "Your Grace. Thank you again for honoring our function." He wasn't a tall fellow, standing a full head shorter than Will and shorter even than Gwendolyn. His voice carried the peculiar warble of Russian softened by years spent in the West, like a block of granite weathered smooth by years of English rain.

"A pleasure, Ambassador," she said. "But I must correct you. While I do have honor, my grace is nonexistent. My husband has proved a suitable provider in other regards, but he has been a crushing disappointment in this area."

Fedotov looked confused.

"The blame lies at my brother's feet," chimed Will. "Selfish fellow, hoarding titles for himself and his wife." He indicated Viola, also on the balcony, where she stood chatting amicably with the ambassador's wife. "She, of course, is 'Her Grace, the Duchess of Aelred.'"

"But I am merely Lady Gwendolyn Beauclerk."

"Formerly *the* Lady Gwendolyn, of course," said Will.

Fedotov looked back and forth between them, like a spectator at a tennis match. Which, in a way, he was.

Taking encouragement from the deepening furrow between the ambassador's eyebrows, Will put on the air of revealing a close confidence. "As I'm sure you can imagine, our marriage was quite the scandal. The daughter of an earl marrying an untitled commoner like myself?"

Which was partially true. Not for the sake of titles, of course; Gwendolyn herself was not a peer. Marrying into the Beauclerks had been the eventual aim of many families since Will and Aubrey had been children. But Will's personal history, rather than the order of his birth, had tarnished the brand.

The ambassador frowned.

Gwendolyn shook her head lightly. "It wouldn't have been quite so scandalous had you allowed the announcements to use your title." She turned to Fedotov. "'Lord William Edward Guthrie Beauclerk,' naturally. But he wouldn't have it. So the announcements looked quite lopsided: 'William Edward Guthrie Beauclerk and the Lady Gwendolyn Wellesley.'"

"But you did compromise in the end, dear." Will's turn to take Fedotov into confidence. "She finally agreed to drop that ghastly 'the' after our nuptials."

"Compromise? I had no choice in the matter, love." Again, an aside to Fedotov: "My husband is merely a lord. And that only by courtesy. Which is why today I am merely Lady Gwendolyn. It's all quite straightforward, you see," she concluded.

A moment passed. The creases of concentration on Fedotov's forehead melted away, and he smiled. He shook a finger at them. "You are having me on. Both of you."

Will shook his head. "We wouldn't dream of it."

Fedotov laughed. "We don't suffer from such complexities in the Soviet Union," he said. "Anybody is free to marry anybody, without consideration of titles and status. That, my friends, is just one of the reasons why we thrive. Everybody is equal."

Again dabbing at the corners of her mouth, Gwendolyn said, "And yet you live in a mansion."

"I beg your pardon?"

"My wife complimented your lovely home," Will covered.

Cherkashin, the cultural attaché, noticed the conversation. He pushed aside the lock of hair that had flopped across his forehead and hastily joined them. Gwendolyn stiffened. Cherkashin lacked the ambassador's gift for chitchat. And his smile never quite touched his eyes. It was a Potemkin smile.

More introductions and niceties all around. Cherkashin whispered into the ambassador's ear. Gwendolyn caught Will's eye; he didn't understand the source of her unease, but he tried to quell it with a wink. It didn't appear to mollify her.

Fedotov nodded. He replied to Cherkashin also in Russian, then turned his attention back to Will and Gwendolyn. "I'm reminded that I had hoped to take advantage of your attendance, *Lord* William—"

Fishhooks of panic jabbed Will in the neck. *Please not in front of Gwendolyn,* he thought.

"—to iron out a tiny business detail. If I could prevail upon your patience, *Lady* Gwendolyn?"

Gwendolyn smiled, saying, "By all means." She said it in the same tone of voice she took when enduring Viola.

Will said, "It won't be a moment, dear."

He watched Gwendolyn in the long gilt-frame mirror along the dining room wall. Graceful as always, she turned to speak with Cherkashin as though their conversation hadn't missed a beat. But he abandoned her to follow Will. She recovered, but not before irritation darkened her face.

Will followed Fedotov downstairs, into the depths of the embassy, where the Soviet Union's diplomatic affairs were conducted in private. He'd never been outside the entryway and the reception hall; only members of the Soviet diplomatic corps were allowed in these corridors. It was a flattering display of amity, but also a bit worrying.

They passed a sturdy walnut door reinforced with steel bands. Quite different from the other doorways they'd passed. Will paused, curious in spite of himself. The guard seated beside the door glared at him.

"This way," said Cherkashin. With one hand he pushed Will away from the door, while with the other he pointed up the corridor.

Fedotov's office was situated at the rear of the house, with a view of Green Park just across Piccadilly; the lights of Buckingham Palace twinkled in the far distance. The office wasn't so decadent as the furnishings upstairs, which were intended for entertaining important visitors, but still not entirely modest. Walnut, leather, brass, even a wet bar. It wasn't all that different from Aubrey's study at the Bestwood estate. Will stifled a little laugh. What difference was there, truly, between peers and a high party officials?

Cherkashin closed the door behind them.

"Your office couriered an itinerary to us yesterday, for next month's trade delegation," said Fedotov.

Will suppressed a happy sigh of relief. This wasn't what he'd feared.

"I remember," he said. "It was satisfactory, I hope?" Leather squeaked as he settled into an armchair.

Fedotov took the seat behind his desk. He looked slightly embarrassed. "Not entirely." He lifted a typed sheet from his mostly empty desk, scanning it. "I know Minister Kalugin, and I can tell you honestly, my friend, he will not enjoy the Wilde production on Wednesday."

Will took the sheet. "But if you're seeking a deeper cultural exchange with Great Britain, you couldn't do better than Oscar Wilde. *The Importance of Being Earnest* is one of his best. Besides which, he was an advocate of socialism."

"Nevertheless . . . While I admire his wit, and of course his politics, there are issues about his lifestyle that would be poorly received by Kalugin."

"Ah." Will pondered this. "Well, there is no shortage of excellent productions in the West End. Some Shaw, perhaps? A staunch socialist, that one."

"I'll leave it to your discretion."

"Very good." Will took a fountain pen from the inner breast pocket of his Savile Row suit and made a note on the itinerary. The ambassador made a similar notation, in Cyrillic, on his own copy.

Cherkashin served himself from the sideboard. Will recognized the *clink* characteristic to fine crystal. "May I pour you a drink?" he asked.

"No," said Will. "Thank you."

Cherkashin snapped his fingers. "I forgot. You're a teetotaler, isn't that right?"

The usage took Will aback. Sometimes Cherkashin's command of English came across far better than he let on. Will didn't correct him; his past history was convoluted, and private. "If you prefer."

Fedotov looked at the itinerary again. "Wednesday for the show? Your brother is hosting a function that evening."

Will glanced at his own copy, and sighed. "Damnation. I thought we'd fixed that." He crossed out a few more lines, added another annotation in the margin. "I'm at a bit of a loss for how that slipped through."

"No matter." Fedotov marked his own copy accordingly.

Cherkashin, sitting in the corner with drink in hand, cleared his throat.

Fedotov said, while making notes on his itinerary, "Speaking of things slipping through, there is another, more delicate matter I'd like to bring to your attention. It's an issue of some embarrassment for us, if I may appeal to your discretion?"

"By all means," said Will, echoing his wife in both words and wariness.

"Recently, two patients escaped from a psychiatric hospital in the Ukraine. A brother and sister. Both very dangerous. They are violent, prone to flights of delusion." Fedotov shook his head sadly. "Runs in the family, I presume. They were undergoing treatments to lessen their antisocial tendencies."

Will said, "And you have reason to believe they're coming here?"

"We don't know where they may be headed. But we do have reason to believe that they've passed through France in the past ten days."

Will frowned. "That's many hundreds of miles from the Ukraine. It's rather difficult to imagine that a pair of nutters like those you describe could travel so far without giving themselves away."

"Don't underestimate this pair. That would be a mistake. If they are headed for Britain, they could be a terrible danger to your countrymen." A rueful smile. "What damage would that do to our hard-won détente, if a pair of Russian maniacs were to start cutting down Her Majesty's innocent subjects?"

"You should alert the authorities," said Will.

Behind him, Cherkashin coughed. He said, "The ambassador would prefer to handle this matter quietly."

Will said, "I fear there's little I can do."

"Of course, of course, my friend." Fedotov waved his hands. "We would never ask you to put yourself or anybody else in harm's way. But if you happen to hear anything?"

Will shrugged. "I suppose it would do no harm to pass it along. They're truly dangerous, this pair?"

"Yes."

"I'd be the last person in Britain to hear anything, but if it puts you at ease, I'll keep my ears open."

"That's all we ask."

Will blew on his annotated itinerary. Satisfied the ink had dried, he folded it in thirds and tucked it in the pocket where he kept his pen. He put his hands on his knees. "Well, then. If there's nothing else?"

They returned upstairs. Across the ballroom, Gwendolyn—once again stuck chatting with Viola—watched the three men with a strange expression on her face. In fifteen years of marriage, he had never seen its like. Will smiled at her. He hoped it was reassuring, and that she didn't detect the guilt undermining it.

What did she suspect? She deserved the truth and so much more.

Soon, he promised himself. *She'll have it soon.*

Just as he had promised himself for months.

three

13 May 1963
Westminster, London, England

Rainwater trickled down the windowpanes of Morgan, Kavanagh, and Kynaston, Solicitors at Law. Earlier in the day, it had trickled down the windowpanes at the bank where Klaus and his sister had arranged a draft on the cash they'd stolen from a number of newspaper stands and small businesses. The thievery had drained another battery.

Klaus was content to watch the rain while Gretel finalized her arrangements with the solicitor. She handed him an envelope; oddly, it wasn't addressed to Reinhardt. This was the second of two letters she had written. Yesterday, she'd slipped out of Reinhardt's flat while he was distracted to mail the first letter, which *was* addressed to him.

The man whom Gretel had just hired wore brown suspenders with blue pinstripes over a crisp white shirt, and a red bow tie. He uncapped a fountain pen, then pulled a sheet of watermarked letterhead from a drawer. Pen poised above the blank page, he looked up to ask, "And when shall we put this in the post for you?"

"The fourteenth of May," said Gretel.

The solicitor blinked. A beat, then: "Tomorrow?"

Gretel laid a hand on the armrest of Klaus's chair. "My brother and I will be occupied tomorrow." Then she leaned forward, as if taking the fellow into her confidence. "A family matter."

Klaus didn't bother to wonder about this. He'd find out soon enough. His sister's machinations no longer spurred his curiosity. They brought only a weary dread.

"Ah. I see," said the solicitor. Clearly he didn't. But he didn't need to. He wrote the mailing date on the blank sheet; confirmed it with Gretel; signed it; handed it to Gretel and Klaus for countersigning and witnessing (she signed as Gretel von Westarp, he followed her lead); clipped the page to the envelope; and summoned his secretary to take the package.

Motor traffic hissed and splashed through rain on the street below. From Klaus's vantage, the pedestrian traffic on the pavement appeared as a mass of black umbrellas, each bobbing up and down to an individual rhythm. Here and there he spotted a break in the pattern, a flash of color or even stripes in the sea of black.

Most of the pedestrians in this part of London were businessmen and government workers: business-suited shock troops primed for financial warfare, wielding briefcases and plain umbrellas. Those with the colorful umbrellas were different. Klaus's eyes followed one in particular, lime green with orange spots. Here and there he caught glimpses of its carrier. She was younger than he, much so, in a red sleeveless dress that ended at her knees. Her galoshes flapped against her legs. There were other flashes of color in the crowd, too, but they didn't capture his interest in quite the same way.

Klaus wondered what it would have felt like to be so carefree at that age. Or was it aimlessness? Was he a better man for always having his purpose defined for him?

"I'm so pleased," said Gretel, smiling. This was the mask she wore when she wanted to charm somebody. She stood. The men followed suit.

The solicitor extended his hand. Klaus shook it. Then the fellow took Gretel's hand, and not for the first time his gaze drifted to the wires twined through her braids.

By way of explanation, Klaus said, "The camps."

Most British knew little of the camps Germany had built in the years before the war. The Soviets had found the camps useful in their own right. So the conquerors had never seen fit to publicize the atrocities.

That left only rumors. Nobody truly knew the situation in Europe, nor had they in many years, but everybody had heard the rumors. Klaus had learned that a subtle reference to such things was enough to goad people into constructing a private narrative to explain Gretel's wires, or his own. It even earned sympathy.

Klaus waited for the inevitable flash of discomfort on the other man's face. Then, to give the fellow a graceful out, he said, "Thank you for your time."

On the way outside, Klaus nicked an umbrella from a stand in the lobby. He handed it to Gretel as they joined the stream of pedestrians on the pavement. The woman in the red dress was long gone. A sigh escaped him, riding a surge of wistfulness that caught him off guard.

He followed the flow of foot traffic. His thoughts were jumbled. Unsettled. They'd crossed several streets, turned a few corners, before he realized he had no destination. Gretel hadn't said anything.

He started to ask her, but stopped himself. They'd run her errands all day, moved according to her purposes. Klaus decided to cling to a few more minutes of aimlessness. Idle time was something new to him. It was seductive.

They passed a park, larger than the one he'd glimpsed from the taxi a few days earlier. "Let's go there," he said, and didn't wait for her approval.

For the most part, the rain meant they had the park almost to themselves. It was a Monday, Klaus reminded himself. He wondered what it would be like to have a job, a responsibility, that didn't occupy every minute of every day. He tried to imagine life as a shopkeeper rather than a research subject, or a soldier, or a secret weapon, or a prisoner. *What does a shopkeeper do when he's not keeping his shop? What is a shopkeeper when not keeping shop?*

What am I?

Walking paths of slate gray gravel meandered through stands of scarlet oak and plane. Fig trees lined a small lake. Klaus chose a path at random. Just to see where it went. Then another, and another.

They passed a stand advertising warm peanuts, salted in the shell. Klaus bought a packet, though he wasn't hungry. They found a bench sheltered from the lessening rain beneath a black mulberry tree. Klaus shared the peanuts with his sister. The rip of paper as they tore open the packet sounded oddly loud in the quiet park. So did the cracking of shells, and Gretel's chewing.

The peanuts were warm, almost hot, which felt wonderful after wandering in the cool drizzle. The shells dusted his fingers with salt. Delicious.

A troop of mounted cavalrymen practiced formations on the parade ground abutting the park. Klaus licked salt from his fingers, listening to the jingle of harnesses, the *clopclopclop* of hooves, the bark of the regimental commander as he called out maneuvers. The members of the ceremonial regiment wore shining helmets with black plumes. The plumes drooped in the rain.

Klaus let his sister have the rest of the peanuts. A strange emotion preoccupied him. Gretel still hatched her plans, still did things according to her own secret desires. That was the same as always. But she was close to her goal now; he could tell. And they were in England, and they were free. This was new.

The unfamiliar feeling, he decided, was contentment. A sense of struggles complete, burdens at rest. A sense that finally, *finally,* he could relax. Both physically and mentally, he could ease his guard. He hadn't felt anything like it since before he'd begun to experience misgivings about the Reichsbehörde, when Doctor von Westarp had ordered him to oversee the construction of ovens for disposing of unsuccessful test subjects.

"We need to think about finding a place to stay," he said. The four nights with Reinhardt had been cramped, uncomfortable, and awkward. Klaus had slept very little; at night, Reinhardt had prowled like a cat, waiting for them both to doze off so that he could steal their batteries.

Gretel said, "No, we don't. That's easy."

"You keep saying that. Why is it easy?"

"Because," she said, pointing past the parade ground, "we're going to turn ourselves in."

My brother and I will be occupied tomorrow.

Klaus realized he'd been in this park before. He'd probably dashed past this very same mulberry tree with Gretel in tow. It had been at night, and very dark, because it was wartime and Britain had shrouded itself in a nationwide blackout. And that meant the building behind the parade ground was the Old Admiralty.

As always, Gretel knew exactly what to say. Knew exactly how to mollify Klaus. He resented her manipulations, even as he succumbed to them.

We're free now, Gretel. I want to stay that way.

We've never been free.

Then why did we escape?

Because we had to be here. Now.

Why now?

There is nothing but now.

We could have escaped at the end of the war. Why did I have to endure so many years at Arzamas?

This thing, this now, wouldn't have happened otherwise.

Why must I get pulled along in your wake?

Because I need your help.

Why?

These are dangerous times, brother. Without you, all is lost. If you do not join me, we are both subject to a loud and terrible doom.

This wasn't the first time she'd spoken of doom. That word had passed her lips before, though he couldn't remember when or where. Long ago. He knew that.

She didn't appeal to brotherly love. Because, he realized, that would have failed. That well had been poisoned; its waters ran alkaline. Instead she appealed to his sense of self-preservation. She had given him the barest taste of a truly free life. They both knew he would endure what he must in the short term for the sake of long-term freedom.

Very well, thought Klaus. *Let us use each other.*

They strolled down the Mall with Buckingham at their backs, passed beneath the Admiralty Arch, swung right on Whitehall. They came to a stop at a marble screen, behind which stood a jumble of what the British called neo-Palladian architecture.

The Old Admiralty building wasn't quite what he remembered from the war. Every entrance had been buttressed with sandbag revetments, blackout curtains had hung in every window. Those were gone, but the sentries remained.

Back then, he'd gained entry by looking the part; he'd worn the uniform of a Royal Navy lieutenant-commander. But here, in Gretel's mystical *now,* he wore no such disguise, and neither did she.

Klaus checked the gauge on his battery harness. They were down to their last two batteries out of the eight they'd carried from Arzamas-16. Visions of Reinhardt, the humble Junkman, flitted through his mind.

She put her small hand in his. Her skin was warm, almost feverish, compared to his own, which must have felt like ice. "Ready, brother?"

"No."

She gave him a squeeze. Klaus took a deep breath. So did Gretel. They ghosted through the screen, the shouting sentry, one wall of the Admiralty proper, and several of the guards summoned by the sentry's alarm.

When they were ringed with nervous men pointing sidearms at them, Gretel squeezed Klaus's hand again. He released his Willenskräfte, rematerializing them both so that she could speak. But he didn't release her. Not yet.

Gretel addressed their wide-eyed captors. "We are poor political prisoners, recently escaped from the Soviet Union. We seek asylum."

Three of the men broke off to confer in a corner. They whispered intensely. Klaus couldn't hear them, but based on their reactions, they clearly had no idea what to do.

Two men departed. One ran down the corridor and another jogged up a stairwell and out of sight. The third returned to the ring of armed men, to preserve the fiction that the intruders were helpless and over-powered.

In German, Klaus whispered, "What now?"

"We wait until news of our arrival reaches the proper ears," said Gretel, responding in kind. "The men we seek control the warlocks. You do remember the warlocks?"

Klaus shivered, remembering a malevolent winter equal parts rage and ice. He remembered British commando teams appearing out of thin air, the few survivors disappearing just as easily. He remembered reports of an invasion fleet devoured by fog in the English Channel.

"Hey," said the first sentry, the man through whom they'd passed. His voice quavered with fear and tension. Now that Klaus wasn't on the move, he took a closer look at the fellow, and realized the sentry was at least twenty years his junior. It was hard to believe that Klaus himself had been that age, and a soldier then. The boy cleared his throat, but his voice betrayed his confusion. "No talking. Or, if you must, speak English. But don't talk."

They waited. Klaus's feet ached. Their captors responded in impotent shouts of alarm and disapproval when he led Gretel to a bench. The men settled down once the pair sat with no obvious intent to go anywhere else.

Gretel shook off his hand. In English she said, "You can relax now. They won't shoot."

Naval officers and business-suited civilians passed through the foyer. The sight of armed sentries surrounding the pair of intruders elicited surprised glances and more than a few frowns.

Klaus studied their surroundings. The interior of the Old Admiralty was unchanged in all but superficial ways. It was still the same rabbit warren of narrow corridors, wood-paneled niches, and semi-hidden doorways he'd encountered when he'd come here to retrieve Gretel.

One of the sentries approached. "Look. This is right embarrassing, I'm sure, but if you've come here with the intent of defecting, or seeking asylum, this is a bloody great mistake. We're the Admiralty. We don't handle that sort of thing."

Gretel said, "We'll wait, thank you."

The rapid clack of footsteps on the parquet floor announced a new arrival. The sentries relaxed when a tall fellow in a charcoal gray suit joined them. Klaus, who understood the mind-set of a military man, recognized the subtle shift of responsibility.

The newcomer's brown eyes widened when he saw Klaus and Gretel. Almost as if he recognized them. He turned to one of the sentries. "Fetch a roll of tape, won't you?"

"Sir?"

"Adhesive tape. Any sort will do."

Then the newcomer took aside another of the men guarding the intruders. They exchanged a few sentences before the guard and one of his companions dashed outside on some other errand.

The new fellow approached the bench. He looked them over, paying particular attention to their heads, necks, and the wires in Gretel's braids. Whoever this man was, he understood the mechanics of the old Reichsbehörde technology, because he said: "I'll need you both to disconnect your batteries." To Gretel, he continued, "I notice they're tucked under your clothing. Do you need a privacy screen?"

Her eyes twinkled with amusement. She shook her head, then gave Klaus a little nod. He unbuttoned his shirt and reached inside. At the same time, Gretel felt through the fabric of her dress for the latch on her battery harness. The latch on Klaus's harness clicked open, as did Gretel's a moment later.

"And now if you would be so kind as to pull the loose ends outside your clothing. Let them hang where I can see them."

Klaus and Gretel complied. She, again, with an air of amusement. The sentries watched with various degrees of alarm and disgust dawning on their faces as they realized the wires were surgical implants.

The first sentry returned with a roll of shimmering black tape. The man in the charcoal gray suit tore off two long strips, handed one to Klaus and the other to Gretel.

"Wrap these around the connectors. Tightly, please."

They did. When Klaus finished, the connector at the end of his wires was a solid bundle of black tape. The tape left his fingers gummy.

"Excellent. Thank you for indulging me," said the man. His smile revealed a dark discoloration on his front teeth. "That should hold until we get you somewhere you can properly remove your harnesses without stripping in public." He turned to address the ring of sentries, who were milling about looking very uncertain about what to do. "I'll handle this from here. You," he said, pointing to one guard, "stay with me. The rest of you may return to your duties."

They escorted Klaus and Gretel down a corridor, up a flight of stairs, along another corridor, and finally into what appeared to be a private office. Antique maps hung from oak-paneled walls. Behind a wide desk, a mullioned window showed the sun dipping under the cloud cover, setting over the park where Klaus had enjoyed warm peanuts. Klaus inhaled the strong, sweet scent of pipe smoke.

The sentry stayed in the corridor; the gray-suited man closed the door behind them. He motioned for Klaus and Gretel to seat themselves in the pair of chairs that fronted the desk. They did.

To Klaus's surprise, their host didn't take the seat behind the desk. Still standing, he said, "My name is Samuel Pethick. But the fellow you truly want to talk to, my superior, isn't here at the moment. I've dispatched a driver to collect Mr. Pembroke. He'll be here shortly.

"In the meantime, perhaps you can start by telling me why you've come here."

Why have *we come here, Gretel?*

But she only said, "We'll wait, thank you."

Klaus felt frustrated and weary again. Gretel's evasion had him ready to take the stranger's side.

Pethick chewed his lip. He said, "You're siblings, correct? The ghost and the oracle. If I'm not mistaken, you've both been here before. And now you're back, in the flesh, after all these years. I wonder why."

Ah. Pethick *had* recognized them downstairs. Klaus wondered how.

After that, they waited in silence. The setting sun sank below the curtain of clouds, filling the office with a few minutes of sunlight before it dipped below the cityscape. Streetlamps flickered to life in the park. Pethick turned on a desk lamp.

Klaus craned an arm over the back of his chair when a man wearing a tuxedo entered the office. He was slightly shorter than Pethick, with a long, narrow face and high eyebrows. It made him appear frozen in a state of permanent surprise. A thatch of wavy auburn hair topped his forehead.

The tuxedo man addressed Pethick. "Well?"

Based on the way Pethick deferred to him, Klaus concluded the newcomer was Pembroke. "They came through the screen, on the Whitehall side. Approximately an hour ago."

"There must be more to it than that, Sam, if you sent an armed matelot to collect me. Which caused quite a bit of consternation, not incidentally."

"Sir, you don't understand." Pethick licked his lips. His gaze darted to the siblings, just for a moment. He looked back at Pembroke, and when he spoke, he precisely enunciated every word. "They came . . . *through* . . . the screen. And the wall. And a handful of sentries."

Pembroke looked again at Klaus and his sister, more carefully than the cursory glance he'd tossed in their direction as he entered. She twirled a finger through her hair, black onyx braided with silver, pretending not to notice how he stared at them. A furrow formed between Pembroke's eyes. It deepened when he came around the desk and saw the disabled wires hanging over their shoulders. A flash of alarm or surprise might have appeared on his face, too, but it was hard to tell.

"Are they—?"

"I believe so, sir."

Pembroke took the seat behind the desk. He laced his fingers, rested his hands before him, and said, "I'm Leslie Pembroke. I believe you've been waiting for me. I would like to know why you've come here, and why you want so very badly to speak with us."

Klaus looked at Gretel. He wanted to know, too.

Gretel looked back and forth between Pembroke at the desk and Pethick, who had moved closer to the window. From her blouse she produced a page torn from the newspaper. She slid it across the desk to Pembroke. Klaus saw she had circled a small article, two short paragraphs under the headline, LANTERN BLAMED FOR GLOUS. FIRE.

"You gentlemen have a problem," she said.

Pembroke glanced at the newspaper, then back at her. "What sort of problem?"

She shook her head. "The warning is free. An explanation of your troubles is not. We'll give you everything we know—" She fixed her stare on Pembroke, saying with emphasis, "I'll tell you what *I* know—after you bring in Raybould Marsh."

Pethick interjected. "What?"

"Raybould Marsh. He worked here, long ago."

Pembroke frowned. "We know who Marsh is."

"Then you should have no trouble finding him, yes?"

13 May 1963
Knightsbridge, London, England

As always, Gwendolyn was up and well into her day, or at the very least finishing breakfast, before Will made it downstairs. Even if there hadn't been a biblical deluge raging outside, she still would have risen before him.

"Good morning, love." A peppery scent wafted up from the empty shell of her soft-boiled egg when he kissed the top of her head. The spiciness mingled not unpleasantly with the lavender smell of her shampoo.

He took his seat beside her at the round inlaid table that served as their dining room. A proper dining room would have had a long table, suitable for entertaining a dozen guests. Will preferred to talk with his wife without resorting to flag semaphore. Their tastes ran more modestly than their peers'. The modest and immodest tables traded places in storage as necessary.

"You were up rather early yesterday." He paused, waiting for a crack of thunder to subside. "I saw neither hide nor hair of you the entire day."

"You were up rather late yesterday," said Gwendolyn. She folded the paper she'd been reading and set it aside. Then she handed him the toast rack.

While he spooned lemon curd on lukewarm toast, Will said, "The ambassador's little soiree lasted entirely longer than I'd have preferred."

She laughed, but ruefully. "I'm the one who found herself cornered by your brother's dreadful wife all evening." Another blast of thunder swallowed the *tink* of her saucer as she set down her teacup. She pointed outside, where squalls of rain gusted past the bay window. "Do you know what we discussed? Window sashes. All evening."

Will lifted the teapot. "I have every confidence you were up to the task."

She nudged him with her elbow, but softly, not enough to make him spill. "You were rather scarce. Why did Fedotov need to speak with you so urgently?"

Their cook, Mrs. Toomre—the eldest daughter of one of his grandfather's servants, one of those who'd raised young Will—came in with a plate of egg, bean, and tomato. She set it before Will; he nodded his appreciation to her.

"I cocked up the schedule for Minister Kalugin's visit. We had to get it squared away." Will took a bite of his toast and washed down the sweet curd with a sip of strong tea. It had steeped just long enough: astringent, but not unpleasantly so.

Gwendolyn frowned. "That was it, then?"

Her doubt elicited new pangs of guilt. "Yes. Why? Is something wrong?"

"I don't like you spending time alone with Cherkashin. I find him thoroughly unpleasant."

Will laughed. "First poor Viola, now Cherkashin. My dear, if you're not careful, I'll begin to think you don't approve of anybody." He meant it as a joke, but she was having none of it.

"He's KGB, you know."

A bead of sweat tickled Will's widow's peak. He tucked into his tomato, hoping to hide his anxiety. *Soon,* he promised himself. *I'll tell you soon, love.* Gwendolyn would understand after he explained things carefully. Wouldn't she?

"Cherkashin? I think you're being a bit oversensitive. Not every cultural attaché is a KGB agent."

"It virtually guarantees he's one of them. Did you see how quickly he scurried across the room when he saw the ambassador talking privately with us? I think he nearly elbowed Lady Spencer in his haste." She shook her head. "He's a dreadful fellow. Be careful around him."

"I give you my word," said Will. But he couldn't bring himself to lie so baldly to his love and savior. Not after all she'd done for him. So he said, truthfully, "I shall avoid him as much as humanly possible."

The caveat wasn't lost on her. Her lips twisted in a moue of disapproval.

Rain thrummed against the windowpanes. Will took up the paper. "Anything interesting today?" he asked.

Gwendolyn pulled the jar of lemon curd closer to her plate. Sounding bored, she said, "The president has declared martial law in the American South. Again." She spooned curd on the last piece of toast. "Von Braun's cosmonauts have fallen silent; no transmissions since they returned to the Space Wheel. Cheltenham FC beat Hereford United three—one." Lightning flashed outside, like a strobe. Over the booming reverberation of thunder, she added, "And today's forecast calls for rain."

"I'll be certain to warn Aubrey, then."

"Yes. Do."

After breakfast, Will took up his briefcase, kissed his wife on the nose, and instructed his driver to take him to work. Within thirty minutes, he was stepping out of the Bentley and dashing up a flight of stairs to the lobby of a Georgian office building. Will paused in the lobby to remove his bowler hat and shake out the umbrella.

The North Atlantic Cross-Cultural Foundation occupied the fourth floor. The lift opened on a reception area with burgundy carpeting, walnut panels, brushed aluminum accents, and thoroughly sterile fluorescent lighting. From behind the reception desk his secretary, Angela, a brunette with a beehive hairstyle said, "Good morning, Lord William."

She insisted on using his courtesy title. In return, he strove for scandalous informality.

"Morning, Angie." Will hung his bowler and overcoat on a rack in the corner. "Messages?"

"Several. A busy start to the day, sir." Will's young secretary flipped through her message pad. "His Grace called, via his assistant, requesting the final schedule for the Minister Kalugin's visit." Flip. "A member of Ambassador Fedotov's staff called. They found a pair of lady's gloves after the gathering two nights ago; might they belong to your wife?" Flip . . .

Will glanced out the window while Angela spoke. He studied the arrangement of curtains on the windows across the street, and blinked. He missed the rest of the messages, contemplating the weather. It was, he supposed, the best time for a covert meeting. But he would have preferred not to go out in that. It was raining stair-rods. Perhaps that was a fitting punishment for flouting Gwendolyn's warning.

"Sir?"

He shook his head, clearing it. "Apologies. You were saying?"

"Shall I phone the embassy regarding the gloves?"

"Ah . . . Yes, please. Thank them for me, but let them know my wife hasn't misplaced anything. And then type up the new schedule, and have it couriered to my brother's staff after I sign off, won't you?"

"It's on your desk, awaiting your approval, sir."

Will smiled as much as he could muster and inclined his head at her, acknowledging her efficiency. Only twenty-four years old, yet Angela was more collected than Will had been at thirty-four. When Gwendolyn had come along. When she had started to fix him.

Inwardly, Will flinched. Their breakfast conversation jangled his nerves like a toothache. He'd meant what he said, yet here he was not two hours later planning to violate the spirit of the thing if not the wording.

But on the other hand, the fact was that he *had* needed fixing. Because he'd been forced to do terrible things by despicable men. And, like the fairy-tale egg man, it had shattered him. Even now when he thought about the things they'd done, the atrocities they'd committed, he felt trapped and breathless. Sometimes the guilt lay so heavy upon him, it pressed the air from his lungs. And in the short term his decision to take the reins, to exorcise his demons, only made the guilt heavier. Because the only solution—arrived at after so many long years—meant betraying Gwendolyn. But if Will was to ever make proper reparation for the evil things he'd done, he'd have to shoulder the burden just a bit longer.

Yes, he had an obligation to his wife. And he'd adhere to the very letter of it. *I shall avoid him as much as humanly possible.* But he also had an obligation to make amends for the deeds of his past. The siren song of atonement was impossible to ignore.

Angela must have seen a hint of the anger playing across his face. "Sir?" She inched backwards; the casters on her chair squeaked. "Is something wrong?"

Will realized he'd been staring at her, staring through her, at events from long ago. He shook his head again. Lightly as he could, he said, "Lost in thought."

This lessened the crease of worry between her eyes, but not the hint of frown at the corners of her mouth. If anything, Angela was perhaps too efficient and too perceptive. She was a good girl; Will regretted he wasn't the upright fellow she thought he was. In his youth, he would have found her just the right sort of bird to talk into vigorous but private indiscretions.

He approached the narrow double doors of his office. "Hold my calls, unless they're from His Grace, please."

"Very good, sir," she said.

He paused with his hand on the handle. "Oh, and Angela? Tea, when you have a moment."

"On your desk, sir."

And it was. Strong, hot, with a fan of lemon slices on the side. He poured a cup, then stood behind his desk, watching rivulets of rainwater trace and retrace patterns on the windowpanes. Water turned the streets below into streams, transformed surrounding rooftops into cataracts.

Two cups later, he hadn't moved. Nor had the storm. Nor had the arrangement of curtains across the street.

He gave the new schedule a cursory examination. It included his annotated changes from the other night. Will initialed it.

Typically, an office of this size, for a person of Will's standing, might have contained a well-stocked sideboard. But Will, who had no use for such things, had instead given the extra space to a two-drawer safe. A bright red potted nasturtium draped its leaves over the burnished steel. He opened the safe as quietly as he could manage, though it was difficult to hide the *clack-clang* of the thick steel door when he wrenched the handle. Will preferred that Angela not know he'd accessed his safe.

The top drawer contained a copy of the foundation's articles of investiture, and quarterly investment portfolios for its endowment. All duplicates of documents that Aubrey himself had in safekeeping.

But the contents of the safe were personal as much as professional. The bottom drawer held copies of Will's legal documents, including his last will and testament (everything to Gwen, thank you very much, except for a few cash disbursements to the help); his marriage license; and his own investment portfolios.

Tucked behind all of that sat a yellowed, wire-bound manuscript. Gwendolyn would murder him, if she knew he'd kept it. But it was necessary. A reminder.

An unmarked file folder lay hidden behind everything else. It was much thinner now than it had been when he'd first compiled the contents. All that remained in the folder were a single sheet of paper and a thirty-year-old photograph. The photo was a rare bonus; he'd had a devil of a time obtaining it. Most of the men he'd profiled had never been photographed, not once.

And this was the last. *Soon,* thought Will. *Soon it will be over, and I'll be free of the past.*

Will closed the safe (*clang-clack*) and spun the combination dial. He tucked the documents in the breast pocket of his suit jacket and exited the office.

"Angela, I'm stepping out for a bit." He handed the initialed schedule to his secretary. She acknowledged this, but otherwise said nothing as he gathered his coat, umbrella, and bowler once more. By now she must have been accustomed to his comings and goings.

Will entered the Tube at South Kensington, and rode the District line to Kew Gardens. He wandered through the magnificent Palm House, that great Victorian cathedral of glass and iron. Not far away, placards announced the imminent rebuilding of the Waterlily House, which had been destroyed during the Blitz.

The rains kept the gardens nearly deserted. If not for Cherkashin—perched on a bench under the boughs of a walnut tree on the Broad

Walk, puffing on a cigarette, looking rather soggy—Will might have had the gardens to himself. He tried to shove the guilt aside.

I am sorry, Gwendolyn. But this must be done. I owe it to the Missing. We all do.

Will checked his surroundings again, saw nobody, and sat. A long, tall shrubbery hid the bench from casual passersby. "I thought we'd agreed that *I* would contact *you*."

Cherkashin flicked his cigarette butt to the ground. It hissed on the wet pavement. He crushed it under the toe of his shoe.

And a rather expensive shoe it is, Will noticed. He knew every shop on Savile Row. *If Gwendolyn were here, she'd have something to say about that.* Thinking of his wife evoked another pang of guilt. He countered it by reminding himself of the evil things the warlocks had done to his countrymen and to him. They had turned him into a murderer. A man who bombed pubs. Derailed trains. Sank barges. All without fear of retribution or punishment.

"We agreed," said Cherkashin, "that you would help us."

"I can't do that hanging from the gallows, can I?"

Cherkashin looked amused. "You needn't worry about that. We can protect you."

"Move to Moscow, shall I?" They rehashed this same argument every time they met. Will found it tedious, but Cherkashin never tired of trying to persuade him to leave Britain. "If you think that's even remotely a possibility, you don't know my wife."

"She'd come with you. Even the most principled people will change their stances, when it's that or die."

"You don't know Gwendolyn. For that matter, neither do you know me."

A gust of wind swirled misty raindrops down Will's collar like a spectral caress. He shivered.

Cherkashin waved off the objection. "You're getting upset over nothing, my friend. It's clear to me that you would never be in any such danger. Your countrymen would never hang the brother of a duke. For you? Merely life in prison." He produced a slim metal case from his raincoat. Will declined the proffered cigarette. Cherkashin shrugged.

"It's one of the benefits of your caste system," he said. The orange flash from his lighter shone on his face. "For those at the top."

Will stood. "I think we're done here."

"Relax, relax." Cherkashin patted the bench. "I apologize. My proud socialist upbringing occasionally gets the better of me."

"I consider it a small mercy," said Will, "that our arrangement comes to an end today." He turned, inspected the surrounding grounds again. Satisfied the gardens were still deserted, and that they could conclude their meeting without witnesses, he sat again. "I won't miss this."

Will produced the documents he'd retrieved from his safe, held them out to Cherkashin, and turned his head. For some reason, he always looked away during the actual handoff; he didn't know why.

"You have heroically fulfilled the tasks of the Motherland," said Cherkashin. The documents disappeared into his coat as quickly as they'd appeared from Will's. "I still can't understand why you refuse compensation. We would be very generous."

"It's not about that." Will stood. "You could never understand."

"As you wish."

Will turned for the Palm House. But he paused before leaving. "The others. They've been brought to justice?"

Cherkashin smirked. "If you prefer to call it that."

Satisfaction wrestled with nausea as Will made his way out of the gardens.

14 May 1963
St. Pancras, London, England

Marsh unclenched his jaw just enough to say, "Yes, sir."

"For the Queen's sake," said Mr. Fitch, "you're not a young man any longer, Raybould."

"No, sir." Marsh's fingers ached from squeezing the handle of a spade. It took a conscious effort to loosen his grip. He managed it by imagining a loop of piano wire digging into Fitch's fat neck.

"I'm not without sympathies." Fitch hooked his thumbs into his belt.

"You know, I was a bit rough, too, in my youth," he said, hiking his trousers over his paunch. "But, by God, man, I left that behind in my twenties."

Marsh and Fitch were nearly the same age. The difference was that Fitch didn't show up to his job with a black eye. He worked in a bank. Marsh was his gardener.

Thunder echoed. A cool gust blew the scent of Fitch's aftershave across the garden. The breeze soothed the dull heat of Marsh's bruised face. He looked up at the leaden sky, wondering if Fitch planned to lecture him until the deluge started.

Probably. He was a religious man.

Fitch continued, "When the war started, I *had* to put that sort of rubbish behind me. We all did, if we were going to beat the Jerries. Did you fight in the war?"

"No, sir," Marsh lied. His hold on the spade tightened enough to flush the blood from his fingers.

"Ah. Well, there it is, then." Fitch pursed his lips, as though the secrets of the universe had been laid open to him. He paced back and forth a bit. "You've never had to learn discipline. Never had to take the measure of your own mettle," he said. "That's what sets a man aright."

"No doubt, sir."

Nodding, trying to look earnest, trying to ignore the anger and humiliation: these might have been some of the most difficult things Marsh had ever done. As if Liv didn't cut him down quite enough at home, Marsh also had to endure abuse from the likes of Fitch. But he couldn't afford to lose another job. Liv had made it clear; she'd leave if it happened again. If she did, he didn't know how he'd care for John by himself. Nurses were out of the question. One, he couldn't afford them, and two, none of John's nannies had ever lasted more than a few weeks. Even when he was a tot.

"When we fought the Jerries, my men knew they could count on me. And I knew the same of them. And that," Fitch proclaimed, "is how we defeated Hitler."

Benjamin Fitch had been a mechanic at a POOL petrol depot in Birmingham. Marsh had looked him up.

Nevertheless, Fitch's attitude—that Britain had engaged the Third Reich in combat, and triumphed—was a common fiction. It was the Great National Lie.

"Not everyone can be a war hero, Raybould. But you can still be a responsible man. When I hire you for a task, I need to know I can count on you to do it. That you'll be here when I expect you to be here."

More thunder. Marsh felt a raindrop, then another, through his thinning hair. He decided to work through the rain. Perhaps Fitch would look on that as an acceptable penance. Miserable, cold, muddy . . . still better than staying at home, frostbitten by Liv's icy hatred.

"Don't worry, sir. You can depend on me," he said. He tried to ignore the ache in his fingers, adding, "I'll be here when you need me."

"Not if you're jailed for brawling."

"I understand, Mr. Fitch."

Fitch harrumphed. "Very well, then." Reluctantly accepting that his point had been made and received, he headed inside. Marsh wondered what sort of work he did at the bank. *You sad little man with your sad little job, badgering the gardener for a bit of excitement.*

Marsh donned his tweed flat cap and set about unloading the pallets of shrubs from the bed of his truck. The Fitches had hired him to rip out a bramble around their garden and replace it with a hedgerow. Warning twinges flared through his back and his problem knee when he hefted the first pallet. A smarter, safer, thing would have been to unload the plants individually. But that wouldn't have challenged him, wouldn't have vented his anger and shame through sheer physical exertion.

The Fitches lived in an expansive neo-Georgian with blistered mustard trim. The gutters, Marsh noticed, had pulled away from one corner of the roof. They neglected their house as much as they neglected their garden. One by one, Marsh lugged the pallets behind the house. All under Fitch's disapproving stare, who monitored his progress from a second-floor window.

Rain dripped from the brim of Marsh's hat and seeped into his sweat-soaked shirt. His knuckles ached in the damp chill. The first hints of arthritis, he knew, brought on by a lifetime spent cracking his knuckles.

Moving the new plants was the easiest bit. Hacking out the old plantings offered a more violent release. The thorny, overgrown bramble became a surrogate for the world, his life, himself. Marsh tore it all to pieces with spade, and shears, and ax. He tossed the remnants into piles, then collected the piles into bundles. The bundles he tied off with lengths of twine cut with his pocketknife. The twine felt scratchy against his skin. Thorns punctured his fingers and scratched his palms, but the rain washed away his blood. The scent of wet earth permeated everything.

The rain sluiced mud and leaves into the holes he dug. It soaked the denim of his boilersuit, too, causing it to constrict against his legs when he kneeled in the muck. Cold mud seeped into his shins and knees. His bad knee throbbed again, worse.

"That's him, down there," said Fitch's voice. Marsh turned. Fitch stood behind the house with two men. He pointed at Marsh from under his umbrella. His prim little smile was a study in self-satisfaction. *I knew it,* it said. *I knew Raybould Marsh was no good.*

The men appeared to thank him, then crossed the lawn. Marsh kept a trowel in one hand, and leaned on the spade to stand. His heart thumped; the pain in his knee and fingers receded. Adrenaline.

Old training took over, a relic from years long past. Marsh wiped the rain from his eyes. Two men, younger than he. The first was a bit taller than Marsh, the second roughly his own height. Both wore suits, not uniforms. Not coppers, then. Friends of the man he'd slugged in the pub? Perhaps. Armed? Perhaps. The fellow on the left could be wearing a shoulder rig.

Fitch followed the newcomers at a discreet distance. Close enough to overhear, however.

Marsh sidled closer to solid ground, away from the muddy ditch created by his efforts to remove the bramble. The men stopped outside the range of his spade.

The taller one said, "Mr. Marsh?"

"I am." Marsh kept an eye on both men. But they stayed together rather than flanking him.

"Raybould Marsh?"

"*Yes*. Now, who the hell are you?" No, they weren't coppers. He almost wished they were. Solicitors? Had they come to serve him papers? Had Liv hired them? Had the neighbors filed another round of complaints about John?

"Sorry if we've caused you alarm," said the first man. He raised his hands, palm out. "We've been in a mad hurry to find you, Mr. Marsh. We've come to ask for your help."

The look on Fitch's face was pure confusion. He'd been expecting a tussle, physical or otherwise. Confirmation that Marsh was well beneath him.

Marsh leaned on the spade, studying the newcomers. A taut silence stretched between Marsh, the newcomers, and nosy Fitch, punctuated only by the pattering rain.

Help? No, not solicitors, then. But the way they carried themselves . . . Government men. Which raised another possibility.

Finally, Marsh said, "It's Milkweed, isn't it?"

And he knew he was right, because the quiet man, the one who hadn't yet spoken, glanced nervously over his shoulder at Fitch. Milkweed: the dirtiest of Whitehall's dirty little secrets. Milkweed: the real reason Britain survived the war. Milkweed: the org for whom Marsh had faced demons and supermen; the org for whose secret war he'd lost his only daughter; the org that had spit him out when he was no longer useful.

"If you'll come with us, sir."

Marsh turned his back on the government men and returned to digging holes in the mud. Over his shoulder he spat, "I don't do that work any longer."

"She said you'd say that."

Marsh froze. Rainwater trickled down his face. Quietly, carefully, he said, "What?"

"The woman who asked for you. She said you'd say that. Also told us to remind you she once said you'd meet again."

The government man was being circumspect in front of Fitch. But it didn't matter. They shared a secret language, Marsh and these agents, and Marsh knew exactly what they were telling him: the woman who had killed his daughter was here, in England, and asking to see him.

Cold rage stabbed through Marsh, like an icicle in the gut. But this was bloody Christmas, wasn't it? He couldn't fix the wreckage of his life. Couldn't mend his shattered marriage. But he could still avenge Agnes. Finally, *finally,* his rage could have an outlet.

He fingered the knife in his pocket.

He turned. "Take me to her."

four

14 May 1963
Knightsbridge, London, England

At first, knowing he'd finally finished the task he set for himself left Will feeling exhausted. He'd obsessed over bringing the warlocks to justice, fantasized about punishing them for so long that when it was done he found himself unmoored. A low-level anxiety, a worry that he'd never see it finished, had been his constant companion. What would replace it? Or was his life bereft of purpose? Did it need a purpose?

But he woke the next morning with a profound sense of closure. It was done. He had made amends. He'd finally banished that dark chapter of his life to the past, left it forever and completely behind him. And this was a bigger thing than he realized; it took a full night's sleep to process it completely. The knowledge he'd endured the last of his secret meetings with Cherkashin was no small relief as well.

The closure became ebullience over the course of the morning. It grew, like an air bubble released from the stygian depths of the ocean rising sunward. It was time to confess to Gwendolyn. She would see the change upon him, the joy of a weight lifted, the relief of reparations paid, and she would understand. She had to understand.

Flowers, he decided, were too perfunctory a gift for such an occasion. Likewise chocolates. A painting was too cumbersome. He lacked an eye for vases and porcelains. Gwendolyn deserved something profound, brilliant, unexpected, beautiful, extravagant and eternal. But not a bribe, he insisted to himself. A thank-you gift. An I-love-you gift. Not a token to soften her anger when she learned of what he'd done. No. Not that.

In the end, after three hours of browsing—with an increasingly hostile taxi driver—he settled on a diamond pendant on a silver necklace. A simple thing, but Gwendolyn's tastes tended toward understatement. He envisioned the pendant sparkling like moonlit dew in the pale hollow of her throat. But what he would say when she asked what had compelled him to do this?

Because, my dear. Thanks to you, I've lived long enough to see the men I loathe utterly destroyed.

No. Perhaps not.

Will was too busy composing his answer to notice anything wrong until the last moment, when the driver's yell snapped him out of his reverie. But by then, the lorry had already careered through the traffic light. It barreled across the intersection and clipped the taxi.

Metal crunched. The car spun. Glass shattered. Fragments pattered against Will's face like sharp hailstones as the impact flung him against the door. Pain erupted in his left arm. He dropped Gwendolyn's gift. He caught a surreal glimpse of shocked bystanders, and the alarmed faces of drivers in the cars behind him braking hard to avoid the accident. It unfolded like a dream, one instant stretching on and on and on while tires screeched and the taxi spun. The taxi crunched to a halt against a lamppost, tossing Will across the seat again.

Ears ringing, head spinning, Will struggled to think. "Let me off here," he slurred. The driver didn't respond.

Will tugged on the door handle, but it didn't budge. He had been sitting on the passenger's side, in the rear. The truck had blasted through the intersection to hit the taxi on the driver's side, near the front, crumpling the frame and the driver's door. Will's door was dented where the taxi pressed against the post. He was wedged in.

Slowly, the outside world came into focus. Bystanders pointed, yelled, called for help. A woman in a yellow mackintosh ran toward a police box down the road. She lost a sandal and stumbled. A man's face appeared where the window had been, saying something Will couldn't understand. Will focused on the man's lips, trying to make sense of the noises he made, something about an accident and doctors and could Will move, but it didn't make any sense. The ringing in his ears became a siren.

He smelled burnt tires, petrol, smoke, and blood.

Smoke. Blood.

For a moment Will was back in the war, trying to negotiate another price while German bombs rained and the Eidolons ground him down with their implacable demands. What price was this? What service have we purchased? It had started small, in the beginning, with auto accidents and the occasional fire.

Rain drizzled through the ruined windows. Something glittered on the floor. Glass. And lying open at Will's feet, a red velvet box. *Pendant.* Will sifted through the debris, searching for a diamond amongst the pulverized glass until blood coated his fingertips.

Two bobbies arrived to pry the mangled taxi apart. They offered him a stretcher, but Will waved them off and wobbled to his feet. They ushered him to an ambulance.

Fare.

He pulled the billfold from his breast pocket, struggled to make his hands work enough to pull out a ten-pound note. The policemen frowned.

"Fare," he managed. Will turned to point at the taxi but lost his balance. Somebody caught him.

"Easy, sir. He's collected his last fare, poor sod."

The fog in Will's head slowly dissipated during the ambulance ride. He spent another three-quarters of an hour at the hospital while a nurse tweezed bits of glass from his face. More surprising was the amount that had gone down his collar. It seemed like half the windscreen tinkled to the linoleum floor when he removed his jacket, and again when he gingerly removed his shirt.

After his abrasions had been sanitized and bandaged and his arm set in a sling, the police wanted a statement. By then he'd recovered his wits enough to realize what had happened. He'd been in an automobile accident. The driver was dead.

Will arrived at home late for dinner, still holding the empty box where Gwendolyn's necklace had been.

14 May 1963
Milkweed Headquarters, London, England

They were stripped of their battery harnesses and kept in the Admiralty cellar overnight. "Protective custody," these men from Milkweed had called it. But Klaus knew the situation for what it was. He and Gretel had become property again, dependent upon others for everything. Prisoners. Helpless.

His new captors were polite, respectful, and indicated a great interest in his well-being. The Reichsbehörde had never been like that. Nor had Sarov. And the food was better than anything at Arzamas-16. But what Klaus truly wanted was out of reach, ripped from him almost before he knew how much he'd yearned for it.

Because of Gretel. But someday . . .

The cell itself was among the sturdiest he'd ever seen. Out of habit, he'd gauged the wall thickness as they'd escorted him through the doorway. It looked to be a good eighteen inches of reinforced concrete; a triviality to Klaus when he embraced his Willenskräfte, but practically impenetrable to anything else. Even sound. Plush, thick-pile carpet covered every inch of the floor (blue), walls (yellow), and ceiling (white). Klaus had the impression his captors had upholstered the cell with anything they could find. The steel door opened and closed on noiseless bearings; it sealed with a *click* and the susurration of rubber baffles.

One sink, one toilet, one cot. No visible grille or duct for air circulation.

Klaus had spent an hour lying on the cot, fighting off the first tendrils of claustrophobia, after that observation.

It was quiet as a coffin. Clearly it had been constructed for that purpose. Why did they need a silent cell? Psychological warfare? Were they trying to break him? Other claustrophobics like him?

The faintest of knocks announced a visitor. By straining his ears, Klaus could just make out the rattle of a key in the lock. The massive door inched open. Pethick, the man who'd first attended to Klaus and Gretel, stood outside. The corridor was carpeted top to bottom.

"Good afternoon," he said in a muted voice.

"Afternoon? I can't tell. My prison has no windows, no clock."

Pethick beckoned him outside. "I do apologize for the accommodations, but they are the best we could do on the spur of the moment." He carried a key ring on a thin chain, much like a pocket watch. The carpet absorbed everything but a faint jingle when Pethick sorted through the dozens of keys on the ring.

"You and your sister—" He stopped before another cell door, pointed to it with another key. "—caught us quite off guard. We might move you to a safe house, depending on circumstances."

Gretel had, of course, been waiting for them. She joined Klaus and Pethick in the corridor. There was an eagerness to her step. And the shadows behind her eyes, those dark currents where her madness lurked, lay dormant. This, for Gretel, was giddiness.

The siblings followed Pethick upstairs. The cellar had changed markedly since Klaus came here as an enemy soldier to rescue Gretel. But he recognized the stairwell. They'd climbed it in the final moments of their escape.

"How are you?" Klaus whispered.

"Cheerful and well rested," said Gretel.

Pethick took them past Pembroke's office. A single door of polished walnut opened on what appeared to be a conference room. It smelled of leather and pipe tobacco. The long, rain-spattered picture window along the west wall offered a view of gray sky and the park shrouded in mist. A dreary day: most of the light came from lamps situated on end tables around the edges of the room, and the brass light fixture suspended over a wide oval table. High-backed leather chairs surrounded the table and flanked a cold hearth at one end of the room.

Pembroke was there, staring out the window. The stem of his pipe—dark wood polished to a glassy finish—rattled against his teeth when he raked it slowly back and forth. He turned when the trio entered.

"We've found your man," he said. "Marsh. They're bringing him in now."

Gretel beamed. *She* is *excited,* thought Klaus.

He didn't share her excitement. He'd succumbed to the same old weary anticipation, alloyed with the special dread that came from knowing Gretel was about to play another of her cards. Cards seemed an apt analogy, but— *After all these years, I still don't know your game, sister.*

Did he care any longer? Only insofar as her secret purpose brought him closer to the life he sought for himself.

He wondered who Marsh was, and why he was so important.

Pembroke and Pethick motioned them toward the pair of chairs across the table from the door. Pembroke seated himself at one end of the table, on Klaus's left. Gretel sat on Klaus's right, in the center of the table. Pethick stood at the far end of the table.

"Perhaps now," said Pembroke, "you'll tell us what this is all about."

"Soon," said Gretel.

Pethick interjected. "We've been rather patient."

Gretel was unimpressed. The look on her face said as much. But these men couldn't read her. Klaus wondered how long she had been waiting for this moment. Years? Decades?

They waited in anxious silence. Klaus looked to the window. The rain had driven even the most stalwart pleasure-seekers from the park. From his vantage in the Admiralty, the park was an emerald enclave, a raft of jade on a slate gray world. Waterlogged and dim, it was glorious, untouchable. Only yesterday he'd sat on that bench, down there, licking warm salt from his fingers and tasting life as a free man. Those wonderful few minutes before Gretel flapped her wings, wrapped him in her eddies, and dragged him along in her wake.

Pethick spoke again, snapping Klaus out of his reverie. "Have you ever met him, sir? Marsh."

"Once. Nine, maybe ten years ago." Pembroke nibbled on his pipe again. "Well. More of a glimpse, really." The adjutant, or whatever role Pethick played for Leslie Pembroke, raised his eyebrows. "At Stephenson's funeral. But he didn't linger after the burial."

Pethick nodded extravagantly, as though this were the most sensible thing in the world. He ran the tip of his tongue along the inside of his upper lip. "I understand they called him 'Stephenson's pet gorilla,' in those days."

Gretel looked offended. She turned her sloe-eyed stare on Pethick. The shadows had returned.

"No, no, Sam. Don't be fooled," said Pembroke. "Yes, he was a bit coarse. And yes, they said that of him. But I suspect it was resentment more than anything else. He came from a very working-class background, you know."

"I didn't."

"Oh, yes. The lore says the old man discovered Marsh as a young hooligan. He broke into the old man's house to pinch his food or some such, according to the stories."

Gretel listened, wide-eyed. Her lips parted slightly, a posture of wonderment. As though she were hearing the childhood secrets of a longtime lover.

Pethick said, "He didn't."

"He did. According to lore. The old man saw potential in him, practically raised him as a son from then on. Sent him to Oxford. Quite a sharp fellow, too. Took two firsts, languages and botany."

"According to lore?"

"According to his file," said Pembroke.

This exchange between Pethick and Pembroke didn't provide Klaus any clues as to why this Marsh fellow was so important to Gretel. But it did give a sense of the person.

Klaus had spent his childhood and early adult years at the Institut Menschlichen Vorsprung (the Institute of Human Advancement), which later became the Reichsbehörde für die Erweiterung Germanischen

Potenzials (the Reich's Authority for the Extension of German Potential), learning how to harness the Götterelektron and perform feats of Willenskräfte. But the Reichsbehörde had been more than a training ground for the Götterelektrongruppe. It had also been a spy school. Which had meant studying the enemy; learning to think like the enemy.

Klaus and Heike had been trained for quiet operations: infiltration, assassination, espionage. And while his one and only mission on foreign soil (in this very building) hadn't been very quiet, Klaus remembered enough of that old training to catch the unstated nuances of what Pembroke said. A low-born man like Marsh wouldn't have been well received among his peers in the intelligence world.

Two quick raps at the door. Gretel sat up, smoothed her braids.

"Enter," called Pembroke.

A new man, somebody Klaus hadn't seen yet, poked his head in the doorway. "He's here, sir."

From the corridor behind him, a muffled, angry voice: "Let me see her, son. Let me see her *now,* or I promise you're going to have a very bad day."

Gretel licked her lips. Pembroke nodded. "Very well." A quick look carried some private communication between Pembroke and his second. Pethick nodded, too. "Bring him in. But be alert."

The door opened more widely. The first man entered and took a spot to the right of the door. He was followed by a second fellow, dressed much the same—overcoat, suit, linen trousers dark with rainwater from the shin down. An unofficial uniform, perhaps. The second man took a spot to the left.

Gretel inhaled. A gasp of delight. Ecstasy.

A sodden, disheveled man barged in after them. He wore denim coveralls over a flannel shirt, every inch dark with rainwater. Long, wide patches of ocher mud caked his knees; he'd been kneeling in wet earth. Rain had plastered his thin hair, dark like wet sand, to his forehead. Tiny beads of water sparkled in the lamplight, suspended on his eyebrows and eyelashes. They dripped when he blinked, tracing rivulets down a craggy face. He had a black eye.

Marsh took three steps into the room, shaking the table with the heavy fall of his work boots. His gaze went straight to Gretel. The corner of her mouth quirked up.

Klaus had never seen so much hatred bottled behind a person's eyes. Not even Reinhardt could summon such rage. Marsh quivered with it, brimmed with it. Klaus inched closer to his sister.

"Hello, darling," said Gretel. "I told you we'd meet again."

Marsh said, "Tell me why, you bitch. Tell me why you killed her."

Klaus started to object. "My sister has never—"

But Marsh cut him off with a single contemptuous glance. "I know you're not that stupid, Klaus."

This took Klaus aback. *He knows me. More than these others, who know my name only by reading it in a file. Who is this man?*

Marsh approached the table. "Williton. Tell me why."

Gretel said, "It was necessary."

"Necessary? Agnes's death was *necessary*? For what? She was *four months old!*"

The men at the door stepped forward, ready to act. Pembroke raised a finger without taking his eyes from Marsh and Gretel. They kept their distance.

Quietly, Klaus tried again. "Gretel, what's Williton?"

Marsh looked at him. "It was a village. Tiny, insignificant speck on the map. We sent our daughter there during the evacuations. Safe as houses. Until September eighteenth, 1940, when your Luftwaffe bombed it into powder." He glared at Gretel. "Bombed it into powder because she advised them to do it."

In a flash, Klaus remembered another meeting much like this one. Instead of Marsh it had been General Field Marshal Keitel, the Führer's chief of staff, bellowing at Gretel. He'd demanded to know why she hadn't forewarned the OKW of the catastrophic failure of Operation Sea Lion. Britain's warlocks had summoned monsters to devour the invasion fleet.

And just like now, she had been unmoved by the gales of fury and indignation directed at her. And just like now, she'd said only that it had been necessary. And then she twisted the conversation, convinced

Keitel that the most important thing in the world was to flatten a little town nobody had ever heard of. And, of course, they had.

Gretel said, "You'll understand, one day soon."

Marsh's face twisted with disgust. He addressed Pembroke for the first time. "Have they been unplugged?"

"Of course."

Marsh took the chair across from Gretel. He sat, sliding a bit back from the table. "I'm here. Talk."

Everyone looked at Gretel. She began by describing, with Klaus's help, their capture by the Soviets at the end of the war. From there she described the immense effort the Soviets had poured into reverse engineering the Reichsbehörde technology: the secret city, the mass graves.

"This is a waste of time," said Marsh. "I warned Stephenson about this over twenty years ago. There's nothing new here." He stood, glaring at the siblings. "She's playing us."

"Let's hear what they have to say before we make that decision, shall we?" Pembroke asked.

Marsh looked at Pembroke, Pethick, Klaus, and Gretel. He cracked his knuckles against his jaw. (*What a strange mannerism,* thought Klaus.) Then he made to retake his seat.

Pembroke relaxed. So did the men at the door.

"Please, continue," he said.

Gretel nodded at him demurely, but her eyes flicked to Marsh, just for a moment, before she picked up her story.

Which was how Klaus happened to be looking at Marsh's hands at the moment he yanked a pocketknife from a compartment of his coveralls. Marsh was halfway across the table in another instant.

He's fast, thought some strange, disconnected part of Klaus's mind. The rest thought, and said, "Gretel!"

Klaus reacted instinctively, calling up the Götterelektron and grabbing Gretel's arm at the same moment.

But, of course, he had no battery.

Gretel's chair tipped sideways, toward Klaus, at the same moment Marsh's momentum knocked her backwards. Klaus displaced his sister just enough for the first thrust of Marsh's blade to miss her throat; her head twisted sideways from the glancing blow of his knuckles, and then a flash of metal emerged through her swaying braid. The impact knocked Gretel out of Klaus's grasp.

Gretel on the floor. Marsh atop her. Blade coming back. Bright flash at her throat.

Pethick got an arm around Marsh's neck, the other grabbing for his wrist. But he couldn't dislodge him. Marsh was too strong. The second thrust nicked her earlobe.

Gretel's head rolled back, her mouth open. She was—

—screaming?

—crying?

—laughing.

My brother and I will be occupied tomorrow. A family matter.

Marsh threw his head backwards. The back of his skull connected with Pethick's face. By then, Klaus was on his feet with one arm hooked under Marsh's extended shoulder and the other around his waist.

Together, he and Pethick wrenched Marsh to his feet, off Gretel. Pethick took the knife. Klaus kneeled over his sister, desperate to know if she were hurt. She answered with more giggling.

Pembroke—who, Klaus realized, hadn't moved an inch during the altercation—looked at the men flanking the door. One had drawn his sidearm. "You didn't search him." A statement, rather than a question, rendered so dispassionately that Klaus suppressed a shudder at the memory of Doctor von Westarp. "You brought a potential hostile inside, and it didn't occur to you to search him."

"We thought he was one of us, sir."

Marsh muttered, "Not in a long bloody time, mate."

Pembroke looked at Pethick, who had disregarded the trickle of blood from his nose long enough to search Marsh.

"He's clean now, sir," he said.

"Shall we take him downstairs, sir?"

Pembroke produced an envelope from inside his tweed jacket. The envelope had *Leslie Pembroke* written on it in Gretel's handwriting. He took the knife from Pethick, sliced the envelope open, and removed the note Gretel had written the previous afternoon in Pembroke's office. His eyes scanned down the lines of Gretel's spidery copperplate.

Then he tossed the note on the table, pointedly landing it in front of Marsh. Marsh's scowl deepened into a vision of pure disgust. Pembroke turned his attention back to the men at the door. He answered their question: "No. We'll have no further problems."

He gestured for everybody to regain their seats. To Marsh, he said in a conversational tone, "If you're quite finished, perhaps now we can hear the rest of their story."

14 May 1963
Milkweed Headquarters, London, England

Pethick escorted Klaus and Gretel back to their cells. Marsh gathered they were being held down in the storerooms. Which was where they'd locked Gretel the first time, after he'd captured her in France.

He amended that thought. *After she* let *me capture her. Why?* Why did she do anything? *Because she is a raven-haired demon, sowing chaos and pain for her own amusement.*

His boots smeared mud on the floor when he followed Pembroke back to his office. Which, Marsh realized with a pang, had been Stephenson's office once upon a time. Same view of St. James' Park, same desk, even the same chairs (leather behind the desk, button-tufted chintz before it). Only the artwork on the walls had changed. Framed prints of antique maps had replaced the watercolors painted by Stephenson's wife, Corrie: Terra Australis for flowering dogwood; Nueva España for magnolia.

Milkweed had been born in an office much like this one, christened from an image on one of those watercolors. Marsh wondered if Pembroke knew that.

Thinking of Stephenson and his wife reminded Marsh of his own wedding. Held in the Stephensons' garden. Corrie had given a watercolor to Liv that evening, as a token; it had hung in their vestibule for years, until a row when Marsh slammed the door just a bit too hard.

The frame shattered on the floor. Liv tossed the painting in the rubbish bin.

Marsh shook his head, trying to clear away memories that clung to him like smoke and old cobwebs.

The smell had changed, too. Now it was the sweet odor of Pembroke's pipe tobacco leaching out of the upholstery, rather than the sharp scent of Stephenson's Lucky Strikes. The pipe seemed an obnoxious affectation on one so young.

But then Marsh realized Pembroke's youth was an illusion created by the perspective of his own age.

Pembroke closed the door. He opened a sideboard, pulled out a bottle and two tumblers.

That's new, too, thought Marsh. *The old man kept his brandy in his desk drawer. Until Will drank it all.*

"I think we could both use a drink," said Pembroke. "You, especially."

"I'm not the one running around like Gretel's lapdog. You must work up bloody great a thirst."

Pembroke poured a generous portion into both glasses. The earth-and-fire scent of scotch tickled Marsh's nose. He set a glass on the desk for Marsh, then took the seat behind it. The casters squeaked.

Marsh squelched into a chair. His sodden boilersuit itched all over.

Pembroke said, "We're on the same side here, Marsh. I am not your enemy."

"You are as long as you're working for Gretel."

"I think you're a bit confused."

Marsh took Gretel's note in his fist, shook it in Pembroke's face. "She's pulling your strings. Jesus Christ, how long did that take? One day?"

Pembroke sipped. He swallowed loudly. "Of course I let things unfold the way they did. It was a perfect opportunity to test her. That's not letting her pull the strings. It's basic tradecraft, and you should recognize that." He sipped again. "Besides, unlike you, I've never seen her ability at work. Not directly. And, you must admit, your attempted assault did unfold precisely as she'd foretold. Chapter and verse. Remarkable."

"I presume you had the presence of mind to disconnect her battery the moment she arrived?"

"Sam did."

Marsh said, "I've seen her do this before. She pulls these things off long after her battery has been removed. So rather than gaping in wonderment, you should be wondering how long she's been planning this. And why."

Pembroke gestured at the letter, stilled balled in Marsh's fist. "I watched her write that."

Marsh threw the paper across the room. He shook his head in disgust. "Jesus." He massaged his temples. "She's playing you."

"She's not the enemy any longer. She's a defector."

"She's not here to help us." Marsh shifted in his chair. The fabric of his drying boilersuit had constricted uncomfortably against his legs.

"The Soviets would never let her off the leash. She's far too valuable to squander as a double agent."

"I didn't say she's working for them. I said she's not here to help us," said Marsh. He drained his glass in two swallows; it was a nice single malt. "Let me spare you months of effort," Marsh whispered. Coughing past the fire in his sinuses, he added, "They never turned her. Her brother, maybe, but never Gretel. Hell, in the end even von Westarp couldn't control her. And he created her."

"It's not a matter of controlling her," said Pembroke. "It's a question of securing her willing cooperation."

"Cooperation? Are you mad? Downstairs you have locked up a man who can walk through walls like a ghost. And his sister, who can read the future as easily as you and I read the goddamned newspaper. Now, you tell me something. Do you honestly believe it took them twenty-odd years to escape?"

Pembroke sighed. "You're probably right." In response to the skepticism on Marsh's face, he said, "Look, I'm not a fool. But I'll happily play the part if it means access to the secrets in her head. If we could know a fraction of the things she knows, we could chart a new course for Britain."

"She's seducing you, and you don't even realize it."

"I'm willing to let her think that. We ought to work together on this, Marsh. Work the problem from both ends. Let Gretel believe I'm her willing pawn. Meanwhile, you unravel what she's really after."

A thrill raced through Marsh. A chance to return to the only life he'd ever fit? But it was replaced just as quickly with irritation bordering on shame. What a sad carrot this was. Pembroke didn't have a fraction of Stephenson's mettle. Gretel would eat him alive.

"You can't outwit her," he said. "You can't outmaneuver her. And if you try, she will dance on your grave."

"I will never trust Gretel. Not after everything I've read about her history."

"You've been into the archives, then."

"Of course I have."

"The archives I retrieved from Germany."

Pembroke paused in mid-sip, pointing at Marsh across the lip of his glass. "That was an incredible piece of work, by the way. Something of a legend in these parts."

Marsh dipped his head slightly, acknowledging the compliment but not enough to dislodge the icy veneer he presented to Pembroke. He asked, "And where exactly are 'these parts' today?"

It was Pembroke's turn to nod, acknowledging the subtext of Marsh's question. "We're back in circulating section T. Have been since . . . forty-five?" He nodded to himself, then plied Marsh with a wry smile. "Stephenson's old purview, if I know my history."

Back before the creation of Milkweed, in the late 1930s, Marsh had been a field agent reporting to Stephenson, who headed the "technological surprise" section of MI6, Britain's Secret Intelligence Service. It was on a mission to Spain during the civil war there that Marsh had stumbled across the greatest technological surprise of the century: the Reichsbehörde. Not long after that, the old man had created Milkweed, handing T-section over to others and even giving up his opportunity at the top of SIS in exchange for free rein to run Milkweed as he pleased.

In those early days, Marsh had thought he'd make a long career of serving the country. He'd never imagined the intelligence world would one day be overrun with twits like Pembroke.

"Still special access, I hope."

"Naturally," said Pembroke. "But there are few of us. Me; Sam, whom you've met; a handful of others. Field agents and technicians. And, of course, you."

Marsh said, "But Milkweed isn't autonomous any longer."

"Well, nearly so." Pembroke shrugged. It reminded Marsh of the old man's peculiar one-armed shrugs. The loneliness hit harder this time. Marsh squirmed. Pembroke continued, "As autonomous as anything in the Service can be these days. This isn't wartime. And there is such a thing as a budget, you know."

"I can't imagine that's been much of a problem for you. How much could you possibly cost the Crown, sitting there and twiddling your thumbs for years on end?"

Pembroke ignored the jab. He shook his head. If anything, he looked almost amused. "So you believe her story, then?"

"I don't believe she's being forthright with us," said Marsh. "But yes, I expect that if you bother to check up on your warlocks, you'll find most of them dead. Just as she claimed." He shook his head. "Every struggle, every sacrifice. Rendered moot by your carelessness."

"Is that so." A strange look came over Pembroke's face. Again, that hint of amusement. It was maddening. Marsh wanted to straighten him out. "If she's right, we have quite a mess on our hands."

Marsh slammed his empty glass on the desk. "Quite a mess? Don't you see what they're doing? They're clearing the board, you imbecile. Your Soviet counterparts have tired of this so-called Cold War. So they're resetting the game."

"That's not the problem to which I refer," said Pembroke. "Because to my mind, the real issue is how the Soviets have managed to track down our men. They excel at hiding, at staying in the shadows. As you may remember."

What Marsh remembered was how Will had taken great lengths— traversing the United Kingdom from north to south, from east to west, and back again—to track down and recruit less than a dozen warlocks for Milkweed. Finding them would have been impossible if not for the cryptic hints found in the journal of Will's grandfather.

Back then, all the world's warlocks wouldn't have filled the chairs in the conference room down the corridor. Now, Marsh feared, they wouldn't fill this office.

It struck Marsh he hadn't considered Will might be one of the victims. He found he was too detached to care one way or the other. Then again, Will's death would have made the news.

Marsh said, "It's bloody obvious. Arzamas-16 has an agent in the country. Gretel said as much. He waltzed in here and took a stroll through your files. Von Westarp had an invisible girl. Or maybe he's like Klaus. Or, for all we know, Klaus and Gretel are behind this. How long have they been in the country? You don't know, do you?"

Once again, that infuriating look passed across Pembroke's face. Marsh clenched his fist.

"I doubt very much that their man has been to the Admiralty. Instead, I'd wager the leak, if there is one, is one of your contemporaries. From the old days," said Pembroke. He glimpsed Marsh's fist, then changed the subject. He opened a drawer and set a file folder on the desk. Marsh recognized the green border of an MI6 personnel file. "You've had a difficult time of it, these past few years."

Marsh disliked the sudden turn to the conversation. And he certainly didn't welcome the attention to his home life. But he kept quiet, waiting to see just how deep a hole Pembroke would dig for himself.

"You've had a number of run-ins. Fighting. Disorderly conduct. Disturbing the peace." Pembroke turned a page. "A long succession of odd jobs. Gardening. Mending. A bit of construction here and there. All aboveboard?" he asked.

But Marsh held his silence.

"I ask only out of curiosity. It's difficult to reconcile your tax records with what we know of your work history. A bit of cash paid under the counter from time to time?" Pembroke shrugged. "I truly couldn't care if you've let a few quid go unreported. You do have two mouths to feed." Another page.

He continued, "Presumably two mouths. Nobody has seen your son in years. Not even the neighbors. Not since the last nanny packed up and quit rather suddenly, from what I gather." Pembroke turned another page in Marsh's file, shaking his head sadly. "Quite a few hospital visits in his early years, though."

Marsh's jaw ached when he ground his molars together. His fingernails dug into his palms; he stopped just short of drawing blood. The effort not to leap across the desk and throttle Pembroke left him physically trembling.

"My son is not on the table for discussion," he managed. His voice trembled with the same effort.

Pembroke looked up, wide-eyed as if surprised to find Marsh upset. "Of course he isn't." The file made a soft clapping sound when he flipped it shut. "Look. I don't raise these issues because I think I can strong-arm you into returning. I know that wouldn't work with you. I'm merely trying to suggest that you might be happier if you returned to the service. Leaving SIS was your great mistake, Marsh."

"It wasn't a mistake," said Marsh. Just as he'd told himself countless times over the years. Perhaps it was even true. Things had been bright, even rosy, when he'd left. He'd yearned to get out, to start over with Liv. His row with the old man at war's end had been the opportunity he'd needed to turn his back on the life of the spy. Jumping at that opportunity was the smart thing. He would have been a fool not to do it.

No. Leaving the service hadn't been a mistake. Marsh's great regret was not coming back. But he'd never admit that to Pembroke.

"Steady pay," said Pembroke. "We'll put you in at what your salary would have been today, had you stayed and continued your record of exemplary service. And, of course, we can have the more colorful incidents expunged from your police record." He pulled the pipe from his breast pocket, gestured vaguely with the stem. "The usual caveats continue to apply. Official Secrets Act and the rest."

Marsh didn't want to acknowledge the thrill he felt. A chance to make up for the failures of the past twenty years . . . "And what would my assignment be?"

"I've already told you." Pembroke produced a tobacco pouch from his desk. Tamping the bowl of his pipe, he said, "Suss out Gretel's intentions. You'd have complete latitude to do so however you see fit. You are the best man for that job."

"I'd be reporting to you, then."

"Yes."

Arthritis flared when Marsh pressed his fingers to his jaw, thinking. Pembroke misinterpreted the gesture.

"You're wondering about me."

"Ever been in combat?"

"No. I was sixteen when the war ended."

"Your predecessor lost an arm in the First World War."

As if it would somehow justify himself, Pembroke said, "My father fought in Egypt."

But Marsh ignored that, instead asking, "And how did you end up here?"

Pembroke, it turned out, was a Cambridge man, recruited into the service directly out of university. He'd taken a starred first in Russian literature, another first in European history, and then went to work analyzing Soviet military tech for MI6. Pencil-and-paper war games. From there, it was but a lateral move into Milkweed.

"In other words," said Marsh, "you're a pencil pusher."

Pembroke sighed. "I think we're starting off on the wrong foot here. If Gretel's right, you're a part of this."

"If Gretel's right, and she always is, you've pissed away Milkweed's reason for existence. Your incompetence has broken the impasse of the past twenty years. The Eidolons were our trump card, the only thing keeping the Soviets at bay. But now, thanks to your bungling, the Eidolons are closed off from us."

"Because I've been twiddling my thumbs."

"Yes."

"If I could convince you the situation isn't quite so dire," Pembroke said, "would you consider returning?"

Consider it? Returning to Milkweed was the single bright spot on the dreary horizon of Marsh's life. He'd left the service after realizing he could either build a life with Liv, or build a career around a futile and poisonous quest for justice. He'd chosen Liv. But their attempts at creating a family had been spectacular failures. And today their marriage was nothing but a lie. He had chosen poorly.

Coming back to SIS wouldn't fix any of that. But it meant a steady income. It meant having a purpose in life. It meant a legitimate excuse to avoid Liv's resentment without enduring tossers like Fitch. And it meant Marsh would be there when Gretel slipped. Everyone slips, eventually.

Marsh hadn't realized how much he'd missed the service until today. "I'll consider it," he said.

"Excellent," said Pembroke, standing. He set the unlit pipe on his desk. "I'd like to show you something."

The Old Admiralty was much as Marsh remembered; only the names on the doors had changed. He noticed that many of the rooms that had belonged to Milkweed in its brief heyday were now storerooms, crammed with old desks, chairs, rolls of carpet, filing cabinets, and the other office detritus that accumulates over the years.

But then they descended a stairwell to a heavy door that looked like the entrance to a bank vault, and the sense of familiarity vanished. This was new.

Pembroke spun the wheel in the center of the door. It moved silently. Even the bolts made barely a whisper when they withdrew. He started to pull the door open, but then he snapped his fingers and stopped. He turned to Marsh.

"I ought to have asked earlier. You're not bleeding anywhere, are you?"

"Bleeding? No."

"You're quite certain?" Pembroke eyed the bruise on Marsh's face. "Your wounds have healed?"

Marsh glanced at the scratches on his hands. "Yes."

"No open cuts? No ulcers?"

"No."

"Very good, then."

The vault door was the first of a pair. They were connected such that the inner door could be opened only when the outer door was locked, and vice versa. Like a castle's sally port, or the air lock on a submersible.

When they emerged in the cellar, Marsh found he didn't recognize anything. The space had been radically altered since last he was down here. The cellar Marsh remembered had been a warren of brick barrel vault passageways. It had been lit by bare lightbulbs hung from wires overhead, and lined with the gray, rivet-studded steel doors of storerooms and bomb shelters. Water stains had mottled the ceiling and cold concrete floor.

It was impossible to know if any of that remained. Thick carpet covered the floor, ceiling, and walls; the walls were studded with angular baffles carved from black plastic foam. Marsh understood at once, by virtue of having spent so much time struggling to perfect John's room. This was soundproofing done right, at the Crown's expense.

Walking was a bit difficult. The thick beige carpet underfoot yielded a good inch beneath every footstep. The storerooms had been replaced with vaults much like the ones they'd passed through on their entrance to the cellar. These were also soundproofed.

Pembroke pointed at two adjacent doors. "Gretel and her brother are in there, and there," he said. Marsh had to listen carefully in order to hear him over the sound of his own beating heart and the blood rushing through his ears. "Do speak freely, however. They can't hear anything that transpires out here, short of mortar fire."

Marsh wondered if Gretel had foreseen this place, this future version of the cellar, during her short incarceration here in 1940. Probably.

He followed Pembroke to the end of a long corridor, around the corner, and down another. The Admiralty cellar adjoined tunnels that ran far past the footprint of the building itself; Marsh guessed they had passed beneath St. James' Park. The world was silent except for footfalls and heartbeats. The carpeted soundproofing changed patterns here and there, from stripes to dots to triangular tilings. Marsh suspected the deepest reaches of this warren had been built earliest, out of scrap materials. Some of this carpeting predated the war.

And then—so suddenly, it seemed impossible—an overpowering mixture of scents filled the air. Watermelon. Bile. An old man's sweat. A foul taste coated Marsh's mouth. His stomach convulsed, as though he'd swallowed mothballs.

They've soundproofed the hell out of things, thought Marsh. *And they're worried about blood.*

Motivated by instinct and old memories, Marsh looked at his watch. It had stopped.

The Eidolons have been here. What is this place?

The soundproofing even muted the jangling of Pembroke's key ring. He fished around for a few moments, then unlocked a door. They entered a standard observation room, the kind used during interrogations and debriefings. A row of chairs and a narrow table faced a single pane of glass that stretched nearly from wall to wall. The chamber was dimly lit, suggesting the glass was a one-way mirror. A lone microphone stood on the table; the wall above the mirror had a speaker grille.

Marsh had expected something like this. The whole environment here in the bowels of the Admiralty had been designed for keeping people in deep isolation. But he hadn't expected the scene on the other side of the looking glass.

It was a primary school classroom.

The place had been done up in bright colors, reds and blues and yellows. On one wall hung a green chalkboard smudged with childish scrawls, snippets of an unknowable language in colored chalks. Above it, a series of placards ran the length of the chalkboard, where a parade of merry zoo animals frolicked among the letters of the alphabet and the digits naught through nine. Cubbyholes filled with stuffed toys and picture books lined another wall, beneath a bright mural of children playing happily on the outline of the United Kingdom. Oddly, the wall directly across from the mirror was papered with maps of the world. Many of the maps focused on Europe and the Soviet Union. The maps were dotted with pushpins.

Roughly a dozen children of both sexes sat at tables or sprawled on cushions or stood off by themselves in ones, twos, and threes. The older ones read. The younger ones played with dolls, wooden blocks, toy trucks, stuffed animals. They ranged in age from perhaps five or six years all the way to their late teens. And they were silent. Each and every one of them.

"These," said Pembroke, "are our warlocks."

Dear God in Heaven, thought Marsh. *What have you done?* "They're just children."

"Not just any children. These children speak Enochian. Indeed, you might say it's their first language. They're more proficient with it than any warlock in centuries," Pembroke said. "Which is why we haven't felt a need to keep tabs on the fellows from your days. They're outdated. No offense, of course."

Marsh pointed at the children. "How?"

"Enochian is the ur-language. Some people have speculated that it's the language of creation, or the music of the spheres." Pembroke shrugged. "We have found that if you raise a child in complete isolation from all human language, insulated from any exposure to it, they naturally revert to Enochian."

"That's barbaric." *You twisted bastards.*

"It's realpolitik. It's the world we live in. It's the price of a free nation."

Marsh watched the children. "Are they prisoners?"

Pembroke became indignant. "I should say not." He hesitated. "That is, not in principle. But they seem to prefer it here. They prefer the silence. They've never indicated a desire to leave."

"Have you asked them?"

"Yes."

"They speak English, too?"

"Of course they do. We end each child's isolation the moment they demonstrate fluency in Enochian," said Pembroke. "Around age four or five, typically. After that we provide them with a superb education. Easily the equal of anything they'd receive in public school."

Marsh couldn't stop watching the children. Pointing through the glass with a jerk of his chin, he asked, "How often do you use them?"

"Just enough to tweak Ivan's nose once in a while. Nothing drastic, mind you. No doubt they suspect Milkweed. And that's the point. To let them know we're here. But their information, whatever its source, is far, far out of date. They don't know who the active warlocks are."

"They didn't until you brought Gretel down here."

"Her cell is so far away, past so many layers of soundproofing, that I could light a stick of dynamite here and she wouldn't be any wiser," said Pembroke.

Marsh shook his head, too disgusted and too weary to argue the point. "What about blood prices? You don't force them to—"

Pembroke snorted. "Please. We're not barbarians. Sam handles the prices. He has men for it." He tugged absently at one ear. "Incidentally, and for the most part, the prices are lower than they were in your day. A benefit of the children's natural fluency, you see."

"How low?"

"Acceptably low," said Pembroke. "After a bit of a rocky start," he admitted.

He unlocked a door beside the mirror, which opened on the classroom. "Let's meet them." When Marsh hesitated, he said, "It's entirely safe."

Marsh stared at the children. "Insulated."

"What is it?"

"You don't have children of your own," said Marsh.

"Your point?"

"My wife and I have taken a newborn home from the hospital on two separate occasions. If there's one thing parents do, it's talk to their children."

Pembroke looked uncomfortable. "These children were orphans. Abandoned."

The flippant explanation didn't begin to address the issue. But before Marsh could dissect the transparent evasion, Pembroke opened the door and stepped through. The children ignored him, and Marsh as well when he followed a few seconds later.

"But in order to *completely* isolate them—"

"Believe me when I tell you, Marsh, that they've been treated extremely well."

As one, the children stopped, straightened, and turned to face the adults. There was something unnerving about the way they moved in unison. Something feral. No—insectile. Alien. Something just a bit like John.

One of the older boys stepped forward. He looked at Marsh, squinting. They all did.

"You are Marsh," he croaked. "The man Marsh."

Instant gooseflesh stippled Marsh's arms and nape. It tingled unpleasantly.

The boy's voice sounded wrong. Deeply wrong. It wasn't just that the boy had the hoarse, gravelly voice of an old man. The ruined voice of an old warlock.

These children, Marsh realized, spoke English with an Enochian accent. If that were somehow possible.

"Yes, I am." Marsh bent, ignoring the constriction of his boilersuit and the crawling of his skin to put himself at equal height with the boy. His knee throbbed. Cheerfully as he could manage, he said, "And who are you?"

But his question was lost under the urgent murmuring of decrepit yet childish voices repeating his name. They said it over and over again, in a variety of speeds and intonations.

"Marsh. Marsh. Marsh. Marsh."

Soon they converged on a single tempo and a single inflection. When they switched to Enochian, it happened instantaneously, in midchant.

Marsh found himself inside a maelstrom of gurgles, shrieks, howls, and rumbles. In the chanting he heard the death of stars and the birth of planets. Inhuman noises from tiny human vessels.

The minute part of him that could still think under that onslaught realized, *This is why they're worried about blood. These children could summon an Eidolon at the drop of a hat.*

He clasped his hands over his ears. So did Pembroke.

And somewhere, somewhen, somebody said, *My God. They've given you a name.*

interlude

Gretel's first set of instructions arrived in the post not two hours after she and her spineless brother moved out. Reinhardt wasn't sorry to see the last of those parasites. The bitch took special enjoyment out of his failed attempts to steal their batteries. Every time Klaus caught him, Gretel was there, watching over his shoulder with that infuriating half-cocked smile of hers.

Reinhardt would scorch that smile away. Someday.

He'd worried that her instructions would be nonsensical. Like everything else about her. But the letter was straightforward and detailed. The first part of her task came with a tight schedule; perhaps she had put her riddles aside to guarantee Reinhardt would finish on time.

Which was how he ended up hurrying out of the flat only to spend hours shivering under a hedge in Kew Gardens, guarding his camera from the incessant rain. She'd provided a description of the men he would photograph, their bench beneath the walnut tree on the Broad Walk, even the angle from which he'd take the photo. The last bit being how he found his hiding place. The only thing she hadn't nailed down for him—probably because she enjoyed the thought of Reinhardt shivering in the rain—was the precise time of the meeting.

Of course, she didn't bother to explain who the men were, or why Reinhardt had to photograph them. But he didn't care about any of that. Gretel could play all the games she wanted as long as he got what he wanted.

Have you forgotten how in the past I delivered your heart's darkest desire?

Once the men had gone their separate ways, Reinhardt did as she said and took one final photograph, this time of the front page of that morning's *Times*. To establish the date, he presumed.

After leaving Kew Gardens, Reinhardt drove until he found a chemist's shop thirty miles from his council estate. It would have been better to develop the film himself, but Reinhardt didn't have access to a darkroom. Nor did he know how to develop film in the first place; the Reichsbehörde had used specialists for menial tasks.

He bribed the chemist to ensure the photos would be ready in a day. Nowhere in her letter did Gretel offer to cover Reinhardt's out-of-pocket expenses.

Gretel was just as specific about the next step as she had been about the mechanics of the photographs: he was to send the package of photos to a particular address on a particular day. But Reinhardt knew better than to use a post office near his home. It stood to reason that the recipient of these photos would be surprised and probably displeased by them. He'd photographed a secret exchange—that much was obvious— and the address Gretel provided was in Westminster. That meant this was political. The recipients would take a long, hard look at the postmark on Reinhardt's package.

So he again drove across London, west this time, to post the package from an office he selected at random. Large enough that he would blend into the crowd, and far enough from his flat to throw any investigators off the trail. For the return address, Reinhardt selected something out of the telephone directory, again at random.

The fat postie behind the counter took Reinhardt's package, and his cash, and then did a double take when he saw the fake return address.

Reinhardt said, "Is there a problem?"

The fat man shook his head. "Ain't that the oddest thing. Just got a package for you in this morning's batch."

"That's impossible," said Reinhardt, although he knew it wasn't. Not for Gretel. "I'm new to the neighborhood."

"I figured as much," said the postman. "I remember your name because I didn't recognize it when the package came through. Reckoned it had to be a mistake. Now how do you fancy that?"

Reinhardt waited until he was safely home to open the package. It contained more fragments of the battery blueprint, and a second letter. He tossed the letter aside, trembling with excitement as he dug out his research journals and the fragments that had arrived with her first letter.

One battery. That's all. Just one was all he needed to slip the leash she'd put around his neck.

The blueprint fragments didn't match up. Gretel had sent the edges of the diagram, but not the center. Typical Gretel. But the addition pointed Reinhardt in the right direction, and he knew that in time he'd fill the gaps via his own investigations.

Exhausted from a long day spent hunched over his desk, he finally turned his attention to Gretel's second letter.

My Dear Reinhardt, it began. *From the time you receive this letter, you have three days to vacate your flat.*

five

16 May 1963
Walworth, London, England

Within two days of his first meeting with Pembroke, Marsh had a salary and an office in the Admiralty building. He told Liv he had an offer to return to work at the Foreign Office, which had been his cover during the war. She expressed no excitement for the improbable resuscitation of his career, only for the prospect of a higher and steadier income. But when he told her that his new situation brought with it long days, she refused to rearrange her own life to accommodate the change. Liv made it clear that somebody had to stay with John in the evenings, and that somebody would be Marsh.

In short, the Milkweed job enlivened their home life. It gave them something new to fight about, rather than rehashing the arguments they'd played out countless times.

"And what about Fitch's garden?" Liv pulled open a drawer, searching for a peeler. Rummaging through the utensils, she added, "You promised him you'd have that done ages ago." She found the peeler and leaned heavily against the drawer; it scraped shut. Marsh hadn't wanted to spend precious cash on new rollers from the local ironmongers. "We're fortunate he tolerates you as much as he does."

Marsh crossed his arms. "Fitch can stuff it," he said.

"Did you tell him that?" She channeled her irritation into the carrots she peeled. A flurry of thin orange strips pelted the sink. "Fat lot of good that'll do us when you cock up this new job and then have to go crawling back to him."

Her utter confidence that he'd make a wreck of things flayed him as surely as if she had scraped the peeler down his bare arms. This wasn't about the new job. It was about finding new ways to hurt each other. Marsh was the symbol for everything Liv hated about her life. Her target. But whom did he blame for how wrong it all went? Liv? John? Himself?

It hadn't always been like this. They'd loved each other so much. . . . There had been a time when his heart beat harder when she entered the room. When she made him feel energized, more alive, willing to fight the world just to win her smile. But now her company was a weight that bent his spine, slumped his shoulders. The fighting made him so damn weary.

Liv pulled her hair back. From his spot leaning against the refrigerator, Marsh could see the flush rising up through the fine hairs at the nape of her neck. It happened when she was passionate about something. Strangely, at that moment, it reminded him of the first time they'd made love, and how afterwards they'd lain nestled together like two spoons on the mattress in Liv's garret at her boarding house. He'd watched the way the blush rose and fell along her neck like tides pulled by his breath.

The memory, so vivid and unsolicited, moved him. He reached for her. In a more civil tone, he said, "This is a good thing. We'll have more money."

She swatted his hand away. Upstairs, John launched into a new round of keening. A breeze rustled threadbare, sun-bleached curtains over the sink. It carried the compost scent of Marsh's garden and the residual ozone tang of that afternoon's storm.

Ian Tregillis

"We won't have more money," she said. "You'll have more money to drink away at the pub. While I'm imprisoned here with him," she said, pointing at the ceiling with the peeler. "Nothing will change."

Why did this have to become yet another battle in their long, point-less war? Somehow, improbably, he had his old job back. Maybe that meant there was a chance to reconnect with Liv. A chance for détente.

He said, "It won't be like that this time. I promise." She sniffed. He sighed.

The faucet broke for what seemed the thousandth time when she went to fill the teapot. Handing Liv a dish towel, Marsh said, "Things will be different. Better."

"For you. But you're not abandoning me to deal with John every hour of the day and night. I have a life outside these walls, Raybould. And I won't sacrifice that."

A life. Is that what you call it? Cuckolding me? My work is more im-portant than your affairs, you tart.

Marsh's jaw ached with the effort to hold his tongue. He forced himself to release the pressure on his teeth before he ground them to powder. A dull throb took root behind his eyeballs.

He wondered, not for the first time, about Liv's lover. It occurred to him that now he was back with SIS, finding the man (men?) would be a trivial task. But then what? A confrontation? Marsh feared it would be even more emasculating to know his identity. Liv deserved what happi-ness she could make for herself, even if it was at his expense. They'd caused each other enough grief. One of them should be happy.

Marsh shook his head. "They need me."

"The Foreign Office needs a pudgy, half-pissed, out-of-shape ex-bureaucrat who hasn't held a steady job in ten years? God save the Queen."

Marsh slammed the door. Again. John's crying receded into the gen-eral noise of the city after two streets; Marsh's flaring temper burned itself down to glowing coals after a dozen.

The streets smelled like rain and pub food. The refuse behind a shabby Spanish restaurant stank of ripe seafood. The neighborhood didn't appear quite as threatening in the early-afternoon sun as it had when the storm clouds rolled through that morning, low and black. Torrents of rain had washed the pavement clean of newspapers and waxed paper chip wrappers. But nothing could wash away the feeling of being watched, of eyes peering out from every dark corner.

Part of him still yearned to work the anger out through his fists. At the mouth of a narrow alleyway, he stopped to contemplate a detour. Faintly, from the shadows behind the rubbish bins, where rainwater still dripped from rusted gutters, the telltale scuffle of shoe leather on pavement reached his ears. That was the sound of somebody sitting up, taking attention, surveying a mark. Marsh cracked his knuckles. But he stopped himself before entering the alley and committing himself to what at best would be a scrap and at worst would be a mugging, a stabbing, a murder.

He had a job now. The only job he'd ever been good for. And turning his back on that meant never knowing why Gretel had killed Agnes.

Marsh took the Tube to Charing Cross.

His office in the Admiralty building overlooked Horse Guards Parade. The Royal Horse Guards were practicing maneuvers when Marsh flopped into the wobbly office chair behind his particleboard desk. He opened the window and spent a few peaceful moments listening to the Yorkshire bark of a regimental commander, the clop of hooves on cobbles, and the jingle of harnesses. The drills continued while Marsh dived into the mounds of folders and papers that had appeared on his desk, as if by magic, since the previous evening. Pembroke had wasted no time getting Marsh plugged into the loop.

The topmost file was a status report on the debriefing of the two "defectors." They'd been questioned separately, and so far their story held. No progress, in other words. But Pembroke had agreed with Marsh's suggestion they be moved to a safe house outside the city center; that had happened this morning, during the storm.

The next batch of paperwork was everything Milkweed had on the old warlocks: names, aliases, wartime achievements, movements, last known whereabouts. Most of the files became quite sparse after the mid-1950s. Marsh guessed the first batch of warlock children had come to fruition then.

Working through its parent organization, SIS, Milkweed had begun the laborious process of corroborating Gretel's claims. But the warlocks were hard men to find, and so it was likely to take weeks before solid conclusions could be drawn. One file did note that the recent fire in the Forest of Dean appeared to have begun in a small cottage deep in the forest. This was consistent with the prewar living arrangement of one of the warlocks. Shapley. Marsh remembered him.

One file stood out from the others by virtue of its size. The accompanying photograph showed a man considerably younger than the one whom Marsh had recently seen on television. The man in the photo had no wrinkles, no bags beneath his eyes. Will Beauclerk had gone underground before the official end of the war; Milkweed agents had tracked his movements through a recurring sequence of dosshouses and hospitals over the course of several years. Will had been a drunkard and a morphine addict when the old man kicked him out of Milkweed. Leaving the service hastened his decline.

Marsh paused. He'd known that Will had been in a bad way. But this . . . It was a miracle the man hadn't killed himself during that time.

The surge of regret caught Marsh unaware. Will had been a close friend. Marsh hadn't realized, until now, how much he missed that friendship. How lonely and isolated the wreckage of his marriage had left him. What kind of man had he become, that he didn't care if an assassin gutted his former friend? The fight with Liv, and his failure to defuse it, had saddled him with a nostalgic melancholy.

The file documented that somehow, miraculously, a sober Will emerged from his long, slow suicide with a wife at his side. The Lady Gwendolyn Wellesley, eldest daughter to the Earl of Portland, had met Will while working as a nurse. The file contained a photo of Gwendolyn. Marsh felt a stab of resentment; he wondered how well she might have preserved her looks into late middle age if she had been taking care of John for all that time, rather than Will. At least Will could crap by himself. Presumably.

Since then, Will had been something of a public figure. Keeping tabs on him was trivial. It wouldn't take much investigative work to know if the brother of the Duke of Aelred had been killed. Reading the newspaper would suffice.

The sun had fallen into evening, sending long shadows across the silent parade ground, when Marsh noticed the mail. A single envelope, filled with something stiff, addressed to Raybould Marsh care of the Admiralty. The handwriting was unfamiliar.

Very few people knew Marsh could be found here. Of those who did, all but two could speak with him at leisure. No need for strange packages.

He started to tear the envelope open with his thumb, as he did with mail at home, but stopped himself. The envelope had been postmarked. Rather than risk tearing or smudging the mark, he fished out his pocket-knife and slit the narrow end of the envelope. Marsh dumped the contents onto his desk. A set of color photographs tumbled out.

They formed a sequence of images, shot from a distance at a low angle, of two men sitting on a bench. The images were slightly blurry and somewhat dark. Marsh found himself wishing he had Stephenson's jeweler's loupe, which the old man had kept from his days analyzing aerial photographs during the First World War. A blurred fringe of green bordered some of the photos, as though they had been shot through a hedge. The final photograph in the batch showed the front page of the *Times,* and the date. The photos had been taken three days earlier.

Marsh turned his attention back to the men. After a few more seconds of study, he knew what these photos were meant to tell him.

"Bugger me," he said.

The man on the left was Will Beauclerk. The man on the right—caught in one of the photos accepting an envelope from Will—Marsh had never seen before. But he didn't need the second man's identity to know how the Soviets had tracked down Milkweed's original warlocks. Will Beauclerk had sold them out.

He felt a fool. Will didn't deserve his concern.

"You son of a bitch."

Pembroke had been right all along: the leaked information was coming out of Milkweed through an insider, not because they'd been compromised by an outsider.

A dozen thoughts raced through Marsh's runaway mind, each

competing for a moment of attention with a flash of insight before he landed on the next conclusion. It all fell together.

Will didn't need Milkweed's files to find the warlocks; those files existed because of Will's effort to find those men in the first place. And the Soviets hadn't done anything about the warlock children, because Will didn't know about them. How could he? He'd been drummed out of Milkweed long ago. His information was out of date.

"You bastard, Will. You unbelievable bastard."

Marsh wanted to scream with rage and weep with envy.

He ached with the need to punish Gretel. He'd lost his own *daughter* to her machinations. Agnes's death had become an unhealed wound, a gangrenous cyst on his marriage. It had weakened the love between Liv and Marsh, poisoned it, to the point where the next insult—their son, John—killed it completely.

But he couldn't exact revenge on his enemy. She was clairvoyant. Untouchable. And that made his a solitary crusade. Even Stephenson had brushed off Marsh's warnings when he returned from Germany with incontrovertible evidence that the Soviets had taken her. Because the war had severely weakened Britain, and Whitehall couldn't risk upsetting its fragile alliance with the USSR. Nobody—not the old man, not Milkweed, not SIS—had lifted a finger to put things right for Marsh.

But later, when Will suddenly decided to have it out with his former colleagues, he had nothing less than the entire KGB jumping to his aid.

It wasn't fair.

Why, Will? Money? Ideology? A bit of both?

A grudge?

The Soviets had found a way to turn him. It probably wasn't difficult. They might have started when Will was a raving, drug-addled lunatic. That's when he was the most vulnerable; Marsh made a mental note to get the SIS lamplighters digging into Gwendolyn Wellesley's past. Family history. Political inclinations. Perhaps they'd find a den of Bolshies.

And, of course, Will's brother was a prominent pro-Soviet figure in the House of Lords. Will oversaw the daily operations of Aubrey's NGO. Meaning the Soviets had plenty of access to the younger Beauclerk.

Everything fit. Marsh knew that when Milkweed dug deeper, it would find more evidence damning Will. Knew it in his gut. He could save a lot of work, and perhaps lives, if he simply confronted the man.

New questions presented themselves: Who was the man photographed with Will? Who took these photographs? Gretel herself? But then why did she go to such elaborate lengths to mail him the photos?

Marsh locked the photographs in his desk. The corridors were empty and silent; most folks had gone home for the evening. But Marsh found Pethick locking up his office, clearly on his way out for the evening. He had a brown mackintosh slung over one arm, and an umbrella threaded through the handle of his briefcase. With his black suit and black umbrella, he looked more like a banker than spy. And that spoke volumes about the current state of Milkweed.

"Good evening," said Pethick. "And he's working late already. Not one to waste time, is he?"

Marsh waved the empty envelope at him. "Where did this come from?"

Pethick shrugged. "The post, I presume."

"How did it get on my desk? Who put it there?"

Pethick studied the envelope for a moment. "We do have regular post service here, you know. And I note this is addressed to you. I'd say that solves it."

"I want you to see something," said Marsh. Pethick followed him back to his office.

When Marsh laid out the photographs for him, Pethick let out a long, low whistle. He scanned them slowly, his gaze sweeping forward and back across the photos.

Marsh asked, "Do you recognize these men?"

Pethick said, "Yes."

"The man on the left is Will Beauclerk. The other?"

"I believe that is Yevgeny Cherkashin. Cultural attaché at the Soviet embassy here in London." Pethick paused to study the date in the *Times* photo. He looked at Marsh. "But in SIS circles, he's known for running the Lincolnshire Poacher network. A handful of Soviet agents spread throughout the United Kingdom."

"Lincolnshire Poacher. Number station?"

Pethick nodded. "Broadcast out of Nice."

Number stations were a simple, secure means of openly sending orders to agents working undercover in foreign countries. The sobriquet described them accurately; the typical number station broadcast consisted of a male or female voice reciting a sequence of numbers. The numbers referred to blocks of a one-time pad. As long as the only copies of the pad belonged to the sender and recipient, and as long as certain precautions were followed during the generation of the pad itself, the messages were essentially unbreakable. Most number stations broadcast at regular intervals, usually at preset times and frequencies on certain days. The Soviet empire had dozens of such stations broadcasting around the world from behind the Iron Curtain. Britain operated stations of its own.

Many number stations commenced or terminated their broadcasts with a few bars of a song or melody. Cherkashin's handlers in Moscow had evidently chosen a British folk song.

"So we know about Cherkashin's network, but we haven't rolled it up," said Marsh. "To avoid tipping our hand?"

Pethick said, "There is that, yes. And, also, the network has fallen silent since—" Pethick scratched his chin. "—hmmm, you'd have to ask the signals chaps down in Sussex to know with certainty. Two years, perhaps?"

"Silent isn't the same as inactive." Marsh jabbed his finger at the stack of files pertaining to the dead warlocks. "Cherkashin has been rather busy."

17 May 1963
Croydon, London, England

The drive to the safe house had taken seemingly forever in slow-moving traffic. Klaus knew they had been moved to a place called Croydon, but beyond the name, he knew very little of the place. He and his sister had huddled near the back of the truck during the move, and what little he could see through the front windshield had been obscured by sheets of rain beneath a coal black sky.

A glimpse of the environs while hustling from the truck to the house suggested a heavily industrial, working-class neighborhood. Dingy brick row houses lined both sides of the street, crowded shoulder to shoulder like empty-eyed beggars glaring at the occupants of passing cars.

Their safe house was outwardly indistinguishable from the others on this street, with the exception of being a corner lot. A redbrick wall surrounded the rear garden. On the inside, the safe house occupied a large footprint. The interior walls separating the safe house and its neighbor had been removed, although the street-side appearance of two separate houses was strictly maintained.

The house reeked of stale cigarette smoke. It was the smell of boredom, of hiding and waiting for days on end. And in Gretel's case, playing rummy.

In addition to Klaus and Gretel, three people occupied the safe house. He gathered that one—a woman named Madeleine, whom he'd glimpsed only briefly upon arrival—lived here semi-permanently, on the other side of the house. Probably to preserve the fiction of a single-family dwelling on that side. She ran the house. The minders who had moved Klaus from the Admiralty building, Anthony and Roger, were charged with keeping an eye over the siblings until replacements arrived to relieve them in a few days. But they weren't immune to boredom. Hence the cards.

Klaus couldn't decide if Gretel was using her power. Like him, she had no battery. But she did win most hands. She responded to the other players' complaints with demure deflections about luck and skill. Klaus knew that tone of voice; she was highly amused.

Klaus didn't participate. But the afternoon's endless card game did tell him something useful. Their minders were British Intelligence, obviously, but they weren't from Milkweed. Only an idiot would knowingly play cards with a precog, even if the stakes were merely plastic chips.

"Damn. There she goes again," said Anthony. He tossed his cards on the scuffed table, knocking the rumpled corduroy blazer from the back of his chair to the floor.

Gretel laughed, and started to protest. Roger cut her off, "Yeah, we know. It's better to have luck than skill."

"It is, truly," she said. "Isn't that so, brother?"

Klaus shrugged noncommittally and went back to peeking through the drapes to watch the street below. He saw nothing funny about being cooped up in a British safe house. The accommodations were better and the attitudes warmer than they had been at Arzamas, but that didn't alter the fact that he was a prisoner again. Because of Gretel.

The street saw little traffic. Sunlight glinted on the pavement alongside the road, where dwindling puddles had been left by the previous day's deluge. Klaus watched not out of expectation for anything specific, but because he knew that sooner or later another cog would slot into place, and Gretel's machinations would advance ever closer to her secret goal. He lived in a state of perpetual dread, waiting for the other shoe to drop. It was wearying, but he was loath to drop his guard.

Klaus spent three hours at the window. He saw one neighbor fail to clean up after her poodle when it crapped on the pavement, and he watched the postman zigzag his way up the street with his satchel banging against his hip. Both times he wondered if they, like he, were unwitting chips in Gretel's great game.

His stomach gurgled. Klaus set aside the vigil in favor of lunch. Madeleine stood at the kitchen counter, spreading marmalade on a piece of toast with quick, precise gestures of the knife blade. She was tall for a woman, nearly Klaus's height, with a mass of chestnut hair that cascaded over her shoulders. She looked up when he entered.

Scrape-scrape-scrape. Aggressive competence.

"Am I allowed in here?" The words left an aftertaste of shame when they left his mouth. It was appalling, how automatically he reverted to the mind-set of a prisoner.

She raised her eyebrows, surprised or amused by the question. Age hadn't yet softened her skin, hadn't yet caused it to sag. Klaus guessed she was roughly ten years younger than he. She asked, "Why wouldn't you be?"

Because I've been a prisoner my entire life, he thought, *and being a prisoner means knowing the boundaries.* He made a show of looking to the blade in her hands. *And more to the point, because you store knives in here.*

He said, "I don't know your rules yet."

"We're not jailers, Klaus," she said.

"Am I free to come and go as I please?"

"Within the house, yes. But you ought not venture outside without escorts."

"Escorts or guards?"

There might have been a glimmer of amusement in her eyes, or perhaps irritation at being second-guessed. She gestured at the refrigerator with her knife. "There's watercress and tomato in there if you fancy a sandwich. Bread's in the pantry."

The house featured a narrow kitchen. He brushed past her on his way to the pantry. She wore a hint of perfume; it smelled clean and light. Somehow, it reminded Klaus of early autumn snowfalls at the Reichsbehörde. Back when the world was black-and-white, when he and his sister stood together against the world.

"Do let us know if you'd like us to obtain something particular from the grocer," she said. "Reasonable requests can usually be accommodated."

The knife in her hand caused the skin between his shoulder blades to itch. A lifetime of training made his body unwilling to turn its back on an armed opponent. He felt her eyes on the back of his head, fixating on the wire bundle that dangled past his shoulder. Marsh had insisted that the siblings wear their wires on the outside at all times, so that any attempts to use them would be noticed immediately. As though Klaus were likely to find compatible batteries stocked in the pantry.

Anticipating the question she wouldn't dream of asking, he trotted out the familiar canard. "It happened in the camps. During the war."

He wondered if she knew he had been a Nazi. Probably. But he said it anyway.

He wondered if she'd had family members killed during the long Blitz. Probably.

He found the bread, and a jar of honey. Madeleine was still watching him when he turned to put them on the counter. "Your sister. Is she settling in well?"

Another curse sounded in the den, followed by Gretel's laughter. "She always does," he sighed.

Madeleine brushed past him again to toss her dirty knife in the sink. Part of him wondered who would be tasked with washing the dishes, while another part of him wondered if she was trying to arouse him. That seemed a likely ploy. And somewhat to his dismay, it worked. He kept his back to her in order to hide this.

She turned to leave before he said anything. "What I said about the grocer applies in general," said Madeleine. "We'll make your stay here more pleasant, if we can. Books, perhaps?"

She's trying to learn more about me, thought Klaus. *Fishing for information.* That was yet more training rising to the surface, the vestige of a youth spent at the Reichsbehörde and a middle age spent at Arzamas-16. But the oldest Klaus, the one who'd come to Britain foolishly thinking it would make him a free man, found he didn't care if Madeleine were fishing or not.

He thought back to what he saw in the park during his taxi ride through London. "Painting supplies," he said over his shoulder. "I'd like painting supplies."

"Are you a painter?"

"No."

This time there definitely was a hint of amusement in her expression. He could tell she wanted him to elaborate, but the bell chimed just then, and so Madeleine went to answer the door. Klaus followed her a minute later, just in time for the argument.

Marsh and Pethick had arrived. To Roger and Anthony, Marsh said, "Having fun? Party's over. Get back to work."

Roger scowled. Pethick pulled out his billfold, removing a five-pound note to cut off Anthony before he could protest: "Take a breather, gents. We need a private few with the guests."

The two minders tossed their cards on the table. Anthony collected his blazer from the floor, took the note from Pethick, and followed

Roger through the garden door behind the house. The hinges needed oiling. Madeleine, Klaus noticed, had also made herself scarce.

Marsh took one of the vacated seats. Gretel pouted at him. "I was going to win that hand, Raybould."

"Don't call me that." He tossed an envelope on the table, scattering the pile of chips she had amassed. Cards fluttered to the tangerine carpet. "What the hell is this?"

Klaus recognized Reinhardt's handwriting. He suppressed the urge to step forward and see firsthand what Gretel's instructions had wrought. But something in his bearing piqued Pethick's curiosity. Pethick sidled up to the kitchen, where Klaus leaned against the doorjamb.

Gretel took the envelope. She studied the postmark for a long moment, as if committing it to memory. Which she was, Klaus knew. Committing it to the memory of a younger version of herself, the Gretel who had foreseen this moment.

What are you doing, sister? What will this new paradox achieve?

After studying the envelope, she tipped it over the table. A set of photographs spilled out, knocking more chips to the floor. Most were of a pair of men sitting on a park bench; Klaus recognized neither of them. One photo was of a newspaper. Gretel scrutinized this as closely as she had the postmark.

Marsh leaned forward. "Well?"

Gretel sifted through the remaining photos. Her gaze lingered over one of the clearer shots. "I haven't seen William in ages," she said.

"Who took these photos?"

Klaus felt Pethick watching him, sidewise. Honey trickled down his fingers, cool and sticky. He took a bite from his sandwich. The bread was stale. He chewed nonchalantly, thinking about anyone but Reinhardt.

"A friend," said Gretel.

Marsh's tone was calm. Measured. "Why so baroque, Gretel? Why not tell us about Will when you came in?"

"Without evidence? Would you have believed me?" Her playful demeanor vanished. She stared at Marsh, bottomless dark eyes boring straight into his. "The woman who killed your daughter?"

Six words that sucked all the air from the room. Pethick and Klaus both turned to watch Marsh. Their breath ought to have steamed in the sudden chill. The silence was so complete, so heavy, that Klaus couldn't hear anything but his own chewing. He realized he wasn't tensing up to grab Gretel, nor preparing to pull her out of harm's way. This time, he was a spectator. Let Gretel fend for herself. She always did.

Marsh held her gaze through the length of several agonizingly long heartbeats. He didn't blink. That impressed Klaus. He'd never known anybody who could stare her down. Not when the madness behind her eyes was so naked to the world.

And, yes, it was madness. Klaus knew that as well as anybody. But there was something else, too. Something previously hidden to him.

No, not hidden. Something he'd never dared to acknowledge before. Gretel had dropped her masks and her pretenses, and for the space of those few heartbeats, he saw his sister's essence.

He saw her heart and soul, darker even than her eyes. He saw the truth of this woman for whom the world and its people were nothing more than tools toward an end. Remorseless, like a chess player sacrificing pieces according to her grand strategy: Rudolf. Heike. Doctor von Westarp. Marsh's daughter. The REGP itself.

Klaus's freedom. Twenty years of his life.

The way Gretel moved through the world . . . it wasn't simple madness. Nor was she misguided, as he'd let himself believe.

Klaus started to laugh. He couldn't help himself. He was the world's greatest fool. After so many years spent struggling to justify Gretel's actions, so much effort expended bending over backwards to give her the benefit of the doubt, the real explanation turned out to be absurdly simple.

Gretel was evil, and she was insane.

Reinhardt could have told him that.

Thinking of Reinhardt sent another wave of hysteria crashing over the feeble breakwaters of his self-control. But it wasn't joyful laughter. It was the laughter of the utterly overwhelmed. The others stared at Klaus. He retreated to the kitchen, wiping tears from his eyes. He breathed deeply until the fit subsided. And then the deeper reality hit.

Klaus doubled over and emptied his stomach into the sink. It took three glasses of water to wash the worst of the taste from his mouth.

Pethick came in. "Are you ill?"

Klaus waved him off with one hand, gulping more water. He swished it around his mouth, then spit the remnants of his gorge into the sink. The cloying scent of honey threatened to evoke a second wave of nausea. Klaus screwed the lid back on the honey jar and tossed the entire thing into the rubbish bin. He walked around Pethick and returned to his spot in the kitchen entryway.

Marsh hadn't moved a hairsbreadth. His body had become a tightly coiled spring, and it wound tighter and tighter with every word Gretel spoke. She broke off when Klaus returned.

"Brother?" she said. "What troubles you?" It was still there, that thing behind her eyes, that alien emotion, bare to the world. She directed it straight at him. And the look in her eyes . . .

Doctor von Westarp, the mad genius who had turned a handful of starving orphans into the pinnacle of German military might, had a way of looking at people. When the doctor directed that dispassionate gaze through his thick glasses, it felt like Klaus was looking up from a microscope slide. The doctor had seen everything around him with a clinical detachment. Not malevolent—it was emotionless—but cold and hyperanalytical. That simple look cowed his mightiest children, long after they had mastered the Götterelektron.

The look on Gretel's face, there in the British safe house, made Klaus miss the doctor.

"Let us not worry about your brother." Marsh snapped, "The photos. Who. Took. Them?"

"Reinhardt." The name passed Klaus's lips as a whisper, floated across the silent room like a feather, and landed on the table with a thud. Pethick stared at Klaus. Marsh draped an arm over the back of his chair. "What was that?"

Klaus coughed. He peeled his gaze away from Gretel. He said, "Reinhardt is your photographer."

Pethick shrugged at Marsh. Marsh looked down, shaking his head slowly, like a man listening to a faint echo. "Reinhardt," he repeated, as though it were vaguely familiar. He looked up, wide-eyed. "Reinhardt from the Reichsbehörde? He's here?"

"Yes."

Marsh stood. To Pethick he said, "Keep working on her." He pointed at Gretel with a thumb over his shoulder. To Klaus he said, "Come with me. Let's talk."

17 May 1963
Knightsbridge, London, England

Gwendolyn took Will's recuperation more seriously than he did. She forbade him from returning to work for several days. And when he refused to stay in bed any longer, she relented only insofar as to arrange him on the Victorian fainting couch in their parlor. She put a jade green porcelain tea service (complete with sliced lemon) within reach of his one free arm, alongside a stack of his beloved Dashiell Hammett novels.

Fixing Will was what she did. Letting Gwendolyn fix him was what he did. This was the center of their relationship, and had been since the beginning.

His fingertips tasted of lemon when he licked them to turn the pages. The collar of his dressing gown caressed his neck with silk; a cotton chenille blanket cushioned the sling and hugged his chest. He could almost forget the pain, so warm and drowsy was the parlor. It was so peaceful, so relaxing, he couldn't quite bring himself to tell Gwendolyn about his arrangement with Cherkashin. Not yet. He'd lost the gift that might have softened the blow. And he was in no shape for something so fraught. He had to be alert. Delivered injudiciously, the confession might color their relationship.

Will told himself he wasn't procrastinating while she pampered him. But he knew better.

Gwendolyn opened a window to admit a cooling draft. He dozed off halfway through *The Thin Man.*

The rap of the door knocker jostled him to wakefulness. The

noise came from both sides of the door simultaneously, through the foyer and the open window. It gave Will a drowsy, inside-out feeling, as though he could perceive everything at once, like the Sphere in *Flatland*.

They had given their housekeeper the day off. He sat up, but Gwendolyn breezed past the parlor on her way to answer the door.

"William Beauclerk, I know you wouldn't dare remove yourself from that spot."

She'd been sculpting. A kerchief held her hair, and a smear of dun-colored clay colored the curve of her jaw under her left ear, where she tended to tug at her hair absently when deep in thought.

Will settled back on the divan. He listened to the door scrape open a moment later.

A long pause. Then Gwendolyn said, "May I help you?"

A man's voice, heard again from both sides of the door, said, "I'm seeking Will Beauclerk."

Gwendolyn, stiffly: "Lord William isn't receiving visitors presently. Kindly call another time." And the door creaked again, but stopped, as though somebody held it back.

"This will not wait," said the visitor. "I'm a colleague of Will's, from—"

"I know who you are," said Gwendolyn. Crisp. Terse.

Who the devil is it? And what the devil is this about? Will tottered to his feet, still woozy from the nap. He tossed aside the blanket, found his slippers, then tied the sash of his dressing gown more tightly about his waist as he shuffled to the foyer. The stranger was hidden from view by Gwendolyn.

"You must be Gwendolyn," he said. She crossed her arms. "Are you Will's wife, his secretary, or his zookeeper?"

"I've told you," she snapped. "He isn't well."

Will said, "Darling? Who is it?"

Gwendolyn spun around, looking alarmed. "William! You must stay off your feet. You know what the doctor told us."

"Doctor?" said Will, confused.

She hustled toward him, keeping herself between Will and the stranger. "Let's get you back into bed before you put yourself in an early grave."

"Grave?"

She took him by the shoulders, ready to march him upstairs. But their visitor stepped into the vacated entryway before she could spin Will around.

The shock of recognition hit him like a brickbat, launched a frisson of panic bounding through his body. The newcomer was a demon from a distant and unlamented past. A harbinger of sorrow. Or was he an opium nightmare, a mirage forged from the heat of Will's fevered imagination?

What if Gwendolyn was nothing but a fantasy, while the real Will Beauclerk still lay sprawled on the floor of a Limehouse tenement with a needle in his arm?

Yet this demon was subject to the passage of time. It had aged just as a real person would have. Even at their most vivid, Will's drug hallucinations had never been meticulous.

Will swallowed. "Pip?"

Marsh said, "Will."

And Gwendolyn sighed. "Damn."

Gwendolyn didn't offer Marsh anything to eat or drink. Or even a place to sit. But he looked as though he wouldn't have accepted either of the former, and he certainly didn't wait for an invitation before taking a seat in the parlor. He perched on the edge of a green baize chair, his fedora balanced on the armrest.

Age hadn't dampened Marsh's intensity. His body looked softer in places; his belly a smidge wider; his hair thinner; his face craggier than it had been when they last saw each other. But those caramel-colored eyes still scanned every room like it was a riddle to be solved. He still carried that air of a man who couldn't stand an unsolved problem. But what unsolved problem did William Beauclerk represent? What crisis precipitated this end to decades of estrangement? Marsh vibrated like an overstretched piano wire.

All Marsh ever did was destroy things. His sudden reappearance, now of all times, filled Will with a nauseating dread. He tried to cover with banter, hoping beyond all reason Marsh wasn't there to talk about Cherkashin. Gwendolyn could see his agitation, but naturally she would have been looking for it. She knew all about the past Marsh and Will shared. Every awful thing they'd done for King and Country.

Every train he had derailed. Every barge he'd sunk. Every pub he'd bombed.

For his part, Marsh seemed to regard Gwendolyn as though she were just another piece of the problem at hand. And he deflected every attempt at small talk with curt answers to Will's questions:

"I see you've met my darling wife."

"Yes."

"And how is Olivia?"

"Older."

The grandmother clock on the mantel *tick-tock*ed loudly in the awkward silence. To his wife, standing beside his chair, Will said, "You would like Olivia. I think you two would get on famously. Quite sharp, that one."

Gwendolyn responded with a noncommittal, "Hmm." Marsh was the focus of her attention, as Will was the focus of his.

Marsh's deflections were insulting; his aggressive demeanor the basest sort of rudeness. Maddening. Here Will was the gentleman, making an overture of friendship to the man who had stood aside and watched while Will destroyed himself. Marsh hadn't lifted a single finger to help when Will needed it. He'd talked Will into diving headlong into the meat grinder they called Milkweed, and then turned his back when Will came out the other side an unrecognizable mess. Somehow, through undeserved good fortune and the intervention of an angel named Gwendolyn, Will had overcome those dark days. But now Marsh had returned to ruin him all over again. And he clearly wasn't leaving until he'd had his say. *Damn the man.*

"Look," said Will, running a thumb across his moist forehead. "Just what is this about, Pip? This clearly isn't a social call. Not after all these years. I do recall you're able to fake social niceties when you must. But you can't be bothered to do so today."

"He's come to take you back," said Gwendolyn. "They need you for something."

Marsh shot her a hard look. Will knew she was right; he saw the gears turning as Marsh reassessed her.

"I will never, never go back to that life, Pip." Will tried and failed to keep the tremor from his voice. Gwendolyn put a hand on his shoulder. "I would rather die."

"Just who do you think you are?" Gwendolyn demanded. "Swanning into William's life after all this time. Did you expect to take him by the wrist and drag him back into the shadows? Never once have you checked on him since you tossed him aside." She emphasized her words with an unladylike finger. "Never once. Not even for the sake of basic human decency."

Marsh ignored her. He turned to Will. "We need to speak privately."

Will considered this. *Maybe he's not here about Cherkashin. Perhaps it's something else.*

"Gwendolyn knows everything about the old days. There are no secrets between us." *Except one . . .*

Marsh studied them both. "Is that so?"

"I know about Milkweed, Mr. Marsh." So icy was Gwendolyn's tone that Will half expected to see hoarfrost creeping across Marsh's body.

Marsh had worked Will into a corner, double damn him. There was nothing to do now but bull forward. If Marsh hadn't come to discuss Cherkashin, this encounter could only strengthen Will's connection with his wife. And if Marsh was here because of Will's recent interactions with the Soviets, then he was already doomed.

"Whatever it is you've come to say, say it to us both."

"If you insist," said Marsh. One hand tugged at something in his breast pocket. "But remember I offered you the courtesy of privacy, as a nod to our previous friendship." His voice dripped with venom. "And you refused it. A stupid bloody fool to the last."

He tossed an envelope at Will's feet. A handful of photographs

spilled out, their glossy colors dull against the deep crimson and tur-
quoise of the Turkish rug. Will gathered them.

Your countrymen would never hang the brother of a duke, he saw
Cherkashin saying.

Panic clutched Will's heart with red-hot talons. He thought he might
hyperventilate. He didn't want to breathe, didn't want to exhale forever
the last wisps of his contented and perfect life.

*Oh, God, what have I lost? I ought to have known. The man destroys
everything.*

Somewhere nearby, the clamor of church bells announced a wedding, or a funeral, or the end of a war.

"William? You've gone pale as snow." Gwendolyn crouched beside
his chair, hand on his wrist, eyes on his face. "What is it?"

"Your husband," said Marsh, "is struggling to explain why he committed high treason."

"What do you mean?" She faltered. "William, what is he talking
about?" She leaned over Will, glancing at the photographs that tumbled
through his fingers.

A long, painful moment stretched between the three of them. When
Gwendolyn found her voice again, it was high and reedy, the faintest
thread of its usual self. "William. Why were you visiting with that dreadful Cherkashin?"

Will stood, scattering the photos and evoking a throb of protest
from his wounded arm as he leapt to her side. "It's not as it appears," he
insisted. "I swear it's not what you're thinking."

"Oh?" said Marsh. "Because it appears as though you've been selling
state secrets to the Soviet Union."

"Dear Lord," whispered Gwendolyn, looking stricken. She staggered
backwards as though she had been. Casters squeaked beneath the ottoman when she dropped on it. "What have you done, William?"

"I wasn't selling them," Will spat over his shoulder at Marsh. To
Gwendolyn he said, as softly as he could manage, "You have to understand, love. Those men, those horrid men, they did so many terrible
things, committed so many evil acts, and when it was over the government treated them as heroes. They never faced justice."

Marsh said, "They saved the country."

"They're war criminals!"

"Criminals," whispered Gwendolyn. Will knew she understood about whom he spoke; only she knew how deeply the wounds went. She would understand why he did it, why he had to do it. Wouldn't she? She had to.

"Milkweed's warlocks," said Marsh. "Your husband has been passing information about them to Soviet agents. Who have in turn systematically murdered them."

Gwendolyn moaned. "Oh, William."

Marsh and his pretensions of righteousness could go hang, for all Will cared. But Gwendolyn had to understand. He clutched her hand as though she were his parachute, his lifeline. As she had been, once upon a time. The pressure to make his point, the white-hot urgency to argue the justice of what he'd done, forced out tears that trickled down his face.

"You know, Gwendolyn, you know what they did to me. You know what they forced me to do," Will sobbed. "How many innocent citizens did I slaughter for those goddamned blood prices?" The tears came steadier, searing hot rivulets trickling along his cheeks. "It was the only way to get justice, Gwendolyn."

Marsh said, "This isn't justice. It's treason."

"It *is* justice." Will swept up that morning's copy of the *Times* from the end table where it sat atop a pile of novels. It was folded in quarters to a half-finished crossword puzzle. He flung the paper at Marsh. "Justice for the Missing."

The Missing: the term had emerged near the war's end, to describe the vast numbers of British civilians who had died or disappeared under strange circumstances. Victims of domestic insurgencies, Nazi saboteurs, and fifth columnists; a vast cryptofascist conspiracy in the British countryside that evaporated without a trace when the Reich crumbled. So said the received wisdom. Few people knew the truth, that the Missing were victims of their own government. Chosen entirely at random by Milkweed's warlocks to satisfy the Eidolons' blood prices. A necessary evil for defending the nation. And Will couldn't live with that.

"You sicken me." Marsh batted the newspaper aside. His voice trembled with rage. "You deserve to be shot. I ought to do it myself." He stood. "I lost everything that ever meant a damn to me, all for the sake of this country. My daughter, my marriage! But I endured because my sacrifice had meant something. We'd saved the Empire. Or so I'd thought until I discovered everything I've worked for has been flushed down the loo. You've handed this country to our enemies on a silver platter, all because you were too weak to live without a pristine conscience."

Marsh reined himself in with a visible effort. He assumed a more reasoned, analytical mode. A problem solver to the last. "You're going to tell us everything about your interactions with Cherkashin. When this started. How you arrange meetings. Where you meet, and how frequently."

"It won't do you any good," said Will. "I'm finished with Cherkashin." He looked at his wife. A tear fell from his chin. "He is a wretched person, Gwendolyn. You've always been right about that."

Marsh frowned. "What do you mean, 'finished'?"

Will sighed. He saw no point in holding anything back. Not now. "I've had my final meeting with Cherkashin. I've given him everything I know. About every warlock who ever worked for Milkweed."

Gwendolyn and Marsh looked at each other. Something passed between them, something beyond the currents of mutual distrust. "Will," said Marsh. As if noticing the injury for the first time, he asked, "What happened to your arm?"

Will looked at his arm cradled in the sling. It still ached, but not nearly so badly as when he'd lost his finger. But what did this have to do with anything? Marsh had come back and in the space of half an hour he'd ripped Will's happy life to shreds, like a brat at the beach kicking apart another child's sand castle. Only now, with the damage irrevocable, when Will's life once again hung in bloody tatters, did he feign even a modicum of concern. Harbinger of sorrow, indeed.

"Automobile accident," said Will.

"Oh, William," said Gwendolyn, her voice heavy with sorrow. "You daft, daft darling."

Marsh shook his head. He ran his hands through his thinning hair. "You truly are a fool."

"What?"

Gwendolyn said, "Don't you see, William? The Soviets haven't finished yet. There's one final warlock."

"They saved you for last," said Marsh.

six

17 May 1963
Milkweed Headquarters, London, England

Marsh refused Will the luxury of an overnight bag. It had to look, for the benefit of any Soviet agents keeping tabs on the Beauclerks' house—a terraced redbrick Queen Anne revival—that Will was merely stepping out for a few hours. This need to maintain appearances was the only thing that made Marsh accede to Will's request for time to change out of his dressing gown and into a suit. Left to his own methods, Marsh would have marched him outside naked.

Gwendolyn stayed behind. To her credit, she accepted the separation gracefully. What on earth could she possibly see in Will?

Nice bit of acting. Both of them. But Marsh wasn't ready to conclude Will had acted alone.

He had taken a Morris Minor from the SIS motor pool on his trip to Will's home in Knightsbridge. He'd chosen the car in case Will became recalcitrant; it had been modified with an iron ring in the floor behind the passenger seat, to which Marsh was prepared to fasten shackles if Will became too much of a problem. But he didn't, and that was for the best, again from the standpoint of not broadcasting the situation to enemy watchers. But it was disappointing all the same. He'd have liked to bloody Will up, just a bit.

Will blinked at the ring. "Planning to haul me back in chains, were you?"

"Hoping you'll give me a reason," said Marsh.

It was their only exchange during the drive to Whitehall. The brilliant sunlight that came streaming through the windscreen couldn't begin to dispel the atmosphere inside the Morris. Beech trees in Hyde Park shimmered with new growth, a chartreuse fringe of tiny leaves. Some of the trees, Marsh suspected, were centuries old. As old as the park itself.

Would it all be destroyed because of Will? Did he know about the children? Had he told Ivan about them?

Will was silent but jumpy. Perhaps his recent accident had left him skittish. He lowered his window. But the susurration of wind through the car couldn't drown out the angry silence. He sank farther and farther into his seat as they approached the Admiralty, until it seemed he truly had deflated. A marine sentry waved them through the screen after Marsh flashed his SIS credentials. Will swallowed audibly.

After the exchange in the car, Will broke his self-imposed silence exactly once. It happened when Marsh took him downstairs, through the massive double doors that led to the soundproofed corridors where the warlock children had been raised. The cell Marsh chose had been recently vacated by Klaus's move to the Croydon safe house. Will looked over the carpeting, the foam baffles, and the rubber gaskets on the doors like a man plunged into a waking nightmare.

"My God," he said. "I didn't imagine it."

Marsh shoved him inside, then slammed the door. It barely made a sound.

He retrieved Will in the morning; Milkweed convened a de facto war council.

Will was already awake. He looked like he hadn't slept. He lay on the cot in his underclothes; the suit lay in one corner of the floor, carefully folded.

He stared lazily at Marsh from the cot, one hand under his head. "I see you're not holding a blindfold," said Will. Speaking around an expansive yawn, he managed to add, "Has the firing squad been held up in traffic?"

"We're going upstairs," said Marsh from the doorway. "You can walk out of this cell clothed, or you can be dragged out half naked." Marsh's knuckles popped when he pressed the backs of his fingers against his jaw. "Either way, you have two minutes to pull yourself together," he said, looking at his watch.

Will sighed. He rolled to his feet, then stretched. His back cracked. He picked up his suit.

Brushing indigo carpet lint from the pin-striped trousers, Will said, "You know, I seem to recall a time when our roles were reversed. When you were staying down here in a bit of self-imposed imprisonment. This cellar was quite different back then. Less carpet. Not so *quiet*." He stepped into the trousers. "Nevertheless, I tried to talk you out of it. Tried to talk some sense into you."

"One minute," said Marsh.

Donning the shirt gave Will much trouble, owing to the sling on his arm. He left one sleeve unbuttoned. Pearlescent buttons glinted in the light. "But of course, you were too busy brooding back then to listen to anybody. Weren't you, Pip? Too busy to realize that everyone around you was falling apart."

Marsh stepped into the cell, ready to grab Will by the neck. "All finished," Will said hastily. "I do thank you for indulging my sartorials," he said. "After all, without my wife, they're all I have now."

"Don't play the victim with me," said Marsh.

What a righteous prig. He put on a brave show, but it didn't hide the tremor in his voice. Will was frightened. As he damn well ought.

How many nights had Marsh lain awake—listening to the mindless keening from the beast in the attic, Liv's side of the bed cold and empty as an open grave—consoling himself that his life had mattered? His efforts had cost him terribly, but he'd done more than most to keep Britain safe and free. That knowledge had kept him going, even when Liv shrank from his touch, when the sight of her freckles repulsed him. And then Will decided to undo everything they'd achieved.

Marsh brought Will to the room where he'd first met Pembroke, where he'd had his reunion with Gretel. The arrival of Marsh and his prisoner brought the total attendance of the war council to six: Marsh, Will, Pembroke, Pethick, Klaus, and Gretel.

The others were waiting for them. A reel-to-reel tape recorder sat in the center of the table. Will did a double take when he saw Klaus and Gretel sitting at the table.

Gretel said, "Hello, William. Has your finger healed?"

Confusion reigned on the faces of the men who didn't understand Gretel's comment. But Marsh knew she'd meant it as an inside joke, as a reference to an experience shared only by him, Will, and Gretel. The raven-haired demon.

Klaus looked at Will's hand. He caressed the stump of his own missing finger.

Will turned to Marsh, his eyes still on her. "Pip? What is this?"

"This is where we try to gauge precisely how much damage you've done to the United Kingdom," said Pembroke.

Marsh took the empty chair across the table from Gretel and Klaus while Will received brusque introductions from Pembroke and Pethick. Gretel smiled at him. He laid his hands on the table as he watched the siblings; the polished rosewood felt like silk beneath his fingertips. Klaus sat rigidly, his posture and body language cutting Gretel from his peripheral vision.

Interesting, thought Marsh. *Wonder if he's aware of it.*

Will sat. "I'll give you my unfettered cooperation in exchange for a pledge that Gwendolyn be excluded from any charges. She had no knowledge of my actions or decisions. I won't see her tarred with the same brush you've prepared for me."

Pembroke said, "Yours is not the position for making requests."

Will crossed his arms. "In that case, I can't help you gentlemen until I've spoken with a solicitor."

"Solicitor?" Pethick chimed in. "All we need do is tell the Crown you've disseminated to known agents of the Soviet Union the most extraordinarily sensitive information pertaining to this nation's security. That you've flagrantly and egregiously violated the Official Secrets Act. All of which is entirely factual, you may note." He sipped from his cup. When he spoke again, his breath smelled of weak tea flavored with anise. "You'll be denied representation because sharing the details of the charges with a civilian solicitor would constitute yet another breach, and cause further risk to the United Kingdom."

A moment passed while Will processed this. His resolve crumbled, leaving in its place an expression both raw and forlorn. The sliver of compassion it evoked from Marsh caught him by surprise. He bludgeoned the compassion back into hiding. Will's betrayal cut too deeply for anything other than anger and indignation.

Quietly, Will said, "I see. Very well, then."

Pembroke opened a ledger. Uncapping a fountain pen, he said, "Begin by telling us your full name. Then recount everything you've shared with Cherkashin. Every piece of information you've passed."

"Sir." Pethick interrupted before Will could start. "May I please ask you to reconsider doing this in front of our guests." He accentuated "guests" with a minute tip of the head toward the siblings.

"Finally," said Marsh. Pembroke's idiotic intransigence on this issue had nearly driven him round the bend. "Thank you, Sam." To Pembroke: "Your adviser is correct. This is idiotic."

Pembroke shook his head. "No, Sam. There's no point in doing this on the q.t. As long as Gretel is involved in this affair, there's no reason to isolate her from our discussions," he said. "Her involvement means she'll know about any actions we take in the future, which in turn means she already knows what decisions we'll come to today."

Gretel acknowledged Pembroke's point with a low nod. Morning sunlight glimmered on her dark eyes. It occurred to Marsh that she was probably accustomed to people speaking about her as though she were absent.

"That is a truly stunning display of specious reasoning," Marsh grumbled.

"In that case," said Pethick, "why not save time and effort and simply ask her what our decisions will be?"

Gretel emerged from her cocoon of amused silence. "But then they wouldn't be your decisions, would they?" She smiled at Pembroke.

He smiled back. "Quite right."

A great weariness settled over Marsh. He rubbed a hand across his eyes. "She's playing you, Leslie."

As a younger man, he would have had the energy to fight this travesty. Tooth and nail. But with age came the need to select his battles wisely. He resigned himself to the fact that today wasn't about fixing Leslie Pembroke, but about assessing the damage Will had done.

Pethick started the recorder with a loud *click*. The reels lurched to life.

Will stopped fidgeting with his sling. "My name is William Edward Guthrie Beauclerk." He recited the names of the warlocks he'd betrayed, along with what he knew about how to find them. The tape recorder reels turned silently, spooling in Will's litany of treacheries; the nib of Pembroke's pen skittered across the pages of his ledger.

After Will finished his monologue, Marsh began the questioning. "Why didn't you use a dead-drop?"

Pembroke: "Was that Cherkashin's idea, to meet in person for these exchanges?"

("If it was, he's a bloody amateur," said Marsh under his breath.)

"No," said Will. "I insisted on delivering the information in person. I wanted to be certain it would land in the hands of people who would . . . act . . . on it." Will looked uncomfortable with the awkward and unconvincing euphemism, as though it had left a foul taste in his mouth.

Good, thought Marsh. *You ought to squirm, traitor.*

Pembroke: "How did you arrange meetings?"

"By placing a flowerpot on my office windowsill."

Marsh: "What was the acknowledgment?"

"A pair of blinds on a window across the way. Different configurations for different responses."

Pethick: "Who chose Kew Gardens?"

"I did."

Gretel's expression betrayed no amusement, no sense that something important had slipped. No sense that Pethick had just given her another piece of information she needed to orchestrate the unmasking of Will's clandestine activities. That she'd foreseen this mistake years ago.

But the questioning continued. "Did he approach you at first? Or did you approach him?"

"He approached me."

"In person, or through an intermediary?"

"In person."

"When? Where?"

"A year ago this spring. At my brother's foundation."

On and on it went. The questioning followed a predictable pattern. Marsh let the drone of conversation wash past him. He knew that Will wouldn't cling to deception now the cat had been hurled out of the bag. He could read it in the slump of Will's shoulders.

The question now was what to do. Piece by piece, Marsh laid out the parts of the puzzle for himself.

One: The Soviets have been killing warlocks.

Conjecture: They're clearing the board for something.

Two: According to Gretel, the Soviets have reverse engineered the old Reichsbehörde technology. The source is unreliable; the information is highly plausible.

Conjecture: Points one and two are related.

Three: The assassin, or assassins, may be a product of the research program at Arzamas-16.

Conjecture: They're field-testing the first batch of new troops. This would follow the procedures established by von Westarp.

Four: Cherkashin's network, Lincolnshire Poacher, is running the assassin. But it has changed its procedures and fallen silent. We've lost track of it.

Conjecture: We are buggered.

He pinched the bridge of his nose, concentrating. The future of Milkweed, and therefore quite possibly of the country, rested with a dozen halfway inhuman children locked in the cellar.

The cellar. What was it Will had said?

My God. I didn't imagine it.

Marsh sat up. "Will," he said, interrupting a question from Pethick, "how did you know about the cellar?"

Will shook his head, processing the sudden change of topic. "The cellar? Oh, you mean—" His eyes flicked over to Gretel. "I witnessed some of that work. Just prior to leaving Milkweed."

"Did you tell Cherkashin about it?" asked Marsh.

"No."

"Why not?"

"I did what I did to bring evil men to justice. Anything else was irrelevant."

"This is important. Does he know about it?"

"To my knowledge, no."

"Are you certain? Did he ever ask about it?"

Will enunciated every word with emphasis. "We never discussed the cellar."

Klaus surprised everybody except his sister by chiming in. "Your worries are misplaced," he said.

The room fell silent. After the space of several heartbeats, Pethick said, "And how do you know that?"

"You worry that this Soviet agent may know of something hidden in the cellar of this building," Klaus said. "He doesn't. If he did, he would have taken it long ago. Or destroyed it."

"What makes you say that?" said Marsh.

Klaus took a deep breath. Like somebody steeling himself to dive headfirst into murky water. "Because I was trained as an assassin, too. It's what you do with somebody who has my ability."

Marsh laid his hands on the table again, thinking very carefully. "So. If things had gone differently, you would have been the Götterelektrongruppe's wetwork specialist?"

"Yes, me. There was another. . . ." Klaus glanced at his sister, just for an instant. A complex expression played over his face. Marsh wondered what passed between the siblings just then. "Heike."

"Heike." The name rattled around in the back of Marsh's mind, dredging up memories of things he'd read long ago. "She could make herself invisible. Is that right?"

"You know about Heike?"

"I've read the Schutzstaffel's operational records of the Reichsbehörde."

Klaus's eyes widened. "Those records disappeared before the end of the war. Our captors at Arzamas spent years searching for them."

"You see, brother?" Gretel broke into a wide smile. She beamed at Marsh, almost like a proud parent. "He's very, very good."

The demon's affections made Marsh bristle. He felt oily. Tainted.

"Getting back to the point," he said. "If you were the Soviet agent, Klaus, how would you destroy something in the cellar of this building?"

"I would walk through a wall, carrying a rucksack filled with high explosives. I would drop through the floor to the cellar. I would find my target, deposit the explosives, and walk out through the explosion." Klaus shook his head. "Because this building hasn't been reduced to rubble, I conclude your Soviet agent hasn't learned about the cellar."

Which was the answer he'd expected from Klaus. But the blood drained from Pembroke's face, and Pethick looked uneasy. The look on Will's face was more cryptic.

Klaus said, "I developed this technique to deal with the *ouvrages* in the Ardennes forest."

"You should have seen him," said Gretel. "Nobody can clear out a pillbox like my brother."

"Of course," said Marsh, "you'd already know this, Leslie, if you'd studied those files properly."

Pembroke cleared his throat. "This is all fascinating, I'm quite certain. But if we could leave the reminiscences for another time, and return to the matter at hand?"

"I know what we need to do," said Marsh.

The conversation at the Admiralty building had raged well into the evening. But though the questioning had stopped for the time being, Will found himself growing anxious again, only partially because of Marsh's plan. He didn't know what would happen when he faced his wife again. Would she even *be* his wife? Why didn't he tell her when he'd had the chance? The look on her face had kept him awake all night. So stricken. So betrayed.

In fact, Gwendolyn looked at Will as though he'd risen from the dead when he returned. She gaped at the sight of Will waltzing in like a free man. The whites of her eyes had taken a reddish cast; the skin under her eyes was dark and puffy.

"William?" she gasped. "What are you doing here?"

"I live here," he said, but his attempt at levity failed. He was too tired, too confused and frightened by Marsh's scheme, too sick with the worry he'd dealt their marriage a terminal blow.

She stepped forward, but didn't take his hand. Her voice dropped to a whisper. "You . . . you haven't escaped, have you? Please tell me you haven't made things worse by running away."

"No," Will said. "I haven't run away." He perched at the edge of the fainting couch. He patted his hand on the couch, but Gwendolyn continued to stand. He sighed. "If you go to the window, you'll see a blue lorry parked up the street a bit. My chaperones, if you will."

Gwendolyn pulled the curtains aside. "They're watching you?"

"Yes." He joined her at the window. She stepped away.

"May we discuss what happened?"

"Discuss what? You lied to me, William."

To that he said, "Yes," because it was the truth, and because he didn't know what else to say.

"You betrayed me. You betrayed the country."

To that he merely nodded. Because he still couldn't bear to hear himself admit it aloud. What he'd done to the warlocks was nothing they hadn't brought upon themselves. It was justice. He knew that down to his marrow. But to have betrayed Gwendolyn, to have driven this wedge between them . . .

Will cursed Marsh and his bloody crusades. Damn him, and double damn that wretched Gretel. Even more than Marsh, she had ruined everything. Why did she care what Will did?

He said, "They were evil men. You know what they did to me." The tears returned. "I had to do something about them. I couldn't bear it any longer. The anger. The shame. The self-hatred."

"What you did," said Gwendolyn, "makes you no better than they." She went upstairs. The bedroom door clicked faintly when she locked it behind her. Will cradled his head in his hands and wept.

The MI6 vehicle didn't leave Knightsbridge when Will stepped out early the next morning. *Too conspicuous,* he assumed. No doubt somebody from the service had an eye on his car during every inch of his journey from home to his office at the foundation. Will suppressed the urge to crane his neck to peer through the rear window, to try to see if his minders were still there. Too much of that might have alarmed the driver.

Oddly enough, he found the constant surveillance almost comforting. He tried not to wonder how his shadowy watchers could possibly intervene in time if another attempt on his life happened as suddenly as the automobile accident. Will reassured himself that as long as SIS needed him, they would keep him alive. It was better than trusting to blind luck, which as Marsh had explained was the only thing that had spared him thus far: Will was a public figure living in the center of London, and so Cherkashin's man had opted for a hands-off approach by staging a very public and very tragic accident. A few seconds' difference and that might have been the case.

Will tried not to think about whether Milkweed would still need him after they'd carried out Marsh's plan.

He arrived at half past nine. Angela, his secretary, looked relieved. "Welcome back, sir," she said. "I worried myself sick after His Grace told me what happened."

Claws of cold, nauseating panic dug into Will's stomach. *Aubrey knows?* He'd hoped he could postpone that particular conversation a bit longer.

But Angela kept smiling at him. As though everything were right with the world. She looked at the sling cradling his arm. "How are you feeling?"

Ah. She meant the accident. Will hadn't returned to work since then. It seemed a lifetime ago.

His voice shook when he said, "This?" He glanced at his arm, wondering how to sound like his old self. "A minor inconvenience," he lied. "But I fear I'll be rubbish with a typewriter for some time."

"That's what I'm for, sir." She took her seat. "Things have piled up a bit since you've been gone. Mostly owing to Minister Kalugin's visit. I've put it all on your desk, sorted by date and urgency. Shall I put tea on?"

"Yes."

Will retreated to his office. He caught himself before he locked the door. *Don't change your routine.* Marsh had emphasized that.

He moved the potted nasturtium from the corner of his desk to the window. The soil was moist. Angela, thoughtful to the last.

The flowers blazed scarlet in the sunlight. Easily visible from the street, for Soviet and British spies alike. A flowerpot in the center of the windowsill: *Urgent meeting requested.*

After that, Will turned his attention to the paperwork stacked in neat piles on his desk. But he made little headway because he glanced across the street every few minutes, waiting for the arrangement of blinds across the street to change. He couldn't concentrate. The simplest documents twisted themselves into indecipherable riddles. He'd spent all night on the rug outside the bedroom door, listening to Gwendolyn's sorrow. He couldn't clear the sound of her tears from his head.

Nothing happened for several hours. Angela brought him a late lunch of tomato sandwiches. He didn't eat.

The afternoon dragged by, one agonizing minute at a time. Did Cherkashin's men know SIS had nabbed him? Did they know Milkweed had him on a leash? Perhaps instead of moving the blinds, they'd shoot him through the window.

He knew it was an irrational fear. They'd never kill him so obviously. Would they? He hunched his shoulders, touching his temple where he imagined a rifle bullet smashing through his skull.

As it did every weekday at five o'clock, the hum of traffic swelled into the controlled chaos of the evening rush. Car horns; the rumble of engines and hiss of tires on asphalt; the unintelligible murmuring of a dozen conversations from pedestrians on the pavement. And as he did every weekday, Will tuned it out.

The blinds moved at twenty past. One up, one down: *Message received. Come immediately.*

The crowds had thinned by the time Will arrived. He was thankful for that; it meant the gardens would close before long, giving him an excuse not to dally with Cherkashin.

Just deliver your message and go, Marsh had said. *And for God's sake, pretend you mean it.*

On his way to Cherkashin's bench, Will passed a young couple strolling arm in arm, a dustman emptying the rubbish bins, and a mother pushing a pram with two infants nestled inside. Who among them were SIS minders? All of them? None of them?

Will arrived before Cherkashin. He seated himself next to a stand of wilted snapdragons; their bare stems cast shadows like needles across the sculpted lawn. A breeze tossed golden petals across the pavement, where they caught on his shoes. The gardeners had laid down new soil in the plots upwind. The world smelled of manure.

The itchy feeling in his temple returned, and it grew with every minute that Cherkashin didn't appear. As though somebody's gaze tickled him through a rifle scope. Will concentrated on the lies that Milkweed had set him loose to tell.

Lincolnshire Poacher is the assassin's link with Moscow, Marsh had said. *We must disable that network before we deal with him. In order to protect the cellar, we must sever the lines of communication.*

Of course, said the other spies, in a fit of pique. *But that's easier said than done.*

But Will knew, from the way Marsh stared at him while he outlined his thoughts, that this segue to the problem was intended for him. The nonspecialist.

Radio triangulation, Marsh continued. *Feed them something hot, too hot for a slow diplomatic pouch, and they'll have to resort to a burst transmission. Find the transmitter, and we have our wedge.*

Of course, said the other spies, in a fit of pique. *We're not amateurs, thank you so very much.*

The trick, said Marsh, *is knowing what to tell them.* And it was here that Will knew he had just become the cheese in a very large mousetrap. Marsh pointed at him. *It's staring us in the face.*

During that long preliminary interrogation—preliminary, because other sessions and other methods were sure to follow—the act of describing Will's interactions with Cherkashin cast them in a new light. The pattern unraveled, as though the spinning reels of the recorder tugged at a loose thread.

The hinting. The probing. Why didn't Cherkashin take all Will's information in one exchange? Why draw it out?

Because he wanted to turn you, William Edward Guthrie Beauclerk. Because he wanted to wrap you up with a bow and send you back to his masters in Moscow. Because he wanted you to oversee the training of brand-new warlocks for the Great Soviet. But you wouldn't play along. So when you convinced him it would never happen, at that final exchange when you condemned to death the last of those wicked old men, so, too, did you condemn yourself.

Cherkashin's footsteps echoed in the gathering dusk. The soft leather soles of his shoes scraped loudly on the pavement. He swung around the bench and fixed Will with that cold, gray-lipped stare. He ran a finger across his forehead, flipping his hair aside; he needed a trim.

Will tensed when Cherkashin's hand snaked into his suit. But the Soviet spy runner retrieved a cigarette and a lighter, rather than a pistol. He dragged deeply. The cigarette tip blazed orange in the shadows.

Cherkashin fixed him with another stare while exhaling. Smoke jetted from his nose like steam from a Chinese dragon. "I thought you were eager to be done with me," he said.

Feed them something hot, Marsh had said.

"Tell me about life in Moscow," said Will.

18 May 1963
Croydon, London, England

Madeleine kept her word. When Klaus turned in for the evening, after returning from the roundtable debriefing of William Beauclerk, he found the center of his bed taken up with a broad, flat package wrapped in brown butcher's paper and twine. He opened it to find a set of water-color paints; half a dozen brushes; a palette; a board; four metal clips; a sheaf of thick, pulpy papers almost two feet square; and three books: *Watercolor Painting for the Novice, Studies in Advanced Watercolor Technique,* and *Watercolor Masters: Dürer to Cézanne.*

The accompanying note said: *Good luck, Klaus —M.*

It made him smile. He cracked open the tin of paints. They had a subtle scent, like rain and soft candle wax.

Klaus stayed up late that night, reading by the light of his bedside lamp. Only later, while drifting to sleep, did he realize he didn't know what to paint. He didn't know how to have a hobby. But he had one now: a simple fact, a thrilling fact. His last thoughts that night were to wonder if the British would try to psychoanalyze him based on his artistic efforts, and to realize he didn't care.

He woke early the next morning. He hurried back to his room with his plate of breakfast. But it was nearly lunchtime before he remembered it, by which time the eggs had congealed and the beans were cold. He was scraping dried egg yolk from his plate to the bin, and wondering how one would create such a precise amber color with watercolors, when Marsh knocked on his door.

"I don't know where she is," said Klaus.

"I don't care about Gretel," said Marsh. "Not at the moment." He beckoned toward the garden. "Let's take a walk."

Klaus sighed. He wanted to return to his books. But he knew this was inevitable. Marsh was obsessed with Gretel; naturally he'd use Klaus as his Rosetta stone. Klaus would never be his own person. He would always be, first and foremost, Gretel's brother. She wove her webs too tightly; the strands stuck fast, and nothing he did would ever scrape them clear. The watercolor obsession was a petty, pointless rebellion. Still, it was his. As long as he had it, he refused to despair. He had to start small.

Roger came in as they stepped out. He said to Marsh, "It's clear, boss."

They startled a pair of starlings. The garden occupied the entire lot behind both houses. Ivy carpeted the brick wall around the garden. (Jade. Vermilion. How to create such colors?) Klaus knew the wall itself was topped with glass shards. A paving-stone walkway meandered past ferns and flower beds (yellow, blue, violet).

Marsh paused, his attention caught by a small maple tree in a wide clay planter. He touched the leaves, turning them gently with puckered knuckles. The waxy green leaves were a dull gray underneath, and mottled with brown. (Warm colors? Cool colors?) Marsh squatted beside the planter and touched the soil, rummaging through the thick layer of last autumn's leaves that had accumulated around the trunk. He pulled out a handful of crumbling leaves, and sifted through them on his palm.

"They need to transplant this," he said to himself. "It'll die soon."

Klaus remembered the way Marsh had been dressed when he'd first arrived at the Admiralty. In a boilersuit with mud on the knees. "You're a gardener?" he asked, surprised.

"Yes." Marsh smiled to himself. Whether it was wry or rueful, Klaus couldn't tell.

"I thought you were a . . . government worker." Klaus knew better than to use the word *spy*.

"I've been that, too."

Marsh grimaced when he stood. He gave the tree's condition one last critical glance. He dropped the dead leaves, wiped his hands on his trousers. He sat on a wrought iron bench with cedar planking, in the shadow of a patinated armillary sundial. Klaus chose to stand.

Marsh said, "Thought you'd want to know we sent a team to the solicitor's office. Another to keep an eye on the flat you identified as Reinhardt's."

Klaus didn't bother to hide his skepticism. "You've captured him?"

"There's no sign of him."

Klaus sighed. It was too much to hope for.

"She warned him, didn't she?"

"I don't know." Klaus shrugged. "Yes."

"Our men had slightly better fortune with the solicitor. They spoke with a chap who remembers a man and woman matching your descriptions. Thus far, your story holds water."

"I have told you the truth."

"Apparently he remembered you quite vividly."

"The wires," said Klaus, absently fingering the bundle that dangled over his shoulder.

"Yes." Marsh frowned, as if something had just occurred to him. More quietly, he said, "Are they painful?"

Klaus blinked. Nobody had ever asked him that before. Nobody had ever worried about his comfort. Who was this strange man? "No. Not any longer."

Marsh nodded. "Your solicitor friend claims he received one letter, preaddressed, to be posted on the following day."

Klaus nodded. "Gretel wrote two letters. The first she posted herself. The second she gave to the solicitor."

"Our problem is that the second letter has already gone out." Marsh's expression became very serious. He leaned forward, elbows on his knees. "I need to know the contents of that letter, Klaus. What does your sister want Reinhardt to do?"

"I do not know."

"Where did the second letter go? Where is he?"

"I do not know. It wasn't addressed to Reinhardt, but probably it was intended for him."

"If you're holding something back," said Marsh, his voice harder than the bricks that built their garden prison, "I'd advise you to re-think it."

"I'll never help her again." Frustration—buried for so long, it might have been fossilized—came surging back to the surface. Something else rode along with it. Something worse. He was alone in the world. He had no friends, no allies, nothing in which to take pride. The Götterelektron had made him insubstantial, but it was the circumstances of his life and his poor decisions that had rendered him a ghost.

But that was too much to admit to this stranger. "I'm ashamed of myself for trusting her as long as I did."

Marsh mulled this over. Almost gently, he asked, "Your Reichsbe-hörde file describes you as fiercely protective of her. What changed?"

Klaus hadn't noticed it earlier, but Marsh pronounced the German flawlessly. *No, you're clearly more than a gardener,* thought Klaus. *You learned German just as we learned to speak English. The natural symmetry of enemies. But we aren't enemies now. We aren't friends. What are we?*

Marsh pressed his point. "Why turn on her after all these years?"

Klaus ran a hand along the pitted bronze of the sundial. Such a lovely, subtle color. Why *did* he turn his back on Gretel? Even though he'd made his decision and knew he was right, it was an uncomfortable thing to articulate. Saying it aloud was an admission that he'd been a blind fool for most of his wasted life.

Klaus sat heavily on the bench, gazing at the space between his shoes. He was quiet for a long time. Marsh didn't interrupt his thoughts. When Klaus did speak again, the weakness in his voice surprised him.

"My sister is a terrible person. I've denied it for too long."

Marsh matched his quiet tone. "But you must have known she had anticipated your rebellion."

This was a question for which Klaus did have an answer, because he'd thought about it a great deal. "That doesn't free me from doing what I think is right."

"Hmmm," said Marsh. He looked thoughtful.

They sat on the bench without speaking, the ex-Nazi and the British spy. The starlings returned. Wind rustled the leaves of the dying maple tree.

"Why is she obsessed with me?" said Marsh.

"I don't know why she did what she did to your daughter." Klaus hesitated, unsure of himself and where he stood with Marsh. "I've rarely learned her reasons for the things she does. And when I have, I sometimes find it was easier not knowing." He shook his head, thinking again of poor Heike. Marsh raised an eyebrow at this, but Klaus didn't feel up to explaining that entire story.

"It's more than my daughter," said Marsh. "It started before that. In Spain." Klaus blinked. Marsh said, "We crossed paths in Barcelona, the three of us. And then again in France, Gretel and I. She wanted to be captured, didn't she?"

"She deserted us that night. You caught her?"

"Yes." Again that little smile appeared on Marsh's face. Rueful, Klaus decided. "And I was there when you rescued her."

Klaus remembered a long chase through the Admiralty cellar. But he also remembered the tables turned several months later. When he chased a man across the grounds of the Reichsbehörde, moonlit snow crunching underfoot, gunfire and explosions echoing around them. That was the night he inhaled the phosphorus smoke that scarred his sinuses.

"You were at the farm the night the doctor died."

Marsh said, "Yes." He watched Klaus warily.

"It was for the best," Klaus admitted. "He was . . . as bad as my sister, in his own way."

Spain. That felt like a lifetime ago. It was.

He shook his head at the perversity of the situation.

Gretel truly was obsessed with this man. The poor, poor bastard.

"I didn't realize her preoccupation ran so deeply. I do not envy you."

What are we? Two unwilling chips in Gretel's game.

The door creaked open. Pembroke stepped into the garden. "There you are," he said around the pipe clenched in his teeth. He removed the pipe and glanced at the sky. "I see why. Lovely day."

Marsh turned to Klaus. Just loud enough to ensure that Pembroke would hear him, he said, *"Pass mal seinetwegen auf. Der glaubt das er Gretel versteht."*

Be careful around him. He believes he understands Gretel.

As Klaus suspected, Marsh's German was perfect.

Pembroke looked bemused. He said, in Russian better than Klaus's, "Что бы он тебе ни говорил, Клаус, имей в виду что не он заправляет нашей славной семейкой, а я."

Whatever he may have told you, Klaus, keep in mind it's not he in charge of our little family, but me.

seven

27 May 1963
Walworth, London, England

The doorbell chimed while they bathed John. Marsh knelt on the floor, ignoring the ache in his knee while he held his son's ankles in the lukewarm water of an aluminum washbasin. Liv ran a sponge across John's bare shoulders and back. Soap dripped into Marsh's hair.

John fidgeted. Water sloshed, dousing Marsh's sleeves where he'd rolled them above the elbow. He tightened his grip and peered down through the gray water. John needed his nails trimmed.

The doorbell chimed again. "Oh, sod off," said Liv under her breath. She handed the sponge to Marsh, who wrung it out in the basin and handed it back. The slightly caustic scent of the soap masked the odor from John's body and the stuffiness of the room. Soundproofing covered the windows, so the room had little in the way of ventilation. Leaving the door open was not an option.

On the third chime, Marsh said, "Please get the door before it drives us mad. I'll hold John for a moment."

Liv dropped the sponge into the basin. She stepped out of the room, drying her hands on the towel slung over her shoulder. She didn't close the door behind her. A moment later, the stairs creaked.

John sniffed. His head swayed back and forth as he sampled the stale air, eyes like flawless white pearls drifting aimlessly inside their sockets. He snuffled at his shoulder, where Liv had touched him.

"She's just stepped out, son."

John's mouth dropped open. He began to moan.

"Shhh, shhh."

The moans rose in pitch and intensity every time John paused to refill his lungs. Soon he would be screeching.

Marsh released John's ankles and stood. "It's all right. She's coming back." He crossed the room to close the door so that the visitor downstairs wouldn't hear John. Leave it to Liv to neglect the door just when John decided to have one of his episodes.

Marsh heard the splash and slapping of bare soles on the floorboards a fraction of a second too late. He tried and failed to slam the door before John bolted past him. It hit John and swung back, sure to leave a bruise.

Sightless, mindless, heedless of his nudity, John charged into the corridor. Marsh followed. He grasped at John, but the soap had left his skin too slick to hold. John smacked face-first into the frame of Liv's bedroom door. The impact sent him sprawling backwards. Floorboards rattled as he landed on his back. It knocked the wind out of John, bringing a moment's respite from his howling.

"John!" Marsh kneeled over him, checking for wounds and bruises. He worried that John may have shattered his nose; if that were the case, they'd have to take him to the hospital, and that could only end in disaster. But John had taken the brunt of the impact on his forehead. He'd have a terrible bruise there, to match the bruises along his arm and torso where the door had hit him. Marsh felt monstrous for that.

The stairs creaked again. Liv stood a few steps below the landing, at Marsh's eye level. She looked at John.

"Is that what you call holding him?"

"You left the bloody door wide open," Marsh said. "Why must the simplest bit of cooperation escape you?"

"One minute!" she yelled, her face carnation pink with anger. "You couldn't hold him for one minute. You can't do anything without my help."

John found his voice again. He howled.

"Your help? I'm the one who feeds John every evening while you're tarting up in the vain hope some drunken tosser will find you attractive."

That took the fight out of her. Liv's lip trembled. Her eyes gleamed, on the verge of overflowing with tears.

There had been a time when he would have laid out any man who spoke so cruelly to Liv. Back when they had been partners. Lovers. Before the love had soured to apathy, then fermented to a vinegar hatred. They were as sharks, constantly circling each other, constantly testing the water for the first taste of blood.

There was only one other person in the world to whom he'd speak with such malice. How had Liv and Gretel come to occupy the same category in his mind? When had that happened? Perhaps he was a monster.

Seeing the pain and shame so plain on her face hurt him worse than any retort she could have hurled in return.

"Liv. I didn't—"

"You have a visitor," she said, her voice barely more than a whisper as she struggled to keep her composure. Then she turned and stomped down the stairs, brushing roughly past Pethick, who had seen everything. A moment later the door to the dining room slammed, hard enough to jostle the framed photographs hanging over the stairs.

Pethick stared at John, who had gone back to snuffling and mewling. He struggled to find his voice. "I've come at a bad time. I'm truly sorry." He turned to leave.

"It's always a bad time," said Marsh. He sighed, deeply ashamed that any outsider would get such an intimate glimpse of his home. This was a family issue, not something for strangers. Especially a man he'd known for less than a month. "Well, you're here now. Lend a hand."

"How?"

Marsh pulled John to his feet, gently guided him back toward the soundproofed room. "Stand in the door. Don't let him past you, if he runs."

Pethick followed Marsh and John down the corridor. He stopped short when he noticed the series of locks on the door, but then after a moment's pause he turned away, pretending he hadn't seen anything unusual. Marsh checked John for broken bones and cracked teeth, but found none. That was a small mercy. He rinsed the soap from John's skin, so that it wouldn't dry and itch. Then he kissed his son on the forehead and dragged the washbasin from the room. John settled in the corner in the fetal position, banging his head against the wall.

"The basin?" asked Pethick, while Marsh flipped through his key ring.

"I'll empty it later," said Marsh. He threw the locks on John's door with a rapid *clack-clack-clack* that came from years of practice. "Follow me," he said.

Downstairs, Marsh paused briefly at the dining room door. Liv's quiet sobbing sounded from inside. He knocked, cleared his throat. "I've taken care of John. I'm stepping outside."

She didn't answer.

It was humid in the shed. Pethick surveyed the setting with a few quick, cursory glances. He seemed a smart chap; the significance of the cot, the books, the electric hot plate, and the dirty dishes couldn't have been lost on him. Not after what he'd seen inside. But he had enough class to pretend he hadn't seen straight to the necrotic heart of Marsh's home life.

But it didn't make Marsh feel any less lowly, didn't cut the stinger from this humiliation. At Milkweed, Marsh was somebody respected. *Something of a legend,* Pembroke had said. But now here he was with his feet of clay where Pethick could see it all.

Marsh pulled out the stool for his visitor and perched on the edge of the cot. He couldn't bring himself to make eye contact with Pethick; he didn't want to see the disgust and pity there. "Well? What is it? You're not here for a social call."

"Lincolnshire Poacher is moving," said Pethick. "Beauclerk's ersatz defection has roused the network."

Marsh allowed himself a small smile. This was a welcome bit of good news on what had been a wretched day thus far. "It worked, then. Where did the signals chaps pinpoint the transmitter? In the embassy?"

"Ah." Pethick looked uncomfortable. "They haven't."

"What do you mean, 'They haven't'? You've just told me it worked."

"I said Cherkashin's network is showing signs of activity. But we haven't heard a peep of transmission."

Marsh rubbed his eyes. It was a mistake; he must have had a bit of soap on his fingertips. Sarcastically, he said, "Were you listening?"

"I promise you that every antenna from here to Wales has been waiting with bated breath for Cherkashin's people to call home. If they'd so much as cleared their throats, we would have heard."

"But they haven't."

"No."

Marsh pulled a handkerchief from his pocket to wipe his stinging, watering eyes. "What evidence have you?"

Pethick said, "They're preparing a safe house, in Lyminster. We've had an eye on it for a number of years. It had been dormant until yesterday."

"Makes sense," said Marsh. "They'd need someplace to keep Will until they're ready to bundle him out of the country."

"That was our conclusion."

Marsh shook his head. "They don't need Moscow to tell them to set up a safe location for Will. Perhaps they're still running silently."

"They can't get Beauclerk out of the country without help from the Continent," said Pethick. "Something like this requires coordination. And," he said, producing a grainy aerial photograph from his pocket, "three days ago, this vessel broke off from the tail end of a shipping convoy rounding the Bay of Biscay. It's been lurking just outside the Channel Islands since Saturday."

Marsh dabbed at his eye until he could see well enough to study the photograph. The aerial photo showed a dark blur on a gray sea, the silhouette of a Soviet vessel. Marsh's service as a naval officer had been

long before the Soviet navy became a menace to the British Empire, so
identifying the vessel was a matter of guesswork. The old man had
always kept a jeweler's loupe on hand for things like this. But if Marsh
had to venture a guess, he'd say the mystery ship was a corvette: a fast,
armed fleet escort vessel.

"Shit," said Marsh.

It meant Ivan didn't intend to take any chances by flying Will out of
the country. Coastal antiaircraft measures could legitimately shoot down
an unmarked airplane in British airspace. But boarding—or, God for-
bid, sinking—a Soviet warship in international waters was the stuff of
shooting wars.

They probably intended to take Will out to sea in a small craft, something that wouldn't appear on radar. Once across the maritime boundary, they'd be free to rendezvous with the corvette. Or, Marsh surmised,
if they truly wanted to wind us up, the ship could be a decoy. They could
be planning to pull Will out by submarine as well.

Marsh strained to read the calendar tacked above his workbench.
"Five days. Not enough time for a diplomatic pouch to make the round
trip to Moscow."

"No."

"Yet Cherkashin has been in touch with his superiors."

"Clearly."

"And we've missed the burst transmission."

"Yes."

In other words, they'd lost their opportunity to roll up the network
and isolate Cherkashin's man.

"What chance have we," said Marsh, "of drawing this out? Get Will
to drag his feet a bit more?"

Pethick took the photograph from Marsh and tucked it back in his
pocket. "Ivan's getting ready to move him very soon. I suspect further
evasions by Beauclerk will be viewed suspiciously."

The fatigued cot springs creaked when Marsh shifted his weight to
stretch. "I feared as much."

Pethick said, "Our guests might know more about this."

"Klaus? I doubt it," said Marsh. "Gretel does, but she's immune to coercion. Von Westarp, the Schutzstaffel, and the NKVD couldn't break her in over forty years of continuous effort. We won't manage in a handful of days."

"They'll want to move him. Sooner rather than later. We need to do something before they call his bluff." Pethick frowned. "It is a bluff, is it not?"

Marsh said, "William Beauclerk is naïve as the day is long. But I do believe him when he says he did what he did for purposes of revenge, not ideology."

"The Soviets won't care if he's a willing defector or not, if they see a chance to send him to Moscow. I don't know him as you do, but I suspect he'd crumble under their questioning." Pethick shrugged. "If they get him, he'll tell them everything he knows about Eidolons and Enochian."

Marsh shook his head. "It won't come to that. Will won't board that ship." He nodded toward the pocket where Pethick had tucked away the reconnaissance photo. "I'll shoot him myself, if need be."

"In the meantime," said Pethick, "Cherkashin's pet killer is still out there. Yours was a good notion, starting at the top, but we're no closer to finding him."

"I know. . . ." Marsh massaged his temples, fostering the warm glow of a new idea. "I suppose this means we'll have to flush out Cherkashin's man directly."

28 May 1963
Croydon, London, England

Klaus found himself waking earlier and earlier. He enjoyed the serenity of dawn, that special time of day when the world was empty but for himself, the songbirds in the garden, and a cup of coffee. His thoughts, he found, were clearest and most creative early in the morning. Thus, within a week of receiving Madeleine's gift, he forged a new routine for himself. He'd wake before dawn, creep downstairs, make breakfast for himself, eat at the window while songbirds serenaded the rising sun and the first rays of sunrise dipped into the garden, then retreat to his bedroom—and his brushes, and his watercolors, and his exercises—before the others appeared.

Properly timed, on a good morning, he could almost pretend that the house was his and his alone. That he had a normal life of his own choosing. But Gretel was the pin to Klaus's soap bubble illusion. The fragility of his imagined life could not hope to withstand her.

Klaus preferred the comforting illusion of solitude to the ugly reality of his sister. Even when she adopted her most pleasant mode. Such as the previous morning, when Gretel had awakened him before dawn to watch a particularly colorful sunrise with her. "Something for you to strive for," she'd said.

A knock sounded on his door around midmorning. Technically, Klaus wasn't permitted (or even able) to lock the door, so knocking was merely a courtesy. One he appreciated; it contributed to the fantasy of normality. Knocking had been unknown at Arzamas.

Klaus set down his brush. He stationed himself between his make-shift easel and the door. "Yes?"

Madeleine poked her head in. The papers tacked to the walls caught her attention. She opened the door more widely and slipped inside, head turning to take in his work.

"You've certainly been busy," she said.

He knew what she saw. Pages covered with wavy lines, straight lines, thick lines, thin lines, solid colors, blended colors. And most of these, he knew objectively, were rendered with a childlike lack of skill. Klaus shrugged, feeling embarrassed by this attention to his personal efforts. It had been a long time since he had tried to acquire a new skill.

"They're nothing," he said. "Exercises. From books."

Madeleine smiled. "I'm pleased to hear it." She gave his exercises another approving glance, then pointed back over her shoulder with one finger. "Marsh is here. Wants to see you and your sister."

Klaus sighed. The debriefings had long ago become tedious, and difficult. *How many times must I say, "I don't know"? They've heard it in English, German, and Russian.*

At least it was Marsh this time. One on one, he was easier to deal with than the others. On the other hand, Marsh became much pricklier in Gretel's presence. But to be fair, so did Klaus.

But Marsh hadn't come for another debriefing session. Instead he ushered Klaus and Gretel to a car parked outside. Pethick sat behind the wheel. Marsh sat in front. The floor behind the front seat, Klaus noticed as he climbed in, had been fitted with an iron ring. A bulky radio set hung beneath the fascia, alongside the driver.

He asked, "Where are you taking us?"

"To frame an old friend," said Gretel. He ignored her.

"To be seen," said Marsh.

Pethick cranked the wheel to inch the car out of its parking spot. He cleared the other cars, then gunned the engine. They pulled away from the safe house. The acceleration sent Gretel sliding across the seat, into Klaus. He pushed her back. She laughed.

Marsh didn't elaborate, and Klaus didn't bother to press him for details.

They entered the heart of London after an uneventful drive. Pethick pulled the car to a stop before the steps of a Georgian office building. Marsh got out and motioned for Klaus and Gretel to do likewise. Pethick stayed in the car.

Marsh shepherded them to the lift. He jabbed the button for the fourth floor, which, according to a brass plate alongside the buttons, housed the NORTH ATLANTIC CROSS-CULTURAL FOUNDATION. The lift floor pressed against the soles of Klaus's shoes; Gretel hummed to herself during the short ride.

They emerged into what struck Klaus as an ultramodern office space, decked out in wood and brushed metal beneath bright fluorescents. Across a swath of burgundy carpet, a young brunette at a reception desk hammered on a typewriter with machine gun efficiency. She wore her hair in a tall mound atop her head. It seemed a popular style these days; Klaus had seen many variations of it since arriving in Britain. She paused when Marsh approached her desk.

"We're here to see Lord William," he said.

She smiled at him, but it faltered when she glimpsed Klaus, and then again when she turned her eyes to Gretel. His sister twined a finger through one wire-wrapped braid.

"I'm afraid he isn't in, sir."

Marsh said, "We'll wait."

"Do you have an appointment?"

"We do now."

The receptionist looked unhappy about this, but there was nothing she could do about it. "Very well, then. May I offer you tea? Coffee?"

"No," said Marsh.

Marsh stood by the windows, gazing at the building across the street. Klaus took a seat in a leather chair beneath an oil painting. An engraved placard affixed to the frame identified the subject as AUBREY BEAUCLERK: a pudgy, balding man who had apparently created the foundation. Klaus knew, based on what he'd heard in the debriefing of William Beauclerk, that Aubrey was his older brother. A member of the peerage.

Gretel settled beside him. She watched him sidewise, and smirked when his gaze kept returning to the receptionist. She leaned over, whispered in his ear. "Isn't she pretty?" she said, nodding toward the receptionist. "Do you think she's attracted to older men?"

The tickle of her breath made his skin crawl. Klaus shrugged her aside again.

It didn't require a genius to understand why Marsh had brought them here. The Soviets had asked William Beauclerk for help in finding the escaped siblings. And it was clear from what Will had said that the Soviets had people watching his office closely, for covert signals. By bringing Klaus here, Marsh had ensured that the Soviet spy network would conclude that the younger Beauclerk had betrayed them.

The question was why. What did Marsh hope to gain from this? Klaus would have asked him, were the two men alone. But they couldn't speak freely in front of the receptionist, nor would Marsh be candid while Gretel was in earshot.

Their wait lasted just long enough for the receptionist to notice Klaus's wires, and for her to cast a few alarmed glances at him and his

sister, before Will arrived. He emerged from the lift, greeted his receptionist, and then paused when he saw Marsh standing at the window.

"Pip?"

Marsh turned. "Hi, Will. We need to have a chat." He gestured at
Klaus and Gretel. "Just the four of us."

Will's shoulders sagged. He had all the presence of a fallen cake.

"They haven't made an appointment," said the receptionist. "But they
insisted on waiting for you."

"Never mind, Angela," said Will, clearly resigned to this turn of
events. "Hold my calls." He unlocked a narrow pair of double doors
and beckoned the others inside. Klaus followed Gretel and Marsh into
Will's office. Will locked the door behind him. Klaus took a seat on the
wicker settee beside the door.

"May I ask what this is about?" Will slipped the key into a pocket of
his herringbone weskit.

"Change of plans," said Marsh. "Your meetings with Cherkashin aren't
having the desired effect."

Gretel crossed the large office to the wide mullioned window overlooking the street below. She made a show of studying the flower on the
windowsill.

Will watched her. He turned to Marsh, his face pale. "You're setting
me up."

"We're forcing their hand," said Marsh.

"Forcing their hand? What in blazes does that mean?"

"We know that your chums, Fedotov and Cherkashin, were hoping
you'd let them know when these two showed their faces outside the
Iron Curtain. We also know your chums like to keep a close eye on your
office window. Convenient means of communicating, that."

So Klaus was right. He could guess the rest without difficulty. But
the details didn't matter. Marsh had chosen to parade Klaus in front of
the people who wanted nothing more than to kill or imprison him. He
might have lacked Gretel's subtlety, but in this they were very much
the same: Both saw Klaus as a tool, a game piece, a chit, and used him
accordingly. Klaus the man didn't matter; only his role in the game.

Gretel plucked a scarlet blossom from the flowerpot. She tucked it into her hair. "It's a lovely view," she said. "Come see, brother."

Klaus didn't move. He looked at Marsh. "Is that why I'm here?"

Marsh nodded. "I won't try to force you, Klaus. She's already let the cat out of the bag. But it would help if you showed yourself, too."

"They don't want me," said Klaus. "It's Gretel they care about."

"If they intend to recapture you both," said Will, "they must realize that's a rather far-fetched hope. Given her . . ." He trailed off, gesturing at Gretel with a languid wave of his hand.

Klaus shook his head. "They've never succeeded in replicating my sister's ability. There is only one Gretel." At this, she smiled. "If the Soviets can't use her, they'll try to ensure that nobody can."

"Again," said Will, "a far-fetched ambition. Given the, ah, circum-stances."

"Of course they won't kill me," said Gretel, still gazing out at the traf-fic below. "I'd never let *that* happen. But in their desperation, they can attempt to limit my resources."

"And that brings us back to you, Will," said Marsh.

Will said, "I rather dislike the look in your eyes."

Klaus sighed. He joined his sister at the window. It wasn't a lovely view. If he stood on his toes, he could just make out a spot of greenery far past the sea of brick chimney pots and spindly television antennae. All the blinds on the windows across the street had been drawn.

Gretel put her head on his shoulder. He shrugged her off again. She smelled like Madeleine. They shared a bathroom; perhaps they used the same hair shampoo.

"I'd gather that just about now," said Marsh, "Cherkashin is receiv-ing a very urgent telephone call, alerting him to the fact you've just re-ceived a visit from a pair of escaped lunatics. But when you don't attempt to set up a meeting with him, he's going to assume you've betrayed him. And that shall make him rather cross."

"What are you doing to me?" Will asked.

Gretel said, "They'll try to kill you."

Will clutched absently at the sling cradling one arm. "You wretched cur. I've done everything you've asked of me."

To Klaus, he sounded petulant. Will's country had trusted him with sensitive information. But he'd traded that information to a hostile nation, and now he acted as though being forced to deal with the consequences of his actions were an outrageous punishment. Punishment? Will had seen nothing of the sort. He had no idea just how fortunate he was. Klaus had spent his entire life in places where a far lesser transgression would have earned a bullet in the head from an officer's pistol, or several days of the doctor's "reconditioning." He shivered at the memory of the old Reichsbehörde incubators, his old coffin box.

The irony of the situation angered Klaus. Enraged him. Will had betrayed the United Kingdom, a place far better than everywhere Klaus had ever lived, to the Soviet Union, a place with an institutional contempt for people like Will. Klaus had spent much of his life yearning for a chance to escape the latter for the former. His was a privileged perspective, if "privilege" was the right word.

Will's naïveté was breathtaking.

Klaus spat, "You are an extremely foolish man."

Both Marsh and Will turned to blink at him in surprise. There may have been a flicker of appreciation on Marsh's face, just as Will stepped back, retreating from the truth.

Marsh said, "It's our only sure method of exposing Cherkashin's man."

"And I'm to be the cheese in the rattrap, am I?"

"Yes."

28 May 1963
Knightsbridge, London, England

Will fell silent for a moment, trying to gather thoughts that sluiced through his mind like water through his fingers. Marsh was trying to have him killed. The man had gone mad with rage. Couldn't anybody see that? But Will had no allies in this room. When he spoke again, his voice cracked. It betrayed the terror he felt as Marsh's plan came into focus. "Gwendolyn?"

"Safe. We moved her this morning."

"You don't waste a moment, do you?"

Another flash of irritation passed over Marsh's face, but a knock sounded at the door before he could unleash a retort. Will sighed inwardly, thankful for the respite, no matter how brief.

He unlocked the door. "Yes, Angela."

His secretary poked her head inside. She looked uncertainly around the room before turning her attention to Will. "Sir, there's a man here to see you. Samuel Pethick?"

Will looked at Marsh, then back to Angela. "Thank you. Let him in."

She ushered Pethick into the crowded office, then pulled the door behind him. Pethick waited for the paneled door to latch shut with an audible *click* before addressing Marsh. "Just got an interesting message over the blower. Our lamplighters down in Lyminster report that Ivan's gone bughouse. Started a few minutes ago. The rats are abandoning ship." He glanced at Klaus and Gretel, who still stood at the window. "I think it worked."

Will realized he hadn't a clue what Pethick was talking about. Nothing the man said made the least bit of sense. And that only deepened the sense of terror, because Will was at the center of it all. How had everything gone so utterly beyond his control? He'd thought he finally put everything in his life right. Yet now he didn't know if he'd survive the week. The carousel of life was spinning out of control, faster and faster, while Will's sweaty fingers lost their grip an inch at a time. Soon he'd be flung into the bushes, where lurked bears and demons.

All because he found the murder of innocent civilians disgusting and inexcusable.

Marsh scowled at Will. "And you think *we* work quickly? Your would-be masters make us a tortoise." To Pethick, he said, "Thanks, Sam. Take the others and wait for us outside, will you? I need a word alone with Will."

Pethick beckoned to Klaus and Gretel, who followed him back into the anteroom without another word. Gretel winked at Will as she passed his desk. It scratched something deep inside him, the hard pit at the center of his fear.

Will waited for the door to *click* closed again. When he and Marsh were alone, he snapped, "How dare you drag my wife into this? She's innocent."

Marsh stood, drew himself to his full height. "You involved her the moment you decided to sell us out."

"Listen to your self-righteousness. Sell you out? I did nothing of the sort. They were evil men. You know it. Not so well as I, and for that you should be damn grateful, but you know it." Marsh snorted. "Milkweed was a sick organization! We did the most heinous things. Why am I the only person willing to admit it?"

"I won't see my sacrifices come to naught just because William bloody Beauclerk decided in a fit of pique to single-handedly rearrange the state of the world." Marsh punctuated his statement with short, sharp jabs of the finger at Will.

That sense of looking upon a coiled spring came over Will as he stared at Marsh, just as it had in the old days. The difference being that Will was now the target of that suppressed power, those barely contained destructive urges. He backed away, wondering if he'd make it to the door if Marsh snapped. The man would beat him to death, and they'd call him a patriot for it. A poor, angry patriot.

"I've already heard this tirade, you know. Yes, yes, your martyrdom is quite impressive," Will said. "Everybody lost something in the war, Pip. You act like your loss is the only one that matters, that your sorrow is unique. Having lost somebody doesn't make you privileged. It makes you British."

"British? There might not be a Britain left after what you've done."

"Dear Lord. You yearn to punish the people responsible for what happened to Agnes. You virtually tremble with the need," said Will. "And yet you'd deny me the same urge to punish wicked people, to set things right. I do believe that is the most hypocritical thing I've heard in many long years." He paused, blinking in the glare from a new flash of insight. "You're not angry because of what I've done. You're envious because I succeeded."

Marsh extended an arm, pointing vigorously at the door. His voice became a harsh whisper. "Gretel still breathes because I have more self-control than you do."

"You sanctimonious ass. Are you lying to me, or yourself? I'd wager you tried to strangle her the moment you saw her. But you failed, didn't you? And so you've decided to show me up, just to assuage your wounded pride. Whisk my wife away while you march me around town until somebody slits my throat. Is that your plan?"

Marsh pinched the bridge of his nose, frowning with the effort not to bellow. "I swear to God, speaking with you is like speaking with a child," he murmured. "Get this through your thick head. I've done you a courtesy, you stupid, chinless toff. Or would you rather Gwendolyn was home when Cherkashin's man comes for you? Because he'll murder her without a second thought."

Oh, God, Gwendolyn. What have I done to you? The urge to argue left Will, but the heat of anger had left his bones soft as candle wax.

Will sat heavily in his armchair. It rolled backwards, bumping to a stop against his safe. "How does this work?"

"We'll nab him at your house, when he comes for you."

"You know, nobody ever thinks to ask the cheese how it feels, after the rat is dead and all is said and done."

"The cheese doesn't get a say in the matter," said Marsh.

"What did your men tell Gwendolyn?"

"That her safety was at stake. Which it is. Because of you."

Will sighed. "She hasn't spoken to me."

"Oh, do stop," said Marsh. "I'll surely weep."

Will glared at him. That was Marsh, self-absorbed to the last. Oblivious of any and all forms of human interaction. Will wondered if the man standing before him knew any emotions aside from the rainbow hues of rage.

"When the circumstances were reversed, I did my best for you," he said. "I tried to save your marriage. Twice, in point of fact."

"Save my—?" Marsh paced. He lost the struggle to control his voice. "Save my marriage? You told us to terminate Liv's pregnancy!"

Will met Marsh's eyes. Quietly, he said, "Was I wrong?"

The dart flew true.

No, I wasn't wrong. I see it in your face, Pip. Will shuddered, as much for the unguarded glimpse of Marsh's despair as for the thought of what it meant. *What sort of abomination lives under your roof?*

Will remembered his blood dripping to moonlit snow, while men screamed and died around him. Remembered the suffocating stink of cordite and the ground-meat remains of James Lorimer. Remembered trying to concentrate, trying to speak Enochian over the chatter of gunfire. Trying to get home. Trying to save Marsh's life.

And he remembered how the Eidolons had changed their price for the return trip. Inflated it, like black marketeers flouting the price of rationed sugar.

The soul of an unborn child.

Back in the present, Marsh said with icy calm, "You'd better get your things in order. They'll come for you soon, and when they do, you'll have to stay dead until we've cleaned every last bit of your mess."

"Will I be allowed to see Gwendolyn?"

"It's easier to mind you both if you're together."

Will stood. He considered pulling his personal documents from the safe, but decided against it. The bank and his attorney had copies, of course, but walking out with this collection of odd characters and a sheaf of papers under his arm would only raise more questions in Angela's mind. Better if he went nonchalantly. As though he didn't know he was toddling off to his own murder. And none of it mattered any longer. All he wanted was to see Gwendolyn.

"I'm ready now," he said. Marsh followed him out of the office.

Pethick sat under the oil painting of Aubrey, next to Klaus. Marsh joined them. Gretel stood alongside the casement window behind Angela's desk, her back to the room.

"I'm stepping out for a bit," said Will.

Angela worked diligently at her desk, acting as if she hadn't heard every word of what must have been a very perplexing row with Marsh. The epitome of professionalism.

"Sir, I know this isn't my place," she said, looking at the men in the corner and briefly over her shoulder at the gypsy woman. Her voice dropped to a whisper. "But your visitors are a bit odd." She pointed toward where Gretel stood behind her. "Especially that one," she mouthed.

Bless you, Angela. Faithful and perceptive to the last, thought Will. *I'll miss you. Aubrey will give you good references.*

"Nothing to worry about." Another flash, this time of inspiration. Will resisted the urge to pat himself on the back. "Refugees," he whispered. "From the European camps."

Angela raised a hand to her mouth. "Oh, dear."

"I'll be out the rest of the day," he said.

"Very good, sir." She returned to her typing.

Will rounded the desk and joined Gretel at the window. "I like this city," she said. She was rather petite, he realized; the top of her head didn't reach his chin. He'd forgotten that.

He leaned over her. "I don't know why you've taken it upon yourself to ruin him," he whispered, nodding at Marsh, "but I won't allow you to do the same to me. I am not your plaything."

Gretel stared up at him, her blank face wide-eyed. She cast a quick glance over her shoulder. Then, seeing that the others were momentarily occupied, she quirked up the corner of her mouth. Her eyes shed their innocent quality, leaving in its place something that chilled him.

"Hop, little bunny."

She plucked the nasturtium blossom from her hair and tucked the stem into Will's breast pocket. It snagged on the silk he'd arranged there. He caught a whiff of the scent.

She reached up, gently laid her hand on his face. Her skin, Will noticed, felt warm. Almost feverish.

Gretel patted his cheek. "Hop, hop, hop."

eight

Klaus knew he was veering into foolishness. Refusing to interact with his sister? Pretending she didn't exist? They lived in the same space; rode in the same vehicles. It was pointless but, more frankly, childish. And so it would be while the British practically treated them as a single entity. He'd never be free of Gretel on his own.

Thus had the seed of an idea taken root while he sat in the foyer of the North Atlantic Cross-Cultural Foundation, waiting for Will and Marsh to finish their argument. It sprouted during the return drive across London. And by the time they returned to the safe house, it had borne fruit.

Everything hinged on Marsh's plan to use Will as bait. If it failed, Klaus's chance at a normal life would die on the vine. But if the plan succeeded with his help . . . Well, then it depended on whether or not Marsh was a man of his word.

Klaus tapped Marsh on the arm as everybody emerged from the Morris. "May I speak with you? Privately?"

He followed Marsh through the house to the garden, leaving Pethick to deal with Gretel. An empty planter stood where Marsh had identified the diseased maple. It had been transplanted, Klaus saw, into the south corner of the garden, in a niche where the walls met. He wondered if Marsh had done that.

Once they were outside, with the rear door firmly closed behind them, Marsh crossed his arms. "Well?"

"The plan you've hatched. You intend to trap the assassin by using a pixie."

Marsh hesitated, just long enough to signify his surprise. He recovered, shrugging noncommittally. "Perhaps."

He doesn't trust me. Nor do I trust him entirely.

"They're aware of that vulnerability," said Klaus. "The Soviets. They used it against us when they occupied the Reichsbehörde. It's how they captured us." He pointed at the house, a vague gesture to imply "us" meant him and his sister.

"We know that. What are you saying?"

"When you captured my sister during the war, you took her battery, yes? Studied it? And from that you derived a design for the pixies."

Marsh frowned. "Is that why she came here? Why she let herself be captured? To give us a battery?"

Klaus had never considered this, but it was plausible. He reappraised Marsh; the man seemed to have given much thought to the complexity of Gretel's machinations. It bordered on an obsession.

"I don't know. But . . ." Klaus trailed off, shaking his head.

". . . It sounds like something she might do?"

"Yes. The purpose of her trip to England was never clear to the rest of us. It served no . . . strategic purpose."

"Hmm." Marsh held his frown, contemplating this. Then he said, "I derailed you. What point were you trying to make regarding the pixies?"

Klaus said, "I understand how the Soviet engineers think. They have anticipated such countermeasures. They have—" He paused, grasping for the right word. "—reinforced the battery and its circuitry." He touched his scalp, where the wires emerged.

"Damn," Marsh whispered. He ran a hand over his face. "I'd feared that was the case." He sighed, shook his head. "What would you have me do, Klaus? It's the only tool at our disposal."

"You're wrong about that. You have another."

"What?"

Klaus took a deep breath. *How long until I regret this? Five years? Five minutes?* But this was a rare opportunity. Better to chart one's own course than to have it dictated by others. How many times in life did Klaus have the opportunity to alter the course of his life? Few indeed.

And so he said: "You have me."

"What?" The sound of Marsh's surprise echoed from the garden walls. It alarmed the handful of blackbirds perched on the eaves of the safe house. They responded with a shrill chorus. "Let me get this clear. Are you volunteering to help us?"

"Yes."

"Why?"

Klaus hesitated, choosing his words carefully. But he knew that only full candor would suffice. "When this is over, I want to have a normal life."

Marsh scoffed at that. "Normal."

Klaus touched his wires, self-consciously aware of the irony. "As normal as possible for somebody in my position."

"You want SIS to furnish you with a cover identity, so that you may live quietly forevermore in the countryside. Is that it?"

"Yes," said Klaus. "A quiet life by myself." He looked at the ground between his feet. "Far away from Gretel. Will you help me have that? In exchange for my aid? I'll never have that quiet future if this country falls."

Marsh cracked his knuckles, wincing as he did so. It seemed to be an unconscious habit. He peered at Klaus through eyes narrowed in thought. "Tell me more about this aid you're offering."

"Every ability requires specialized training. I can't tell you what the man you seek will be able to do. But I can tell you that he'll have been trained to fight against firearms, explosives, mortars, tanks, airplanes, knives, mines, mundane soldiers." Klaus looked at Marsh, to emphasize his point. "I am familiar with the training he'll have received."

"You were part of it."

"Yes."

A notable number of the fatalities at Doctor von Westarp's farm happened in the first weeks, or hours, or moments of a subject's first tentative embrace of the Willenskräfte. The boy who had slightly preceded Klaus in developing the ability to pass through solid objects died soon after its first manifestation, before everybody understood the implications of the ability. He dematerialized, fell through the earth, and presumably suffocated somewhere deep underground. Nobody, not even the doctor, had considered that transparency to matter required careful attention to gravity as well.

The technicians never succeeded in recovering the boy's body. Klaus remembered his name was Oskar.

The men and women who ran Arzamas-16 had made it very clear to Klaus that it was in his best interests to foresee any such mishaps, to warn the technicians and subjects.

Marsh said, "And?"

"He won't have been trained to fight his comrades. He won't know how to fight somebody like me."

Marsh looked skeptical. "And you do?"

"I don't know how much you understand about the atmosphere at the Reichsbehörde. It was not a convivial place. There was much friction between us. All of us."

It felt so wrong, discussing such personal issues with this former enemy. The details of his formative years, the influences that molded his psyche, his relationship to the Götterelektron . . . these were the most intimate details of Klaus's life. The flames in which he had been forged. Telling Madeleine about his sex life—from the prescribed couplings at the farm to the institutionalized prostitution at Arzamas and every shameful fantasy he'd ever entertained in between—would have been less uncomfortable. Less soul baring.

Yet he'd never become the man he wanted to be, living the life he wanted to have, if he continued to guard himself so rabidly. Klaus forced himself to endure the self-humiliation. Extending this trust to Marsh was the price for escaping Gretel.

A potential reward well worth the effort. So he plunged forward.

"And when I was young, when I believed in Doctor von Westarp without reservation, I was determined to rise to the top. I spent much time devising tactics for battling with Reinhardt, Rudolf, Kammler, and the rest. So that I would be prepared, if and when the moment came.

"Everybody did it. We evaluated each other, measured each other. Thought about how to fight one another, how to kill one another.

"Except my sister. There's no fighting her."

At this, Marsh bristled. "Nobody is invincible."

Perhaps your understanding of Gretel doesn't run as deeply as I had thought.

A flash of chestnut caught Klaus's eye. Madeleine stood at the kitchen window, her attention focused on the sink. She looked up and treated him to a moment's smile before returning to her task. He thought he smelled dish soap. She spoke with a woman Klaus didn't recognize.

Klaus said, "Have I once again made a fool of myself? Or will you help me?"

"I'll never believe your sister hasn't arranged this."

"Whether she has or not is irrelevant," said Klaus. "I'm not doing this for her. I'm doing this in spite of her."

A raven perched on the sundial, cawing loudly. Its talons scraped along the pitted bronze. The sight of the raven dislodged a dreamy image from the recesses of Klaus's memory. Something about a hay wagon, in a forest.

It gave him a sense of what he wanted to capture in watercolor. Not the image, yet, but the feeling. Something foreboding. Portentous. He couldn't quite articulate it to himself, but he knew it would come in time.

"How can I know you won't run off the moment we return your battery?"

"You can't."

Marsh thought about this. Then he said, "I can't promise anything, Klaus."

"I know."

"In that case," said Marsh, "I accept your offer. Thank you."

He extended his hand. They shook.

28 May 1963
Knightsbridge, London, England

It amounted to house arrest, the interminable wait for Will's murderer to arrive.

Echoes and shadows filled the hole left by Gwendolyn's absence. The house, once modest by the standards of Will's peers, now felt cavernous. Cold. Empty. Sepulchral. Like a mausoleum waiting for its unruly resident to settle down.

All this in spite of the handful of workers who passed through the passage that had been cut through the west wall of the dining room, to the adjoining residence. The neighbors on that side, the Ashton-Clarkes, had been quietly evacuated before sunrise. As had the rest of the crescent, on the pretense of a gas leak. Will had given the same explanation to Mrs. Toomre when he sent her home.

By late afternoon, it looked as though Will and Gwendolyn had hired Genghis Khan to remodel the house. Milkweed men tore into every wall to dig out the electrical mains. The silk wallpaper, carefully chosen by Gwendolyn, hung in tatters. Fine tufts of green and silver thread bobbed on imperceptible drafts. Plaster dust caked the floors like wheat flour in the kitchen of a hyperactive baker; it crunched underfoot, ground itself into the rugs. Even the pantry had suffered. Long, rippled gouges revealed the pale heart of oaken floorboards, tracing the path where the Milkweed boffins had dragged their crates into place. The crates contained coils, wires, and electrical equipment with names and purposes unknown to Will. Equipment they assembled and spliced into the exposed electrical mains. Where once the house had carried the earthy scent of Gwendolyn's potting clay, now it stank of sawdust and plaster.

And the physical destruction of their home was a bellwether for the condition of their marriage. Every broken floorboard symbolized the broken trust; every grenade a manifestation of the bomb he'd dropped by not confessing to Gwendolyn. Yes, Marsh's chums had destroyed the house, but Will himself had gutted the marriage.

He sat in the shadows of a reading alcove, hugging his knees in the recess of a bay window that overlooked the green space enclosed by the crescent. It was the only spot in the house where he didn't have to dance aside, or offer apologies every few moments. Gwendolyn had selected thick, French-pleated curtains for this window. They did an excellent job hiding the dismantlement of their home.

He remembered the pixies Lorimer had built. Presumably, the gutting of Will's house served a similar purpose.

Who, Will wondered, would pay to rehabilitate the house after Marsh caught his man? To whom did the house belong? Would Milkweed allow his wife to keep it, or had the title been requisitioned for purposes of national security?

Will's tea had gone lukewarm beneath a faint dusting of plaster. He drank it anyway. The plaster made it chalky. The cup rattled against the saucer when he set it down, like a burst of Morse code telegraphing his anxiety to the world.

The workmen cleared out near sunset, hastily disappearing back through their hole like the March Hare. The last two maneuvered a teak-wood credenza into place behind them, hiding their escape route. Three men stayed behind: Marsh, of course; a Milkweed agent named Anthony, a large man with acne scars on his face; and, most surprisingly, Klaus.

"What happens now?"

"You keep to your bloody routine," said Marsh from the shadows of the dining room. "Eat as you normally do, when you normally do, and retire likewise."

"You want me to eat dinner and put myself to bed?"

"Yes. Cherkashin's man will be watching your windows, watching the lights come on and off as you move through the house. Been doing it for days or even weeks, if he's good."

Will suppressed a shiver. How many times had this phantom killer watched Gwendolyn come and go?

"He may come to the front door, posing as a visitor," said another voice from the shadows. This voice carried a German accent.

Will said, "Roped you into joining the fun, did he, Klaus?"

"Don't worry about him," Marsh snapped. "Be thankful he wants to see the end of this as badly as we do."

Will dined alone. His dinner consisted of marinated lamb shank with mint jelly, green beans with almond slivers, and a sweet potato soufflé. Mrs. Toomre had planned two such servings before the faux evacuation sent her home to Swansea for the foreseeable future. If he didn't die in his sleep tonight, Will would eat Gwendolyn's portion tomorrow.

Marsh and Anthony staked out different rooms downstairs, while Klaus took a seat in a corner of Will's bedroom. The idea being, apparently, that Klaus would pull Will to safety at the first hint of trouble.

Will didn't like the sound of that.

Occasionally one of the others would come upstairs to check in with Klaus. Will found he could distinguish the men from their breathing and how they trod the stairs. Anthony fidgeted, shifting his weight from one foot to the other, eliciting creaks from the floorboards. Klaus made the slightest of rasps when he inhaled. Only Marsh was perfectly silent, a shadow brooding in the darkness.

The drowsy part of Will's mind marveled at the twisted set of circumstances. Klaus was one of the reasons Milkweed had been created; a formidable enemy, whose existence had goaded Marsh and the old man to extreme measures. Klaus's spectacular foray into the Admiralty building to free Gretel had prompted Will to track down and recruit Britain's warlocks for the war effort. Those had been frightening days; time's passage hadn't blunted Will's memory. It wasn't so different from now, the sweaty anxiety, the dodgy sensation of teetering on the razor edge of panic. The impotent worry that any moment they'd be overrun by dozens of Klauses, and all the others on the Tarragona filmstrip.

Yet now Will found he much preferred to have this former enemy looking after his well-being rather than his former friend and ally. Part of him secretly feared that Marsh might succumb to rage and slit Will's throat in the middle of the night. If nothing else, the Nazis knew discipline.

Will whispered, "Why are you doing this, Klaus? How terribly did Marsh twist your arm?"

"He didn't," said Klaus. But he didn't elaborate.

Later, Will caught a snippet of whispered conversation.

"I recognize you. From the safe house."

"I reckon so."

"You played cards with my sister. For hours."

This was followed by a chuckle and what might have been the susurration of fabric, like corduroy. "Commander Marsh's orders. Wanted us to test her limits a bit. Glad it weren't for real quid, though."

Sometime past midnight, the play of headlights shone through the drapes and danced along the ceiling of the bedroom as a lone car rounded the crescent. Will, who had been sleeping lightly if at all, sat bolt upright.

Klaus's radio squawked to life. Will recognized Pembroke's voice. "Stand by."

The quiet somehow became more complete, more oppressive, as every person in the house held his breath. Klaus plugged in; the *click* ricocheted through the pregnant silence. The Milkweed men covertly monitoring the street gave a running commentary on the passing car. Sweat trickled down Will's arms.

"Two occupants . . . A man and a woman . . . They're slowing. . . . They've stopped before number twenty-three. . . . They're consulting a map, looks like they're having a row. . . . They're pulling out. . . . Stand down. Stand down."

The adrenaline surge kept Will awake most of the rest of the night. But he did doze off, eventually, and woke the next morning slightly surprised to find himself still alive.

Will even snored like a toff. Marsh made this observation when he went upstairs to relieve Klaus. Sunrise peeked through the blinds of Will's bedroom. It had been a long, frustrating night.

"Knock off for a few, Klaus. Sleep it off if you're able. We'll rest in shifts."

Klaus stood. It sounded like every joint in his arms and legs cracked. He yawned, rubbed his eyes.

"Have you budged from that spot this entire night?"

"No," said Klaus.

Well, thought Marsh. *That's Nazi discipline for you.*

"You can rack out on the couch downstairs," he said. Klaus nodded, yawned again, and tromped down the stairs. Marsh tapped Will's shoulder. "Oy. Get up."

Will mumbled. Marsh poked him harder. "Get up."

Will blinked at him blearily. "Pip?" He took a moment to survey his surroundings. In a raspy voice he said, "I still live, I see."

"For the moment."

"Well. Thank heavens for quiet nights, then."

Marsh waited outside the master bath while Will showered and shaved. Surveying the bedroom, he realized that Will slept with silk sheets on his king-sized, four-poster bed. That single set probably cost more than all the sheets and towels in Marsh's house, combined.

The surge of resentment tasted like bile on the back of Marsh's tongue. Every crystal light fixture, every sterling silver teaspoon, grated like a draft of cold air on a cracked tooth. Just the previous morning, he and Liv had fought over whether they could afford to hire a plumber to fix the kitchen sink.

And to think that Will was the poorer Beauclerk brother. Marsh doubted Aubrey's lifestyle was any less opulent, in spite of his affection for socialism. He'd have to ask Klaus the Russian word for "hypocrite."

Will emerged from the steamy bathroom in his dressing gown, hair wet, face pink from the razor. He hadn't slept well; Marsh could read it in the darkened skin beneath his eyes. But the bags weren't so pronounced as they had been in the days after Will had discovered morphine. An errant thought tainted with guilt; Marsh punched it aside.

Will opened a wardrobe. He sifted through the clothes hung inside, critically examining each pair of trousers. Likewise the shirts. This went on for a full minute.

"Oh, for Christ's sake," said Marsh. "You're not meeting the bloody Queen today."

"And what am I doing today?" Will put a set of clothes on the bed and began to dress. It was an awkward process. Milkweed's medic had dispensed with Will's sling, but Will still moved gingerly, favoring the arm. Marsh rolled his eyes; the doc had suggested the original injury hadn't been more than a mild sprain.

"When does your secretary arrive at the foundation in the morning?"

"I haven't a clue." Goaded by Marsh's snort of impatience, Will added, "Angela is always there before me."

"Why am I not surprised," said Marsh.

"Why the interest in Angela? She's too young for you."

"You're calling in sick today."

"Ah."

"We suspect Cherkashin may have your phones tapped."

A pause. And then, more quietly, "I see."

"It might speed things along, if they think you'll be home alone all day."

"Yes. Nothing could be more vexing than a tardy assassin. Very uncouth, taking his time like this."

"I haven't slept. Don't try my patience."

Will fell silent while he struggled to dress. As he fumbled the last button through its hole, he said, "I want to see the end of this as much as you. I won't see Gwendolyn until then."

Marsh followed him down the stairs. "I can't begin to imagine what she sees in you."

"Neither can I, Pip."

Downstairs, they found Klaus stretched out and breathing deeply on the fainting couch in the parlor. The scent of eggs and bacon wafted out of the kitchen. Anthony had taken it upon himself to scrounge up breakfast for the beleaguered team. Marsh's stomach grumbled. He'd neglected to eat dinner during the hectic rush to turn Will's home into a trap.

"You're lucky she found you when she did," said Marsh.

Will said, "Nobody understands that better than I."

The radio squawked again that afternoon, rousing Will from a fitful nap in the reading alcove. Unlike Marsh and the others, who had been napping in shifts and resorting to generous helpings of tea and coffee to stay alert, Will had no reason to force himself awake. He'd dozed through much of the morning and early afternoon. His dreams had been feverish, still life montages of being buried alive.

As it had during the previous night's false alarm, a burst of static preceded a transmission from the SIS lorry parked down the crescent. Marsh, Klaus, and Anthony tensed, turning their attention to the two-way handset situated on the dining room table alongside several Mills bombs. Will drew a shuddery breath.

"Stand by," announced the tinny, disembodied voice. Pethick, rather than Pembroke this time; perhaps the SIS lorry had a cot.

A shadow slipped across the curtains of the bay window as a vehicle pulled to a stop on the street outside. Will resisted the urge to peek.

"It's a lorry," said their eyes outside. "National gas." Gas distribution had been nationalized in the mid-forties.

"Single occupant. He's getting out. Dressed as a workman." Anthony pulled his sidearm; Marsh did likewise, then pointed from Klaus to Will to the stairs. Will followed Klaus up to the master bedroom, where the second radio handset took up the running commentary.

"He's giving the crescent a good look over, both directions. . . ."

Klaus plugged in. Will looked at the wall. He swallowed. The boundary separating the Beauclerk household from the Ashton-Clarke household, through which the rattle of plumbing and the occasional muffled voice had escaped over the years, now seemed impassable. Impregnable.

"He's crossing the street, approaching the door."

Klaus glanced at the gauge on his battery. He frowned.

It turned Will's knees to jelly. "Look," he said. "If there's a problem, perhaps we should rethink—"

"Go! Go! *Go!*" The radio squealed, overdriven by the urgency and excitement in Pethick's voice.

Klaus grabbed Will's arm. An electric tingle suffused his body, made his mouth taste as though he'd been sucking on a ha'penny. Klaus pulled Will behind him. Will tried to object, tried to break away, but Klaus's grip was too firm. The wall engulfed Klaus.

Wallpaper, plaster, timber, and paint passed through Will's eyes, bones, brain, and heart. Buried alive. He panicked, overwhelmed by claustrophobia. But his screams only expelled ghostly air from ephemeral lungs.

And then he was out again, staggering through the neighbors' bedroom. He needed to catch his breath but Klaus wouldn't stop. They passed through another wall. And another. And another. Each residence took Will closer to the SIS lorry, and closer to blacking out.

They stumbled to a halt in an unfamiliar master bathroom. A towel lay crumpled alongside a safety razor and a white porcelain sink dusted with the black detritus of somebody's beard. Klaus released him.

"Get outside!" he said.

Will doubled over, sucking down air. "I hope never to do that again," he gasped.

But Klaus had already disappeared.

Marsh crouched in the shadows behind the stairwell, which gave him a clear view of the foyer. A man stood on the landing, his features blurred by the frosted panes.

Anthony hid behind the green baize chair in the parlor, Browning pistol at the ready.

The silhouette on the landing turned, as if surveying the street again. The doorknob rattled. Marsh laid a finger on the light switch.

The stranger's hand ghosted through the door at the same moment the radio gave the order for Klaus to move. The phantom hand felt around the inside of the doorframe, and then turned the latch.

He's like Klaus, thought Marsh. *So much for our traps.*

The door swung open. Cherkashin's man stepped soundlessly into the foyer. He wore the uniform of a gas company workman, complete with boilersuit and tool belt. Silhouetted by the afternoon glare, his features were invisible to Marsh. Marsh squinted, straining for any sign of wires snaking down the man's collar, but could see none. Perhaps they were subcutaneous, as Klaus had warned.

Cherkashin's man turned to close the door behind him, but froze when he glimpsed the exposed electrical mains.

Marsh flipped the switch.

For an instant the walls trembled with a tremendous buzzing as if packed with lightning and hornets. The chandelier above the foyer exploded at the center of an electric-blue flash. It showered the intruder with shards of broken crystal. An ozone tang filled the house, sharp enough to sting.

And now he knows we're wise to him.

Marsh blinked rapidly; the flash from the chandelier had imprinted green afterimages in the corners of his vision. He needed to see clearly, to gauge whether the improvised pixie had worked. The assassin shook his head as if trying to clear it. Crystal fragments tinkled to the floor when he brushed himself off, the only sound in the aftermath of the blast. Marsh held his breath.

The debris didn't pass through your body. Are you disabled, or merely surprised?

The assassin turned his attention toward the shadows of the darkened house. Slowly. Deliberately. He wasn't dazed, and he wasn't retreating.

God damn it. The pixie needed just under a minute to recharge. Marsh reached for one of the Mills bombs on his belt, mentally reviewing what Klaus had confirmed for him. *Have to do this the hard way. Keep him insubstantial until he needs to draw a breath.*

From the parlor he heard the bump of a chair shouldered aside, and Anthony saying, "Don't move."

Heat shimmer engulfed the assassin. Anthony screamed. Tufts of torn silk wallpaper fluttered like gossamer pennants in the sudden updraft before flaring into ash.

"Shit!" The oath escaped Marsh before he could catch himself. It drew the assassin's attention. He looked in Marsh's direction, frowning.

Marsh fumbled for the second light switch. It triggered a pair of antipersonnel mines embedded in opposite walls just as the Soviet agent stepped between them. The hail of shrapnel flashed into incandescent vapor.

Marsh threw himself backwards, behind the stairwell, as a surge of superheated air flashed through his hiding spot. It charred the exposed timbers in the walls. His sinuses, throat, and chest erupted in blistering pain, scorched by the effort to breathe impossibly hot air. Tears trickled down his face.

What else *can this bastard do?*

He pressed himself into the corner, trying and failing to shield himself from the assault. *What now? What now?* Pain extinguished his concentration.

Marsh realized he'd made a fatal mistake. He'd cornered himself. Because he was thinking like a frightened gardener, not a field agent. Too many years had passed. They'd made him soft. Careless. He remembered Krasnopolsky, the poor sod burning to death in the lobby of a Spanish hotel. And here he was, almost twenty-five years later, about to share the same fate.

Keep him busy. . . . Something hot and salty coated Marsh's tongue when he coughed. . . . *His abilities don't matter. . . .* He gagged . . . . *Just drain the battery. Any way possible.*

The walls crackled with flames. Marsh heard the slow, steady clomp of work boots on marble and the jingling of a tool belt as Will's would-be killer drew closer.

Marsh pulled his sidearm. It was warm to the touch.

The assassin said, "Where is William Beauclerk?"

The assassin glanced contemptuously at the Browning in Marsh's hand. The barrel sagged. Marsh dropped the ruined gun before it scorched his hand.

"Where," repeated the assassin, "is William Beauclerk?"

Marsh fumbled for a Mills bomb, knowing full well he wouldn't survive the detonation, but hoping it would take the assassin with him. He managed to get a finger on the pin at the same moment Klaus blew through the ceiling like a ghostly cannonball.

Klaus left Will gasping for breath in a residence on the far end of the crescent. He doubled back toward where Marsh and Anthony lay in wait.

Smoke and heat stung his nose the moment he emerged through the wall into Will's house. It meant the improvised pixie had failed. But it also meant Klaus knew exactly how to deal with the Soviet agent: using the same strategy he'd developed for fighting Reinhardt. It had worked well, the one time he'd been forced to use it.

He crouched behind the balustrade of the second-floor landing, peering down through the shimmering waves of heat that poured from the Soviet agent. The updraft wafted the stink of charred pork to him; someone had died.

The agent said, in a quiet, almost conversational tone, "Where is William Beauclerk?"

Klaus realized the man was addressing Marsh, who had taken a hiding spot behind the stairwell in order to watch the foyer. The gauge on Klaus's harness rested just at the boundary between green and yellow; pulling Will halfway around the crescent had taxed the old battery.

The assassin kept advancing. He repeated his question. Marsh was cornered.

Klaus embraced his Willenskräfte and leapt at the Soviet agent. He willed himself transparent to the walls, the ceiling, the balustrade, the landing, and most of all *heat*. But not the floor. He landed a few paces behind the assassin, skidding on ash-slick marble.

The assassin whirled to face him. Ripples of heat distorted the expression on his face. But the irritation on his face turned to surprise, then disdain, as if he recognized Klaus. Klaus didn't know this man, but Arzamas-16 had become a large place over the years. Much larger than the old Reichsbehörde.

Klaus gritted his teeth against the inevitable burn to his fingertips. He lunged, arm outstretched and fingers splayed, ready to snag his opponent's wires on the way through his body. The Soviets, he knew, implanted them subcutaneously. Marsh and Pembroke wanted the assassin disabled and alive, suitable for questioning. Klaus found that wildly optimistic. He aimed for the man's neck; if he missed the wire, it still gave him a chance of plucking at the carotid artery.

The assassin saw Klaus's advance. The heat shimmer winked out—

—and his entire body became insubstantial. Klaus's fingertips passed through it all without resistance, unable to snag anything.

He does what I do? Scheisse!

Klaus skidded to another halt, and spun to face the assassin while his mind raced. This man must have represented a tremendous leap in the Arzamas technology. Two manifestations of the Willenskräfte in the same body? Dual uses for the same Götterelektron? Even the mad genius von Westarp had never spoken of such a thing.

How do I fight myself? Reeling with the need to reassess and restrategize, Klaus backed off. He put himself just outside what he gauged to be the other ghost's leaping distance. The two men circled each other, heedless of walls, fire, and other obstructions.

The first tendrils of exhaustion, the slow burn of pent-up breath, raked Klaus's chest. There had been a time, long ago, when he'd routinely held his breath for minutes at a stretch. But he shoved aside the introspection to concentrate on the growing pressure in his chest.

If he shares my ability, he also shares my weakness. He can't breathe like this.

Marsh leapt out of his hiding spot. He darted through insubstantial Klaus and the equally ghostly assassin on his way to the dining room. There was nothing he could do.

Klaus and the assassin evaluated each other. It was a standoff. The first man to succumb to the ache in his lungs, to chance a hasty breath, would get a ghostly hand in the throat or heart.

Klaus passed through a burning wall. Golden flames on the exposed beams grew as quickly as the burning in his chest. The effort to hold his breath drew beads of ephemeral sweat on his forehead; it stung his eyes.

The Soviet agent showed no sign of strain. He watched Klaus with placid, unblinking eyes. Much as Klaus might have watched the other man many years ago, had their roles been reversed.

He bit his tongue, pursed his lips as the flush rose in his face. The old Reichsbehörde training failed him. All the tricks he'd learned—counting his heartbeats, willing blood from his limbs to his head—were useless against another copy of himself. And time had long since eroded the benefits of the physical training in his youth.

The Soviet agent frowned. He looked unconcerned. And that was when Klaus noticed the swell and ebb of his opponent's chest.

The son of a bitch was breathing. Insubstantial, yet breathing.

Their eyes met. The agent sighed as though bored.

Scheisse.

Klaus dived through the burning wall. He released the Götterelek-tron before he tumbled to the floor of the adjoining home, exhaling with an explosive sigh.

The pop of gunshots rang from next door.

Because SIS had evacuated the crescent before sunrise, the blinds and drapes were still drawn. They covered the windows as effectively as black-out curtains.

Will ran into an armchair where a door leading from the master bed-room to the corridor ought to have been. He sprawled face-first on a hard floor. Brick? It scraped his skin, tore his trousers. The chair flipped over, landing on him with a crash.

He thrashed, convinced that Cherkashin's man had tackled him, be-fore regaining his senses enough to extricate himself. He struggled to his feet. An end table and lamp wobbled next to the toppled chair, barely visible in the shadows. Will steadied them. He pulled the lamp chain. (Tiffany glass, azure dragonflies. Strange, the details that grab a person in desperate moments.)

The light lasted just long enough for him to realize this end unit of the crescent had been extensively remodeled. But then the lamp died with an audible *pop*. It startled Will. The lamp shattered on the floor.

Will found the corridor. He stumbled down the staircase, his knees still rubbery from the residual fear of being entombed alive. His foot-steps echoed in the cavernous vestibule. Any moment, he'd be discov-ered. Murdered.

He fumbled the locks open. But the door swung inward only a few inches before slamming to a halt. More precious seconds ticked away while Will heaved on the door. It wouldn't move. He didn't notice the chain until he'd tried several times to force the door. He yanked the chain out of its slot, threw the door wide, tripped over the sill, and stag-gered outside.

Marsh crouched in the dining room, watching helplessly while the German and Soviet supermen circled each other. Turning his head, swallowing, even breathing—every flexion of his wounded throat threatened to overwhelm him with agony. But the job wasn't finished.

Shit, shit, shit. How many things can this bastard do?

He was a ghost, like Klaus, and a salamander, like Reinhardt. What next? Would he become invisible? Fly? Tear the house apart with his mind?

And he was immune to EMP.

Flames spread from the foyer. They danced along the banister, up the stairs. Heat raked Marsh's face; he flipped the dining room table on its side, momentarily shielding himself from the flames. He thought about what he'd seen at the moment of Klaus's attack.

The corona had blinked out when the Soviet agent switched between his abilities. More than that. He'd flickered . . . as if he'd reverted to his normal form, just for an instant, before changing from salamander to ghost.

He can't be both at once.

Marsh kept his head low, ducking behind furniture as he scrambled to the parlor. There, half charred and reeking of pork, Anthony's body lay inside a circle of ash. He'd drawn his pistol before he died. Intense heat had constricted his flesh, curling his fingers into a skeletal grip; slivers of white bone peeked through cracks in the blackened muscle. The surge that had killed him had also ignited the window sashes. Draperies fell in burning clumps to the floor, past panes of sagging glass.

The Browning was hot to the touch, like the rest of Anthony. But the barrel hadn't wilted. The blast had been directed at his body rather than his weapon. Marsh peeled the dead man's fingers away, snapping them as necessary.

He returned to the foyer just in time to see Klaus dive through an adjoining wall. Marsh squeezed off a shot.

The bullet passed through the Soviet agent. It lodged in the wall through which Klaus had escaped, raising a puff of plaster that disappeared into the rising smoke. The agent turned, frowning. He saw Marsh. He flickered.

Marsh fired again, a fraction of a second too late. A shimmering corona engulfed the other man at the same instant Marsh pulled the trigger.

The bullet vaporized in a flash of violet light. The Soviet assassin stepped backwards, steadying himself.

"Where is William Beauclerk?" he said. His voice was calm, muted by the whoosh of his corona's updraft and the crackling of the burning house.

Marsh retreated. He fired again, and again. He'd missed his chance to kill the monster now advancing on him; all he could do was try to outlast the battery. Smoke tickled his ruined throat. He coughed. A new round of pain nearly caused him to black out.

"I grow tired of this," said the fiend. "Tell me. What have you done with William?" He stalked Marsh into the parlor.

Fumbling for the pin on the Mills bomb at his belt, Marsh stumbled past Anthony's body. The Soviet agent loomed over him, wreathed in flames like a demon.

Somewhere outside, tires screeched on pavement. The agent's head jerked up. He stared past Marsh, to the ruined windows and the street beyond.

"Ah. Never mind," he said. "Wait here." Then he turned and ran for the foyer.

Marsh cursed. He scrambled after the other man.

"Will!" he croaked. The burns had given his voice a gravel-and-whiskey rasp. Pain drove him to his knees. "Watch out!"

The street was empty.

"Damnation," Will gasped.

Where's the bloody lorry?

Pembroke will be waiting for you, they'd told him. *Just hop inside and ride to safety. Easy-peasy.*

A handful of parked cars lined the long, straight leg of the crescent. But nothing large enough to hide a surveillance team. Will glanced the other way, past the wide horseshoe curve of deserted town houses.

There. Across the crescent. Idling outside the *other* end unit, a boxy green Morris Oxford van painted with an advert for a gardening service.

Klaus had taken him out the wrong end. Or Pembroke had cocked it up, switched things around. Either way, Will found himself standing in the open, several hundred yards from his easy-peasy ride to safety.

And between the two, his own house. Where firelight flickered in the windows. Where plumes of smoke roiled through the wide-open front door.

Will waved his arms. "Hi, hi!" he yelled. "I'm here!"

The van didn't budge.

"Sod it all." Will sprinted across the street. "Good show, Pip," he muttered. "Very well done."

A low, wrought iron railing lined the park occupying the open space at the center of the crescent. He tripped over it. An ornamental spike snagged Will's trouser leg. He stumbled across the park, trailing the torn hem and still waving his arms.

"Hi, hi, over here!"

The crackle of sporadic gunfire echoed across the park. Will hit the earth. He covered his head and tried to make himself as small as possible. Much as he had during that terrible night in Germany so many Decembers ago.

The gunfire trailed off. Will allowed himself a peek across the park. The van still hadn't moved.

"Oh, yes, you're doing a brilliant job, aren't you?"

He took a deep breath, thought fleetingly of Gwendolyn, and set off on another sprint. Will had just passed his former house—which was burning like Crystal Palace now—when the van finally lurched forward with a grinding of gears. It zipped around the bend, nearly tipping when it swerved around a car parked too far from the curb.

It skidded to a halt between Will and the burning town house. The side door banged open. Pembroke leaned out, beckoning at him.

An unfamiliar voice yelled, "Will! Watch out!"

Will hopped the railing again and dashed across the street. He'd come within a few paces of the van when the asphalt softened underfoot. It pulled at his shoes. He staggered. Pembroke caught his hand. Shimmering waves of heat came surging around the van, making a mirage of the crescent beyond.

Klaus sagged against the wall, struggling to catch his breath. His chest ached. The wall grew warmer by the moment; the fire was spreading out of control.

He hacked up a gobbet of blood. It splattered on the floor. Breathing too hard irritated his damaged sinuses.

Breathing while insubstantial. He spit again. *Multiple abilities.* He stood. *What else haven't you told us, sister?*

Another flurry of gunshots. Klaus knew that was Marsh attempting to keep the Soviet agent busy, to force him to keep drawing on his battery. But Cherkashin's man drew upon the Götterelektron with wild abandon; Klaus hadn't seen such an extravagant demonstration of Willenskräfte since the Ardennes forest. The assassin's battery must have held a stupendous amount of charge.

Klaus glanced at his own battery. The needle rested a hairsbreadth above the red. Meaning the battery would soon fail.

But. If Marsh could keep their opponent occupied for just a few more seconds, long enough for Klaus to slip in behind him . . .

Ear pressed to the warm wall, he listened for another gunshot. It would give him a rough idea of Marsh's location, assuming the man still lived. Klaus would have to guess as to where the other man stood.

Crack. Another shot. Klaus inhaled deeply. But then the SIS van screeched to a halt on the street outside.

That wasn't supposed to happen. It ought to have been far away by now.

He glimpsed Will running for the van. Which meant the assassin was bound to see him as well.

Klaus called up his Willenskräfte in midstride. The copper taste filled his mouth again. He passed through the unfamiliar dining room like a ghostly wind and hit the street hard, heading for the van.

Every footstep was a struggle against passing out. The pain was becoming too much for Marsh to bear. But he staggered outside, following the Soviet agent down the stairs to street level.

The killer blazed brightly now, a vaguely human shadow wrapped in searing luminescence. Flames erupted from wooden window boxes while the calendulas inside shriveled and blackened. Iron handrails sagged in his wake. His passage even rendered the granite steps uncomfortably hot.

He was heading for the van. As was Will.

Marsh lobbed a Mills bomb. It disappeared in the corona. Explosives were pointless; even if the heat didn't destroy the grenade, the shrapnel would vaporize before it could touch the fucker. Marsh needed something larger.

He glanced up and down the crescent, desperately looking for anything useful.

The assassin strode to the curb. Asphalt bubbled beneath his boots. A wall of shimmering air spread from his corona, roiling toward the van. It splashed like a wave where it hit the vehicle, blackening and bubbling the paint.

Klaus leapt into the furnace.

The Götterelektron surged through Klaus's body. He funneled it through his outstretched fingers into the bumper. He willed the van and its human contents transparent to the hellish assault.

It was a momentary reprieve.

He watched the gauge needle sink deeper into the red. Current ebbed and surged through Klaus's wires. He struggled to keep the flow consistent, grappled with the sputtering death throes of his battery. He'd carried the battery all the way from Arzamas, but it was ready to fail.

The Soviet agent redoubled his efforts. Klaus and the van became an island in a lake of bubbling asphalt.

The van couldn't leave without Klaus inside; it would burn the moment he broke contact. But he couldn't move. Wrangling current from the dying battery took every bit of concentration he could muster.

Do something, Marsh. Do it now.

The needle sank deeper.

Come on. Come on.

Deeper.

There.

Marsh reloaded Anthony's pistol while sprinting past a row of parked cars toward a yellow sign marked with a bold "H." It indicated the location of metal plate in the street, and the fire hydrant beneath it.

The hydrant plate had a narrow hole for admitting a fireman's wrench. Marsh jammed the barrel into the hole and fired three shots. Next he twisted the pistol and heaved, using it as a lever to flip the plate open. Everything stank of melted asphalt.

He dropped a Mills bomb into the hydrant chamber. Then he kicked out the driver-side window of a black soft-top Triumph and took cover behind the driver-side door.

A muffled *whump* shook the street. A thirty-foot geyser erupted from the shattered water main. Marsh braced himself against the curb, lifted the hydrant plate, and angled it into the plume. The torrent drenched the street with cold rain, engulfing the Soviet agent in a cloud of steam.

Artificial rain fell in sheets. Water sizzled on the asphalt beneath the van. It soaked Klaus intermittently as his battery coughed up the last of its current.

He pounded on the van. With the last of his breath he managed, "Go! While he's blind!"

The driver revved the engine before throwing the van into gear. It jumped forward, rematerialized, then lurched to a crawl. Klaus threw himself clear of the roiling steam before filling his tortured lungs.

Flaming tires churned through soft asphalt. For a moment it looked as though the van wouldn't break free. But it gained just enough traction to inch forward. It accelerated. Ruined tires *slap-slap-slapped* on the solid roadway. They'd be driving on the rims before they reached the end of the crescent.

The van wouldn't get them very far, but it would get them away.

Marsh scrambled inside the Triumph. He hadn't boosted many cars in his youth, having preferred motorbikes, but the principle was the same. Precious seconds ticked away while the steam dissipated and he fiddled under the steering column with arthritic fingers.

The car sputtered to life. Marsh slammed it into gear and stomped the gas pedal.

It was a gamble. A gamble that the assassin hadn't flown away. That he hadn't become a ghost. That he wouldn't quit until Will was dead.

Marsh aimed for the heart of the cloud.

Inferno.

Agony.

Impact.

Darkness.

interlude

. . . three days to vacate your flat.
They will come for you. Flee.

The wood-dry scent of burnt toast tickled Reinhardt's nose. He used a fork to flip the bread slice sizzling on his electric skillet. Toast and jam, twice a day; that was his diet since abandoning the council estate flat. He couldn't afford anything else. Most of his cash had gone into the pockets of a Jew landlord, in the form of a deposit on a flat in Whitechapel.

Reinhardt had abandoned most of his electronic supplies at the flat. In the course of a single frantic night, he'd lost the collection amassed over years—decades—of painstaking work. There had been barely enough room in his car for the essentials.

But he didn't need his entire collection. Not any longer. He hadn't yet reconciled the findings in his own journals with Gretel's blueprint fragments, but he could infer the extent of the missing information. It wasn't unlike piecing together a picture puzzle: he knew the shape of the hole, and it was small.

The bread blackened while he reread Gretel's letter.

Yes, they know you're here. And no, dear Reinhardt, I am not the one who betrays you. It is my brother. He means well, but he doesn't understand. He doesn't understand what you and I are accomplishing.

"You and I?"

Each time he reached that line, his fingers twitched with the urge to crumple the letter and toss it away. But he didn't, because—

We're close now. If only you could see what I do. It's glorious.

"Of course I am, you gypsy lunatic."

He speared the bread and tossed it on a dinner plate. The Jew had threatened to evict him if he popped another fuse, so he took care to twist the hot plate control in the proper direction when turning it off. Reinhardt spread a spoonful of marmalade on the toast.

There is but one obstacle remaining. His name is Leslie Pembroke. . . .

From there she launched, finally, into more straightforward details. At least this time she didn't want things done yesterday.

He chewed, studying the photographs tacked on the wall. These he'd taken of his own accord, from the comfort of his own car, rather than from some miserable hiding spot in a rainy park. Pembroke leaving his house. Pembroke hailing a taxicab. Pembroke and his wife arriving at the theater.

Reinhardt didn't know who this man was, nor why he was so important to Gretel. He didn't care.

nine

I t's the children," said Pethick. "They're acting strangely."

Gwendolyn used the interruption as an excuse to sidestep another stillborn conversation. After Marsh had revealed Will's secret dealings with Cherkashin, it didn't seem possible Gwendolyn could have become any cooler, any more distant. He felt no warmth when her gaze touched him, read no affection in her body language. But she'd been forced to leave their home, by men she did not know. Will hadn't even been present for that. Another earthquake, widening the chasm between them.

Of course, they left it to him to tell her their house had been destroyed, along with most of their belongings. If before her demeanor had been cool, now it was frosty. Eye contact hurt like grabbing an iron railing on the coldest January night. Her body language had been rewritten in an indecipherable script. The chasm grew wider still.

The forced proximity made things so much worse. The crowded safe house didn't lend itself to the private, heartfelt conversations for which Will yearned; neither did it offer the physical separation that Gwendolyn needed. The closer he approached—physically, emotionally—the harder she pushed away. Like a pair of magnets, constantly repulsing one another.

And yet for all of that, she had adapted to the new circumstances with remarkable aplomb. Far better than Will had. She'd gone from weekly whist games and regular dinners with a duke to sharing a bathroom with the insane and somewhat disturbing product of a defunct Nazi experiment. Will knew his wife well enough to know the imperturbable grace was affected. But that was Gwendolyn. British to the very bottom of her soul.

Will watched as she retreated through the kitchen and out the back door to the garden. Klaus stood near the sundial with watercolors and an easel. Gwendolyn settled on a bench shaded by thick clumps of ivy carpeting the brick wall. A breeze rustled the ivy, teased her hair. Klaus nodded at her; she returned the greeting. Will wondered what they found in common, what point of conversational reference they shared.

Pethick cleared his throat. He had begun to run his tongue along the inside of his upper lip, looking bored. Will frowned at him. *Ah, yes. The children.* "And I'm to check on the poor demonic waifs. Is that so?"

This had been inevitable. He'd known that sooner or later Milkweed would make him their intermediary with the children in the Admiralty cellar. He'd known it from the moment Marsh had taken him downstairs.

"It would be a help. I'm headed there, to work with them a bit. We need your expert opinion."

Will raised an eyebrow. "Work with them?" Pethick didn't elaborate. "Very well, I'll tag along and take a peek into your cabinet of horrors. Would this be Pip's idea? Another punishment for me?"

Pethick shook his head. "He hasn't awoken yet. Still touch and go, from what I've heard."

That worried Will. For some reason unclear to him, he found he didn't want Raybould Marsh's name on the long list of people who had died because of him. He didn't even like Marsh, or the man he had become. But Will already had innocent British blood on his hands.

Will studied them. He flexed his fingers. Sometimes it amazed him that they should appear so clean. They ought to be mottled crimson, the nails caked and black. Stained down to the bone after all these years.

Out damned spot, and the rest.

And there was new blood as well, to Gwendolyn's point of view. Where he saw justice, she saw . . . Well, if not exactly murder, something equally reprehensible.

Will's memory of the escape was spotty. He'd been close to blacking out, unable to breathe while Klaus held the van insubstantial. The resulting headache, a low-level throb behind his eyeballs, had lingered for two days. Pembroke and Klaus had explained the details of his death after he had been reunited with Gwendolyn at the safe house. Will had read his own obituary in the previous morning's *Times*. It was longer than he'd expected, but generally favorable.

His funeral had been held that morning. Closed casket, of course, since the gas main explosion hadn't left a recognizable body. A pang of sorrow robbed him of breath; he wished he could see his brother again.

I'm sorry, Aubrey.

Forcing his thoughts back to Marsh, Will said, "He'll come around."

Pethick said, "Hope so. He's prickly, but he's good. Haven't worked with anyone quite like him."

"I'm quite certain that's true," said Will. He scratched a sudden itch at the stump of his missing finger. *My God. They've given you a name. . . .*

Will shivered. "You say they're acting strangely. How so?"

"Nurses say they're agitated. Excited," said Pethick. "They've been unruly."

What constituted normal for a ten-year-old warlock? The world hadn't seen such a thing in centuries. And doubtless was better for it.

"Children acting like children?" Will clucked his tongue. "Well, we certainly can't have that."

Pethick glared at him. "I asked politely. I didn't—"

"I know, I know," said Will. "It's not a request, and you didn't have to be polite about it. May I tell my wife I'm stepping out?"

"Of course."

Gwendolyn still chatted with Klaus. She broke off when Will leaned out the door.

He smiled at Klaus. The man had, after all, saved his life. Klaus had even apologized for mistakenly taking Will to the wrong end of the townhouse crescent. Will thought that was very decent of him.

He said, "You'll be ready for your own exhibition soon."

Klaus gave him a tired nod.

"Love, I'm stepping out for a bit. I'll return in an hour or two." He glanced at Pethick, who nodded.

"As you must," she said, each word limned in hoarfrost. And then resumed her conversation with Klaus.

Will wore green corduroy trousers and a teal shirt for the trip to the Admiralty. Partially because his entire wardrobe had been destroyed, and thus he had to avail himself of the limited selection at the Croydon house, but also because he had to dress as a different person in case anybody glimpsed him getting in or out of the car. He felt naked without his bowler. Strange, the things one misses.

Pethick drove. The Morris had darkened windows.

Before they entered the Admiralty basement, Pethick asked if Will were bleeding. (No.) Had he any unhealed wounds? Too many to count.

The arrangements were much as Will had expected, and no less terrible for it. Milkweed had strived for a veneer of normalcy in its mockery of a primary school classroom. The children's ages ranged more widely than he had expected. The oldest ones, perhaps in their late teens, might have been among the first to "graduate"; the youngest, the prodigies, were barely more than toddlers. Will's skin felt ready to crawl straight off his body, slink across the room, and shiver in a dark corner.

Shades of Dover, Will thought. That trip to the coast with Stephenson, back in the summer of '40, was where the seeds of this loathsome practice had been sown. Where Will had reluctantly explained the historical relationship between children and Enochian to the old man.

Quibble as he might over the fates of Hargreaves and those other bastards, there was no denying that the responsibility for this scene lay squarely at Will's feet. This was abuse. The psychological mutilation of children. And it was his doing.

He wanted to vomit. Some things were never acceptable under any circumstances.

Unacceptable, under any circumstances. Gwendolyn had said the same thing to him.

Will pulled out a chair. He dropped into it.

"Oh, Gwendolyn," he whispered.

Pethick said, "I beg your pardon?"

Will shook his head. "Unpleasant thought."

At this, Pethick looked alarmed. He thought Will meant the children. "What?"

"Never mind."

There was no excusing what had been done to these children. That was the bare, bald truth. And like a plunge into an icy river, the abrupt change of perspective stole his breath, constricted his chest. Will was no different from the men who had done this. No justification would ever acquit him of the things he'd done. He had to accept responsibility if he ever wanted to redeem himself and regain Gwendolyn's trust.

Will watched the children through a partition of one-way glass. They were a rambunctious lot. Running, yelling, playing. Even the oldest kids were part of the chaos, shouting and whirling, contributing to the controlled pandemonium of playtime. One could almost believe they were normal children, if not for the odd timbre to their voices. A layperson might have thought they were the victims of a rare degenerative disease, some strange illness that caused these children to speak with the ruined voices of haggard old men. But to Will's ears, the disturbing resonances revealed a first language that was not English. Not human.

A ghostly odor wafted through the viewing gallery just then. Hot sand; wet pasteboard; grapes left too long in the sun. A phantom mélange.

Pethick nodded at the children. "You see?"

"I see children playing. Deeply damaged children, but at least they're still able to play now and again."

"This isn't normal. They're typically quiet."

"Seen but not heard. That's how it should be, eh?"

Pethick leveled a hard stare at Will. "They do not," he said, "*frolic.*"

"I'm sorry to tell you this, but it appears they do," said Will, pointing at the window. Pethick glanced at his wounded hand. Will hid it away in a pocket, feeling self-conscious. He continued, "Nobody has performed this barbarous experiment for hundreds of years. Because it *is* barbarous. But leaving that aside for the moment, there's no way for you to know what's normal for these children. There are no records. Only scant hearsay."

"I have a new tasking for the children. Normally I would do this over the intercom—" He pointed at a microphone, and a speaker grille above the windowpane. "—but I think it would be best if you met the children directly. To take a closer look."

Tasking? That was a euphemism Will had hoped to never hear again. He tried to swallow the lump in his throat. It wouldn't move. A rivulet of sweat tickled the underside of his arm. "I will never," he managed, "participate in another negotiation."

Pethick didn't acknowledge this. He unlocked the door separating the viewing gallery from the "classroom." Will took a deep breath before following.

Will had never in his life felt at ease around tykes and tots. Gwendolyn said he had a knack for it, but he'd never seen any such indication. He didn't know how to converse with regular children. And he hadn't the faintest of inklings how to approach these.

He needn't have worried. The children ignored them.

Pethick frowned. He stepped around a pair of children who twirled in a circle—arms linked and caterwauling—to approach the maps hanging across from the one-way mirror.

Will followed him. The maps depicted the entire globe, although the emphasis was clearly on the Soviet Union. He inferred that the pushpins represented locations targeted by various "taskings." They were mostly confined to the sprawling USSR. But a handful of additional pins were scattered elsewhere, seemingly at random: Tanganyika Territory, the American Southwest, Nepal . . . even the Midlands—not far from

Bestwood, in fact. On the wall above the maps, somebody had taped a spread of pages from an American magazine, *Life,* containing an effusive article about the Soviet moon program. A handful of artist's renderings of the space station in orbit accompanied the article (rather well-done, though the artist's name, Bonestell, was a tad morbid). These, too, had pins.

"You've certainly kept them busy," said Will.

"This is odd," said Pethick. "The children have been moving pins about." He pointed at the pin in the United States. It was stuck firmly in the "x" of NEW MEXICO. "We've never done any taskings in America." He pointed at a few other pins. "Or here. Or here."

"Children play. Even I know that."

Pethick clapped, twice. "Hello, children," he said. That got their attention. The worst of the playtime chaos subsided after a few moments. The children turned to look at Pethick.

"Hello, Samuel," said one of the older boys. He stretched the word into three distinct syllables. *Sam-you-ell.* He looked at Will. "You are not alone, Samuel."

The boy spoke with an odd cadence. Random, like the flickering of starlight.

"This is William."

Will donned the bravest, most deceitful smile he could manage. He waved to the children.

The boy glanced at the network of thin white scars spiderwebbing Will's hand. He tipped his head, looking at Will sideways. "Are you one of us?"

Pethick said, "William is a friend. He's here to watch us today. Are you ready to work, children?"

They gathered around Pethick like fidgety ducklings. Will fell out of their worldview as quickly as he'd entered it. He backed away and slouched against a far wall. Partially to put more distance between himself and those horrible children, and partially to observe the process more clearly. Dread became a cannonball in his stomach.

Pethick fished around in the breast pocket of his suit coat and produced a pin. "Now," said Pethick, "whose turn is it today?"

A girl stepped forward. Her hair, wild and wavy corn silk, just brushed the ruffled shoulders of a lacy pink frock. The top of her head wouldn't have reached Will's waist, were they to stand together. Her round face still carried a hint of baby fat.

Will rubbed his eyes, wishing he could leave. But Pethick held the keys to the sally port at the bottom of the stairwell. Will dabbed his forehead with a handkerchief.

The girl offered her hand to Pethick. She made no sound, showed no discomfort, when he poked her index finger with the needle. He released her. She squeezed her fingertip until a crimson drop stained her pale skin.

Pethick wiped the pin clean. "And who remembers where Baikonur Cosmodrome is located?"

A handful of children went to the map of the south-central Soviet Union. They pointed to a bare section of the Kazakh SSR, a bit east of the Aral Sea.

"Well done," Pethick said. He assumed a more somber tone. "Now, children. The evil men, the ones who seek to harm us, they intend to launch another rocket soon." He pointed to the *Life* magazine illustrations. "It must fail."

"Rocket fail," said the boy who had greeted Pethick.

"Rocket fail," said the bleeding girl.

"Rocket fail," said the rest.

Another rivulet of sweat dripped from Will's underarm. It trickled down his side, hot like ice.

The boy repeated himself. The others responded, each child with a different cadence and intonation. But each in a manner that accentuated his or her unnatural accent. Brought it to the fore. The chorus continued with slowly increasing tempo until the children converged upon a single rhythm. They switched to Enochian in midchant.

Will was buffeted by a howling maelstrom of inhuman language. The rumbles, the gurgles, the fury of newborn stars and the death cries of galaxies ancient beyond knowing . . . everything an echo of his old life.

And all incomprehensible. It made no sense. Granted, his Enochian was rusty. More than that: cursed and abandoned. Yet he found himself struggling to attain even a fingerhold on this eldritch grammar of intent.

One facet of the problem was old and familiar. Enochian was far too ancient to encompass a concept like "rocket." During the war, Milkweed's warlocks had spent countless hours devising workable circumlocutions in order to express the things they needed. It was difficult, dangerous work. These children had been at this long enough—judging from the maps and pushpins—that they'd devised their own shorthand. An Enochian creole.

Will strained to make sense of the pandemonium. It was as though these children spoke a different dialect of Enochian, although he knew that was impossible. Dialects were a human construct. Part of it, he realized, was that these children spoke Enochian without inhibition. They were raised on it; perhaps they even *thought* in Enochian. But if they held the grammar in their minds, stored it in brains pulsing with human blood—

His train of thought progressed no further. Shadows cast by the fluorescents in the ceiling writhed and shuddered; the floor canted. The air assumed the cloy of rot and tingle of aftershave, making it a chore to breathe. A vast consciousness filled the room. Cold and crushing, darker than the bottom of the sea.

The children had called forth an Eidolon almost as easily as they might have called for their mothers. Which perhaps, in a way, they had. Another terrifying thought.

The Eidolon spoke. Its voice was the thunder of creation and the silence of a lifeless universe. Even the children could produce only a pale imitation of pure Enochian. They were, after all, merely flesh. But that wasn't all. The Eidolon sounded different from every other negotiation he'd attended. Beyond the enormity of its presence, beyond the ever-present undercurrent of malice, it sounded . . . agitated. If he hadn't known better, he might have said it was excited. Impatient. He trembled.

Will turned his back on the Enochian call-and-response of the negotiation. He staggered into the viewing gallery, closed the door behind him, and huddled in a chair. After a moment he reached up and ripped the wire out of the speaker above the one-way glass. Killing the speaker did nothing to keep out the Eidolon, didn't insulate the gallery from the fact of its presence. There was no insulating oneself from something that brushed the world through cracks in time and space.

One part of the negotiation came across clearly. The blood price: three souls. Milkweed would buy this act of sabotage with the blood of three innocent civilians. Poor, unsuspecting sods chosen at random by Pethick and his team of killers.

What will it be, Sam? Will you set fire to somebody's house? Cut the brake lines on an omnibus? Or perhaps you can arrange for a piece of masonry, a molded cornice, to topple loose and smash into the flow of pedestrians along Shaftesbury. A well-aimed corbel could easily take out a couple strolling hand in hand.

All for the greater good of the British Empire.

Will drew his knees up to his chest and wrapped long arms around his legs. But hugging himself didn't chase the chill away, didn't lessen his shivering.

He sat that way until the Eidolon departed. Pethick appeared to thank the children. The children resumed the activities they'd been pursuing when the adults had arrived. As though the past half hour hadn't happened at all.

Pethick entered the viewing gallery. "Well?"

"Your problem isn't the children. It's the Eidolons. Something has worked them into a frenzy."

2 June 1963
Croydon, London, England

It surprised Klaus that Gwendolyn would choose to converse with him at all, much less be pleasant about it. He knew little about her. Only that she was married to Will, that she now lived in hiding, and that she shared a bathroom with Gretel.

But she didn't mention any of that. She complimented his painting. (She wasn't a convincing liar.) When he asked, she explained the upcoming celebration of the Queen's Birthday, which he had seen mentioned on the television. (A strange thing, that television. Klaus had known of the idea, but he'd never actually seen one until his arrival in Britain.) And she surprised him by revealing a passing familiarity with the German philosophers: Goethe, Schiller, Nietzsche.

Klaus had been exposed to quite enough of Nietzsche in his youth. He felt no desire to spend another minute ruminating over *Zarathustra* or *The Gay Science*. But Schiller! Doctor von Westarp had included Schiller in the reading curriculum at the farm, though he hadn't pounded the point home as obsessively as he had with Nietzsche. The doctor had emphasized Schiller's notion of *Pflicht und Neigung,* the harmony of duty and inclination.

Those lessons had returned to Klaus over the past few weeks. Schiller had much to say about beauty and freedom.

Do you have a beautiful soul, Gwendolyn? Do I? Does any living person?
Gretel didn't. That he knew for certain.

Gwendolyn broke off in midsentence when Will leaned outside. He smiled at Klaus, pronounced another well-meaning lie about his painting ability. Klaus understood Will's overtures; he had, after all, participated in saving the man's life. But the platitudes grated on him.

For one thing, he wished he could be alone, to paint in solitude. But more maddening was how nobody said a word about the agreement he'd made with Marsh prior to the battle with Will's would-be assassin. Neither Pethick nor Pembroke had shown any indication that they even knew of the deal, much less that they'd honor it. Once again, Klaus had chosen to trust the wrong person. Marsh has used him just as efficiently as Gretel might. Klaus's one attempt to inform his own destiny had been a pointless failure. He'd never be free.

He gave Will a polite nod, then rinsed his brush in a jar while Will and Gwendolyn had a brief awkward exchange. Madeleine had cleaned the empty marmalade jar before presenting it to him as a supplement to his painting supplies. It was useful.

Will departed. The closing door sent a gust of air across the garden, rattling the easel. Klaus lunged for the canvas, which sent his disconnected wires flying in a wild arc about his head. It made him feel conspicuous. Vulnerable. Especially in front of a stranger.

After steadying the easel, he turned his back to Gwendolyn. Then he moved the wires so that the bundle dangled down his chest, where she wouldn't see them.

"You needn't be ashamed."

Klaus concentrated on painting. Clean, steady strokes.

Gwendolyn said, "You weren't a victim of the camps, were you? You were part of that project, during the war. William explained it to me."

Her voice carried a tremor of wistfulness. He glanced over his shoulder to study her face. There was, around her eyes, a minute crack in her façade. Gwendolyn put up a good front, but it was just that. A front.

"He told me all about the war," she continued. "About Milkweed. About the Reichsbehörde."

Ah. So that was why she had come outside.

He told you about it, but you've never seen *it. And you want to. You want to understand the incomprehensible things that have brought you here. To witness firsthand the things that ripped your life apart.*

Klaus focused his attention on the easel. "It wasn't a wartime project. The war was only the end of it."

"The incredible things he told me. They're all true, aren't they?"

"I don't know what he told you," said Klaus. He chose a finer brush and moistened its tip in a tin of ivory black.

"He described a group of Germans who could . . . do things. Things that other people couldn't."

"Did he confess that he also belonged to such a group? A group of men capable of unnatural things?"

She answered with a slow, melancholy nod. "And that they did wretched things for the sake of this country. Of that I have no doubt." She paused, choosing her words. "William was ill for a long time after the war. I knew he meant the things he said. He believed every incredible word of it. But it was *so* incredible, the entire story. I've always wondered if parts of it had perhaps been the illness speaking."

"You want to see a demonstration."

Gwendolyn drew a long, shuddery breath. "Yes."

Klaus shook his head. "I have no battery."

"Oh," she said. One syllable fraught with so much disappointment. "I very much would have liked. . . ." She trailed off.

"I cannot help you," he said.

She fell silent after that. The wind picked up. Open blue sky retreated before a line of ash gray clouds that came scudding from the west. The wind smelled of summer rain. Diffuse sunlight brightened and dimmed through the shifting cloud cover. It made it difficult to gauge colors correctly. What was meant to be purple black became jet black one moment, midnight blue the next.

Klaus tore the sheet from the canvas. His painted ravens lacked the dark iridescence of the real birds. Pathetic imitations. Wet watercolors trickled down his fingers when he crumpled the paper.

"What a shame," said Gwendolyn. "I wanted to see the finished product."

"It's nothing. An image from an old dream."

The first misty raindrops fell while Klaus assembled his painting supplies. Gwendolyn held the door while he carried them inside.

"I understand you were part of the group that saved my husband. Thank you," she said.

She retired to her room. The mist became a summer shower. Klaus washed his hands at the kitchen sink while rain sluiced between the paving stones of the garden.

He could hear the television in the next room. Something about the United States. Klaus peeked from the kitchen. Gretel sat on the floor, braiding her hair while the screen showed images of tatterdemalion men and women standing in long lines for bread, or pleading for work. The American Depression was well into its fourth decade. The scene changed to New York, where vast crowds of people jostled for a rare spot in the emigration lottery.

Klaus stowed his supplies a few minutes before Pembroke arrived for the next debriefing session. Normally he left the questioning to Pethick and Marsh. Pethick alone had run the previous session, since Marsh was incapacitated. The other Milkweed agents, Roger and deceased Anthony, had been excluded from the sessions from the be-ginning.

Madeleine had set a tea service, a plate of finger sandwiches, and a reel-to-reel tape recorder on the low walnut table in the den. She pointed at Klaus's hand and winked before closing the paneled door behind herself, leaving the two men to their conversation. He'd missed a spot; his damaged ring finger was stained a muddy brown. The stain felt slick on his rough skin.

Would Pembroke believe him if he explained the deal he'd made with Marsh? Cooperation in the ambush for a new identity? No. The only wit-ness to their agreement was in the hospital, maimed and unconscious.

"Let's begin, shall we?" Pembroke activated the recorder. *Clunk.* He opened his ledger, uncapped a fountain pen. The scent of sweet pipe tobacco wafted out of his clothing.

Klaus nibbled on a sandwich. It was damp and salty.

Pembroke's opening question was an abrupt departure from the line of investigation built over previous sessions. That questioning had been focused on the work at Arzamas-16.

"Tell me, Klaus. On the day the Red Army occupied the REGP, in 1941, where were the Twins?"

3 June 1963
Lambeth, London, England

Consciousness returned slowly. The struggle to become alert felt like swimming up for air after a deep plunge in a lake of treacle. Gradu-ally, the haze of fever dreams and painkillers receded, replaced by something that might have been awareness. Moments of lucidity came and went, punctuated by sleep, sedation, fire, pain.

Shadows. Sounds. Textures. Smells. Perceptions of the outside world flickered through Marsh's awareness like fragments of a burnt and bro-ken filmstrip.

Bedside whispers. Footsteps echoing on a hard floor. The odor of antiseptic.

Something rough and wet on his face. Itching. Cloth?

Something sharp in his arm. Stabbing. Needle?

Something warm, almost hot, in his hand. Holding it. Soft fingers, caressing his.

Liv.

His mouth was a desert. He worked up enough saliva to wet his tongue. He swallowed.

The saliva became sandpaper. Worse. Liquid fire trickled down his throat. He coughed. A bomb went off in his esophagus. Raked his windpipe with shrapnel.

A whisper tickled his ear. "Don't try to speak, darling. You've been badly injured."

Gretel.

Marsh ripped his hand out of her grasp. The needles in his arm pinched him, punished him for moving. He sank back into the pillows, still groggy from sedation.

"The doctors thought you might not recover," Gretel said. "But I assured them you would."

He remembered the fight at Will's town house. Remembered how their plan had failed. Remembered the Soviet agent killing Anthony, beating seven shades of shit out of them. Remembered boosting a car, driving it at a man who blazed like the sun. Nothing after that.

He didn't know how long he'd been under. A day? Felt like longer.

He cracked his eyes open. His right eye opened freely. Cold, sterile hospital light flooded painfully into his blurry, dark-adapted vision. Opening the left was more difficult. It creaked open, pushing against inflexible tissue and stiff adhesive. A swath of gauze bandages traced the side of his face and neck.

He was in a private room, with a window looking out on the corridor. A lady strode past the window too quickly for him to see her properly. A nurse, or a perhaps a nun.

"How long?" His voice came out in an unrecognizable rasp. He coughed again. The pain made his head swim. He nearly blacked out. A fingertip brushed his lips.

Gretel said, "You've burned your throat. Use this." She held up a writing slate, like the kind he'd used as a schoolboy. A dusty, gray black writing surface in a wooden frame, with a moist sponge hanging from one corner and a piece of chalk from another. She placed it on his stomach.

The door opened. Roger peeked inside. He frowned at Gretel, suspicious of her. "Thought I heard something." His expression brightened when he saw Marsh. "Ho! Welcome back, boss. I figured you'd gone for a Burton."

Marsh tipped his head in Gretel's direction, then frowned at Roger, shrugging.

"She said you'd be comin' round today. Said she oughta be here."

You don't work for her. Marsh underlined it. Twice.

At least Roger had the grace to look sheepish. "The boss wanted me keeping an eye on you. So I was comin' here anyway."

How long? he wrote.

Gretel said, "Four days."

Four days!

Wife? he wrote.

"Don't worry," said Roger. "She knows you're here. We notified her, uh, when we thought you'd kick. She's been stopping by every day."

"Poor Liv," said Gretel.

Tap, tap, tap went the chalk: *Where?*

"St. Thomas's," said Roger.

"He needs rest," said Gretel. She took the slate, hooked it over the railing of his hospital bed. To Roger's questioning glance, Marsh closed his eyes and nodded.

Marsh woke an indeterminate time later, again with somebody's fingers twined in his.

He opened his eyes. The room was dark; somebody had turned off the overhead lights. The corridor lights had been dimmed as well. Night, then. The gauze on his face was cool and moist; it had been replaced while he slept.

Liv sat alongside his bed, silhouetted by the soft glow through the window. Her eyes glimmered. Her face was puffy from crying, milky skin slackened by age; wisps of auburn hair had escaped from where she'd pulled it back. Liv dropped his hand and pushed away, retreating into her chair, when she saw his open eyes studying her.

"Liv," he managed. The blackness almost took him again.

"They say you've scarred your vocal cords. That your voice will sound like that from now on." She raised one hand hesitantly, as if to touch him again. "And your face . . ." She pulled her hand back, let it drop to her lap.

"Liv," he croaked again. The world went purple around the edges.

"This is the sort of thing that happens to bureaucrats at the Foreign Office, is it? Occupational hazard? Is that what I'm to believe?"

How could he explain this to her? Perhaps it was a side effect of the painkillers, but he couldn't see a way to reconcile this with his cover. He'd been a better liar in his youth.

"I'm not a fool, Raybould. First you turn up in the hospital, burned and dying. And then I hear on the telly that poor Will is dead, killed in a gas main explosion."

They didn't own a television. He wondered where she had heard this.

Well. At least Milkweed had managed to construct a suitable cover story for the events in Knightsbridge.

"You've always been so angry. Did you . . ." Liv's voice dropped to a hoarse whisper. "Did you murder Will? Did you burn his house down?"

"No!" The shout tore something. Marsh coughed on the hot, salty trickle in the back of his throat. Next came a chunk of something soft and bitter. He struggled to swallow it without sicking up. Time passed while he rallied the strength to open his eyes again.

Liv stood. "I thought I was a widow." She crossed her arms beneath her breasts, as if hugging herself. She paced, down one side of his bed and up the other. "I've told you, Raybould. I won't let you abandon me with John. I can't care for him by myself. I won't."

She paused in the shadows at the foot of his bed. "Don't you *dare* leave me. Not with John."

He tried to say, "I wouldn't if I could." But the agony of speech overwhelmed him.

He didn't recognize his own voice. He couldn't tell if Liv understood him. But her bottom lip trembled, there in the half light at the end of the bed.

Only now, when he couldn't speak, did he long for a real conversation with Liv. So many things he wanted to say, needed to say . . . The look on her face, the tremor in her voice, her footsteps when she paced all told him she felt the same need. Things left long unsaid had almost become forever unsaid. He wondered if things would change between them.

She sniffled. "They had me do up the forms for my widow's pension."

Marsh nodded. He had negotiated that into his deal with Pembroke, as a precaution in case something happened to him while unraveling Gretel's web. As it very nearly had.

Liv perched on the edge of the chair at Marsh's bedside, like a bird ready to take flight. She didn't hold his hand.

Marsh's attending physician was a tall and amiable Irishman named Butler, whose frequent smiling revealed a gap between his front teeth. Butler's medical career had begun during the war, treating downed RAF pilots. Those few who survived the Luftwaffe and the crashes often suffered from massive second- and third-degree burns over much of their bodies. Marsh's injuries, he insisted, were petty in comparison.

They didn't feel petty. Particularly after Butler dialed back the morphine dosage. The boric acid in Marsh's bandages went from hardly noticeable to a minor itch to pins and needles raging across half his face. Swallowing became painful enough to make him wince. Sleep became difficult.

Pembroke placed a small potted fern on the bedside stand; the long, feathery leaves drooped over the edge of the table. Marsh watched through his eyelashes while Pembroke stood hesitantly alongside the bed, unsure of whether he ought to stay or leave. Marsh opened his eyes and motioned for him to sit.

Pembroke said, "Your doctor tells me you're a 'right tough bastard.'"
He cracked a smile. "I'd have to agree with his diagnosis. Though I'm
not a physician."

Marsh's shrug tugged on the sutures beneath the bandages along his
neck. It hurt.

"It was touch and go for a bit, but you'll be out of here before long.
I must say, I'm glad for that. You've done a remarkable job." He laid a
hand on Marsh's shoulder. "Quick thinking, using the water main. The
lot of us would be nothing but ash now if not for your resourcefulness."
He took his hand back. "We were grossly unprepared for Cherkashin's
man. And for that, I apologize."

Marsh lifted the slate from its resting place on his bed rail. *Will?* he
wrote.

"Safe," said Pembroke. "Officially he's dead, of course. The fire provided a convenient cover story."

The sponge had dried out. Marsh moistened it in the cup of water on
the bedside stand before wiping the slate clean. *Klaus?*

"He came through without a scratch. I've thanked him as well."

Next to Klaus's name, Marsh added, *Arrangement?*

Pembroke looked puzzled. "Arrangement?" He shook his head.
"No. I've made no arrangements with him."

Apparently Klaus hadn't brought up the deal he'd struck with
Marsh. There wouldn't have been any point, had Marsh died in the hospital. Marsh lacked the patience to spell out their deal on the tiny slate;
Klaus would have to wait a few more days until Marsh could speak
without shredding his vocal cords.

Assassin? Marsh erased this immediately after flashing it to Pembroke,
lest a nurse or doctor enter.

Again, Pembroke shook his head. "There wasn't much left, after you
drove into him. That chap melted half the bonnet before you made contact; his body was fused into the metal. It was hard enough getting you
out of that wreck and into an ambulance without compromising the situation. But we managed to get a tarpaulin over the car quickly enough.
We loaded the entire mess onto a flatbed lorry and hauled it to a ware-
house down on the docks." Marsh nodded; he knew the place, an SIS

holding. The sutures throbbed again. "We've loaded the place with dry ice, to preserve the remains, but . . ."

Marsh closed his eyes. He sagged back into his pillows. So much for learning anything useful.

"Lincolnshire Poacher remains silent."

Marsh sighed. Of course it would be.

"But," said Pembroke, "speaking of which, we think we know how Cherkashin is communicating with his handlers back in Moscow."

Marsh raised his eyebrows.

"Klaus has confirmed the Soviets captured one of the Twins during the raid on von Westarp's farm. He claims to have seen her loaded onto a truck."

Marsh rolled his eyes, slammed his head back into his pillow. A suture popped. *The Twins. Of course, of course, of course.*

Doctor von Westarp had labored for decades in his quest to capture Nietzsche's "will to power." At the foundling home he ran as a front for gruesome medical experiments, he went to horrific lengths to sculpt an Overman from the soft clay of abandoned children. And years later, under the patronage of Heinrich Himmler, he succeeded. By 1939 he'd created four men and four women capable of impossible feats: Gretel, Klaus, Reinhardt, Kammler, Rudolf, Heike, and a pair of nameless identical twins.

The Twins had a very specific ability, but a damn useful one. They saw through each other's eyes, heard through each other's ears, each feeling everything the other did. They were useless for combat. But they were a superb channel for ultra-secure communications. With one Twin in Berlin and her sister stationed elsewhere, the German High Command was free to relay the most sensitive orders and receive the most detailed reports without recourse to encryption or burst transmissions.

Marsh's mind raced. He broke the chalk in his haste to scrawl, *The other?*

The broken fragment clicked on the floor. It rolled beneath the cot, leaving a faint powdery trail.

Pembroke said, "He doesn't know where the Jerries had her stationed.

But. Hard to believe she wasn't somewhere in Europe. Perhaps even Germany. It's a safe bet Ivan has her, too."

Of course he did. Hindsight made it bloody obvious. Why hadn't he reread the archives, scoured the Schutzstaffel operational records he'd retrieved from Germany? He ought to have refreshed his memory the day he returned to Milkweed. If he had, he'd have made the connection at once. But he'd refused to admit to himself that he'd gone soft, that he needed a refresher. That his prime was well in the past.

But none of that mattered now. The Soviets' slow, methodical elimination of the original Milkweed warlocks suggested they were gearing up for something. Something big. Marsh had warned Pembroke about this. And now they knew, based on the Knightsbridge debacle, that Arzamas-16 had succeeded in re-creating and improving the original REGP technology.

Taken as a whole, it meant Ivan planned to unveil the Communist equivalent of the SS's Götterelektrongruppe. To make the world tremble before the inexorable might of the Soviet Union.

But that hadn't happened yet. If it had, Pembroke wouldn't have wasted time with small talk and pleasantries. What stayed Ivan's hand? Cherkashin and his handlers had saved Will for last, and now Will was dead, as far as the outside world was concerned. For what were they waiting?

Alongside *The other?* Marsh drew an arrow pointing to *Will's death,* and another arrow from that to *Confirmation?*

Pembroke nodded. "Yes. That was our conclusion. Our friend Cherkashin runs a tight ship, doesn't he? Not one for breaking protocol."

Deducing that protocol wasn't difficult for somebody well versed in tradecraft. Will's death had been all over the news. No doubt Cherkashin had heard of it. So had his handlers in Moscow. But it could be elaborate subterfuge. Disinformation. So they wouldn't act until he personally confirmed Will's death, via the Twins, and Cherkashin wouldn't do that until he'd received his own confirmation from the assassin.

Which was a shame. The children down in the Admiralty basement would make a nasty surprise for the Soviets. Milkweed was poised to chop Ivan off at the knees, if only he'd step into the open.

But they could coax him out. If only they had one of the Twins . . .

And Marsh knew exactly where to find her. He thought back to Will's debriefing sessions. They'd questioned him at length about the embassy. Which is how Will had come to mention the guard posted outside a steel-banded door.

Tap, tap, tap went the chalk while Marsh outlined his idea to Pembroke.

Gretel returned. She tried to take Marsh's hand again. He pulled away. "Don't touch me," he managed.

"Rest your voice," she said. "Use this." She rested the slate on his lap again.

Don't touch me, he wrote.

"Your bandages come off today," said Gretel.

Why are you here?

She frowned, as though it were obvious. "Your bandages come off today."

He started to call for Roger, but raising his voice tossed him into another choking fit. He swallowed blood and flecks of sour tissue. Gretel put a hand on his chest and gently pushed him back to the pillows. "Relax."

Her hand felt warm through the thin fabric of his hospital gown. It lingered. Marsh couldn't reach up to knock it away without tugging painfully on a needle or his sutures. She smiled at him.

"—weaned from the painkillers entirely over the next several weeks, though it may be difficult."

The door opened. Dr. Butler held it for Liv, apparently while discussing Marsh's care. She entered, nodding halfheartedly as she took in the doctor's instructions. Gretel's hand dropped to her lap.

Oh, no, thought Marsh. *Not now!*

They had a chance to reconnect. It wasn't his imagination. He'd felt it during Liv's visit. She'd held his hand while he slept. But Gretel's presence may have already destroyed the thaw in his relationship with Liv.

Liv began to ask Butler a question, but stopped when she saw Gretel sitting on the edge of Marsh's bed. "Who is this bint? Your girlfriend?"

Gretel stood. "Hello, Olivia. Raybould and I work together." She took Liv's hand in both of hers. "I'm so pleased to finally meet you."

Liv frowned at her. But the glare met Gretel's eyes only for a moment. She flinched away when she saw the wires. She hugged herself again.

"Well, isn't the Foreign Office a truly fascinating place," she murmured. More loudly, she said, "I didn't realize you fancy Jerry girls. *Raybould.*"

How on God's earth could he explain Gretel? Liv, please meet Hitler's secret weapon. She's insane, cold-blooded, and clairvoyant. She's been obsessed with me longer than I've known you. Nobody knows why.

Gretel killed our daughter.

Sod it all for a game of soldiers, he decided. *Liv deserves the truth.*

He steeled himself against the inevitable pain. "Gretel—," he began, but Butler cut him off by laying a friendly hand over his mouth.

"Not yet. Give your voice another day's rest. Use the slate if you must." To the women, he said, "He mustn't get too worked up before I remove the bandages and sutures."

Gretel slid her arm into the crook of Liv's elbow. Liv flinched again. "Let's step outside while the doctor cares for your husband."

Marsh tried to yell through Butler's hand. "Get away from her!" But yelling merely distorted his ruined voice, and the doctor's hand muffled it into meaningless noise.

Liv paused, frowning. Gretel nudged her toward the door. Butler pulled a syringe from the pocket of his long white coat. He uncapped it with his teeth and spit the plastic cap aside.

"Look," he whispered, leaning over Marsh to slide the needle into his shoulder, "I'm sure it's quite distressing, your wife and mistress meeting like this, but what's done is done." His thumb depressed the plunger. "You must relax."

"Liv, don't let that bitch get her claws into you," Marsh mumbled.

When he woke, Liv and Gretel were gone. The doctor stood over him.

"We're finished," he said. "How do you feel?"

Marsh stared up at him through bleary eyes. He blinked groggily. *Finished? Oh. The bandages.*

He reached up to touch his face. His fingers traced a furrow of scar tissue that extended from the corner of his left eye to the edge of his jaw and across his throat. It was hard and smooth, like a leather coat forgotten in a rainstorm and dried in the sun. The skin beneath his fingertips felt nothing.

"Easy, easy," Butler said. He held a shaving mirror in one hand. "It's important for you to accept that your body image is going to change. That takes time. But it's equally important to remember you're the same man you were prior to your automobile accident." With that, he handed the mirror to Marsh.

He didn't recognize himself. The mirror shattered on the floor.

The scar was longer and wider than he expected. An ugly furrow of puckered flesh covered half his face. The damaged skin was shiny and pink where it had burned, and cleaved down the center where the sutures had held it together. Now it itched like mad.

Butler said, "I advise you against shaving, for the time being. Further irritations to your skin could cause keloid scarring."

The warning was unnecessary. Marsh had already decided to grow a beard. With luck, it would hide the worst of his scars, lessen his disfigurement.

He dressed while Butler explained how to clean and care for his scars. The instructions didn't register, because Marsh was fixated on finding Liv and getting her away from Gretel. His foot bounced impatiently on the linoleum floor while Butler wrote two prescriptions, one for antibiotics and the other for painkillers.

Marsh managed a growly, "Thank you," before hurrying from the room.

Liv and Gretel were seated on a bench in the corridor, where everything smelled of sterilizing bleach. Liv was slumped against the smaller woman, head on her shoulder. Gretel had an arm around Liv. Liv shuddered. Her eyes were red, as was her runny nose.

"I had such high hopes, that day in the garden. . . . Everything was supposed to be perfect and wonderful from then on," said Liv, her voice heavy with the release of pent-up sorrow. Gretel hugged her. "It was before the war started. Before Williton . . ." She fidgeted with a scrap of pasteboard in her lap.

It stopped Marsh in his tracks. Liv had carried the evacuation tag receipt in her handbag ever since the day they'd said good-bye to their infant daughter at Paddington Station, back during the worst days of the Blitz. It was the other half of the perforated tag they'd clipped to Agnes's clothing. The evacuee number was still faintly visible on the creased and worn pasteboard: *21417.*

Gretel whispered to Liv. Liv shuddered again. Gretel gently offered a handkerchief to wipe away her tears.

Marsh knew in an instant what had happened while he'd been sedated. Gretel had given his wife the sympathetic ear she'd long missed. Gretel had looked ahead (how many years?) and foreseen a path for slipping her poisoned nettles around Liv's heart. In return, Liv unburdened herself to Gretel, confessed feelings she'd never expressed even to her own husband. And along the way, she unwittingly gave Gretel everything she needed to know in order to orchestrate the bombing raid that had killed their infant daughter.

Gretel had known so much about them during those confusing days in 1940 . . . and it had all come from Liv. Today. In 1963.

It staggered him, this first peek behind the curtain. Even his rage quailed when confronted by the sheer scope of Gretel's manipulations. The world was her loom; she weaved paradox and sorrow in equal measure.

You miserable bitch. Marsh's hands curled into fists, his physical agony forgotten. He started forward again, savoring the release, anticipating the sensation of wrapping his fingers through her wires, feeling the electrodes crack their way out of her skull like hatchling chicks on Easter.

Gretel saw him. Liv felt her shift; she looked up. Her face was a mask of grief and confusion.

He recognized the depth of that sorrow because he met it in the mirror every morning. But Liv didn't recognize him. Not through the scars, the tears, and the fog of memory. Not for several heartbeats.

Which was just enough time for his rage to become an impotent fury. He couldn't drag Gretel out of the hospital by her braids. Not without telling Liv the truth about what she'd just done. That this, combined with Gretel's madness, was what had killed Agnes.

It would break Liv.

Marsh knew he couldn't do that. Even if the price was losing his chance to reconnect with Liv and to finally have his revenge on Gretel. He couldn't subject Liv to that much self-hatred.

Gretel studied his ruined face and smiled.

ten

8 June 1963
Croydon, London, England

Marsh's release from the hospital was the pebble that started an avalanche. Events unfolded quickly after he returned to the safe house. They had to. This year's celebration of the Queen's Birthday fell on the third Saturday of June. It made for a hard deadline, just nine days after Marsh returned.

At least, Will thought it was Marsh. The man called himself Marsh, acted like Marsh, even cracked his knuckles like Marsh. But the hospital had been a cocoon, housing a ghastly metamorphosis. The sandpaper rasp where his voice had been; the ugly wreck of his face, etched with a serpentine scar; the salt-and-pepper stubble where before he'd always been clean-shaven. Speaking more than a few sentences at a time caused him to flinch. He moved gingerly, even eating and swallowing with measured deliberation. And, like the man he'd always been, he bore the burden stoically. Alone.

But sometimes, when he thought nobody was watching, Marsh would sag against a desk or wall or chair, and toss another painkiller tablet into his mouth. Will, who knew something of finding escape in painkillers, watched him. In Will's case, it had been to escape a quiet, invisible agony. Marsh's agony was seared into his face for all to see.

Marsh had become the physical embodiment of Will's self-delusion. An unassailable contradiction to the comforting lies Will had told himself. Will had justified his arrangement with Cherkashin by convincing himself the only victims were the warlocks themselves: men who deserved their fates.

But Marsh's disfigurement was a direct result of Will's actions. Did he deserve that fate?

No.

Will had done this. Marsh wasn't dead (they called it miraculous, but they didn't know just how stubborn he could be), but his blood still stained Will's hands. Will's recklessness had maimed an innocent man. Marsh had become a mirror, an enchanted looking glass, reflecting a hideous truth behind Will's beautiful lies. Thanks to Gwendolyn, Will had begun to overcome his wounds. But Marsh would never overcome this. There was no healing it.

Will had entered this venture cloaked in righteous self-pity. The cloak fit no longer.

He wondered what Marsh had told Liv. Will had taken such a fancy to her, so long ago. And though he hadn't thought much about her in the intervening years, he found he couldn't bear the thought of Liv blaming him for what had become of her husband. Although, of course, she ought.

Will had his own part to play in Milkweed's preparations. If things worked according to plan over the next several days, the tenor of the negotiations was going to change. It was Will's job to ensure the children weathered the transition smoothly. Being dead, he no longer had access to the safe in his office at the foundation. But Stephenson—that cold, methodical bastard—had of course seen fit to copy the master lexicon Will had assembled from the individual journals of the warlocks recruited for the war effort. Pethick retrieved a copy from the Admiralty vault on their next visit to the children.

The work came with unintentional and unwelcome consequences. If Marsh's situation was enough to shatter Will's self-delusion, every minute spent in the Admiralty cellar made it more difficult for Will to believe himself a victim of the past. Those awful children were the true victims. Of abuses that sprang directly from Will's own actions. His evasions, the adroit self-justifications, these failed in that demonic class-room.

Will admitted everything to Gwendolyn, one evening in the safe house.

He sprawled on a sofa in the den, long legs dangling over the edge while the top of his head nudged up against her leg. It was the first time she'd let him touch her since the day Marsh had appeared on their doorstep. They held that arrangement a long time while he owned his actions.

"You were right. I am sorry."

She twirled a finger through his thinning hair. "Do you know what I think?" she said.

"That your father might have been on to something when he ordered you to reject my marriage proposal?"

A sad smile touched her lips. From Will's vantage, peering at her upside down, it looked like a grimace. "I think the only way out of this is forward."

This from the woman who had nearly tossed Marsh out on the street when she believed he'd come to ask Will to work for Milkweed again. Did she no longer feel protective of him? Surely she realized forward meant turning a blind eye toward further blood prices? He felt cold. Naked. But Gwendolyn had yet to be wrong about such things. Her wisdom outstripped his own.

Will drew a long, shuddery breath. He was frightened, and weary from the effort to relearn something he'd abandoned long ago. "I prom-ised myself I'd never speak Enochian again."

Gwendolyn absently tucked a lock of hair behind her ear. "Perhaps you won't have to."

"Perhaps. But Pip wants me there when they try to bring her across." The plan to reunite the Twins contributed to Will's growing sense of dread. It drew inevitable comparison to the wartime raid on the REGP. Which to Marsh's mind meant success was virtually guaranteed. After all, while the raid itself had been a monumental cock-up, courtesy of Gretel, the coming and going had worked. Marsh didn't know just how close the Eidolons had come to stranding the last surviving members of the raid in Germany. Will had never told him about it. Which sooner than later would make an uncomfortable conversation.

"And for the rest," Will added. Marsh's plan came in two parts.

"He trusts you."

"I rather doubt Pip trusts anybody. He doesn't know the children. Doesn't understand them. But I'm the devil he does know."

"Needs must when the devil drives," she quoted.

"Speaking of whom," said Will. He turned his head slightly and nodded, quietly drawing her attention toward the staircase. Gretel descended slowly, her attention fixed on one of the books she'd requested Madeleine find for her, Shirer's *Rise and Fall of the Third Reich.* She and Gwendolyn nodded amiably at each other.

They waited until Gretel passed out of earshot. Gwendolyn whispered, "Can she truly do what they say?"

Will thought about this. "Yes. I believe so."

He arched his back, stretching until his chest cracked. He'd spent too many hours hunched over the lexicon. He sat up. "So. Am I forgiven?"

Gwendolyn looked as if she'd swallowed something sour. "William. You committed *treason.* Men have died."

It went without saying that his cooperation in Milkweed's efforts was the price he had to pay if he wished to avoid lifetime incarceration. Although whether it would truly keep him out of prison remained to be seen. He had the impression Klaus had made his own agreement and now wondered whether anything would come of it.

"I don't give a toss if Britain forgives me," said Will. "Only that you do." He sighed. His breath carried a lingering taste of the ginger tea he'd taken to calm his stomach. "Do you?"

She stared at him for a long moment before shaking her head. "Not yet." Gwendolyn touched his knee. "But you are improving." She kissed him on the cheek, then rose to leave.

"Gwendolyn?" he said. "I'm frightened."

Accepting that he had been wrong meant also accepting the world was not improved by his actions. That the world was no safer for him and Gwendolyn. If the Soviets decided to give it another go, what could Marsh and his ilk truly do to protect them? But that wasn't what kept Will awake at night.

She sat again. "Frightened."

"Of what's coming. Of what they'll make me do, make me witness. I'm afraid this will break me again." He bowed his head, unable to meet her gaze. "And I'm terrified there will be nobody to pick up the pieces this time."

She took his hand, laid an arm around his shoulders, pulled him close.

9 June 1963
Mayfair, London, England

The plan was complicated, and it was urgent. A bad combination.

It was crucial they put things in motion prior to the conclusion of the annual Queen's Birthday celebration. But the real difficulties weren't in the timeline, nor the resources that SIS had to wrangle on such short notice.

The second-largest difficulty was mathematics.

The largest was securing Klaus's cooperation.

Marsh stood inside a stand of silver limes, watching the tents, pavilions, and grandstands rising like toadstools in Green Park. Though the morning's drizzle had given way to bright sunlight shimmering in the puddles along the Broad Walk, he still wore his mackintosh. By turning up the collar and tipping the fedora to shade his face, he could hide the worst of his scars from random passersby. He hoped the beard would help, when it came in fully. He looked a proper fool—and felt it, too, as the sun rose higher and the summer humidity asserted itself—but it was better than the alternative.

People stared at him now. He would never be inconspicuous again.

At the moment, his beard was nothing more than heavy stubble. It itched, particularly along the ragged edges of his scars. He rubbed his face, then winced.

His career in foreign ops was officially dead. Marsh reminded himself that he'd turned his back on that life long before, but somehow this felt more final. Something fundamental had changed, far beyond his physical appearance.

Liv would never touch him again. Touch him? She recoiled from him now. What woman wouldn't?

The rising heat made the park smell pleasantly damp. It mingled with the petrol fumes from lorries and omnibuses rumbling along Piccadilly. The traffic lurched forward an inch at a time, restricted to a single lane. Road crews patched holes on Piccadilly and several surrounding streets in anticipation of Saturday's crowds. Earlier that morning, before the breeze had died off, the roadwork had wafted the unpleasant stink of hot tar across the park. Marsh preferred the smell of old rain. He wished for a rain hard and pure enough to cleanse his life of all its mistakes.

On his left, across the wide expanse of Green Park, stood Buckingham Palace and the Palace Gardens. The palace itself was a jumble of the so-called revived classic style dating from the time of George IV, plainer additions and alterations made during Victoria's reign, and modern additions dating from after the Blitz. Before him, past the pavilions and slightly off to his right, across the snarled traffic along Piccadilly, stood the Soviet Embassy.

Ostensibly, the temporary structures in Green Park were there to accommodate the crowds expected for the Queen's Birthday. And so it would appear to any curious onlookers from the embassy.

Secretly, however, they existed to hide a new trench from those same onlookers. Just as the road crews—all manned by SIS agents, including Roger—were a cover for surveying, measuring, grading, and marking Half Moon Street according to figures from the maths boffins.

Simple physics, the boffins had said. *Assuming you chaps have done your figures correctly.*

That depended upon having an accurate layout of the embassy.

Which Milkweed didn't have. They had the original designs, dating from the building's construction, and Will's testimony. But it was wise to assume the Soviets had altered the internal layout for their own purposes. Or for spite.

SIS didn't have a man inside the Soviet Embassy. Thus, Pembroke had funneled requests via his superiors to their colleagues in MI5. Milkweed was a mystery to the rest of the British intelligence community, which knew only that the tiny, semiautonomous organization was deep black, and that its rare requests were to be afforded the highest priority. MI5 had provided an updated floor plan. It came with no guarantees, but it was consistent with Will's recollection as to the location of the guarded door.

Satisfied that preparations here were under way, and resigned to the fact he couldn't speed them along, Marsh returned to the Admiralty. He couldn't in good conscience ask more of Klaus without first apprising Pembroke of the agreement they'd struck prior to the operation at Will's town house. He'd been trying to do so for the past day.

Marsh knocked on Pembroke's door. No answer. He knocked again and, on receiving no answer, tried the knob. It was locked.

Pethick poked his head out of his own office. "He hasn't been in today," he said. "Nor yesterday."

"Where is he?" Marsh enunciated his question carefully. People found it difficult to understand his altered voice.

Pethick stepped into the corridor. "Probably off smoothing ruffled feathers." He crossed his arms and leaned against the doorjamb. "There have been quite a few of late. The new operation isn't helping."

Marsh reached up to crack his knuckles against his jaw and winced when he touched his scar. It would be a difficult habit to break.

"Ruffled feathers?" he asked. The jagged ache he'd learned to dread wedged itself in his throat.

"First," said Pethick, "Milkweed came this close—" He held his forefingers a centimeter apart. "—to burning down half of Knightsbridge. No explanation given. And now we've made a point of blowing the Queen's Birthday far out of proportion this year. Thirty-seven is a rather odd number for such a large production, isn't it?"

Marsh shrugged. "Ten years since the coronation." A fortunate hap-penstance. It lent plausibility to the celebration.

Pethick said, "Even we can't tell the Crown what to do. We advise. The Crown listens, if it so chooses."

Marsh shook his head. "Somebody had better listen, if we're to avoid a war," he muttered. "When he returns, tell Pembroke I need to speak with him, please?"

"I will," said Pethick. "Where can he find you?"

"I'm off to beg Klaus for a bloody great favor. But first I'll check on Will," said Marsh with a nod to the floor. It hurt.

Pethick fished out his basement key. Handing it to Marsh, he asked, "Has he shared his concerns with you about the children? I mean the Eidolons, rather."

Marsh rolled his eyes. "Yes."

"What do you make of it?"

"I think Will would say anything to get out of this."

"He struck me as sincere."

"No doubt he was. Will excels at lying to himself."

"I do understand you two have a history," said Pethick. "But for what it's worth, he has been cooperating."

"Good. He's come to understand he has no choice." Marsh set off down the corridor. Over his shoulder he said, "Perhaps his wife set him straight."

Marsh spent a few minutes in the Milkweed vault before going downstairs. While there, he chewed another painkiller. The conversa-tion with Pethick left Marsh feeling like he'd attempted to gargle hot pitch. But he still had Will and Klaus to deal with.

He found Will in the observation room, hunched over a lexicon. An odd expression crossed the dead man's face when he looked at Marsh; Marsh was growing accustomed to that. But the children in the adjoin-ing room were too rowdy for the adults to converse easily. Rather than speak over the half-human–half-Enochian din, Marsh gestured Will into the soundproofed corridor outside. Silence engulfed them as soon as the door whispered shut behind Will.

Will said, "How are you feeling, Pip?"

"Leaving aside the constant sensation of choking on a razor blade?"

"Ah . . . no. I only meant to say . . . Look, Pip. I am sorry about what happened. In spite of our disagreements, I wouldn't have wanted . . . Well. You didn't deserve this."

"Found religion, have you?"

"I'm sorry my actions led to this."

"It's a bit late to have a crisis of conscience. If you'd thought about what you were doing, truly thought about it, none of this would have happened." *I wouldn't be fit for the bloody circus,* Marsh wanted to add.

Will blinked. "You're right. I only—"

"Words won't fix this, so don't bother. Can the children do it?"

"There's very little they can't do." Will fidgeted. He was nervous. "But I am concerned."

"Pethick will handle the blood price. You won't have to do anything. He has specialists for that." Marsh gathered that Pethick's men carried vials of the children's blood when carrying out payments. He wondered what possible cover could explain *that.*

"And that's fortunate for the both of us." Will's voice hardened. It matched the flinty look in his eyes as he said, "There is nothing on this earth you could do that would force me to carry out one single blood price. I've done quite enough of that."

Had Will suddenly grown a spine? Apparently. What had become of the man? First remorse, then a spine . . . But Marsh doubted he couldn't make Will cooperate, if it came down to that. Will had weak spots, like any person. But since the point was moot, Marsh decided to let it pass.

Very well. Let the man think he's had his moral victory, if it will grease the wheels.

"My understanding," said Marsh, "is that the children excel at keeping the prices acceptably low."

"Oh, listen to you," Will snorted. "There is no such thing as an acceptable level of state-sanctioned murder. But taking it for granted that Pethick's men won't balk at sabotaging airplanes and burning down crowded dance halls, there is another concern.

"There may be complications when we attempt to reunite the Twins."

"How complicated can it be? You did this before when you were half soused."

Will flinched. Marsh tried to rein in his irritation, but the pain made it difficult. No point in enraging Will; he was the only living warlock ever to have witnessed a teleportation. Milkweed needed him. But why let that go to Will's head?

Marsh said, "It's a one-way trip for one person. Simpler than the last time we used the Eidolons to move people about."

Will straightened his shoulders, as though steeling himself for something. It made Marsh weary. He didn't have the strength for another round of Will's drama, whether apologetic or moralistic.

"I must tell you something about that night in Germany. Getting home wasn't as easy as you think." Will hesitated, looking for the right words. "When it became clear the venture had gone into a cocked hat, I called upon the Eidolons to fulfill the second half of our agreement. They refused to bring us home, Pip."

A prickling sensation crept across the nape of Marsh's neck. Refused?

"That isn't possible. We had an agreement. You and the others negotiated and paid for it." Marsh didn't understand the nuances of the system, but this much he did know. Negotiation, price, action: that's how it worked.

Will said, "Yes, we did. Nevertheless. When it came time to leave, the Eidolons changed the price for the return trip. They wanted something else."

Something else? But Will had managed to bring them home. Which meant . . . Why had Will seen fit to begin this conversation with an apology? The prickling sensation sent tendrils down Marsh's spine.

Quietly, calmly, he asked, "What did you give them?"

"I didn't understand—"

"What did you give them, Will?"

"They demanded the soul of an unborn child. I agreed."

The prickle on Marsh's spine became a sickening rot in his stomach. Will had to be mistaken. He had to be.

Marsh protested. "What does that mean? That's gibberish, the province of clergy. It isn't something *you* can dole out."

Will hesitated. He took a half step backwards. "Under the circumstances of the moment, which were rather pressing as you may recall, I was speaking for the both of us."

Marsh still remembered the sensation of falling through the crawlspaces of the universe. Remembered how the Eidolons had twined themselves through every particle of his being. How they'd studied him. Disassembled him. Past, present, and future.

No. Not him. His future progeny. His son.

That's what had been wrong with John all these years. He was empty. Soulless.

Marsh struggled but failed to keep his voice level. "You gave them my son," he growled, swallowing blood. It curdled in his stomach.

Will raised his hands, palm out, trying to mollify him. "I didn't know what it meant. There wasn't time to suss it out. I didn't know until much later, when I saw that Liv was pregnant again."

Anger overwhelmed the throbbing pain in Marsh's jaw. He cracked his knuckles. "You gave them my son."

"I saved your life."

Marsh stepped forward, fist clenched. Will retreated.

No, said his conscience. It spoke with Liv's voice. *Not here. You mustn't shed blood so close to the children. It's too dangerous. . . . Your throat is bleeding. You must leave, now. Get away from the children before your blood summons something. The Eidolons have an affinity for you.*

"Have you any idea how it's been for us? Our son . . ."

Dear God. How many times over the years had he wondered how things had gone so terribly wrong? Now, suddenly, he knew the answer. An answer more direct than he'd ever thought possible. But knowing didn't help. It didn't do a damn thing. He couldn't share this with Liv. It didn't show him how to fix John. It changed nothing, and that was the most frustrating thing of all.

"I had no choice," said Will. "I had to do it."

"Liv can't stand to be under the same roof. With me, with him. Can't stand what our life became. She boffs other men just to hurt me." Marsh advanced on Will again. "And now you tell me it's all because of what *you* did on that night?"

Will retreated again, looking horrified. His voice came out as a whisper. "I didn't know what would happen."

"Can you undo it? Can you fix John?"

"No," said Will.

Marsh shoved him against the wall. The taller man fell back against a soundproofing baffle; the foam and carpet cushioned his fall.

Marsh stared down at him. "Get it right next time."

9 June 1963
Croydon, London, England

Klaus kept painting while Marsh spoke. It was difficult to understand his raspy voice. On top of that, he was angry about something, which meant he spoke quickly. Marsh paced while he laid out his idea and made his plea.

The Twins. Marsh spoke of them as game pieces. Or Gretel's plastic chips. They were the other pair of siblings raised by Doctor von Westarp. Closer than any two people could ever be, yet separated by hundreds or thousands of miles for most of their lives. Always apart, because their ability demanded it.

He'd sometimes wondered what happened to them. They'd always been the gentlest souls at the REGP. Klaus felt slightly ashamed that he hadn't appreciated that in his youth. Instead, he'd sneered at it. Confused it with weakness. Uselessness. He didn't know if they'd both survived and been put to use, or if one or both had been executed to keep them from being used. But as the long, gray years had dragged on at Arzamas-16, it became easier to forget the old life.

Their situation—assuming they still lived—was almost certainly worse than Klaus's. And they deserved it even less. Helping them could be an atonement for the foolish man he'd been in his youth. Another break with his past, more freedom from the anchors holding him down.

But Marsh's plan was reckless. The man didn't understand just how dangerous it was. The slightest miscalculation and . . . Marsh had never seen somebody swallowed forever by the cold earth. Klaus had. Of all the terrible ways death could take a person, live burial was the only one to give Klaus screaming nightmares.

Thinking of all the ways the plan could go wrong set Klaus's breath to puffing in desperate gasps. He didn't want to think about it. He didn't have to. It was moot.

The setting sun cast Marsh's shadow across the easel. Klaus said, "You're in my light."

Marsh stepped closer to the sundial at the center of the safe house garden. "Well? What do you think?"

I think you're a madman, thought Klaus. *I think your plan is reckless. And that you're gambling with my life.*

But he said, "We had an agreement."

"We still do," said Marsh. "I've been trying to discuss it with Pembroke ever since leaving the hospital. He hasn't been in."

"You might have mentioned it to him before you nearly died. How convenient it would have been if you'd taken our agreement to the grave."

Yes, Marsh was angry. He opened his mouth as if to argue, but stopped himself. He collected his thoughts, calmed himself with visible effort. "Yes. You're right. I ought to have reported it to Pembroke before we went to Will's house. Now. I am asking for a favor. It is the last thing I will ask of you. We already owe you a new identity. If you help me with this, I will personally go around Pembroke and see it done the same day. You will never have to see your sister again."

Klaus should have been released from the safe house by now. He would have been, if Marsh had kept his word. He'd risked his life in the belief he'd be, if not exactly free by now, no longer cooped up with his sister. Independent.

"I don't know if I can trust you," he said.

"Oh, you can, brother."

The kitchen door creaked shut behind Gretel. She strode across slate paving stones on bare feet. The hem of her skirt exposed bony ankles, the olive skin spiderwebbed with darker veins. She stopped before an azalea bush. It was in full bloom, a riot of lavender blossoms.

She leaned forward and pushed her face into the mass of flowers. Her chest swelled with breath; she let it out with a rapturous sigh.

Gretel set to work on the bush, delicately trimming away blossoms with a pair of scissors. She had picked up her old hobby of drying and pressing flowers. One of her arrangements stood on the kitchen windowsill. Madeleine had scrounged up the vase.

"Our Raybould is a man of his word," Gretel said.

They ignored her. Klaus asked Marsh, "You believe both Twins are alive?"

"Yes."

"If I did this, it would be for them." Those poor, helpless girls. It ate at Klaus, that he'd willfully forgotten them for the sake of his own comfort. "But it's pointless. I can't. My battery died in the battle at William's house." The technicians at the REGP had designed the lithium-ion batteries to be rechargeable, but that required special equipment. Klaus felt no disappointment.

Marsh unzipped the satchel he'd carried into the garden. Klaus recognized at once the final battery he and Gretel had stolen from the Arzamas vault. The gauge indicated a nearly full charge. It must have been the battery Gretel had worn on the day they turned themselves in. She'd never used it. Conveniently.

Klaus chewed his lip, thinking. Was it worth the risk? Klaus was willing to do almost anything in order to end his life as a prisoner. But Marsh's plan was profoundly dangerous. Given the choice, and if not for Gretel, Klaus would rather rot here than risk suffocating somewhere beneath London. But not risking it, not granting Marsh's favor, meant losing another chance to escape her. It was no choice at all.

What the hell, he thought.

"Gretel," he said. She glanced up from the azaleas. He steeled himself before looking in her eyes. "Tell me the truth. Will this work?"

Did she look sad? Amused? Concerned? Mischievous? Damn that sphinx.

She gathered her flowers and scissors in one hand. The other hand she laid on his elbow. "Yes. You will have a safe landing."

"And after?"

"You'll get what you want." Her eyes gleamed. "As will we all."

She said it the way she announced every prophecy. Baldly. Matter-of-factly. Did he believe her? If this were true, he'd never again have to watch the shadows coiling behind her dark eyes.

"Well," said Marsh. "There you have it, then." His old voice would have dripped with sarcasm. His new voice didn't allow such subtleties.

Klaus turned away from her. To Marsh, he said, "I want to leave the moment it's finished. Whether or not this works, I will not return here."

"Done."

The sun had fallen behind the garden wall. It meant an end to painting for the day; the best light was gone.

"Walk me through your plan. Every step," said Klaus.

Marsh said, "There's a map in the house."

To Marsh's credit, Klaus found no obvious problems with the plan, no showstoppers. Except, of course, the sheer reckless audacity of it.

Klaus required three pieces of equipment for his part in the operation. The battery worked. As did the net and the wristwatch.

Marsh's plan required only a few seconds of Willenskräfte. But they had to be perfectly synchronized and executed with precision. Klaus practiced until dozens and dozens of trial runs, flickering in and out of substantiality, threatened to damage the aged battery. The gauge needle dropped with every rehearsal. Klaus called an end to practice before the battery became unstable.

After that, the only thing left was to wait for nightfall. So preoccupied was he with preparations that it wasn't until evening when he realized the sun had risen and set on the last day he'd ever see his sister. If the plan worked, Marsh would let him leave. If it failed, he'd be dead.

The thought swirled up a turbulent cascade of emotions. No regret. No remorse. But melancholy, and wistfulness, and a sense that this was closure without catharsis. The great, long journey of his life was coming to an end, soon to be replaced by the beginning of another. For good or ill, Gretel had been his traveling companion—more honestly, the captain, the driver—from the time of his earliest memories. And now he'd be going on without her.

He felt excited by the prospect, but to his surprise, it also saddened him. Not because he'd soon see the last of her, but because in the end she hadn't been the sister he'd thought she was.

Klaus knocked on her door a few hours before leaving with Marsh. He'd nap until just before they departed. He didn't need to pack; they'd come to England with a few batteries, a handful of money, and the clothes on their backs. He was sorry he couldn't take the books and painting supplies Madeleine had kindly provided, but he wasn't about to take keepsakes on a mission.

Klaus smiled to himself. The very suggestion would have caused Standartenführer Pabst to choke on indignation. Strange. He hadn't thought about Pabst in many, many years.

Gretel said, "Come in, Klaus."

How rare for her to address him by name. She knew why he'd come.

Opening the door released a whiff of attar into the corridor. She'd decorated her room with flowers from the garden. She sat cross-legged on her bed. Her blossoms stood in milk bottles and hung skewed from tacks in the walls. Spindly stems poked from books, like wax paper sandwiches pressed between volumes of T. S. Eliot.

"I came to say good-bye," he said.

She watched him. She didn't move, or speak, or blink.

He sighed and turned away.

"Wait," she said.

He faced her again. "Well?"

Gretel stood. She said, "I'm remembering this. Remembering you as you are at this moment. For the past."

"Good-bye, Gretel."

She did something he didn't expect: She hugged him. Tightly. And kissed him on the cheek.

"Thank you," she whispered.

Warmth? Humanity? Hints of a soul? Where had Gretel hidden it all these years? Damn her.

Klaus knew, much as he tried to convince himself otherwise, that he'd miss her. Even though he'd stopped loving her, part of him would still miss her. But he'd made his choice. Nothing to do now but move forward.

He passed Madeleine's door on the way downstairs. He hesitated, considered saying good-bye to her, too. No. Starting over meant a clean break.

Marsh woke him an hour past midnight. Klaus made one final test of his equipment before climbing into the Morris parked on the street outside the safe house. He sat in the rear, on the passenger side. He buckled his lap belt, knowing he'd need it. The tight pressure on his stomach worsened the anxiety.

The early hour made for a quick drive into the heart of the city. London was deep in its slumber. Streetlights illuminated a city devoid of human activity. It wasn't difficult to imagine it had been emptied by evacuation, or plague. The few cars they passed might have been ghosts roaming through a silent cityscape.

"We're almost there," said Marsh. "Are you ready?"

"Yes." Klaus's stomach was so full of butterflies that he half expected one to escape when he opened his mouth.

Buckingham Palace loomed over them as they zipped past the gate. Klaus glimpsed gold and iron gleaming in the light of electric torches. Marsh took the car through a roundabout surrounding an immense piece of statuary; Klaus guessed it was a memorial to a past monarch.

They skirted St. James' Park for a few heartbeats. *Strange,* thought Klaus. That park was like a lodestone, drawing him back again and again. Marsh wrenched the wheel, and they plunged into the jumble of London streets.

He brought the car to a halt a few minutes later. They idled at the curb. Marsh lifted the handset of the two-way wireless mounted under the fascia. He announced, "In position." Then he hung the handset back on its cradle.

"Remember. Three seconds," Marsh said.

"I remember," said Klaus. But he checked the wristwatch just the same. "Do you remember your part?"

"Yes."

"And our agreement?"

Marsh opened the glove compartment. He pulled out a thin valise of burgundy leather. "Cash, identity papers, and the lease for a flat in Aylesbury. Just remember it'll take me a few minutes to ditch the car and get back to the park." He returned the valise to the glove compartment.

The radio squawked to life. "One, clear." It meant traffic was clear on Half Moon Street. A moment later a different voice said, "Two, clear." Nothing coming down Piccadilly, either.

A third voice said, "Go." And Marsh did.

He slammed the car into gear, hard enough to shove Klaus back into his seat. The underpowered Morris engine whined in protest. Klaus concentrated on his breathing, trying not to let the butterflies overwhelm him as the car finally picked up speed and careered around the corner onto Half Moon. The maneuver would have sent him sliding across the seat—and out of alignment—if he hadn't fastened the belt.

They passed the first traffic barrel set out by the impostor road crews. It was an acceleration marker. But Marsh didn't break off, meaning he had the car up to speed.

The embassy appeared through the windshield. It grew larger by the moment.

They flew past the second barrel. Marsh didn't waver.

The engine hum rose in pitch as they climbed the subtle incline left behind by the SIS road work. This was the final alignment. Klaus laid a finger on his wristwatch.

The embassy looked much larger than Klaus had imagined. It dwarfed all the arguments he'd used to convince himself this was a good idea. It wasn't a good idea. It was a terrible idea. It was insane. As the building loomed closer, he looked up, just for a moment, and saw what might have been a television antenna. Antenna?

He remembered the Arzamas fail-safes.

Klaus said, "How do we know—?"

But then they were crossing the mark the road crew had painted on the street. Marsh swerved. He hit the brakes and bellowed, *"Now!"*

Klaus pressed the stem of his watch at the same instant he embraced his Willenskräfte, and then he was flying toward the Soviet Embassy on a ballistic trajectory. The tall iron fence around the embassy blurred past him at over forty miles per hour.

He unfurled the fine mesh net on a towline behind him. Like him, it was insubstantial, meaning there was no wind to force it open. Klaus opened it with a flick of his wrists while coasting through what might have been a kitchen.

Three seconds after he pressed the stem, his watch vibrated. A regular alarm would have been useless, because it couldn't have made a sound in its ghostly form. But Klaus could feel it shaking on his ghostly wrist.

He willed himself and the net to flicker, ever so briefly, at the apex of his trajectory. He slowed; the net wasn't empty now.

And then he was out of the embassy, gliding across Piccadilly on the descent into Green Park. He tipped sideways to avoid the edge of the trench. The net resisted him. He'd snagged something on this fishing expedition.

He rematerialized just before hitting the first layer of air bags hidden beneath one of the pavilions. They burst, slowing him. *Fwump.* He dematerialized again to let the net and its contents pass through him. He glimpsed an arm, a leg, pieces of a cot, and half a cinder block.

Then he was substantial again, bumping and rolling to a stop along the trench floor while a second and third set of air bags ruptured. *Fwump. Fwump.*

Twelve seconds had passed since Marsh applied the brakes. But Klaus wasn't done, and he had to work quickly.

Dizzy, disoriented, he gained his feet. He followed the dim light of an electric torch to the end of the trench. Trapped in the net, beneath a jumble of bedding and concrete, a woman flailed.

Frantically, spasmodically. Because she was terrified. How could she not be?

Klaus peeled the net away. "You're safe," he said in German. He repeated it over and over while tossing aside the debris. Miraculously, she hadn't broken any limbs; he could tell from the flailing. But fresh cuts and bruises bloomed on her porcelain-pale skin owing to the violence of her extraction.

Her mouth opened in a silent scream. She was mute. As was her twin sister.

Klaus put his hands to the sides of her face, gently brushing aside the bundle of wires dangling from her scalp. Marsh was right: she wore a battery harness even in her sleep. Because Moscow might decide to send an urgent message at any time of the day or night.

"You're safe. It's me, Klaus. Do you remember me?"

The Twin writhed in his grasp. She stared. Confused, uncomprehending.

"Klaus! From the farm!"

She frowned, pulling away.

"I've rescued you," he said. Which was true, more or less. He hoped. "I'm sorry it had to be so sudden. We couldn't get a warning to you."

Her brow furrowed; her struggles flagged.

Klaus? she mouthed. She looked no less confused. And perhaps even more frightened. The last time he'd had any meaningful interaction with either of the Twins, it was before the war, when he and Reinhardt had vied for the doctor's favor. He'd been young and arrogant. A killer. How could she know he was a different man now?

"Yes. It's me." Klaus put an arm around her, helping her to sit up. She flinched away from his touch. He'd forgotten the sisters' eyes were two different colors. One blue, one brown. A side effect of the doctor's experiments.

They darted left, right, down, and up. She took in the earthen walls of the trench and the crude oak timbers. *Where? How?* she mouthed.

"You must listen to me. We have very little time." He looked first into the brown eye, and then the blue. "Am I speaking to both of you?"

She frowned again, eyes narrowed in concentration. Her head shook slowly. Concentration became disbelief, then a new fear. She trembled.

Klaus had never worked with the Twins, but her reaction was easy to interpret. She'd lost contact with her sister, and now she was panicking because she was too confused to think properly.

Poor girl. Klaus leaned forward; she flinched again.

"I'm not going to touch you. I want to inspect your wires and your harness."

The hunch in her shoulders dropped by a fraction of an inch. Klaus inspected her battery. It wasn't a Reichsbehörde design, but rather a hybrid between the original technology and the assassin's implants. The Soviets had upgraded the Twins' equipment for better durability and longevity in the field. Klaus had received no such upgrades, since they had intended for him to spend the rest of his life at Arzamas-16. And, of course, their captors had never dared to make even the smallest alterations to Gretel's equipment. She was too valuable.

The gauge showed two thirds of the charge remaining. The three-pronged banana plug from her wires (this, too, differed from his own) sat firmly in the connector, with the safety latch snapped over it. Klaus traced the wires to her head; halfway back he found a sharp kink where fine strands of copper poked through the insulation. That, too, had been replaced by the Soviets. Probably many times. A small spasm racked the Twin when he brushed the frayed strands with his finger.

"Sorry."

His own battery had begun to fail, sputtering out the last remnants of its charge. He disconnected it. Then he carefully peeled the insulation away from the kink with his fingernails, just enough to let him unwrap the insulation around the break. Naked copper gleamed in the torch-light. Rolling the segment of bare wire between his thumb and forefinger rebraided the strands enough to restore the flow of current. It would need solder and a proper splice later, but the repair would hold for now.

He'd done this to his own wires countless times. They all had.

"Better? Am I speaking to both of you now?"

She tried again. The panic became trembling relief. She nodded.

That was one problem solved. But how had her sister reacted to all of this? Had she already raised the alarm back in Moscow?

"Listen. This is urgent. I'm working with people who can reunite you. You can be free. Both of you."

A look of shock passed across her face. And, he imagined, across an identical face thousands of miles away. It dissolved into disbelief, and then hope so earnest, it hurt to behold.

"I know what it's like," he confessed. He couldn't help it. The look on her face . . . "I was held at Arzamas."

We know, she mouthed.

"I know you have no reason to trust me. I promise you can be to-gether again, and soon. But for this to work, you mustn't let the Soviets know what has happened." He studied her eyes again, wishing he could see the other Twin. "Do you understand? The Soviets mustn't know what has happened until they find you missing."

The Twin's multicolored gaze lost its focus while she mulled things over with her sister. She nodded emphatically.

"Good." Klaus tried to give her a reassuring smile. "They'll be here soon."

She shivered. Though it was June, it was also the middle of the night, and the ground was damp. She'd been sleeping when he snatched her out of bed. Most of her blanket had made the transit with her. Klaus gathered it up and covered her.

They waited. Somewhere, a cricket chirped.

"Reinhardt is here in England," he said. "As is my sister. Try to avoid them both if you can."

Confusion twisted the Twin's face.

"Long story," he said.

The cricket, and a post-adrenaline crash, lulled Klaus into drowsi-ness. More time passed. Finally, a ladder propped at the far end of the trench creaked beneath a set of work boots. Marsh joined them a few moments later, followed closely by Pethick and a third man whom Klaus didn't recognize.

Marsh sighed with relief when he saw the Twin. *"Guten Morgen,"* he said. He carried a writing slate, a paper bag, and the valise from the car.

He handed the valise to Klaus. "Thank you. And good luck," said Marsh. Klaus checked the contents. Marsh had kept his word. In return, Klaus removed the dead battery from his harness and handed it to Marsh.

It was a weight off his shoulders, literally and figuratively. The last time he'd ever wear a battery. But no pangs of sentimentality accompa-nied the realization. Klaus had earned this. He wouldn't miss the cop-pery taste of von Westarp's legacy.

Marsh offered his hand. Klaus took it. "Thank you," he said. "Her wires have been damaged, but they'll hold."

Klaus crouched beside the Twin. Switching back to German, he said, "You can trust this man. Soon you'll both be safe. I'm leaving now. Good-bye."

Klaus climbed the ladder while Marsh introduced himself to the Twin, also in fluent German: "My name is Marsh. And I need your help."

That was all Klaus heard, because then he emerged from the pavilion into the park. It was lovely. Peaceful. Moonlight limned all the greenery with silver. He could have almost imagined it was his own private preserve. But he didn't linger.

A lone taxi idled along the broad walk on the east side of the park. Klaus climbed in.

The SIS driver said, "Where to, mate?"

Klaus thought about this. "Anywhere," he said.

eleven

She didn't have a name. According to the records, von Westarp and his cronies in the SS had referred to them only as "1" and "2." The Soviets had done likewise, prompted by the tattoos inside their left wrists. Marsh asked her how she referred to herself, but she struggled to convey that in writing. He gathered that the Twins shared a sense of identity altogether alien to what regular people could comprehend.

Which worked to Milkweed's advantage. The Twins wanted desperately to be together again. That was clear. Marsh hoped the promise of reunion was sufficient to earn their cooperation.

He struggled to stay awake while the doctor gave the Twin a cursory examination. He hadn't had a decent night's sleep since leaving the hospital. Lying down irritated his injuries and caused a tickle at the back of his throat. The tickle often grew into a cough severe enough to leave Marsh retching into the waste bin beside his cot.

The doctor declared the Twin fit for travel. She'd been knocked around quite violently during the extraction, but she was otherwise as fit as could be expected. That was a small mercy; things might have gone pear-shaped in any one of dozens of ways. More than anything, the woman was confused and skittish. Understandably.

Marsh had stuffed some of Liv's old clothes into a grocer's sack the previous evening. When he opened the sack, he discovered it smelled like his wife from the days when she had been young and beautiful. Odd, that something forgotten for so long could become so desperately valuable. But Marsh shoved aside the pangs of sorrow to concentrate on the job. The woman Klaus had fished from the embassy was taller than Liv, and a little thinner, but Marsh offered her the chance to change out of her sleeping clothes.

She'd begun to strip even before Marsh and Pethick could turn away. No sense of privacy or modesty. Marsh inadvertently glimpsed a smattering of scars and old surgical wounds. Another legacy of von Westarp's farm.

In minutes they were crossing dew-damp grass to a waiting van. Traffic had picked up a bit, but it was still early enough that they made it to the Admiralty in good time. Sunrise was little more than a salmon-colored smear on a charcoal horizon when they arrived.

The plan had been to send the counterfeit message from Pembroke's office. Location was immaterial to the Twin's ability to relay things to her sister. But doing it from the other logical choice, the basement, wasn't wise; there was a danger the Twins might report what they saw, possibly warning Ivan that the warlocks weren't extinct.

Always assume the enemy is smarter than you. Stephenson had taught him that.

But Pembroke's office was locked and dark. Pethick had to use his key. He and Marsh exchanged a look of concern—this didn't smell right—but they held their tongues. Marsh ushered the Twin into a chair. She declined with a small nod when Marsh offered to pour her a scotch from Pembroke's sideboard. He helped himself to a swallow of the single malt, but regretted it. It burned like lava on the way down.

Chalk tapped on the slate as the Twin wrote, in German, *Did Klaus tell the truth?* It was the first thing she'd said without prompting. Marsh hoped that was a good sign.

"You'll be together sooner than you think," he said. "When do they come for you in the morning?"

When they feel like it, she wrote.

That meant they still had time. The dull glow of sunrise had only just begun to penetrate the city. From Pethick's office window, Marsh saw streetlamps wink out along the edges of St. James' Park. Green Park lay somewhere in the gray beyond that. Where even now SIS crews labored inside tents and pavilions to fill the landing trench and erase any sign of its existence prior to the celebrations on Saturday.

Pethick used Pembroke's telephone to summon a boffin to give the Twin's wires a once-over. He arrived with a small toolbox, a soldering iron, a coil of copper wire, and a roll of electrical tape. He set to work turning Klaus's makeshift splice into a permanent repair.

Marsh beckoned Pethick into the corridor. He waited until they were out of the Twin's earshot before asking, "Where the hell is he?"

"I thought he'd be here by now," said Pethick. "This isn't like Leslie."

"Have you tried ringing him?"

Pethick nodded. "I have several telephone operators quite cross with me. No answer."

"Something's wrong."

"Yes."

"Send somebody to his home," said Marsh.

Pethick asked, "Do you think he's in trouble?"

"I think Gretel arranged this. So, yes."

"What could she be doing?"

What point in speculation? Either they'd find out, or they wouldn't. He glanced at his watch. "We're running out of time. Let's do what we came here to do."

Pethick went to his own office. From there he'd call around to dispatch somebody to Pembroke's house; he'd also monitor the listening stations. If Cherkashin discovered the Twin missing before Milkweed could set things into motion, he'd have no choice but to transmit an emergency broadcast to Moscow. The stations would attempt to jam that transmission, and ring Pethick immediately.

Marsh returned to Pembroke's office, where the technician put the finishing touches on the Twin's wire. He bit off a length of black electrical tape and deftly wrapped it around the repair. The sickly-sweet odor of solder flux mingled with the earth-and-fire taste of Pembroke's scotch.

Marsh sat beside her, in the second of the two armchairs arranged before Pembroke's desk. He asked, "Better now?"

She nodded. *No static,* she wrote.

"Excellent. Are you comfortable? Warm enough?"

Another nod.

As soon as the technician had departed and closed the door behind him, Marsh spoke in earnest. "Are you both ready?" How eerie to converse with two people sharing a single set of eyes and ears.

Another nod.

"You've both been extremely patient this morning. More than I would be were our roles reversed. Thank you."

She shrugged. Most of their adult life had been spent waiting to send and receive messages. They were, to the people who owned them, a useful tool and nothing more.

Marsh took a deep breath and launched into his pitch: "We know Cherkashin is using the pair of you to report on a series of political assassinations. Elderly men, living in the countryside."

The Twin nodded.

"What you might not know is that these killings have been carried out in preparation for an attack on Britain, or its holdings. But Cherkashin's masters back in Moscow have been waiting for one final report before putting their plan into motion." It was too late to turn back; they'd hit that point when he punched the brakes on Half Moon Street. So he forged ahead. "But here's the thing of it: We want the attack to proceed."

This surprised her. *Why?*

He shook his head. "That's unimportant. What does matter is that you can put it in motion by making the Soviets believe that final report has arrived. We presume that since you've been the conduit for those reports, you know how they are phrased."

The Twin looked past him. A distant look clouded her mismatched eyes while she conferred with her sister. Unsettling. Marsh had read the files, but that wasn't a patch on actually seeing the Twins in action.

She wore the chalk down to its final nub, writing, *We can do that. Then you'll reunite us?*

Marsh handed her a fresh piece of chalk. "What about rotating code phrases? Are you certain you can deliver the appropriate message?"

We have the system committed to memory. It hasn't changed in years.

Which meant the Soviets had grown complacent. Utterly convinced that they were running rings around the feeble British Empire. Which, until recently, they had been. So much the better. But:

"Aren't they concerned you'll produce counterfeit messages of your own? Or corrupt real messages?"

We tried that once. To escape.

"And?"

The Twin shook her head. *Only once.* Marsh recalled the old wounds and scars. Perhaps they weren't all vestiges of von Westarp's experimentation. Impatiently, she erased the slate with the heel of her fist. Quickly she scrawled: *You'll reunite us after?*

"Yes."

He didn't tell them that Milkweed planned to pull the distant sister to England regardless of whether they cooperated in the subterfuge. In the end it didn't matter what message they sent. Because whether or not Ivan took the bait, the Twins were far too potent a resource for the enemy to possess. Milkweed wouldn't let that continue.

Ideally, they'd extract the second Twin from the USSR after Ivan had committed to his course of action, so that Milkweed could chop him off at the knees, breaking the Cold War's precarious stalemate. If Ivan didn't fall for it, pulling her out would tip their hand: Britain still had warlocks aplenty. Good-bye sterling opportunity. And the Cold War would continue as before: a long, grinding struggle, leading to the slow erosion of the British Empire.

How? she wrote.

Marsh tried to give her a reassuring smile. His own scars probably didn't help. "You'll find out soon enough." He looked outside. The Admiralty building cast a long shadow across St. James', where sunlight flowed like syrup. The sun had risen.

"We haven't much time. We must begin."

We're summoning the others.

"Announcing an incoming message?" said Marsh.

She nodded.

Ten minutes passed, or perhaps a quarter hour. She raised a hand when he became impatient. A few moments later she wrote, *They're here. We're doing it now.* More waiting.

The Twins were two ends of an invisible tether, tying Marsh to his enemies. Could they sense him?

Marsh stood. He paced while, presumably, the Twins reported the death of Lord William Beauclerk. Sunlight like molten gold glinted on the lake in St. James'. "What are they saying? Do they believe you?"

She wrote quickly now. Marsh read over her shoulder: *They're suspicious. Long delay.*

He tried to picture the scene in Moscow. How many people stood at the other end of this game of Chinese whispers? Were they party? Military? KGB? Representatives of Arzamas-16? All of the above?

Marsh and Pethick had consulted with a handful of SIS's top experts on the Soviet Union while preparing the script for this operation. But the best responses, they deduced, were common sense:

"Tell them their agent had to maintain a very low profile. That the British had laid a trap for him. He didn't dare move until he was certain he'd evaded them." Just as his orders almost certainly dictated.

The response came quickly: *Trap?*

"The British were lying in wait at the target's home." The more truth a lie contains, the easier it goes down. Another lesson from the old man. It was the honey coating for this poisoned pill: "The British were very desperate to protect the target."

There followed another long pause. Marsh stood at the window, too deep in concentration to see outside. He cracked his knuckles. The *tap-tap-tap* of chalk on slate pulled him back beside the Twin.

Arguing. Some want to move forward. Some think the mission was a failure. The chalk snapped in half as she added, *Too public.*

Cherkashin's bosses had seen the publicized reports of Will's death.

"Remind them the world believes the target died in a gas main explosion. The arson investigation concluded as much." Because, of course, SIS had ensured it would. "Nothing has been compromised."

The distant expression settled over the Twin's face again. Marsh held his breath. Forever passed.

She blinked, shook her head, and took up the chalk once more. *They're leaving. No decision. Still arguing.*

Disappointing, but expected.

She wrote, *Now you'll do it?*

Marsh said, "Very soon. But we have to wait in case they return for follow-up questions." Her eyebrows pulled together in a deep frown. Did she think he'd lied to her? "Please be patient," he pleaded.

If they waited too long, Cherkashin might raise the alarm and Moscow would abandon its attack plans. But the same would happen if Milkweed extracted the other Twin too quickly. Marsh glanced at his watch again.

Either way, they'd have their answer soon.

11 June 1963
Milkweed Headquarters, London, England

Roger fetched Will from the Croydon safe house just after dawn. Will rode to the Admiralty in the Morris with the darkened window glass.

He asked, "Well? What happened?"

"They got her," said Roger, downshifting as the car leaned around a corner. "Bit of a miracle, if you ask me."

Will yawned. "Bully for Pip." He'd barely slept, for fear that today would be the day he violated a long-standing vow to himself. "He's always had a flair for the dramatic."

"I bet ol' Ivan never saw this coming."

Past another yawn, Will said, "Oh, yes. Undoubtedly."

Roger showed his identification to the sentries manning the Admiralty screen. He parked the car at the foot of the wide marble stairs. The rising sun tinted the pale building with gold. Will stepped from the car. His shadow rippled up the stairs, as if escorting him inside.

Will drew a deep breath to hold the collywobbles at bay. He hoped today's events would prove Gwendolyn correct. Perhaps he'd be spared the worst of it; perhaps he wouldn't have to speak any Enochian. After all, that was the children's job. But he knew better. This was Milkweed, after all, and Milkweed left nobody unscathed. It would chew him, and swallow him, and cough him up again. But this time there might not be a Gwendolyn to catch him.

They stopped at Pethick's office to retrieve the key to the cellar. Marsh and, presumably, the Twin were firmly ensconced behind the locked door to Pembroke's office. Pethick was on the telephone when Roger and Will entered.

"You're quite certain there's no answer? . . . Get inside. Find anything that might tell us where Leslie's gone. . . . Look, I don't care if he lives in the bloody Taj Mahal. Just get in. . . . Yes, I'll take responsibility. Ring me the moment you have something."

He dropped the handset on its cradle, hard enough to make the bells hum.

Roger said, "Trouble?"

"Leslie's gone missing," said Pethick.

Will hadn't interacted with Pembroke much since those first intensive debriefings just after Marsh collared him. When Pembroke came to the safe house, it was mostly to question Klaus and Gretel.

Will said, "That's troubling."

Pethick sighed. He dug out a key and handed it to Will.

Will imagined how he and Marsh might have reacted, had Stephenson suddenly vanished while Milkweed was on the verge of a major operation. It *was* rather suspicious, and compounded Will's sense of dread. This was not right. But he knew better than to think it might scuttle the day's plans, so he left the worrying to Pethick and resigned himself to spending the rest of the day in the cellar.

The pall of unease hanging over Will thickened into coal black thunderheads of despair when he checked on the children.

Finger paint had been splashed across the observation window. Picture books had spilled from an overturned bookcase. Torn pages littered the floor. They'd shredded their cushions; goose down swirled around their feet, piled up in the corners like snowdrifts. The maps hung in tatters. And in the midst of the destruction, the children virtually bounced off the walls while screaming themselves hoarse in a hodgepodge of English and Enochian.

The children, Will knew, took their emotional cues from the Eidolons. Insofar as cosmic entities had emotions; Will had always been unclear on that point. He doubted any of the other warlocks could have given a definitive answer.

Something was very, very wrong. Pembroke just happened to go missing while the Eidolons decided to throw a tantrum? No mere coincidence, this. The Eidolons saw everything at once, everywhere. Not as a chain of discrete events through time and space. A stone, a pond, and the ripples were all the same to them.

But which parts are the ripples, and which parts the stone? Will wondered.

When they weren't communing with demons, the children were subject to the limitations of their human bodies. The youngest succumbed to weariness first. Pandemonium descended into bedlam, and then into mere chaos. It was as though a cyclone had passed through the classroom, whipping the children into a frenzy, but now it had passed, taking their appetite for mischief along with it. Several children were snoring, sprawled on torn cushions or huddled together on the floor, when Marsh brought the Twin downstairs.

Like Klaus, Gretel, and the other men and women whom Will had glimpsed in the Tarragona filmstrip, the poor woman had a bundle of wires trailing from her skull. But the first thing Will noticed was her eyes. They didn't match. He wondered if her sister shared that unusual trait.

"Well, hello there," he said. "My name is William."

Behind the Twin, Marsh slashed one hand through the air in a frantic "cut it out" motion. *Ah. Yes. Just do my job, shall I? Pretend she's a useful tool and nothing more?*

Will ignored him. "I understand you've had a rather trying morning."

Marsh said something in German, ostensibly translating for the Twin. She spared a moment from surveying the surroundings, the expression on her face growing more puzzled by the moment, to nod at Will. He recognized the slate she carried; Marsh had used it sporadically during the first few days after he returned from the hospital. A single word had been printed on the slate in block letters, and underlined: *BITTE?*

Will had only a smattering of German, but the meaning came across just the same. She begged Marsh to deliver on his promise. Will suspected she might change her mind after the Eidolons gave her a once-over.

Marsh frowned at the observation window, where streaks of green, purple, and red trickled down the pane to mix into a dull brown along the sash. "What the hell is this? What did you tell them?"

Will pulled him aside. He whispered, "I told you they were agitated, didn't I? Well, here's your proof. They had already torn the place to shreds when I arrived."

"They look exhausted. Can they still do what we need?"

Will made an effort to keep his voice level. "Perhaps we ought to rethink this. First Pembroke goes missing, and then the Eidolons whip the children into a frenzy. Don't you think this is a bit troubling?"

Marsh shook his head. "The Eidolons had nothing to do with Pembroke. It's Gretel. I'd swear my life on it."

Damn the stubborn fool. "You may very well be, if this isn't a coincidence."

"We'll worry about it later." Marsh pointed at the Twin. "You need to get her sister here, now. We can't risk having them tell Ivan about you and this place."

"You don't trust them."

"Of course not."

Will asked, "Pethick's done his part?"

The words tasted like ash. He leaned against the wall, took steadying breaths, trying not to sick up.

The Eidolons had demanded eight new blood maps for today's work. Eight innocent civilians killed or maimed by their own government. Will hated himself for knowing this and not shouting it from the rooftops. One can either condemn atrocities, or be an accessory to them. Will had done both in his life.

The last time Milkweed had attempted a teleportation, Will and the other warlocks had been forced to derail entire trains in order to meet the Eidolons' price.

Marsh nodded. He still favored the wounded side of his neck when he moved. "The prices have been paid. For this, and for what comes later."

Will couldn't think of any further way to stall. And the poor woman looked desperately sad. So he said, "Let's get this behind us then."

He ushered Marsh and the Twin through the door to the classroom. The few children who weren't dead asleep ignored the newcomer, much as they'd ignored Will the first time he'd come here. But Marsh's arrival brought their stupor to an end. The older children nudged the younger ones.

"The man Marsh is here."

A few blinks, a few rubbed eyes, and soon the entire class was on its feet. As one, they crowded around Marsh and the Twin, who looked deeply uncertain about this.

"The man Marsh is here," repeated the oldest. The others repeated Marsh's human name. It became a chant.

"Children." Will clapped. The chanting continued, faster. Will clapped again. *"Children!"*

They stopped. They looked at Will. "Hello, William," said the boy who'd recognized Marsh. *Will-ee-am.*

"Hello, children." He cast a glance at the Twin. She looked shaken. He tried to give her a reassuring smile. Marsh spoke to her in what was probably the most soothing tone his ruined voice could manage. Will returned his attention to the children.

"Do you remember when I told you about my friend, whose twin sister is lost and alone?"

A handful of children nodded. The rest watched him with dull eyes.

Will held a hand out to the Twin. She came forward.

"Here she is. Isn't she nice?" From the corner of his mouth, Will added, "Wave to the children, please." Marsh translated; she managed a trembling, halfhearted wave.

"But our friend here," said Will, "is quite sad. She misses her sister very much." He looked around at the assortment of cherubic faces. "I think we should bring her sister here. Don't you?"

Will had tied himself in knots over the wording of the negotiation. He'd opted for the clearest, most specific statement possible. It was crucial the children understood exactly what he wanted, lest he wind up with a two-headed grotesquery screaming itself to death on the classroom floor. They sought to *reunite* the Twins, but not *unify* them. Such was the danger. Without sufficiently considered phrasing, the Eidolons might very well try to stuff both women into the same body. It was all the same to the demons. Will hoped he'd circumvented that, but still felt queasy. She seemed decent.

"Bring her here," said one of the oldest boys.

"Bring her here," said the girl in the pink frock.

More children picked up this new chant. New voices joined in each iteration.

Will fished inside a pocket of his waistcoat for a safety pin. Raising his voice to speak over the chanting, he said, "I have to prick her finger. Her sister must draw her own blood as well. The tiniest drop will suffice."

She looked even more confused and doubtful when Marsh relayed the instructions. But she let Will stab the pad of her index finger. He squeezed, gently, until a scarlet bead welled from the puncture. Meanwhile, her expression went a bit slack. The children picked up the tempo.

The Twin winced. Marsh asked her something in German. She nodded. "It's done," he said.

The last children joined the chorus. As before, they switched seamlessly from English to Enochian: inhuman syllables built from the howls of dying galaxies, the sizzle of starlight, the thunder of creation, the silence of an empty universe. Terror replaced apprehension on the Twin's face.

Something entered the room. It oozed in through the fissures between one instant and the next. That dreadfully familiar pressure, that suffocating sense of a vast intelligence suffused their surroundings. Even the air felt thicker, heavier. More real. The floor rippled underfoot, as the geometry of the world flowed like soft candle wax around the searing reality of the Eidolon.

The children burbled in Enochian. They spoke in unison, their precision inhuman. Will still hadn't cracked the deep structure of their creole, but the surface meaning cascaded through the chthonic rumbles. They called up a prior negotiation, put it to the Eidolon's attention.

It responded in kind. As the surface of the sun to a smoldering campfire, so, too, was the pure Enochian of an Eidolon to that filtered through human flesh. There was a deep structure here as well—undercurrents of impatience and agitation churning a malevolent sea.

The Twin clamped her hands over her ears. The slate fell from her trembling fingers. It bounced: once, twice, then made an impossibly slow pirouette before coming to rest suspended on a single corner.

Will shifted his weight again, buffeted by the howl of Enochian. He listened.

Commingled blood. A price paid. Somewhere in London, a pair of window-washers had tumbled to their deaths when their scaffolding failed. Scaffolding sabotaged by Pethick's men and marked with specks of the warlock children's blood. Elsewhere, a chain had snapped at a shipyard, crushing two men. And an accident on the Tube had killed five and wounded eleven.

Commingled blood maps. Another sliver of the world handed to the Eidolons. Milkweed had overpaid, but the Eidolons never made change.

The negotiation and blood price were complete. Now it was the Eidolon's turn. It agreed to this task in the language of creation, using grammar like a chisel that sculpted reality.

Will nodded at Marsh. Marsh took the Twin's wrist and pulled her hand toward the children. A red streak marred her ear where she'd pressed her fingers. Blood dripped to the floor, loud as a scream.

The Eidolon found her blood. It read the map, traced the boundaries of her existence, and *saw* her.

Terror distorted her features, revealed rings of eggshell white around her mismatched eyes. Her knees gave out. Marsh caught her.

Almost done. Now for the trick that made this entire venture possible. A loophole that would enable the warlock children to retrieve a person they'd never met.

Identical twins. Identical blood.

All that remained was to make the connection and bring it to the Eidolon's attention.

See this, said the children. *Two bodies, one blood.*

"Quickly now," Will managed. "She has to connect with her sister. While it's watching her."

Marsh whispered in the Twin's bloodied ear. Will couldn't imagine how she could concentrate under that cosmic scrutiny. But she was stronger, far stronger, than she looked. Her fear-wide eyes glazed over as she once again called up that thing Klaus called *Willenskräfte* to build a bridge of willpower to her sister.

And that's when everything went to hell.

The undercurrent of agitation from the Eidolon erupted into a tsunami of rage. Will dropped to his knees, his concentration shattered by the onslaught. Even the children staggered beneath the tidal wave of celestial indignation. They screamed, curling into fetal balls as they hit the floor.

The Twin lay unconscious, dragged to the center of the maelstrom. Marsh crawled forward. He tried to grab her, but the Eidolonic fury had shredded the space and time around her to confetti.

A silent explosion. The Eidolon withdrew, and the world reverted to its shadow-puppet reality. Two women lay on the floor, where eons earlier there had been only one.

Marsh scrambled to their sides. He checked their pulses, their shallow breathing. The new arrival sat up, unsteadily, with Marsh's help. Her sister's eyelids fluttered.

A stillness had descended upon the classroom, broken only by scattered sniffling and crying. Will crouched beside the nearest children. Roused them, reassured them.

The Twins huddled in the corner. They held each other. Will wanted to believe their tears came from the joy of being reunited. But he knew better.

11 June 1963
Milkweed Headquarters, London, England

The Twins were disoriented, and unsteady on their feet. As was Marsh after the ordeal in the classroom. He worried the Eidolons might have left the Twins permanently addled. Several men who had participated in the raid on von Westarp's farm had gone mad during the transit to Germany. It was difficult to diagnose the mutes; their silence made them seem perpetually withdrawn. How did trauma manifest?

In one morning, Milkweed had stolen two of Ivan's most precious toys. Marsh hoped they hadn't lobotomized two innocents in the process. Knowing this was all for the greater good did nothing to assuage the pangs of guilt. The women were victims of von Westarp, the Schuztstaffel, Arzamas-16. But no longer. Perhaps some tiny measure of good could come of this. But the thought didn't relieve the pounding pressure behind Marsh's eyes.

Almost done, he told himself. *Just a little more.*

Gently, he took one Twin's arm across his shoulders to help her to her feet. Will did likewise. They escorted the women upstairs, where Roger waited for them. Marsh collected both batteries; like Klaus, the Twins relinquished them without any hint of regret. Their equipment differed from what Klaus and Gretel wore.

Marsh introduced the Twins to Roger. "He'll take you someplace safe," he said. They nodded. Their faces, Marsh realized, were mirror images of each other. Both had mismatched eyes, but one pair was blue/brown and the other brown/blue.

Roger asked, "Croydon?"

"Yes," Marsh said.

Roger sighed, rubbed the nape of his neck. "Getting a bit crowded out there."

"Madeleine will just have to make do."

The Twins showed no interest in this exchange. They held hands, resolutely determined to stay together, when they followed Roger to his car.

Will waited until the trio disappeared around a corner before saying, "I warned you something wasn't right with the Eidolons. Don't pretend you didn't notice."

Marsh fished another painkiller tablet out of his pocket. It crackled between his molars. The astringent taste made the muscles in his jaw clench up, like biting into a lemon. It always hurt to swallow, but the tablet dulled the worst of the pain in his throat. He tried to savor the minor relief; he'd be out of tablets soon enough. The morning's adventures had spawned a blistering headache.

"The Eidolon didn't like it when they contacted each other," he said.

"Obviously."

"Why not?"

"I can't begin to guess. But let's be glad we needn't do that again. And I think we should call upon the children as sparingly as possible."

Maybe, just maybe, Will had a point for once. Marsh had experienced the Eidolons before, felt their contempt for the stain of humanity. But this . . . He shook off the unease. Events were too far along; they were committed. Indecision was deadly. "We're almost done. Rest up. And make certain the children are ready."

Will frowned. He raised his hands as if to argue. But he studied Marsh's face for a few seconds; then his shoulders slumped. "Captain Ahab had nothing on you," he muttered. Will handed over the cellar key, trudged downstairs, and locked the sally port behind him.

Marsh knocked on Pethick's door, but didn't wait before entering. The urbane Cornishman was slumped over his desk, cradling his forehead with one hand and holding the telephone to his ear with the other. His face was flushed, and he'd loosened his tie.

Marsh knew what this meant. He took a seat as weariness seeped into his bones.

"Keep me posted," said Pethick. He tossed the handset back on its cradle. His chair creaked in protest when he stretched his arms and legs.

"Pembroke's dead." Marsh didn't ask.

Pethick nodded. "I sent a lamplighter team into his house. The place had been turned over. It appears Leslie and his wife surprised a burglar several nights ago."

"We both know this wasn't a random accident," said Marsh. "This reeks of Gretel. I'd wager anything Reinhardt had been waiting for them."

"Most likely."

He'd warned Pembroke. *She will dance on your grave,* he'd said. Pembroke hadn't listened and now he was dead. But would it have made a difference if he had listened?

The pain and weariness sank deeper, past Marsh's bones and into the marrow. Fighting Gretel made as much sense as fighting the wind. Resisting her was like trying to push back the tide. And yet that was his job.

"I suppose," said Pethick, "this means you're in charge now." He slid a key across the desk. It differed from the cellar key. Marsh turned the cold metal in his hand. Pethick said, "Leslie's office. Yours, now. I'll arrange to have your effects moved."

To Marsh's mind, it wasn't Leslie Pembroke's office he stood to inherit. It was John Stephenson's office.

I miss you, old man. He set the key on the desk. A flick of the finger sent it spinning back to Pethick. *But Lord knows I never wanted your job.*

"You've been here the longest," he said.

Pethick replied, "Longest, perhaps, but not earliest. Like it or not, you have the seniority." He pushed the key back across the desk.

Seniority. That's just another way of saying I'm *Milkweed's old man now. A tired old man.*

Marsh said, "This is what she wants, you know."

"As long as we both know it, what difference does it make? And to be perfectly blunt," said Pethick, "my hands—" His telephone rang, as if on cue. "—are quite full at the moment."

He lifted the receiver. "Pethick." He listened for a few seconds. "Very good. Make certain they maintain as long as possible."

He set the receiver down again. "I think Cherkashin has just noticed his girl is missing. We started jamming a few minutes ago."

Which meant SIS transceiver stations throughout the countryside were pumping out broadband radio hash at full power. Cherkashin's warning to Moscow would disappear in the noise.

Pethick gave a mirthless laugh. "Perhaps I ought to send a car to the embassy. If he's smart, he'll turn himself in to us before he's summoned to Moscow."

But Marsh didn't feel like sharing the joke. "We have both Twins. Roger's taking them to the safe house."

Pethick massaged his temples, stretching smooth the crow's-feet at the corners of his eyes. "And now?"

"We stick to the plan, and hope Ivan takes the bait."

Marsh stood. It was harder than it should have been. He carried a heavier yoke now, a burden that hadn't been his just a few minutes earlier. Stephenson had been such a towering presence in Marsh's life, now gone these many years. His was a heavy ghost newly cleaved to Marsh. He added the new key to his ring, alongside the cellar key.

"Notify me if anything changes."

"Where will you be?"

"Home," Marsh rasped. "I haven't slept in two days."

Head throbbing with each heartbeat, Marsh trudged along cracked and weathered pavement. His thoughts were jumbled, his mind unsettled. His worries together carried a weight that bowed his shoulders. Like a dog chasing its tail, he spun himself through the same path again and again.

The Soviets. The Eidolons. Pembroke. Gretel.

She had to be waiting for something. But what? He would return to Croydon when he was rested and alert. He had tricked Gretel once, caught her off guard, however briefly. Perhaps he could do it again. But not if he was exhausted. If her mask slipped, or she dropped one of her cryptic comments, he had to be alert enough to catch it.

Swirling thoughts pushed everything to the periphery of his awareness. Thus, as he approached his house, he had only a vague sense that something had changed. He paused with his hand on the door handle. Smooth brass cooled his fingertips while he listened. Recognition came to him slowly, tenuously, like fragments of a long-forgotten dream.

Liv. Singing to herself.

She hadn't sung in the house since John had been an infant. It agitated him, made him howl, no matter how softly she made her music. He always knew.

Marsh closed his eyes, concentrating.

Yes, that was Liv. And John was silent. Not a peep. Marsh's homemade soundproofing wasn't that effective.

He removed his shoes in the vestibule after closing the door as quietly as he was able. He paused at the edge of the den, still listening. The familiar clunk of the pipes as Liv ran the water; the *click-click-whoosh* as she lit the gas hob; the whistle of the teakettle. Liv sang through it all. A melancholy piece; he didn't recognize it. But he imagined she might have picked up any number of melodies she'd never shared. . . . Marsh had always thought their son killed her love of music. Perhaps she had just hidden it away. Or shared it with others. He wondered if she sang for the aftershave men.

Liv's silverbell voice made his chest ache. He'd tried and failed many times to forget the sound of it. Hearing it now brought back so many unwelcome memories. Memories of himself as a young man, his heart not yet rusted and cobwebbed. Memories of lying in bed with Liv, their infant daughter snuggled between them. Liv in her WAAF uniform; Liv taking it off . . . Another man's life.

Why was John so quiet?

He tiptoed backwards through the den. He took the stairs slowly, one at a time, stepping at the edges so they wouldn't creak. The key ring jangled when he took it from the hook beside the door. But John didn't stir, even when Marsh turned the locks.

His son lay naked in the center of the floor. He was curled in the fetal position, hands clamped over his ears. Just as the children at the Admiralty had done when the Twins somehow enraged the Eidolon. A short, shallow breath swelled John's chest; it came out in a little wheeze through his nose. He had a bit of congestion.

John wasn't a warlock child. He couldn't speak English, much less Enochian. He was the furthest thing from those children in the Admiralty cellar. And yet, here he was, reacting as they had.

The soul of an unborn child.

Will had known all along. *All these years, wondering what had gone wrong with John. Blaming ourselves. Blaming each other.*

But the Eidolons had done this. True demons, more inscrutable than even Gretel. This curse came from beyond any human interaction, beyond any human comprehension, beyond any hope of revenge.

"He's been like that for hours."

Marsh started. Beside him, Liv continued, "He let out a terrible shriek, clear as day. I came up when I heard the thump." She shook her head. "He hasn't moved since."

Looking at her twisted the tight skin along his throat. Liv stood close enough that he could smell the rose blossom tea on her breath. She stared straight ahead, choosing to see John rather than Marsh's ruined face.

It wasn't unusual for John to do a single thing for hours on end. Rocking. Knocking. Howling. But not for him to be still and silent like this. He made noise even in his sleep. Marsh wondered from time to time about the nightmares that sometimes plagued his son.

"When did this happen?" he asked.

Liv shrugged. She still wouldn't look at him. She hadn't, much, since he'd come home from the hospital. "Midmorning. Nine or ten."

Marsh didn't know exactly when they'd brought the second Twin over, because clocks and watches were useless in the vicinity of an Eidolon. But it fit the time frame. He'd have to ask Will about this.

He almost said this last aloud, but caught himself in the nick of time as he remembered Liv believed Will dead. What was one more secret on top of everything else?

Liv closed the door. She tossed the locks with practiced ease. "Put you on the night shift, did they?"

By which she meant he'd been gone all night plus most of the previous day, and now he was home at noon.

"I came home for a lie down. I'm not feeling well."

"Oh," she said. This time she did look at him. A flicker of what might have been concern formed a crease between her eyebrows. She held that look for a beat before returning downstairs.

The stairs were too great an obstacle between him and the cot in his shed. Stephenson's ghost was far too heavy to carry much farther without rest. He paused at the open door to the bedroom he ostensibly shared with Liv. The sheets were rumpled on her side of the mattress, untouched on his. To hell with things; this was his, too. Marsh kicked off his shoes en route to the bed. He dropped most of the rest of his clothes in a heap on the floor.

The cool, smooth sheets soothed his aching scars. He lay on his side, cradling his head on the pillow so as not to put pressure on his face. After a moment he took the other pillow, too. It smelled of Liv. Stray strands of her hair tickled the parts of his face that retained feeling.

He awoke after sunset. His nap had been deep and dreamless. The throbbing pain behind his eyes had receded to a dull ache. Several moments of disorientation passed between realizing he wasn't in the shed and remembering he was in the bedroom. Liv's bedroom.

John had roused himself. Banging and mewling sounded from his room up the corridor. The soundproofing muted most of the vocalizations, but it couldn't stop the floorboards from rattling beneath his stomping feet. Well. Whatever had caused him to curl up and fall silent, it had passed.

And the boy needed to eat. It was probably past time for his dinner. Marsh tossed aside the covers, gathering his strength for a trip downstairs to see if Liv had left some food prepared for John before leaving for the evening.

He struggled to find his clothes in the darkened bedroom. He hadn't bothered to pull the blinds, but the illumination from the streetlamps merely cast a dim yellow rectangle on the ceiling. He'd managed to find his shirt but no trousers when the overhead light clicked on.

Liv stood in the doorway with a tray. They stared at each other in surprise. Marsh, wounded and indecent, felt surprised because the sun had set yet Liv was home; Liv looked harried and embarrassed, perhaps because he was wounded and indecent.

"You're home," he blurted, at the same moment she said, "You're up."

Another awkward silence. Liv broke it: "I made soup," she said, indicating the tray. It held a bowl, a piece of black bread, and a spoon. She stepped into the room. Marsh sat on the edge of the bed. He felt self-conscious without his trousers, and then mournful that such would be his reaction to appearing undressed before his wife.

"You're home," he repeated, because the surprise hadn't left him, and he didn't know what else to say.

She turned her head away, gave a halfhearted shrug. "I thought I'd stay in."

He stared at her. Something had changed, but he didn't understand.

Liv hefted the tray again. "It's getting cold." The timbre of embarrassment tarnished her silver voice.

"Oh. Right." His stomach rumbled at the smell of food. Slowly, uncertainly, he pulled himself back into bed. She waited for him to pull the covers across himself, then set the tray on his lap.

"Thank you," he said. And then he tucked in, because he discovered he was ravenous. Liv sat in the armchair beside the wardrobe and watched him eat.

John thumped more loudly. Marsh started to get up, but Liv raised a hand. "I fed him while you slept."

Marsh nodded. He tore off a piece of bread and dunked it in the bowl. The soup was warm but not salty. It soothed the persistent ache in his throat. Salt was painful.

"You weren't home last night," she said.

"Work," he said around a mouthful of wet bread.

A thought struck him. Rumpled sheets. He realized that Liv had stayed home last night. But in a strange reversal, *he* had been gone all night, leaving her to wonder.

"Was Gretel there?"

So that was it. "She isn't my lover, Liv. If you believe anything, believe that."

"I know it. I know. She explained things to me."

He nearly dropped his spoon. "She did?"

"She said there was a lot of friction between you. That you should be warmer to her. But you're not, because of the pain."

Marsh gritted his teeth. How long had they talked in the hospital? Gretel might have tested a hundred variations of the conversation, a thousand, foreseeing every variation, every outcome, until she knew how to educe the precise reactions she wanted from Liv.

"It's complicated," he muttered.

"Why?"

He didn't answer. Instead, he concentrated on spooning the last drops of soup from the bowl. How could Marsh explain this? How could he tell her that Agnes had died in the past because Liv had confided to Gretel in the present? How could he condemn Liv to a life inside that impregnable grief?

Liv changed the subject. "Is she married?"

"What?"

"She mentioned a Klaus. I thought . . ."

The spoon rang against ceramic while he fished out the last piece of carrot. "Klaus isn't her husband," he managed. "He's her brother."

"Oh," said Liv. She looked momentarily confused by that. "Do you think they would . . ." She trailed off again. "Maybe we could have dinner. The four of us."

"What?" This time he did drop the spoon.

"I like Gretel. She's easy to talk to."

Oh dear God. Marsh was at a loss for how to navigate this minefield. On the one hand, his estranged wife was telling him in so many words that she wanted to be around him, at least a little bit. And that hadn't happened in a very long time. It should have brought him happiness. But the joy and hope were corrupted, tainted with suspicion. This otherwise welcome change had come about because of Gretel. Even here, even now, the monster's fingerprints smudged his life. She cast her shadow even on the delicate private interactions of a strained marriage.

"Please don't ask this of me, Liv. Not Gretel."

"I want to have friends again. Real friends."

She had gone to Will's funeral. Will had been touched by that. The funeral and the interaction with Gretel had together left their marks on Liv. They'd forced her to confront a loneliness she'd buried long ago. And Marsh, seeing it so plain on his wife for the first time, felt a gentle connection to her because he carried the same burden. They were twins in sorrow and regret. Two halves of a sundered life.

"Me, too. But not Gretel. It's impossible."

"What about her brother?"

"Klaus?" He was certainly the lesser of two evils. And to be fair, he'd been a fairly good bloke. But: "He's good. But he's gone. He isn't here any longer."

"Oh," said Liv. "How sad. Gretel must be lonely." She stood and took the tray with its empty bowl.

"Thank you for the soup," said Marsh. "I feel better."

"Rest," she said. He settled back under the covers. Liv turned off the light on her way out. But she stood in the corridor and watched him until he fell asleep.

11 June 1963
Milkweed Headquarters, London, England

The children hadn't recovered from their ordeal with the Twins by the time Milkweed received confirmation the Soviets were on the move. But Moscow had taken Marsh's bait, and thus it fell to Will to spring the trap.

Moscow believed the final warlock had been eliminated. And that without the power of the Eidolons on its side, Britain no longer had an effective deterrent against Soviet aggression. No way to defend the Empire, no hope of clinging to its holdings.

Naturally, the USSR went straight for the low-hanging fruit.

Just hours after the Twins' false message, Soviet forces spilled into Iran. The speed of the Kremlin's response surprised nobody. The troop buildup had been in place for weeks. They'd been waiting, poised for the moment the path opened to them. Armored columns plunged deep into the country in a socialist version of the blitzkrieg, ready to claim the rich Persian oil fields for the Great Soviet. So greedy was the Kremlin that they were committed to this path before they realized the Moscow Twin had disappeared. Once again, as SIS analysts had predicted.

Iranian and British forces together attempted to resist the incursion. Under normal conditions, they would have been able to hold out for a long time, because preparing for this eventuality had long been a key element of Britain's strategy in the region.

But this was not a normal conflict, because the attack also marked the world debut of an entirely new fighting force. Hundreds of Arzamas shock troops spearheaded the invasion.

Which meant they were concentrated and vulnerable to an Eidolonic counterattack.

It was all playing out according to Marsh's plan.

twelve

12 June 1963
Aylesbury, Buckinghamshire, England

When dissimilar metals touch in the presence of a conductive medium, the result is a small but measurable voltage. The effect was discovered by Luigi Galvani in the late eighteenth century. It was rediscovered by Klaus on the morning of his first full day as a free man.

He'd arrived at his new flat by early afternoon. The package from Marsh contained the key and a lease already signed under Klaus's new identity, Hans Kannenberg. (He made a mental note to practice his new signature.) The flat was a corner unit over a greengrocer, with an oriel window that overlooked the grocer's awning at the intersection of two lanes lined with shops. The long wooden floorboards creaked with every footstep; the bedroom wainscoting had a prominent mouse hole; the kitchen had only one tiny cupboard for storage. It was, he supposed, quaint.

And luxurious compared to Klaus's expectations: the flat had a private bath. He'd taken it for granted he'd be given a room in a boarding house, forced to share a communal bathroom with a host of other residents.

Never in his entire life had Klaus enjoyed a private bathroom. It didn't matter if the rest of the building turned out to be a rattrap. At least it would be his private rattrap.

He spent most of that first afternoon pacing through the flat. *His* flat. A fact that defeated him. He didn't want to leave, didn't want to stop running his hands along the walls, for fear that it would all disappear if he did.

But as afternoon slid into evening, the hunger pangs reminded Klaus he hadn't eaten since the previous night. He ventured outside and caught the greengrocer as he was closing shop; Klaus spent some of the cash from Marsh's package in return for a tomato, a cucumber, a head of lettuce, and a surprised glance at his wires. Klaus spotted a butcher's shop down the road, just closed for the day. He knocked on the display window. The butcher unlocked the door; Klaus ducked in and managed to get another double take along with the last lamb chop. Neither shop had mint jelly on hand. He'd wondered at Will's dinner in Knightsbridge, the fresh smell of the mint and the bloody scent of rare lamb. Klaus hadn't eaten lamb since the days when he'd been the doctor's favorite.

He rejected the memory, ashamed of it, vowing never to revisit it. Ancient history. Life began anew today.

On the way back, Klaus passed a newspaper stand. A deliveryman stood on the back of a truck, carelessly tossing down bundles of the evening edition. Klaus jumped aside to avoid a flying bundle, toppling a pile of papers in the process. The seller apologetically gathered up Klaus's groceries while Klaus restacked the papers. Again, the sight of Klaus's wires evoked a small frown and shudder.

Klaus glimpsed the front page while self-consciously offering his own apologies. More coverage of the situation in Iran: the Soviet columns had made great progress toward the refineries of the south in an improbably short time, but stopped abruptly. Klaus couldn't stop himself from idle speculation; he couldn't help but wonder how many Arzamas troops rode at the vanguard of that incursion.

No further incidents interrupted his return home. Only later did he realize he hadn't instinctively reached for the Götterelektron during the near miss with the newspaper deliveryman. His training and his old life were fading into the distance. That pleased him greatly. For the first time, his future was what he made it. He would never become a junk man.

He entered the flat hungry and eager to cook his own meal in his own home. But as he set his groceries on the small countertop beside the refrigerator, he realized he had no dishes. No cutlery, no glasses, no pots, no pans. He ate the tomato like an apple, over the sink. The juice ran down his chin, sharp enough to sting a nascent cold sore at the corner of his lips. Klaus resolved to spend more of his Milkweed cash the next day, and to cook a real meal for himself the next evening. He would eventually have to find a job. But that could wait.

He spent the night on a bare mattress, but let himself sleep in. That was also something he'd rarely experienced. At both the Reichsbehörde and Arzamas-16, his daily regimen had been tightly controlled, any opportunities for sloth ruthlessly chopped out and tossed aside.

Klaus ran the hottest shower he could. As with so many other household necessities, he had no soap, no shampoo, no towel; the medicine cabinet was empty but for a rusty straight razor left behind by a previous resident. But that wasn't the point. This was *his* shower. He filled his lungs with steam and stood under the pounding hot rain until it became a cold drizzle.

The cracked gray tiles of the bathroom floor turned treacherously slick beneath his feet. Rivulets of water streamed out of his hair, pooling in the mildewed gaps between the tiles. Steam had condensed into a fine silvery mist across the mirror. Klaus wiped a hand along the cool glass, flicked the water into the sink.

Mirror and morning light together showed him the truth: He was a fiftyish man with nothing to show for all those years, turning softer with every passing day, and eternally defined by the wires embedded in his skull. He thought back to his brief shopping trip the previous evening. The greengrocer, the butcher, and the newspaper vendor hadn't seen Klaus the man so much as they'd seen a man with wires.

It had been surprisingly easy to overcome his own reluctance to venture into public without a disguise. But it wasn't enough. No amount of self-confidence, of forced goodwill, would ever put people at ease when faced with such ugliness. Gretel relied upon her manipulative charm.

The wires were a tether, forever chaining him to his old life. He'd seen it three times in the space of a quarter hour.

Klaus tested the straight razor with his thumb. The blade hadn't been properly stropped since long before it was abandoned. But close to the hinge it still retained a cutting edge. Not sharp, but perhaps good enough for sawing through strands of woven copper.

He used his fingernails to peel away several inches of insulation. Next, Klaus gripped the razor handle in one hand and flipped the blade backwards so that the dull side pressed against his knuckles. He clenched the wires in his free fist and pulled them taut enough to tug unpleasantly against the steel fasteners in his skull.

Klaus held that posture while he studied himself in the mirror. The wires had been a part of him—part of his physical space, his body image, the way he moved through the world—for most of his life. He was as unconsciously aware of his wires as he was of his own fingers and toes. Was this self-mutilation? Self-hatred? He erased all doubts by thinking of Reinhardt, who scoured church rummage sales in search of a lost godhood, who sought to revive something long dead from broken radios and bits of scrap.

Beads of condensation trickled along the gleaming wire. Klaus touched it with the razor. His tongue curled beneath the taste of copper. It became an overpowering stench of rotten eggs in the moment before a convulsion racked his arms and broke the connection.

Klaus dropped the razor and retched into the sink.

Stray electrical currents had triggered random pathways in his brain. How on earth did Reinhardt experiment on himself with substantial voltages? How did he stand it?

A painful cramp twisted his gut. His empty stomach had produced only a handful of tomato seeds that lay sprinkled across the white porcelain. The hunger pangs returned with a vengeance.

It took several breaths to clear away the sickening phantom odor. Klaus gathered up the razor, steeled himself, and tried again. This time the galvanic currents brought forth flashes of light bright enough to bleach out the room, like magnesium flares, and the sensation of a wolf gnawing on his foot. Klaus withstood the convulsions until the wolf's fangs prized his ankle bones apart.

He dropped the razor again and lurched against the bathroom door. The razor handle cracked on the tiles. He slid down to a crouch over the space of several shuddery breaths. Klaus ran a hand over his ankle, simultaneously surprised that it could hold his weight and that the hallucination had been so vivid. He shivered. All of the shower steam had condensed away, leaving something thin and chilly where the air had been.

The mirror showed his wires dangling by a final few strands. Klaus felt the weight of the broken wires—his superfluous limb, his tail, his chains—jerking and swaying like a windswept pendulum. He gazed down at the broken razor, then back at the damaged wires.

Cupping the plug in his palm, he gently wrapped the length of wire around his fist. Klaus stared himself in the eye, and counted aloud.

"One.

"Two."

On three, he passed out.

Some time later he came to his senses, sprawled on the cold tile floor with a length of loose wire coiled around his fist. Something wet and warm trickled through his hair; his fingers came back tinted red. At first he thought he'd opened a wound in his skull, cracked it like an egg by ripping out the implanted electrodes. But no. He'd knocked his head on the tiles when he passed out.

Somewhere, somebody rapped knuckles against solid wood in a quick and emphatic staccato. Another hallucination?

No. The straight razor still lay where he'd dropped it. And when he ran his fingers through his hair, he found a stub where the wires had been.

More banging. Knocking. At his door.

Klaus grabbed the sink and hauled himself to his feet, naked and shivering. The blow to his head had left him dizzy. He studied the mirror, and for the first time in memory he saw himself as himself, without wires or Willenskräfte. Just a man. Not a prisoner, not a spy, not a game piece, not a fallen god. Just Klaus.

Finally. And after years too numerous to remember.

The delay brought more pounding from the entryway. His aching head throbbed in time with the knocking. He gathered up his trousers, slipped them on, snatched his shirt from the hook behind the bathroom door, and padded woozily into the den. He buttoned the shirt while crossing to the door.

He opened it just as Madeleine raised her fist for another flurry of knocks.

A canvas sack hung from her elbow. Tall paper tubes bulged from one end of the sack.

He stared, dumbfounded.

Madeleine extended her arm, holding the sack toward him. "You forgot these," she said.

13 June 1963
Milkweed Headquarters, London, England

Pethick summoned Will back to the Admiralty two days after he and the children sprang Marsh's trap. Had something gone wrong? Was he being called on the carpet?

Will asked Roger, who once again played the role of taxi driver. But Roger shook his head. "Got a package. Figured you should be there to see it."

Will pressed him for details, but he wouldn't elaborate. When they arrived, they found the others gathered in Marsh's office—Will shuddered—formerly Pembroke's office. Poor Pembroke. Murdered in his own home? Will could imagine it; what a terrifying way to die. A death he came very near to experiencing.

Someone had wheeled in a film projector. An empty film canister lay open on Marsh's desk. Pethick snapped a reel onto the spindle and threaded film into the machine while Marsh pulled the blinds and set up a screen.

Will said, "Dare I ask what this is about, Pip?"

Marsh tapped a finger on the canister. "This came by special courier tonight. Straight from Tehran."

Pethick finished with the projector. He rubbed his hands together. To Marsh, he said, "Very good. Let's see if your plan worked."

Roger turned off the overhead lights. Marsh took the seat behind his desk; Roger took the other chair. Will leaned against the door, arms crossed.

Pethick flipped a switch. The projector clattered to life. The film began with the Crown seal, and this notice:

MILKWEED / JACKDAW

MOST SECRET

UNAUTHORISED DISSEMINATION OF THE INFORMATION CONTAINED IN THIS FILM CONSTITUTES TREASON AGAINST THE UNITED KINGDOM OF GREAT BRITAIN AND NORTHERN IRELAND AS DEFINED BY PARLIAMENT IN THE OFFICIAL SECRETS ACT OF 1951. PUNISHMENT UP TO AND INCLUDING EXECUTION MAY RESULT.

MILKWEED / JACKDAW

Will had seen this same warning once before. He didn't find it so intimidating the second time around. Unauthorized dissemination? Treason? He lived on the other side of that boilerplate.

A shaky camera panned across a distant desert plain. The angle put the camera at elevation; a mountain range bordered the desert. A plume of dust hovered above the desert floor like an enormous rooster tail. The camera zoomed in on the head of the plume. Extreme magnification rendered the view shakier and blurrier, but not so much that Will couldn't make out the red stars marking the tanks and armored transports that sped silently across the plain.

But the lead vehicle appeared to be nothing more than a cargo truck. The canvas covering had been removed from the cargo bed, and a handful of men and women stood on the back of the truck. They wore goggles and balaclavas to shield themselves from the dust.

The camera spun, swaying across the empty sky for a moment before focusing on a trio of fighter jets streaking over the plain to meet the column. Will couldn't identify the planes, but they bore the markings of the RAF. Quick cuts between the jets and the truck. The passengers stared at the oncoming fighters. Two of the planes erupted in white-blue fireballs. The third suddenly underwent a spectacular disintegration, as if it had slammed into an invisible wall. Flaming debris rained on the desert. The Soviet column hadn't slowed one bit.

The view cut back to the distant perspective. Time had passed, because now the column was miles closer to the camera. More debris littered the plain behind the Soviets; oily smoke rose from a line of burnt and mangled tanks. The Soviet column hadn't slowed, hadn't broken formation. It had been joined by half a dozen others. All pristine.

And then the wind picked up.

It was subtle at first, just a steady breeze that dissipated the smoke and stretched the rooster tail plume into long fingers of dust. But in moments the breeze swelled into a raging sandstorm. Hundred-foot dust devils spun like dervishes, dancing before a churning wall of wind and dust. The cyclones took impossible shapes, angular and misshapen, as they sped toward the Soviet formation. The camera zoomed on the weather front. It, too, was filled with non-Euclidean shadows. The center of the storm was black and lightless. The feeble sunlight that skirted the periphery of the storm oozed across the foothills of the mountains like crimson syrup.

The sandstorm loomed over the Soviet column, like a wave on the verge of breaking. The figures in the leading vehicle gestured at the unnatural storm. The film blurred. Will suspected, based on the experience with the Twins, the Arzamas troops had provoked the Eidolons to greater rage. The Eidolonic weather front engulfed the Soviet forces.

Another cut back to the original view of the desert plain. No plumes, no debris, no storms. Will thought for a moment the film had jumped back to the beginning. But then the camera zoomed and panned across the plain once more. The desert had been scoured clean. The camera paused on what appeared to be the barrel of a tank sticking out of the sand. Elsewhere, the sun shone on a handful of pale, sandblasted bones.

Roger grunted in approval. "Take that, you bloody commies."

Pethick stifled something that might have been a laugh.

Another cut, and the landscape changed. Another Soviet column, another unnatural weather front. This time it left the Arzamas troops encased in ice.

And so it went. Variations on this theme spooled out before them for the next ten minutes while the atmosphere in the room grew lighter and lighter and Will's disgust grew deeper and deeper.

The projector spit out the last few inches of film. Stunned silence gave way to the *flap-flap-flap* of the takeup reel. The sudden glare of the bright white screen hurt Will's dark-adapted eyes; he squinted and turned away.

When Marsh turned on the overhead lights, he was grinning like the Cheshire cat. It was a ghoulish look on that ruined face. Pethick, Roger, and Marsh congratulated one another. They treated Will as though he were the hero of the hour.

Pethick took his hand and shook it vigorously. "Excellent work," he said. Roger did likewise.

And it was Marsh of all people who actually clapped Will on the back. "Well done, Will. Very well done."

Their mood was nothing less than celebratory. Nobody noticed that Will had gone pale, or the way he trembled when he stood.

"Your tea must be quite ready by now."

Will jumped, startled from his contemplation of the moonlit garden. He turned in the silvery shadows by the window to find Gwendolyn silhouetted in the doorway.

"Steeping it for an hour is a bit excessive," she said, entering the lightless kitchen. "Unless your tastes have changed."

The teapot porcelain felt lukewarm beneath his fingers; a toe-curling whiff of Indian tea escaped when he cracked the lid. And the lemon he'd retrieved from the pantry still sat whole on the cutting board, beside a clean knife. How long had he stood here? The moon had moved almost a third of the length of the garden wall since he'd started the tea.

He'd been thinking about the film from Tehran. And the fact nobody recognized its deeply troubling implications.

"I lost track of the time," he said. He frowned. "It can't be an hour."

Gwendolyn said, "I've been waiting for you to return since you slipped out of bed." She pulled her dressing gown about herself as she settled on a tall stool at the counter. She didn't bother with the lights.

"I woke you. I'm sorry."

The queasiness in the pit of Will's stomach had banished any hope of sleep. He'd finally relented after midnight, and carefully eased out of bed so as not to disturb Gwendolyn. The warmth of her body beside him, the slow and measured susurration of her breathing—things he'd missed for so desperately long, yet now he couldn't enjoy them, couldn't relish them. His mind and heart were too unsettled. Ever since Marsh had dragged Will back to Milkweed, he'd been plagued by the sense of unseen currents swirling in the murky depths. Unseen and perilous. Uncharted hazards contriving to smash all comers against deadly shoals.

Yes, the fear had begun when Marsh revealed Will's deal with Cherkashin. But compared to what followed, that seemed almost quaint. For one, Gretel's part in all of this had yet to become clear. Had she really killed Pembroke? Why? Why were the children acting so strangely? And then that film . . . It all fit together somehow. He knew it. They were hints of something bigger, like stray currents swirling together to spawn a whirlpool. But dragging them down to what?

The dread and anticipation lay on Will just as heavily as they had early in the war. He felt much as he did after realizing Stephenson and Whitehall would turn a blind eye to anything the warlocks did.

Gwendolyn scoffed. "Hardly. Our cozy little house is getting cozier by the day. A smart woman breakfasts at half three. To beat the rush. Any later, and there's a queue for the ladies' convenience."

She had a point. Gwendolyn shared a bathroom with four other women now that the Twins had arrived. Meanwhile the men's bathroom saw less use after Klaus's departure.

Madeleine had received the Twins at the safe house with forced good grace, although the crease at the bridge of her nose betrayed a faint irritation. She put the Twins up in the room recently vacated by Klaus. Will helped her wrestle a second bed from the cellar, while Gwendolyn gathered Klaus's paintings and the supplies he'd left behind. Madeleine made a point of insisting this be done carefully.

It was like living in a university dormitory. Or a barracks. But unlike those situations, there was no end in sight for this. Even worse was knowing that Will would never be able to take Gwendolyn back home, to their old life. Their real home, their wonderful Queen Anne town house with its humble breakfast table, had burned to cinders. The result of a long chain of Will's terrible decisions.

When Gwendolyn had first told Will (with uncharacteristic shyness) that she missed sleeping beside him, part of him had wondered if this were intended as a space-saving measure. A favor for Madeleine. But he'd been willing to take anything that would soothe the ache where her companionship, her partnership, had been. Especially if, as he feared, those unseen currents were to pull them apart sooner than later.

He took the teapot and cutting board to the counter. "I am sorry, love. For all of this."

"I won't be sorry to see the last of this house," she admitted. "I've begun to feel a bit déclassé without a bit of copper dangling from my head." Juice misted his face and stung his eye when Gwendolyn took the knife to the lemon.

Will knew just how much she must have disliked the crowded safe house to prompt even the smallest concession of discomfort. She was, if nothing else, a proper British lady to the last.

"Well." He lifted a pair of chipped teacups from hooks under the cupboard. "It's done now, everything Marsh wanted. I've met the conditions Milkweed set for me in lieu of incarceration. So we ought to have an answer soon, assuming Marsh doesn't move the finish line."

And assuming, he didn't add, *fate doesn't render Marsh's intentions irrelevant.* Which, as long as Gretel kept her true purpose hidden, it almost certainly would.

Nobody had told him whether they'd continue the public fiction of

William Beauclerk's untimely demise. He saw no reason for it. Now that the children had unleashed Marsh's Eidolonic counterattack on the Soviet Union's Arzamas shock troops in Iran, the continued existence of Britain's warlocks was no longer a secret.

Will's thoughts again returned to the film from Iran. He shuddered. The whole adventure called Milkweed had begun with another film-strip back in 1939. Oh, for those carefree days.

Milkweed had put Ivan in his place and the Queen was safe in her palace. And yet . . .

He filled both cups, slid one to Gwendolyn. He sipped, then made a face. It was strong enough to wake the dead. And unpleasantly cool besides. But he drank it anyway.

Gwendolyn tucked a slice of lemon on the lip of his cup. She partly read his thoughts. "And the prospect of reuniting with Aubrey makes you too giddy to sleep?"

Will set his elbows on the countertop and stared into the cup he held beneath his chin. "Something's wrong, Gwendolyn. Deeply wrong."

She frowned. "Tell me."

And so he did.

At issue were the "taskings" Pethick had presented to the children before Will had come along. It was those tasks, those maps stippled with their damned pushpins, that kept Will up all night. Because in dealing with the Eidolons, one cannot simply point to a map on the wall. It was all the same to them: teacups, soldiers, dying stars. Human blood was the only map that carried meaning for the Eidolons.

With a drop of somebody's blood, the Eidolons could track that person's trajectory through the universe, through time and space, like omniscient bloodhounds. Blood enabled them to *see* people. To see things at a human scale, so incomprehensibly limited compared to the vastness of the Eidolons' purview. And with a bit of (expensive) coaxing, they could be made to see the places through which that person had traveled.

Gretel had grown up at Doctor von Westarp's farm. The Eidolons had seen Gretel, and thus the farm. And so Milkweed's warlocks had been able to send commando teams there. For all the good *that* did.

Marsh had been a lieutenant commander in the Royal Navy. He'd sailed through the English Channel countless times. The Eidolons had seen him—

(*Why* did *they give him a name?*)

—and thus had seen the Channel. And so Milkweed's warlocks had been able to conjure a blockade that held off the German invasion. . . .

Will faltered. He covered by taking a long sip of cool tea. Gwendolyn squeezed his hand, knowing he was remembering the Hart and Hearth. She understood how "blood price" had become a euphemism for mass murder.

Freezing the Wehrmacht had been the most difficult and the most risky. Marsh had traveled extensively in Europe, as had Will, Stephenson, and a number of the other Milkweed conscripts. But it was still a patchwork affair, overlaying their travels in the past with German troop deployments in the present. Hargreaves and the rest must have done some fast talking to pull that off; Will didn't know the details, because he'd been drummed out, incapable of functioning without alcohol and morphine, before they'd made it work.

He did know that Milkweed had paid the highest blood prices of the war effort in order to blanket Europe with ice. He also knew it was the closest they'd ever come to breaking the rules, to letting the Eidolons slip their leash. One misstep, one slip of the tongue, one piece of faulty grammar might have allowed the Eidolons to kill directly. To start collecting blood maps on their own.

And then the war wouldn't have mattered at all.

Will shook his head, returned to the present.

Without Middle Eastern oil, the British Empire would falter. And the Soviets had their own sprawling empire to fuel. So a strike at the oil fields had long been inevitable; the troop buildup had begun weeks ago. The USSR had intentionally tipped its own hand because it was ready and eager to unveil its elite Arzamas troops, to showcase its mastery of the same technology that had made Gretel and the rest. It didn't take a master spy or a military prodigy to suss this out.

It had been easy to anticipate the attack. But for the Eidolons to participate in the defense, they needed localized blood. Thus Milkweed had taken advantage of the troop buildup in the region to prepare relevant blood maps. The simplest thing would have been to send secret blood samples along with the supply shipments. Warlock blood would work best. Pembroke and Pethick, two peas in a pod, undoubtedly had generous stores of the children's blood at hand for just these occasions. In fact, now that Will thought about it, the practice of keeping warlocks' blood on file probably didn't begin with the peas.

Stephenson would have foreseen this need.

Oh, yes. The old man would have looked past the end of the war to see the Cold War taking shape. He would have anticipated great upheavals in the geopolitical landscape, upheavals with the potential to render Milkweed powerless unless it had the power to bring the Eidolons to bear whenever and wherever necessary.

Oh, yes. Will had never considered this before, but now it seemed obvious. Stephenson had probably obtained blood samples from all the original warlocks. Will wondered if Milkweed still had his blood in cold storage somewhere.

What a violation. Disgusting, arrogant, unacceptable.

He'd take it up with Pethick.

He paused while Gwendolyn refilled her cup, then his. She stifled a yawn and motioned for him to continue.

"So now," said Will, "let me ask you: Doesn't it seem out of character for our dear Pip to leave things unfinished? Because at the end of the day, there will be no final, definitive victory as long as Arzamas-16 stands."

Even Will could see that was the next logical step. He'd braced himself for just such a demand from Marsh and Pethick. Yet it hadn't happened. Why?

Gwendolyn said, "But you've answered your own question, love. They would do it if they could. But they haven't, so they can't. Implying they have no collocated blood, to use your charming phrase, with which to guide the Eidolons." She wrung another lemon slice over her cup. Moonlight silvered the dusting of gray at her temples when she shrugged. There seemed to be more gray in her hair these days. "Arzamas is probably more secure than Khrushchev's knickers. More secure than the Baikonur Cosmodrome, apparently."

Will had to concede that it wasn't impossible. Waltzing into the rocket facility was exactly the sort of thing a young Marsh might have attempted, had he been fluent in Russian.

"Perhaps," he said. "But the maps, Gwendolyn. They're full of push-pins. Or they were, before the tykes went barmy and tore the place to shreds."

"They've been busy." She pursed her lips as she finished off her cup. Perhaps owing to too much lemon, overly strong tea, or both. She rinsed her cup with a trickle of water so as not to rattle the plumbing in the wee hours of the morning.

But this was all beside the point. So Will repeated what Pethick had said, the first time they had gone to the cellar together.

" 'This is odd,' he said. 'The children have been moving pins about.' And then looked more closely. 'We've never done any taskings here, or here.' "

"Where?" Gwendolyn asked.

"All over," said Will. "Do you remember the last time we had dinner with Aubrey and Viola? There had been that terrible disruption to rail service in the Midlands. We clucked our tongues about it at length."

"Yes."

"The children had put a pin there."

"Oh." She sat again. "It could be a coincidence."

"As I thought when I first noticed it. But as I said, that was before the children went barmy. Driven into a frenzy by the Eidolons."

"You believe the children weren't moving pins about at random," she said. "Something had happened there."

Will nodded. "I think the Eidolons have become worked up over something. And their agitation is leaking out like ripples from a stone tossed into a pond. Spreading across the world, backward and for-ward."

Gwendolyn sounded less and less convinced by her own arguments, but she continued to offer them. "But, love, you've spent a great deal of time in the Midlands. If they do have your blood on file, and if they've used it, this could be a side effect."

"Perhaps. But I am utterly confident no warlock has ever paid a visit to Tanganyika." Will spread his hands widely to emphasize his point. "Or, for that matter, Santa Fe bloody New Mexico."

"What are you saying?"

"I believe Pethick when he says Milkweed hasn't conducted such operations. But I also think the children sense something imminent. And the mystery events are echoes of something that hasn't happened yet."

They both fell silent after that. Will held his wife while a cold, pink sun rose slowly over London.

14 June 1963
Croydon, London, England

Marsh took his time preparing the reel-to-reel recorder. Not to provoke a sense of anxiety; he knew Gretel was beyond any form of intimidation. But the extra minute meant more time to think. More time to consider conversational gambits, opening volleys. More time to try to shake off incipient illness. The injuries, long days, and heavy burdens had caught him up. He'd awoken with a slight fever.

The scents of fresh wood oil from the glossy walnut table and lubricant from the recorder mixed unpleasantly with the aftertaste of the tomatoes and sausages Marsh had fried for breakfast. He and Liv had eaten in silence, but at least they'd eaten together. It was a start. Her sharp edges and cutting wit weren't on display, but it didn't soften the blow when her gaze darted to the wounds peeking from beneath his beard, or when she flinched away from his touch. Liv had broken the silence to mention Gretel again; Marsh went to work before the discussion became an argument.

It was a start.

The glazing bars in the den's window cast jumbled shadows across Gretel's face. She stared at the ivy-covered wall outside with sloe eyes aglimmer. But she'd abandoned her usual air of cryptic amusement. No faint quirk of the lips today: she was smiling. She almost never did that.

Will, slumped in the corner behind Gretel, looking like seven kinds of hell. Marsh might have suspected Will had taken up the bottle again, except he knew Will wasn't nearly clever enough to pull that off under his wife's nose. The man hadn't slept. He'd given a long and animated explanation why.

Which had jarred something loose. A long-forgotten and overlooked memory now stirred Marsh's churning thoughts.

And what would my assignment be? he'd asked Pembroke.

I've already told you. Suss out Gretel's intentions.

The flimsy magnetized tape clung awkwardly to Marsh's fingertips. He threaded it through the machine, pulled the free end to the hub of empty reel, and turned the reel just enough to take up the slack. Marsh adjusted the microphone so that it sat exactly in the center of the table between himself and Gretel. Needles on the recorder swung erratically in their lighted windows when he nudged the microphone closer to Gretel. The recording heads jerked into place with a solid *thunk* when he started the recorder.

Gretel pulled her attention from the window. She looked at Marsh with eyebrows raised and the hint of a smile tugging at the corners of her eyes.

"The beard suits you. Very rugged."

Marsh ignored her. "We know you're waiting for something. That much has been obvious since your arrival. Naturally we've obsessed over what it might be."

Her expression didn't change. As of course it wouldn't. He chose to make it easier on himself by pretending she wasn't endowed with god-like precognition. *Everybody slips,* he reminded himself. *She isn't God.*

God? Marsh hadn't set foot in a church since John's birth. Nor had Liv. Their faith in the divine had withered in light of the overwhelming evidence of its absence.

Gretel can't be right one hundred percent of the time, he told himself. *I refuse to live in a clockwork universe.*

He continued, "Why did Leslie Pembroke have to die? And why go to such lengths to inveigle cooperation from Reinhardt? That must have been quite a feat, since he despises you so."

"Is that what my brother told you?"

"It's what Reinhardt told us."

She shook her head. "Oh, Raybould. Lies do not suit you."

Marsh shrugged. "We'll find him soon enough—"

"No, you won't."

"—and when we do, he'll finger you for your part in Pembroke's murder. In light of your defection, asylum, and newfound allegiance to the Crown, I'll personally see that treason is added to the charges. That means the gallows for you."

Will chimed in. "He means every word of it, you know. He's quite fond of nabbing people for treason. Bit of a crusade, you might say."

Gretel's eyes didn't leave Marsh, but she cocked her head to one side, making it clear she addressed Will. "Would you like to know your wife's deepest thoughts and feelings about this entire affair? It would be no trouble."

Will mustered his dignity, but his voice quavered. He feared Gretel. "We share everything. There's nothing you could tell me I don't already know about Gwendolyn, and vice versa."

"Are you certain?" said Gretel. "It would be the easiest thing in the world to know if you're right. People open up to me. Isn't that right, Raybould?"

"Leave Liv out of this," Marsh growled.

Will frowned, knowing he'd missed something.

"I find Gwendolyn in the kitchen, while she fixes a salad for dinner." Will paled as Gretel began to rattle off her nonchalant prophecy. "I begin by asking her to pass a—"

Marsh rapped his knuckles on the table. The needles jumped again. "That's enough." To Will, who was visibly shaken, he said, "Don't let her get under your skin. She's toying with you. She's not wearing a battery."

"Yes." Will paused. He looked chagrined. "Of course."

Marsh tried to swallow a growing ache, and winced. His injuries had become a caltrop lodged in his throat. He braced himself, then forced his words out, flogging them like cavalry crossing the no-man's-land of his broken voice.

"I think it was a mistake for us to wonder what you've been waiting for. Rather than concentrating on *what* you're doing, we should be asking ourselves *why* you're doing it."

He leaned across the table. "You forget that I've seen behind your mask."

At this, Gretel frowned.

"You present a front to the world, an air of imperturbable serenity. And you play it well, I'll give you that. So everybody accepts it. Even Klaus."

Gretel said, "I hope Madeleine looks after him."

Marsh ignored the deflection. "But it's all just an act, isn't it? You're not fearless. No. Because I know one thing that terrifies you. The Eidolons."

Was there the tiniest shift in the set of her jaw? A minute hardening in the lines around her eyes? A stillness?

"Back in '40, when Will and I put you in front of that Eidolon—naïvely assuming the Reichsbehörde was a haven for Jerry warlocks—you clenched my arm tight enough to draw blood with your nails." He gestured at her hands; she kept her nails short. "Gretel, pale and trembling. No longer an oracle. Just a girl again. That's what I remembered after all these years."

Marsh rolled back his sleeve, peering at his forearm. There, faintly visible under the graying hair, were three pale crescent-shaped marks where Gretel's nails had bitten deep. "But I thought nothing of it in that moment. Because my blood ran freely, which of course meant the Eidolon could see me as well."

"Ah, yes," said Gretel. "Your mysterious *name*."

Will sat up. "Do you know what it means?"

"Haven't your children translated it for you?"

The men shared a look. "They can't," Will muttered. "Or won't."

"Don't worry," she said. She glanced at Will over her shoulder. "I'm sure you'll find it enlightening."

Marsh pulled the conversation back on track. "I'd forgotten all about that incident until today." Marsh nodded at Will. "Will tells me the Eidolons have gone halfway round the bend. Like somebody has lobbed a bloody great boulder into their quiet little duck pond.

"Now, who, I wonder, could do a thing like that?"

Gretel yawned. She made a show of stretching, arching her back like a young woman trying to catch a lad's attention. He realized she was doing exactly that, for his benefit. Marsh shuddered with revulsion. Gretel craned her neck to look at the clock ticking atop the empty bookcase.

"Well," she said. "I've stalled you long enough." She stood. "We must leave now."

Marsh and Will shared another look. For his part, Will looked perplexed, and even a bit indignant. Which was more or less how Marsh felt.

"We're not done here," said Marsh. He made his point by reaching under the table with one leg to kick Gretel's chair toward her.

"If we don't leave now, we'll have a terrible time making it to the Admiralty." She nodded, as if to reassure him. "But you'll have my help, of course."

Marsh frowned. It came as nausea, the sick dread that he'd been outmaneuvered again. This warred with the anger and loathing he always felt in Gretel's presence. Fever sweat made the world slippery. He couldn't grab it, couldn't wrestle it down, couldn't force it to make sense. "Oh, I see. So I'm taking you to the Admiralty now, am I?"

"Yes."

"Why?"

"Because," she said just as Roger burst breathlessly into the room, "it has fallen under attack."

Roger said, "Boss! Just got a call on the blower. Sounds like half of Whitehall is up in flames."

"What? When did this happen?" Marsh was already on his feet, clenching Gretel's elbow with one hand and beckoning to Will with the other.

"Just now! All at once! Coordinated attack."

"By whom?" said Will, scrambling out of the chair.

"Dunno. Line went dead before I could get an answer."

They moved into the corridor beyond the den, like a rugby scrum with Marsh at the center.

To Roger, Marsh said, "Stay here and man the wireless." The house had a transmitter and receiver for communicating with other SIS outposts in cases of emergency. This qualified. "Arm yourself, do a head count, help Madeleine batten down the hatches."

"She isn't here," Roger said.

But Marsh was already moving on. To Will and Gretel, he said, "You two, with me."

Will started to protest: "Gwendolyn—"

"Is safer here. But if this is the children's doing, I need you with me."

They hurried across the entryway to the front door. Gwendolyn trotted halfway down the stairs behind them. "William? Where are you going?"

Will turned, dashed up the stairs. "I'll be back soon, love. Not to worry."

"Such a commotion. Why?"

He kissed her, a peck on the cheek. "Stay away from the windows." A look of deep concern crossed her face.

"We're going, *now*," said Marsh. His gravelly voice made everything sound like a command. Which was useful at times. He pulled Gretel after him, down the stairs to the Morris parked on the street. He opened the passenger-side door and pushed her inside. Will hopped in back as Marsh started the engine.

And then they were off, driving toward the heart of London, where distant sirens echoed and the first plumes of smoke darkened the sky.

The wireless mounted beneath the fascia provided sporadic updates and panicked speculations during the drive. A Soviet invasion, said some. An uprising of fifth columnists, said others. But whatever was happening, it was killing witnesses and severing communication lines faster than they could provide reliable reports. And London wasn't the only place under attack. The list of besieged cities grew by the minute: Manchester, Edinburgh, Birmingham, Leeds, Glasgow, Sheffield . . . All burned.

Gretel took it all in with prim satisfaction. She looked *proud*. She made a little sigh of triumph with each new report, or each time the situation worsened.

"What the hell have you done?" Marsh cranked the wheel. The car skidded through a roundabout, sending Gretel's braids flying.

She caught and smoothed them. "I've done nothing."

He had to bite off his retort while he maneuvered the car around a bobby directing traffic past a collision.

A cacophony of alarms, shrieking sirens, popping gunfire, even the *chuff-chuff-chuff* of antiaircraft weapons engulfed them as they approached Westminster. The noise, the chaos, the smoke . . . Marsh could have sworn he was back in the Blitz again. Back before Luftwaffe bombs had cratered great swaths of the city, before rebuilding had turned London into a different place, broke its links with the past.

The city was burning. Dozens of fires. Rising spontaneously, spread across the heart of London. Flames engulfed office buildings, banks, hospitals, police stations, post offices. People fled the conflagrations, heads bent low beneath dark, billowing smoke, with shirts and scarves pressed to their mouths.

Bankers fled from falling debris, vainly shielding themselves with briefcases and umbrellas. And there was a lot of debris; whole buildings had been pulverized, seemingly at random.

Doctors and nurses herded their patients—those who could move— outside crushed and burning hospitals.

Office workers poured into the streets, snarling traffic in their haste to escape the smoke and heat.

Fire. "Is this why you sent the blueprints to Reinhardt? So that he could start this?"

Gretel said, "Reinhardt has never been this effective. Even in his best form."

No. If there was one thing they had learned from the debacle in Knightsbridge, it was that the Germans were no longer masters of the Willenskräfte. And the reports coming from other cities proved a single Reinhardt wasn't behind this attack. But that left just two possibilities, both far worse than a rampaging Reinhardt.

Marsh glanced into the rearview. "Are the children doing this?"

Will said, "I—"

Gretel shouted, "Stop!"

Marsh reacted without thinking and punched the brakes. The car screeched to a halt just as the masonry façade peeled away from the top floors of a burning six-story building. A rain of bricks and mortar pounded the street hard enough to shake the Morris. The car creaked on its suspension.

"How fortunate she's not wearing a battery," Will muttered.

Gretel smirked. "Back up. Second left," she said.

Marsh threw the car into reverse. Dust swirled around them, blown aloft on updrafts from the surrounding fires. How long before the fires coalesced into a single conflagration, a fire storm that turned London to ash?

Marsh repeated his question, though he feared he already knew the answer: "Will. Is it the children?"

"I think not. I don't see . . ." Will gasped just then, as Marsh swerved around the corner hard enough to throw Will crashing against his sore arm. Gretel clucked her tongue. "I said *second* left."

Marsh shifted again and accelerated down a side street. His thoughts raced along with the overtaxed engine. No, it wasn't the children doing this. Marsh had seen the Eidolons at work when he'd traveled through frozen Germany near the end of the war. This was different.

"Ah, Pip?"

This felt like human malevolence. There was nothing supernatural about it. Which meant—

"*Pip!*"

Marsh almost missed the figure standing in the center of the road because she was cloaked in flames. Not the flames of the buildings burning to either side, nor the flames of the debris littering the street, but the flames she conjured from thin air. Marsh hit the brakes and again threw the car into reverse, but not before the woman in the street turned and noticed the car. A grin spread across her face as his shimmering nimbus disappeared.

"Shit!"

Marsh pressed his foot to the floor, but the car moved upward instead of backwards. The wheels spun uselessly over the asphalt as the Arzamas saboteur willed the car aloft. Marsh thought fleetingly of Kammler, whom he had personally witnessed in action at the Reichsbehörde. The Morris bounced a foot above the roadway, swaying back and forth as though the woman lifting them was checking her grip before giving the whole thing a great heave.

Will yelped. He rolled into a ball, hugging his knees to his chest. He didn't notice that Gretel seemed annoyed but otherwise unconcerned.

Marsh, knowing she would never let anything unfortunate befall herself, tried to relax.

A police van skidded to a halt behind the Arzamas agent. Two officers jumped out, pointed pistols at her. She turned to face them. The car fell. The impact wrenched Marsh's neck and the small of his back. The undercarriage echoed with ominous creaks.

The policemen's gunfire sounded like Christmas crackers from a distant party, improbably weak compared to the *whoosh* of fire and the groaning of the car's abused suspension.

Gretel glared at Marsh. "Second. Left."

He hated the thought of following Gretel's directions. But he adhered to her advice for the rest of the drive. Without access to her prescience, traversing the war zone would have been impossible. The Soviet attack was concentrated here; the streets were thick with smoke, rubble, and combat. Meanwhile the Arzamas sleeper cells methodically eradicated the defenders and tore the city apart. Marsh and his passengers glimpsed more and more of the agents at work as they neared Whitehall.

Ivan tricked us. Outplayed us.

Iran was a diversion. We didn't eliminate their Arzamas troops in Iran. They've been here in Britain all along. Hundreds of sleeper agents, waiting patiently for their orders.

Marsh trembled with adrenaline and inconsolable rage. His greatest fear unfolded all around him, and the fever lent a surreal immediacy to the destruction of Britain. Made it hyperreal. Everything he'd ever fought for, destroyed in one afternoon. Every sacrifice he'd endured, rendered pointless. And the single fact that had kept him going through all the dark years—knowing that the things he'd done had kept Britain alive and free—was soon to be a quaint fantasy.

He'd let himself believe he was good at this. But in the end, he'd failed Britain, just as he'd failed at everything else. His most dire, most spectacular failure.

Gretel warned him just in time to avoid a trio of fire trucks headed toward Buckingham Palace. The center of the lead truck imploded spontaneously as if punched by an enormous, invisible fist. It slewed and tumbled down the Mall, like a rusted tin kicked by a schoolboy. The following trucks collided with the crumpled vehicle in a chain reaction. The wreckage blocked access to the north side of St. James' Park, closing off their shortest route to the Admiralty.

Wreckage brought about by Gretel's impenetrable machinations. By a tragedy she engineered. But why?

She directed him east, a few streets south of the park.

Marsh wanted to lash out at her. Strangle her, smash her head against the windshield glass until she explained herself. But driving required more and more of his attention. And most infuriating of all was the fact they wouldn't make it a quarter mile without her guidance. He needed her help. She had made him dependent upon her. And nothing would ever scrape away the rancid, oily feeling.

These bastards will obliterate everything that has ever meant a damn. Everything that has ever lent any meaning and purpose to my life. Every halfhearted reason I could muster for enduring my awful life is getting ripped away.

Gretel had planned the trip carefully. She took them straight through the epicenter of the destruction. Getting to the Old Admiralty building meant threading a needle.

They sped past the pineapple finial on the west end of the mangled Lambeth Bridge. The bridge's steel center span lay twisted in the Thames. Farther downstream, the current lapped against the shattered ruins of Westminster Bridge. Veering north up Millbank, Marsh watched flames engulf Westminster Abbey on their left and the Houses of Parliament to the right.

A pair of figures spiraled up through the air around the Perpendicular Gothic filigrees of Victoria Tower. They tossed explosives. Gouts of white-hot flame followed in their wake, blowing out the mullioned windows and cracking the stone.

Of course they would single out Victoria Tower; it held five centuries of parliamentary records. Britain's heritage of governance. Erased in a few seconds.

Britain was dying.

Murdered before Marsh's eyes.

Will witnessed the spectacle, too. "And they can fly."

Which explained the antiaircraft fire.

"Rudolf could fly." Gretel nodded, as if confiding something. "He died before you could meet him," she added, sounding not entirely sad about it.

As they approached Parliament Square, Marsh remembered following this same route with Stephenson long, long ago. He had just returned from Spain with fragments of a charred filmstrip and no idea where the puzzle would lead. The two of them had created Milkweed that very afternoon. And as he had ridden in the old man's Rolls-Royce, watching Victoria Tower glide past them wreathed in fog and lamplight, he'd never imagined how much the world could change within a single lifetime. Surely Britain would always stand, so long as men like Marsh did the work to make it so.

And he would. He had the power to stop this.

He swung the Morris around the square. They made a short jaunt west toward St. James' while Gretel called a string of warnings ("Veer left!" "Right!" "Slower!" "Faster!") to evade the attacks of Willenskräfte hurled at them. More screeching came from the abused undercarriage as Marsh sent the car banging over the curb and scraping around the iron partition at the south end of Horse Guards Road, and then it was a dead run past the smoldering crater where Downing Street had been to the parade ground behind the Old Admiralty.

Marine sentries had taken positions on the ground, forming a thin defensive perimeter. But there had been no time for sandbags and revetments. They stood in the open, looking confused but determined, useless rifles held at the ready. Pethick oversaw several pairs of marines, who were erecting pixies. The devices looked little different from Lorimer's original design.

The Arzamas attackers were eliminating their targets in order of priority. Milkweed had to be on that list.

Two sentries tracked the approaching car with their rifle barrels.

Marsh leapt out of the car with the motor still running. The sentries recognized him and waved him through without a word. He half shoved, half dragged Will and Gretel into the building.

Pethick's office door stood wide open. He'd left in a hurry, as evidenced by the phone hanging off the cradle. The vault also stood open; the pixies had come from there.

But Pethick was immaterial. Marsh was the old man now. With Pembroke dead, it all fell on his shoulders. He'd returned to Milkweed with the job of untangling Gretel's web. But that hardly mattered now.

It was Marsh's job to fix this problem. And he would.

Marsh bounded down the stairs two at a time. Gretel and Will followed him to the Admiralty cellar. Will threw himself against the door as Marsh unlocked it.

14 June 1963
Milkweed Headquarters, London, England

Will said, "The children haven't done this. I think that much is clear."

He disliked the children, but they were innocent in this. They didn't deserve to get gunned down because of a misunderstanding.

"I know," said Marsh. Rage blazed in his unfocused eyes, beneath a cryogenic sheen of icy determination. Sweat glistened on his pale forehead. Will shuddered with apprehension. The look on Marsh's face . . . the man would do anything to stop the tragedy unfolding outside. Anything at all, and damn the consequences. He was too angry to think clearly.

Quietly, he asked, "Why are we here, Pip?"

"Get out of my way."

Will raised his hands, palm out. Unthreatening. "Just tell me what you intend. So I can help you."

Marsh pointed upstairs with one hand while with the other he twisted the wheel that released the lock mechanism. "We have to end this."

"Yes. We do." Will focused on keeping an even tone. The last thing he wanted was to turn Marsh against him, or to make Marsh think he wasn't a willing ally. "But how do we manage that?"

Marsh didn't answer. The cellar door sprang open with the *clack* of great steel bolts. Will stumbled to keep his footing when the heavy door bumped against him.

He took Gretel by the arm. "What will he do?"

The corner of her mouth quirked up. "He'll do what he must to protect his country."

The look in her eyes was worse than that in Marsh's. She knew exactly what Marsh intended, because she had been nudging events in this direction since the beginning.

"Oh, no."

"Oh, yes."

Marsh had already set off toward the children. Will bounded after him, his footing unsteady on the thick carpet. The soundproofing made his protests sound thin, ineffectual.

"Please, Pip. I am begging you. Do not do this."

But Marsh didn't drop a stride. "Those bastards outside stand to do more damage to London in one afternoon than the Luftwaffe did in one year. Either we do something this instant, or by sunrise Britain will cease to exist." He brushed Will aside. Fury burned through the sheen of self-control. "I will not let that happen!"

"You can't just wipe them out."

"If you haven't noticed, we're embroiled in a rather one-sided shooting war. People die. There's nothing criminal about defending ourselves."

Will grabbed Marsh's arm, pulled him around. "Damn it, man! I'm not talking about the moral implications. There is a single sacrosanct rule by which all warlocks are bound. You know this! Yet you're a hairsbreadth from making those children violate it. And they'll do it because they don't know any better and because they think you're some sort of mythic figure."

Marsh yanked free of Will's grasp. They reached the door to the observation room. Will jumped in front of Marsh. "I have told you again, and again, and again, since the earliest days of Milkweed. Since you first consulted me. What is the one thing I've always warned you against? One must never, ever use the Eidolons to kill."

He lowered his voice, trying to sound like a counselor rather than an adversary. "We couldn't end the war in one stroke. And we can't end this so easily."

"We'll see about that," Marsh growled.

Will knew that appealing to logic was merely grasping at straws. But he tried again. "How are you going to seek them out? You don't have blood maps for the Soviets."

"Don't need 'em."

That took Will aback. "What?"

Marsh pointed at Gretel. "She's terrified of the Eidolons. Why? The Eidolons went berserk when the Twins communicated with each other. Why? Because, Will. Here's another thing you're always prattling on about: 'The Eidolons are beings of pure volition.' Pure willpower. You've said it countless times. How do Gretel and the others do what they do? Von Westarp called it *die Willenskräfte*. That's 'willpower' to you and me."

My God, thought Will. The Reichsbehörde technology poked the Eidolons right where they lived.

"And right now there's no end of willpower getting flung about. Enough to level London," Marsh said.

"The Soviets call it *сила воли*," said Gretel. She smiled, as though this might be helpful.

"We don't need blood maps," Marsh concluded. "The Eidolons can't help but see the Arzamas agents. They must blaze like magnesium flares to the Eidolons."

Oh, hell. Marsh was right.

Gretel said, "He's very, very good. Isn't he?"

Will braced himself against the door. "I still can't let you do this."

Marsh pulled his sidearm. "Get out of the way, Will. I won't ask again."

Will knew he meant it. He swallowed and shook his head, wishing he had taken time for a longer good-bye with Gwendolyn. Wishing she could see him doing the right thing, finally, at the bitter end. He hoped she understood how much he loved her. "You'll have to shoot me dead. Because that's the only way I'll let this happen."

Marsh stepped forward.

"No," said Gretel. They both turned to stare at her. "If you want to fix things, William mustn't die."

Marsh considered this for several beats of Will's racing heart. He holstered his Browning in the rig beneath his arm. Will released a shuddery breath. Though it had surely saved his life, Will found himself appalled at how easily Marsh heeded Gretel's advice.

"Dear Lord," Will said. "Do you even see what's happening here? You're doing everything she wants. She has made you her puppet. You. Of all people."

Marsh grabbed the taller man by the collar. His breath was hot and sour as an unhealed wound. "I am not a puppet. I have free will. And I choose to do this."

Will tried to put up a struggle, but it was little use. Marsh overpowered his feeble resistance. Will found himself sprawled facedown on the carpet as Marsh barged into the observation room.

Will rolled to his feet. He followed, but too late. Marsh slammed the connecting door to the classroom. Will threw himself against it, but it didn't budge. Marsh had wedged something under the handle.

"The man Marsh is here," said the muted, ruined voice of a warlock child. The children began to chant.

"No!"

Will's fists barely rattled the paint-smeared observation window. He lifted a chair, swung it against the glass. It connected with a solid *clank* that didn't scratch the window but sent a painful reverberation back into his wrists. He dropped the chair.

Marsh bellowed in his own ruined voice. The dividing wall muted his voice, too. "Children, children!" He clapped for their attention. The chanting died off.

Gretel watched with a blank expression on her face.

"Why are you letting this happen?" Will asked. "Don't you know what will happen if he does this?"

She frowned, as though he'd just said something spectacularly dim. "Of course I do."

"The bad men are here," said Marsh. "In London. They're attacking us right now. They'll be in this building, in your home, in moments.

I can't stop them." He paused. "They want to kill us. Me, and all of you."

If that garnered a reaction from the children, it was too quiet for Will to make it out.

He pounded on the glass again. "Children! It's me, William! Don't listen to him!"

Marsh continued. "But you can stop them. You can make the bad men disappear. Can you do that for me?"

Apparently they felt they could, because the children took up another chant.

"Bad men disappear," said a girl.

"Bad men disappear," said a boy.

"Bad men disappear," said the group.

Will racked his brain for an alternative. "Bad men freeze!" he yelled.

The children found a single cadence. "Bad men disappear," they chanted.

"Bad men freeze," Will countered.

They switched to Enochian. Will did, too. But they were peerless in their mastery of Enochian. Even at his best, he never could have matched them. He hadn't spoken Enochian in decades. The impossible syllables wrenched his jaw, raked his tongue, cracked against his teeth. He couldn't formulate the grammar. It all came out as gibberish. The alien words disintegrated like splinters of glass wedged in his lips.

Will doubled over. "Please, no," he whispered.

An Eidolon arrived. Its eager assent shook the world and tasted like rose petals strewn on a virgin's grave.

14 June 1963
Milkweed Headquarters, London, England

The Eidolon came and went so quickly that Marsh thought at first the negotiation had failed. Had he been wrong about using Willenskräfte in lieu of blood maps? If so, then what? They had no hope of obtaining the necessary samples from the Arzamas agents. It would require killing or incapacitating them, but if they could manage that, they wouldn't have needed the Eidolons' help in the first place.

"Bad men disappeared," said the oldest boy.

Marsh asked, "Did it work? Is it done?"

"Bad men disappeared," repeated the little girl with corn silk hair.

He removed the chair from where he'd wedged it under the door handle, and stepped into the observation room. Will sat slumped in one corner, long arms around his legs and his forehead pressed against his knees. Gretel, as always, was unreadable.

"What have you done?" Will whispered.

Marsh returned upstairs. Will lumbered to his feet and followed, along with Gretel.

It wasn't until he'd emerged from the cellar and its countless layers of soundproofing that Marsh realized the sounds of the dying city had changed. Sirens still blared across the city, and roiling smoke still darkened the sky. But the sounds of combat had disappeared. No more gunfire. And the city's antiaircraft batteries had fallen silent.

From his office, with its view of the parade ground, Marsh saw the marine sentries milling about, looking no less confused than they had earlier. He could tell from the scorch marks and shrapnel that two of the pixies had been fired. Marsh opened the window and called to Pethick. Pethick, surprised to see him, acknowledged with a wave. He told the men to maintain their positions near the pixies before he came inside. He joined Marsh, Will, and Gretel a moment later.

Acrid smoke from dozens of fires wafted through the open window. It stung the eyes and irritated Marsh's throat. He closed the window again, but not before succumbing to a coughing spasm. The fever burned freely now, tossing him high and light-headed on its updraft.

His gambit had worked. He had saved Britain.

"They're gone," Pethick reported. He looked pale. His tie hung loose; the collar of his cream-colored shirt was stained with sweat. He shook his head, confused by what he was reporting. "The Arzamas saboteurs have retreated."

Marsh said, "No. Not retreated."

"Then where have they gone?"

"Dead," said Marsh. "Disintegrated. What have you." He shrugged. "What?"

"The children," said Gretel.

"Oh, dear." Pethick took a chair. His skin went even paler. "Leslie and I were under the impression that such a thing was forbidden. Too dangerous."

"It is," said Will. He'd sprawled in a chair, one leg thrown carelessly over an armrest.

Pethick narrowed his eyes at Gretel. "Leslie wouldn't have done this. He would have prevented it, wouldn't he?"

Will glared at Marsh. "With good reason."

This was Marsh's triumph. He wouldn't let them step all over it. "Perhaps you don't like my methods, but I had no choice. It was this or be destroyed."

Will looked unconvinced.

Pethick turned on Gretel. "You should know that your failure to warn us about this attack could be construed as levying war against the Sovereign. We might make a case for treason," he said. "Or treachery."

"You see?" said Will, lazily waving one finger in the air. He sounded half pissed. "I did say they were quite keen on it."

Gretel looked unimpressed. Then she looked at the telephone on the corner of Marsh's desk.

"Ivan will regroup," Marsh told Pethick. "We can't assume they've committed all of the Arzamas troops to this operation. We—"

The telephone rang. Will started. Marsh and Pethick shared a glance. Pethick shrugged in response to the implied question; few people had Marsh's work line.

Marsh picked up the receiver, wondering if the safe house had fallen under attack. "Yes," he said.

"Raybould? Is that you?" said a high, reedy voice on the verge of tears.

Marsh straightened in his chair, thrown again into high alert. His mind raced. Had the Arzamas agents attacked his home?

"Liv? What's wrong?"

"It's John. He's . . ."

"What about John?"

Her voice trembled. "Come home."

"Tell me what happened. Are you hurt?"

"He's different. Please," she said faintly, "come home." *Click.*

"Liv?" But she was gone, her terror replaced with the clicking of the line.

Marsh stood to leave without another word, but thought better of it. John was somehow connected to the children and the Eidolons. Connected by something the Eidolons had done even before Liv and Marsh had conceived him. If Marsh's extreme actions to eradicate the Soviet saboteurs had changed John somehow, that meant something significant had changed for the Eidolons as well.

What if Will had been right all along? Was this what Gretel wanted?

The implication left him feeling queasy, as though his stomach were full of mothballs.

He needed an expert. "Will." Marsh beckoned at him. "Come with me."

"If I'm going to die soon, I'd much rather do so in Gwendolyn's arms than your own. No offense, of course."

Marsh squinted, pinched the bridge of his nose. His voice emerged as a whisper. "Please."

Will regained his feet. "Well. In that case."

To Pethick, Marsh said, "Watch her."

"Don't worry. I'll wait here for your return," Gretel said. She pointed toward the door with one dainty finger. "I'll be just down the corridor."

Will said, "Pip, do you—?"

"Go," said Gretel. She waved them off with a fluttering hand. "Hop, hop, hop."

Their car still stood on the parade ground, at the end of two long skid marks etched in the gravel. The marines had had the consideration to turn the engine off and close the doors, but they'd left the keys inside.

Though the attack had been thwarted, getting across the river to Walworth was a chore. Fires still raged across London. Marsh had to weave around rubble and dodge emergency vehicles. In addition to Lambeth and Westminster bridges, Waterloo and Blackfriars had been destroyed as well, snarling traffic worse than anything since the Blitz.

He crossed the Thames at Southwark. Things improved slightly with distance from the city center, but still it took far too long to get home.

It gave Marsh time to describe Liv's call. Will said nothing. But based on how vigorously he chewed his lip, he didn't like what he'd heard.

Marsh spent the rest of the drive cursing the traffic and wondering what had happened to Liv. Perhaps he was overreacting; perhaps it was nothing to do with the Eidolons. Had John overpowered her? Broken out of his room again? Out of the house? Had somebody seen a bruised and naked man escaping from Marsh's house, and decided to call the police? No. The coppers had bigger concerns today.

Marsh parked the car with two tires on the pavement. He shoved the gate open and dashed to the front door. Will lagged behind.

Marsh fished out his house key but the door was unlocked. From the entryway, Marsh called, "Liv?"

No answer. But he found her sitting on the sofa in the den. Her face was pale as flour. She wasn't alone. A man sat across from her, his back to Marsh.

His matted hair, his ears, the mole on the nape of his neck: it all looked impossibly familiar. But the man sat perfectly still, perfectly quiet. He was clothed, too; he wore one of Marsh's shirts and a pair of his trousers.

This wasn't happening. It was a fever dream.

Liv glanced up from the visitor. She looked relieved to see Marsh. "Raybould," she whispered.

"What's happened? Who is this?"

The visitor stood. He turned, facing Marsh with empty, colorless eyes.

No. It couldn't be. But it was John.

"Hello, Father."

interlude

For once, the crazy bitch was true to her word.

Reinhardt had dreaded checking his post office box for fear of finding another rambling missive with instructions for more incomprehensible errands. But Gretel had specifically stated she needed two favors, and Reinhardt had completed them both. So it appeared she truly intended to leave him alone, now that he had killed Leslie Pembroke and his fat excuse for a hausfrau.

The wife had put up more of a fight than Pembroke himself. That cow had nearly crushed Reinhardt by falling atop him as he strangled her. Pembroke had gone down quickly when Reinhardt dented his temple with a candlestick. Twice, for good measure. But Reinhardt had taken his time after finishing Gretel's part of the errand. Clearly the Pembrokes were not without means, and so it proved worthwhile to loot the premises. He'd made off with quite a bit of cash, some jewelry, and even a small wireless set for spare parts. He did, after all, want to make it look like a burglary.

It meant having enough money to keep the Jew landlord at bay, to eat real food again, and to replace a few supplies. Reinhardt splurged on an external-frame rucksack in anticipation of his imminent and long-sought success. Free of further interruptions, he threw himself back into his research. Gretel hadn't sent the entire blueprint. But the hole in this puzzle, the missing piece that would forever reunite him with the Götterelektron, grew smaller by the day.

And then, not long after midnight on a night like countless others, it all fell into place.

The circuit diagrams in his journal matched the blueprint fragments from Gretel. And the missing part, the part he'd reverse engineered by himself, fit naturally. Current flowed into his skull easier than water through a pipe. No convulsions, no hallucinations, no pain. Just the coppery taste of the Götterelektron.

And delivered exactly as required for energizing his Willenskräfte. He started small, wary after so many failures, so many painful near misses. But he could tell it was different this time. It felt right. More satisfying than any whore he'd ever bedded. Better even than Heike.

Nothing more than a slight heat shimmer at first, roiling in the palm of his hand. Then the other hand. Next, a single violet flame no longer than the tip of his finger. Reinhardt made it dance. It jumped from one finger to the next, slowly up one hand and down the other.

Tears trickled down his face, but they evaporated in the heat of his vindication.

He couldn't summon the same agility he'd had in his youth. Too many years without practice. But that would change soon. Now, he'd do nothing but practice. He'd be his old self in no time.

He didn't sleep that night. The thrill was an electric hum in his blood. And there was all the work of documenting his triumph. He spent hours on three copies of the circuit diagram, each annotated with every detail: wire gauges, serial numbers, even the make and model of the televisions and radios from which he'd taken parts. One copy he'd keep on his person, for repairs in the field; copies two and three he would stash in safe-deposit boxes. Reinhardt supplemented the documentation with photographs of the circuit board.

After that, he converted the working design into a portable format. His own design would never be so compact as the original Reichsbehörde technology, nor would it be rechargeable. The rucksack offered enough space for one board split into two layers, with wooden spacers for ventilation. He filled the smaller pockets with tools and spare parts. This project took until midmorning, because each slight alteration to the circuit layout required testing to ensure it wouldn't hinder his ability to call up the Götterelektron.

The finished package was damn heavy. Reinhardt hefted it, settled the straps over his shoulders, and plugged in. He made one last test of the final arrangement—lighting candles, flashing pots of water into steam—while moving about the flat. Everything worked the way it was meant to. The rucksack was awkward, far more so than the original batteries, but the tingling embrace of the Götterelektron was worth any inconvenience.

He was Richard the electrician no longer. He was Reinhardt the salamander. Once more a god.

No more wigs. No more Junkman.

Junkman. Reinhardt had long known the first thing he'd do with a working battery. He'd return to East Ham and show those brats at the council estate just who the Junkman really was. He'd once told them that they'd burn. Today, finally, he'd make good on that promise to himself. Perhaps eventually he'd find Gretel and her lickspittle brother. But the children came first.

He had to remove the rucksack to drive. He laid it on the passenger seat. He'd gone halfway to East Ham when behind him the heart of London erupted into a cacophony of distant alarms and sirens. If he hadn't known better, he might have sworn the rhythmic booming came from antiaircraft guns.

But unless the Soviets had finally decided to occupy this dirty, dinky little island, or bomb it into submission, that seemed unlikely. Some tragedy going on downtown, he decided. Perhaps more gas main explosions.

He worried that if something serious were happening, the children's parents might have ushered them inside. The council estate cellars doubled as bomb shelters. But his fears were allayed when he pulled into the car park. A dozen of the rotten whelps played in the adjacent vacant lot. Reinhardt recognized most of them.

And they recognized his car straightaway. As he'd hoped they would. He laughed to himself as he climbed out, thinking the children were drawn to the sight of the Junkman like moths to a flame. How very true.

"Lookee this!" said one of the boys. "It's Junkman, come back to visit us!"

"We missed ya, Junkman!"

"Junkman!"

"Rubbish bin man!"

Reinhardt donned the rucksack. Over the years, when he had fantasized about this moment, he often wondered what he'd say. But in the end, he decided to let the fire speak for him.

And so he did.

"Junkman, trash man, rubbish bin man!"

He searched their faces, looking for the ringleader, the boy who had convinced the others to pelt Reinhardt with snowballs in winter and mud in the spring. That boy stood at the center of a semicircle of jeering brats.

"What's in the bag, Junkman? Got us some treats?"

Reinhardt pointed at him with an outstretched arm.

The boy's flesh erupted in white-hot flames. There wasn't much sound to it, just a little *pop* as the violent reaction sucked down liters of air in an instant. An updraft ripped the breath from his crackling lungs, so he didn't even scream. A wave of furnace heat blew the other children aside and blistered the paint on Reinhardt's car. The burning boy staggered just a few steps before his bones crumbled to ash. He collapsed in a blackened heap, stinking of charred pork. It was over in seconds.

Reinhardt laughed. That's when the screaming started.

The children tried to run away, to escape, fleeing in a dozen directions. But Reinhardt herded them together with geysers of flame conjured from the damp earth. He took his time, toying with the children, running them in circles until they doubled over in exhaustion.

More than once, a passerby or somebody from the estate witnessed the fire and tried to help. Reinhardt cut short that interference. This was his celebration and it would last as long as he wanted. He expected witnesses to call the local fire station, but no fire trucks ever arrived.

It wasn't quite so fun once his tormentors were too exhausted to run and scream. Reinhardt picked them off one by one while they tried to crawl away. Sometimes he ignited their clothes, letting their panic fan the flames for him. Others he surrounded with slowly contracting rings of fire.

Every punishment he could imagine. Every punishment they deserved.

Reinhardt was down to the final pair of children when his rucksack stopped working. The gauge he'd rigged still showed plenty of charge, and he could still feel the tingling Götterelektron surge into his skull. But it was as though he aimed his Willenskräfte into a bottomless hole.

Something absorbed it. Quenched it. Devoured it.

He'd never encountered this problem before.

And then he felt it: a titanic malevolence. His fires ebbed and flowed, moaned and howled. The flames assumed impossible shapes. Angular, crystalline, non-Euclidean geometries.

Reinhardt remembered the unnatural winter that had hastened the war's end. The wind had shrieked with supernatural anger; the snowdrifts had sculpted themselves into shapes that hurt the mind to behold. Similar reports had come from the weather spotters in the Channel during the run-up to the failed invasion of Britain. It had all been the warlocks' doing. They had sent their demons to barricade the sea and, later, to freeze the Reich.

But it was different this time. In the past, that undercurrent of malice had always snarled and growled from a safe distance, like the pacing of a caged tiger.

There was no cage today.

Reinhardt forgot the children. Forgot about revenge. He shrugged off his rucksack and started to run.

But it was too late. He had marked himself, and *something* had seen him. It was drawn to his Willenskräfte, like a moth to his flame.

But this was no moth. It was a horror.

Reinhardt's final thought, the instant before demons erased him from existence: *That bitch.*

thirteen

14 June 1963
Walworth, London, England

John's eyes shone like rifts in a blackout curtain before a full moon.

Marsh retreated from the pale, unblinking gaze. He grasped for words, struggled to force each breath past the ice in his chest. Why didn't his breath come out in a cloud? It was so cold. . . .

"John?"

"You call us that," said the thing wearing his son's body. Its breath tasted like starlight.

It looked Marsh up and down, moving John's head with awkward, inhuman motions. Insectile motions. It studied the room, staring randomly at various elements: the carpet; the mantel; the molding over the doors; Liv. All just objects.

"Limited," it said. "This realm where you—" It paused, as though looking for a concept. "—exist."

Its voice sounded so *normal*. So human. But the inflections were wrong, the emphasis random. Like music written by a spider. And its presence carried the same pressure, the same sense of something vast and terrible that accompanied the Eidolons. Marsh's repulsion, the urge to run and hide, hit just as urgently here, now, as it had during any negotiation he'd ever witnessed. This thing standing here in the form of his son was just the tip of a dread reality.

Will stumbled into the den after Marsh. Liv's eyes, already wide with fear, opened further. Her lips parted.

"You're dead," she whispered.

Will managed an inelegant bow. "Olivia, my dear. It's been much too long."

But Marsh focused on John. Slowly, carefully, fearing the answer, he asked, "To whom am I speaking?"

"You cannot say our name. Even your—" Another pause, more alien body language. "—warlocks cannot." The thing in John's body managed a decent approximation of a sneer when pronouncing "warlocks." Air hissed through Will's teeth as he inhaled.

Liv looked from Marsh to Will and back. She said, "What is this? What is he talking about?"

Marsh asked her, "Are you hurt?"

"No." She stared up at their son and hugged herself. Her teeth chattered.

She didn't appear to be bleeding. Marsh wondered if that would buy her any time.

To John, he said, "Why are you here?"

Another voice joined John's. "WE ARE EVERYWHERE."

"What have you done to my son?"

John paused again, surveyed its body with the same disturbing awkwardness. But its motions were becoming more fluid, its speech less halting. The things in John's body were becoming accustomed to it.

"WE EMPTIED THIS VESSEL. FOR US."

Marsh and Will shared a look. *The soul of an unborn child.*

"Why?"

"TO SEE THIS PLACE. IT DIFFERS FROM THE OUTSIDE."

Each time it spoke, another voice joined the chorus. More monsters looked through what had once been John's eyes. Marsh was fairly certain that if he'd had anything to drink in the past few hours, he'd have pissed himself right then.

"Stop it, John! Stop it!" yelled Liv. "Stop talking like that." She stood, faced Marsh. "Both of you!"

Liv's flour-pale features blushed red with fear and frustration, dark enough to hide her freckles. There were new lines at the corners of her eyes and around her mouth that he hadn't noticed before. Terror widened her eyes, ringed them with white. She trembled as she hugged herself, violently, as though a cyclone blew through the forest of her soul. Perhaps it did—John possessed, Will back from the dead . . . Liv deserved to understand this.

But Marsh knew he couldn't risk an explanation. He had to engage John. He didn't know how long the Eidolons would inhabit John, but it seemed that as long as they did, they weren't eradicating Liv, or Britain, or him. And if there was any hope of preventing it, Will needed to hear this.

"Why do you need to see us?"

"PERSPECTIVE. DEMARCATION." Another pause. "WE SEEK YOUR MAPS. BUT YOUR EXTENT IS LIMITED."

Will sat on the ottoman, hard enough to elicit a creak of protest from its wooden legs.

Marsh's bad knee flared with pain. He staggered, slumped against the wall. In the moment before impact he found himself suspended in the gap between sterile knowledge and abject terror, like the moment between touching a hot stove and feeling the pain.

Will was right. Marsh had shattered the deep structure of the cosmos. Unleashed something. But there had been no other way. He'd had no choice. Had he?

Liv's voice, impossibly small, said, "Raybould?"

Marsh struggled to continue the conversation, to keep trying. "That wasn't our agreement."

Liv said, "Agreement?"

"ERASE THE VIOLATIONS," said the infernal choir. "WE SEEK THEM, ERASE THEM, READ THEIR MAPS. FIND MORE MAPS. THE CYCLE GROWS."

"You've completed the task we asked of you. You've found them all."

John didn't respond. Instead it stiffened and turned on its heels. It faced into the northeast corner of the room. John's choir voice swelled with legion presences. It reverberated with undertones of Enochian when it said, "ANOTHER."

Liv clamped her hands over her ears. She leaned over and released a wet, burbling cough. The sour stink of vomit permeated the room.

Marsh took her in his arms. The corner of her mouth glistened with dark spittle. She huddled against him, turned away from John. He asked, "Another what, John?"

"VIOLATION. ERASED."

Marsh looked at Will. Will shrugged.

"That's it, then. You've found them all."

"NO. WE KEEP LOOKING."

"Why?"

"YOUR EXISTENCE IS LIMITED YET YOU EXPRESS INTENT. YOU SHOULD NOT."

We are a stain upon the cosmos, thought Marsh. *And now they're going to fix us.*

"I think—" Will cleared his throat and tried again. His voice still came out quietly: "I think they're looking for something specific."

Something, or someone?

Liv wept into her hands. "Make it stop," she moaned.

Marsh asked, "Are you looking for somebody in particular?"

"THERE IS ONE WHO HURTS US MOST. UNLIKE THE OTHERS. MORE POWERFUL. MORE SUBTLE. MORE PAINFUL TO US," said the Eidolon-thing in John's body. It sniffed, sampling the air with a machine gun burst of short, sharp inhalations, just as John sometimes did. "WE CANNOT SEE THAT ONE. BUT WE SEEK IT."

"Raybould," Liv moaned, "what is he talking about?"

Gretel.

Marsh remembered his first conversation with Pembroke. A month ago he'd said, *She pulls these things off long after her battery has been removed. So rather than gaping in wonderment, you should be wondering how long she's been planning this.*

Gretel worked according to memory, following a plan she'd devised years ago. Why? Because she was hiding from the Eidolons. She knew they'd break free, and she didn't want to be caught actively using her ability when they came a-knocking.

Except. They slipped the leash *because* of her doing. It made no sense. But he saw an opening, a thread of hope:

"I know the one you mean," said Marsh. "If I give her to you, will you leave?"

"WE ARE EVERYWHERE."

"Will you abandon this," he said anxiously, waved one hand at John's body, "perspective? Stop taking maps?"

"NO."

Liv sobbed. The demon in her den had just declared it would never return to hell. Marsh struggled not to sob along with her.

Will released a long, ragged sigh. "You already have her map," he said, referring to Gretel. "We gave it to you long ago. Why haven't you erased her?"

"LONG AGO." John tilted its head again, as if confused by the suggestion that twenty years was somehow significant. Did Eidolons know amusement? Or was it merely annoyed? "IT HIDES. ITS MAP IS A WEB. TANGLED. WE CLEAVE IT."

Gretel wasn't using her power, which meant she didn't stand out to the Eidolons. And though they had sampled her blood in the past, unraveling that map through the tangled web of her machinations, through all the futures she had decided, all the fates she had discarded, was slowing them down. But they did have her blood, and they'd find her eventually.

Which raised another sickening question. How long until they snuffed Marsh? They'd also had his blood map since 1940.

How were they still having this conversation?

Marsh ushered Liv behind him, placing himself between her and John. A meaningless protective gesture, should the Eidolons decide to end this. But even after everything they'd said and done to each other, he couldn't bear the thought of leaving Liv naked to the Eidolons like that.

"Why haven't you taken us yet?"

John swiveled again. Its movements were perfectly fluid now. Still unnatural, but no longer awkward. It fixed Marsh with chalky eyes. "YOUR MAP DIFFERS. IT FASCINATES US. YOUR MAP IS A CIRCLE. A BROKEN SPIRAL. NONLINEAR. NOT LIKE THE OTHER LIMITEDS."

"What do you mean, nonlinear?"

"YOU ARE DISTINCT. WE RENDER YOUR DISTINCTION IN LANGUAGE. TO KNOW IT."

"Ah . . ." Will hugged his knees to his chest. He rested his chin on one knee, staring intently at John, eyes narrowed in concentration.

In other words, Marsh knew, *you've given me a name.*

John brushed past them to approach the window. Liv trembled. Its physical body still smelled of musk and sour milk; their son had been overdue for another bath when the Eidolons put him to the purpose for which they had created him. Marsh wondered if the things inside John noticed.

An empty child. A vessel for the Eidolons to see the world through human eyes. A scout of the human scale, directing the apocalypse for beings who couldn't perceive the distinction between a humble house in Walworth and the churning heart of a star ten million years dead.

"I SEE AS YOU DO," said John, holding aside a curtain with the back of its wrist. "I SHARE WHAT I SEE. HOUSES. STREET." It dropped the curtain. "BEYOND THAT, NEIGHBORHOOD. CITY. NATION." It turned. "YOUR WORLD."

They were getting what they sought. A clear view of the human world. Soon, the view would be clear enough for the Eidolons to start eradicating en masse the human stains that offended them so very much.

Would death happen quickly? Painlessly? All at once, like blowing out a candle? Or would the end come as a creeping shadow?

Marsh tried to prolong the conversation with John. But the enormity of what had happened—of what he had done; of what Gretel had deftly manipulated him into doing—left him too tired for ideas. No amount of cleverness could fix this. Fever simmered in his brain; hoarfrost coated his veins. Marsh hadn't shit himself yet, but that seemed a miracle. The faint odor of urine joined the smell of Liv's vomit.

John's chorus-voice hit a crescendo. *"WE SEE,"* it said. And then it vanished.

Liv gasped. Marsh caught her.

"What was that?" she whispered. "Where did he go?"

"I don't know." He lowered Liv to the sofa. A small wet spot had formed on her dress.

"John spoke," she said. Her breath made his eyes water.

Marsh didn't know what to say. He nodded.

"He was talking nonsense, but you understood him." She shoved him away. She was crying. "You understood him!"

"I—"

"I've gone mad." Liv ran her hands through her hair. One lock came free of the hairpins and bobbed over her forehead. "My son is a monster." She glanced at Will. "And I'm seeing ghosts. I must be mad."

"I assure you, I am not a ghost," said Will, his voice shaky. "Yet." He stared at where John had disappeared.

Marsh took her gently by the shoulders. "Liv—"

"Don't *touch* me!" She shoved him away more violently. He banged his shoulder against the mantel, ringing the chimes of a wound-down clock. Shrieking left her voice hoarse. "You spoke to that, that *thing,* as though you knew it. As though you understood." Liv dodged his outstretched fingers. "Stay away from me."

"Olivia," said Will, still distracted.

"Don't speak to me," she sobbed. "You're not real." She ran up the stairs. The bedroom door slammed.

The fever redoubled its efforts to burn Marsh's brain to a cinder. He staggered to the sofa. It was as good a place as any to die. Perhaps, if he could muster the energy later, he'd go out to the garden shed. That had been his home as much as anywhere these past twenty years.

Liv pounded down the stairs a few minutes later. She'd changed her dress, done her lips, put her hair back in place. She carried her handbag, too. Had she not heard about the disasters in the city? All across Britain?

"Liv, please stay," Marsh called.

But she didn't pause before throwing open the front door and heading outside. Even now, at the end of the world, she couldn't spare a word for him. It cut more deeply than anything else she'd ever said or done. Worse than what the fire had done to his face and throat. He'd have given anything for her to stay. Just a little longer. He didn't want to die alone. But she didn't want to die in his presence. So much for their fragile, tentative reconnection. If it had ever existed. He'd been a fool to think it had.

Marsh listened to the creak of the gate. Soon, Liv's footsteps receded into the din of the sirens and alarms still echoing across the city. He wondered if she might have stayed had she understood what was happening. Probably not, he decided. Liv wouldn't have chosen to die alone any more than Marsh did, but that's effectively what would have happened if she had stayed at home with him. Dying alone was his fate, and the knowledge wearied him.

With John gone, she might have been inclined to spend more time at home. If only the world wasn't gut shot and rapidly bleeding out.

So this is it, then, thought Marsh. *Sleeping alone at the end of the world. A final insult for a wasted life. What a fitting send-off.*

Minutes passed while Will and Marsh sat in silence. They shared the understanding of doomed men. The amity of the condemned.

A small part of Marsh wrestled with the question of Gretel. Like a dog gnawing a soup bone down to splinters, he couldn't let it go. Why? Why work so patiently for so many years solely to bring events to this point? Why engineer history to bring about this apocalyptic finale? Decades of nudging, wheedling, watching, correcting, adjusting—just to take the world down with her when she died? There were easier ways to commit suicide. Marsh would have happily strangled her a dozen times over.

It didn't make sense.

But the rest of Marsh didn't care any longer. He'd done everything he could for his country. Perhaps it had been too much, perhaps too little, but he had nothing more to give. He had strived his best, but he had failed. His heart was weary, his body old, his head light, his face ruined. He had no fight left in him. And there was no fighting the Eidolons.

His stubborn refusal to admit defeat had doomed everybody. The enormity of that failure was too much to swallow. Too much to digest before the end came.

He only hoped it would be painless. He'd had enough of pain. He was ready to stop hurting.

Marsh stood. "Come on. I'll take you to Gwendolyn. Before it . . ." He swallowed the lump in his throat. "Before it starts."

He decided he couldn't face another night—one last night, the last night of anything—alone in the garden shed. Marsh considered a stop at the pub after dropping Will at the safe house. If the world lasted that long. It had been weeks since he'd been tossed out for fighting. They'd probably let him in if he kept his fists to himself this time. Easy enough. He was too weary for rage.

Will didn't move. "Circle," he mumbled.

Marsh sighed. "Doesn't matter what it said. Nothing we can do about it now."

And he believed that, but for the niggling voice in the back of his head.

Gretel. Why did she do this? Why the long game? What vision of the future could have prompted her to facilitate the end of the world? To guarantee there *was* no future? What was worse than this?

It was all so out of character for her. She always had a solution. Always had an escape . . . Or was this just as it appeared? The woman was insane. Evil. And von Westarp had given her a god's power.

No. He shook his head, tried to clear it. *I'm just an old man. A tired old man, dying alone because my wife can't abide my company even at the end of the world.*

He snapped his fingers. "Let's go."

"Broken spiral," Will murmured. He looked up at Marsh. "Do you know what I'm remembering?"

Marsh sighed again, rubbed his beard. Sickness rumbled in his gut. "I don't have the energy for this. I just want a pint before the demons take me."

Will continued as if Marsh hadn't spoken. "Our little jaunt to Germany. You made a very compelling case for it, didn't you? It was the easiest thing in the world for the Eidolons to fling us several hundred miles in an instant." He stretched, unlimbered his long arms from around his knees. "That trip was also a circle, you know." He traced a wobbly semi-circle in the air, with his finger: "From here to there in the blink of an eye." He completed the circle, saying, "And back again. A circle through space. And yet the Eidolons never bothered to name *me*." He paused. "At the time I thought the entire idea was the height of madness. But perhaps our failure was a lack of ambition."

Will offered an invisible spider-thread of hope, but all Marsh felt was the sting of dread and the comfort of surrender. He'd been coming to terms with death and he didn't have the energy for anything more. He didn't have the energy to unravel another layer of Gretel's machinations. He was ill. He was ready to die.

Please, no more. There can't be more to do. I'm weary, and I don't care any longer.

"What are you saying?"

"I finally understand your name, Pip. I know what it means and why they gave it to you." Will shook his head. Marsh couldn't tell if it was a gesture of awe or pity.

"Fine. Just tell me."

"What if Gretel had foreseen a way to stop this?"

"Stop this? She caused this. She's been aiming for this since the beginning."

"Yes. The beginning. But when was that, exactly? How long ago?" Now it was Will's turn to stand. "I think we ought to return to the Admiralty. She said she'd be waiting for us. But we haven't much time."

Time.

No. Marsh fell back on the sofa, stomach churning with mothball sickliness. He hated Will's line of reasoning and refused to follow along. It frightened him too much. More than he feared dying alone, he feared the thought that Gretel's plans for him extended beyond the end of the world.

Marsh shook his head. "I can't do this."

"I know you better than that, Pip. I know you can't bear the thought of dying with an unsolved puzzle on your hands. Even if you won't admit it to yourself."

When had Will become the strong one? Damn him.

"But Gwendolyn," Marsh tried.

"We have an understanding. Don't you want a straight answer out of Gretel? After everything that has happened? I do."

"I want this to be finished."

"It may be. But let's hear what she has to say. One last time." Will extended a hand, offered to help Marsh up.

"One last time." Marsh took Will's hand and struggled to his feet. "To know why."

The din of sirens, panic, and chaos still clamored across the city. Less than three hours had passed since he'd issued the order to kill the Soviet saboteurs. Not enough time to put out every fire, assess the damage, spin a cover story. No sweeping this under the rug as a gas main explosion. Too many witnesses. Marsh knew there were people gathered amidst the wreckage of Whitehall, probably at that very moment, striving to concoct a plausible cover story. Because it was their job, and the poor sods didn't know the world was dying. Didn't know the Eidolons were poised to snuff them all.

In spite of the noise, the atmosphere on the streets was hushed. Expectant. As though the entire neighborhood had drawn a ragged breath and, like a tuberculosis patient, struggled to hold it through the tightness in its chest. As did the rest of the city, Marsh reckoned. As he did, too.

They listened to reports coming over the wireless as they made their way back through the snarl of London traffic. Reliable information was spotty; SIS was patching reports together from the BBC and other news outlets.

"Disturbances" was the word of the hour. A "disturbance" had cleared away the surprise attacks. (So much for a cover story.) But now disturbances were reported elsewhere. Patches of rapidly spreading darkness over the Midlands, in the American Southwest, Tanganyika, India, the former Germany.

Ripples, coalescing at random. Forward and backward from the moment when Marsh heaved a boulder into the duck pond.

Germany. Not far from Weimar was Marsh's guess. There was

probably another "disturbance" centered on Arzamas-16, too, but of course no such news was forthcoming from the Soviet Union. He imagined men and women like Will's assassin trying in vain to fight the Eidolons, unaware that their efforts only attracted and enraged the demons.

Unlike Gretel, who had gone to tremendous lengths to hide herself from the Eidolons. All for naught. Why?

The Eidolons lived outside of space and time. They perceived Marsh as a circle. A spiral. An Ouroboros.

This hadn't begun when Gretel returned from the Soviet Union. She'd put this in motion long, long before. The catastrophic open conflict between Arzamas-16 and Milkweed had been inevitable at least since the end of the war. Perhaps earlier.

But how do you stop something inevitable?

You can't. You must head it off before it starts. By going back to the beginning, to nip it in the bud.

That's what she wanted. But Marsh wouldn't give it to her. That bint could die with all the rest.

But not before she told him why.

A cold wind swept the city. They crossed the Thames again, headed back toward the heart of the chaos. Bobbies stood at major intersections, ostensibly to direct traffic and keep the crowds of panicked Londoners at bay. But the officers' silver whistles hung unused about their necks while they gaped at the sky like everybody else.

"Look," said Will. He pointed north.

Toward where an ink black sky boiled above the Midlands. It held a darkness more complete than any storm clouds, darker than any moonless midnight, more thorough than the wartime blackouts. This wasn't darkness caused by the absence of light. It was the absence of existence. Primal chaos. The darkness of oblivion.

Roiling. Churning. Spreading.

Growing exponentially, as the Eidolons perceived more and more of the human world.

"Dear God," Will whispered. "Aubrey."

The marines had abandoned their posts by the time Marsh and Will returned to the Admiralty. The remaining pixies stood unmanned, some upright, but most lying skew-whiff across the parade ground by virtue of a growing gale.

The howling wind blew north. Toward the vacuum of nonexistence created by the Eidolons.

They found Pethick alone in Pembroke's office. He'd helped himself to the bottle in the sideboard. His tie lay coiled on the floor.

"If you've come to plead with the children to save us, it's too late," he said. "Eidolons gobbled 'em up."

"Where's Gretel?" said Marsh.

Pethick sneered at him. "She killed Leslie because he wouldn't have pulled the trigger. He was a good man." He tossed back a finger's-worth of scotch. A glistening trail of spittle dangled from his lips to the mouth of the bottle. "You've killed us all. Bloody gorilla."

A shudder of distaste flashed across Will's face. He saw an echo of himself in Pethick's collapse.

Will said, "We need to find her."

Pethick sloshed scotch across the desk when he gestured to the corridor with the bottle. "Waiting. Happy as Larry." He wiped the back of his hand across his mouth.

And she was. They found her in one of the old Milkweed rooms that had been reduced to dusty storage after the war. She sat in a broken office chair, bare feet propped on the edge of a metal desk, wiggling her toes. The hem of her dress hung from pale and bony ankles.

Without preamble, Marsh said, "I won't do it. I won't go back. I'd rather stay here and watch you die."

"Ah." She clapped and spun her chair in a circle, braids windmilling about her head. "So you finally understand why *they* named you. I knew you would. Eventually."

"I don't understand a damn thing," Marsh rasped. "I know you're terrified of the Eidolons. And yet you forced my hand, forced me to unleash them to combat a menace you engineered. You let the Reichsbehörde fall to the Red Army so that this would happen. You destroyed the world with your long game."

She pouted, looking hurt. "I didn't make this happen."

Will said, "You've manipulated us since day one."

"Of course I did," said Gretel. "I had to. There has never been a future where the Eidolons didn't roam free. Not a single one. Our doom was sealed the day Herr Doktor von Westarp created his orphanage. It led inexorably to the technology that made us," she said, one hand laid demurely at the base of her throat. "And once Britain learned of his work, Milkweed also became unavoidable. For how else could you withstand the likes of us without the warlocks to defend you? You couldn't."

"My God," said Will.

Marsh shook his head. "Lies. Why go to such effort if the end result was inevitable?"

"There were countless ways this end might have come about. In many time lines, it happens much earlier, during the war: 1941, '42, '43. Those were the most difficult to avoid." She looked at Will. "Almost as difficult as keeping you alive long enough to do your part. Fortunately for me, Gwendolyn carried that burden until I returned." She shrugged, unmoved by Will's indignation. "But sooner or later, all time lines pointed to the same conclusion: that no matter what I did, no matter how I strived, I would die when the Eidolons destroyed the world.

"So I chose to forge a *new* time line. One where that will not happen."

The corner of her mouth quirked up. She fixed a lopsided half grin at Marsh. "And I made certain that when the end came to pass, you would be poised to save me."

Marsh laughed. To Will, he said, "She believes I'm going to save her." He shook his head. "No. You'll die with the rest of us."

"Of course you won't do it for me." She spoke slowly, as though wanting to be certain her point came across. Her dark eyes turned cold. "You'll do it for Agnes."

Beside him, Will fell deathly still. Silence filled the room, broken only by the howling wind.

"What?" Marsh rasped.

"If you go back," Gretel said, "you can save Agnes."

Marsh staggered against a dusty filing cabinet, feeling as if he'd been poleaxed.

His infant daughter. Long dead and sorely lamented. The unhealed wound he'd carried for so many years was nothing more than an incentive to do Gretel's bidding. Bait.

Because Gretel knew there was one thing Marsh still cared about. One thing he'd fight for. The thing he mourned every day: his family.

Dear God. Even at the end of the world, there was no pulling free of the hooks she'd buried in his heart.

He'd always burned with the need to know why Gretel had murdered his daughter. He'd believed that understanding the tragedy would somehow make it bearable. But knowing the answer hurt more than all the wondering, all the blame and sleepless nights.

Will said, "You monster."

She crossed the room to lay a hand on Marsh's arm. "Do you see, darling? It was regrettable, but necessary. I did say you'd understand."

Marsh's fist caught her full on the mouth with a wet *crack*. The punch snapped her head around, sent her sprawling on the floor. A cloud of dust swirled around her.

She climbed to her feet. Blood trickled down her chin from her nose and the corner of her mouth. She pressed a hand to the wound, inspected her blood, held her glistening red fingertips out for Will and Marsh to see.

"Yes," she said. "This will be sufficient."

And in that moment, Marsh hated himself more than he ever had during all the cold, lonely nights in the garden shed. Not for belting a woman. She deserved it more than any man he'd ever decked. He'd done far worse to men who'd earned far less.

He hated himself because he knew he'd buckle. Knew he'd give in. Because as much as he despised Gretel, he missed Agnes more. Missed the Liv that had loved him. Missed his wife, his lover. Missed the family life he'd touched so briefly.

I want my family back.

Will must have seen the decision in his eyes.

"Pip," he said, "there's a problem. Two problems. I can't send you back. The Eidolons have everything they want now. They don't need us to feed them blood prices. What could we possibly offer in a negotiation that would secure their cooperation to send you back?"

Gretel smoothed her braids. She twirled one end, dangling the unused battery connector like a pendulum.

Marsh said, "We give them Gretel."

Will blinked. "Ah. Right. How selfless of her." He frowned. "You'll die along with the rest of us. This is no victory."

Gretel shrugged. "A tiny sacrifice for my greater good. This *body* will die," she said, "but my consciousness will continue in the new time line. Everything I know, she will know. Everything I am, she will be. And she will be free of the Eidolons."

"But that's still a different person! Your death—"

Marsh interrupted. "We don't have time for a bloody philosophy seminar!"

Will said, "There's still a problem, Pip. We're missing the most important bit. We need a blood bridge. An anchor. Something to link the here and now with the here and then." He waved his hands wildly, trying to make his point. "Like the stone during our raid on the farm. One object in two places simultaneously, linking our location in Britain with our location in Germany." Marsh stared at the stump of Will's missing finger. "But we don't have anything analogous for sending you through time. . . ."

Will trailed off, frowning at his wounded hand as if noticing it for the first time. He and Marsh stared at each other, then around the room. The room Gretel had chosen.

They turned their eyes to the floor. Beneath a thick layer of dust, the floorboards were scuffed from years of furniture hauled carelessly in and out. Marsh tried to remember how things had been arranged twenty years earlier. Outside, the wind shrieked more fiercely.

There.

Marsh grabbed the metal desk where Gretel had propped her feet, lifted one end, and heaved it aside. It crashed into a gunmetal gray filing cabinet. The empty cabinet toppled sideways, sliding against a roll of carpet and gouging the plaster wall. Marsh dropped to all fours, gritting his teeth as the pain flared in his knee again. A splinter lodged in his palm as he swept the dust away with his hands. He pursed his lips and blew to clear off the fine layer of grit trapped in the wood grain. He swept and puffed, swept and puffed, until he found what he sought.

A bloodstain. Brown with age.

His knee twinged again as he stood. The stab of pain stole Marsh's breath away. He pointed at the stain, panting, "Here's your blood bridge."

Will stooped to get a better look at the floor. He squinted. "Is that what I think it is?"

"Your fingertip fell right there when I cut it off." Will winced at the memory. "Your blood stained the floor."

Will surveyed their surroundings again. "This room—"

"—is where we showed Gretel to the Eidolons." The building groaned under the assault of the wailing wind. Somewhere, a door slammed. Marsh raised his ruined voice. "Will this work?"

"Yes," said Gretel.

"I, I think so," Will stammered. "Perhaps. Probably."

Marsh said, "Then get prepared."

He dashed outside, into the corridor that led to the Milkweed vault. As he passed the exterior offices, those with windows overlooking the parade ground and St. James' Park, he saw the spreading darkness had reached London. Streetlamps cast a feeble yellow glow into the Eidolonic night. Wind whipped the lake in the park to a froth; leaves fluttered from the mulberry trees like confetti in a cyclone. But worst of all was how the noise had changed.

Faintly audible over the wind: the sirens had been replaced with screaming. The end of the world didn't come with the crackling of fire or the quiet hiss of ice. It came with thousands of voices raised in fear.

Marsh spun the vault dial through the combination as quickly as he could. He heaved the massive door aside. It smashed against the wall and shook the floor. Light spilled into the vault from the corridor. It illuminated the cabinets that held pixie blueprints; a cloven stone; Enochian lexicons; a photograph of a farmhouse; the Tarragona filmstrip; Schutzstaffel operational records . . .

A handful of batteries stood together on one shelf. Two of them were newer than the others—Soviet redesigns of the original Reichsbehörde model, taken from the Twins. The other batteries also formed a matching pair. These were older, their gauges showing total charge depletion: the batteries taken from Klaus and Gretel when they'd arrived weeks earlier. Klaus had used one during the battle at Will's house, and the other to rescue the Twin.

But there, alone in the corner, long forgotten under dusty cobwebs, stood the final Reichsbehörde battery. The battery Gretel had been wearing in France the day Marsh captured her. The battery she'd purposely left behind during her brief incarceration, knowing she'd need it again on the day the world ended in 1963.

Marsh snatched the battery and ran back to Will and Gretel. He didn't close the vault behind him. There was no point. In a few more minutes there would be no London, no Admiralty, no vault. Nobody left to steal state secrets.

He again glanced outside on his way back. There was nothing to see. Even the dim glow of the streetlamps had disappeared. Darkness had enveloped the Admiralty building.

He returned to the storage room just as Will smeared a bloody handprint on the floor over the old bloodstain. A smear of red darkened his lower lip; he'd bitten his hand.

Gretel reached toward Marsh. He lobbed the battery into her outstretched fingers. She tried to hide the trembling of her hands as she caught it. In moments the Eidolons would see her, erase her from existence. The one thing that frightened her in all the world. But she embraced that fate so that a younger version of herself, the Gretel of the past, the Gretel of an alternative time line, could survive. Her entire plan amounted to one long, elaborate suicide. Will was right. Only a madwoman would embrace such a fate.

Even if Marsh did find a way to somehow avert this catastrophe. But first, he'd find a way to save Agnes. Save Liv, save his marriage. What point in saving the world—a world—if he couldn't have that tiny piece of it for himself?

This world, however, was doomed. Along with everybody in it. This

Liv, the Liv to whom he'd been married for so long, whom he'd loved and loathed in equal measure, had no future. She was dead already. Her entire life had been a pointless prologue to nothing. And he was abandoning her. The guilt threatened to hobble him. It grew worse when he thought of all the things he'd never get to say, all the words he'd never get to take back. . . .

Marsh asked, "Ready?"

Will's nod was not entirely convincing. "Have you truly thought about this? We're doing this at the spur of the moment. This isn't a simple trip to Germany, Pip. You haven't had time to prepare."

"We don't *have* time!" Marsh yelled. He pointed to the walls. "The darkness is right outside."

Marsh clamped his teeth on the inside of his lower lip. The taste of salt and iron coated his tongue. He spit on the floor, at the spot where Will's past and present blood mingled together. Fever and headache throbbed in his skull to the beat of his racing heart.

Will reached into a pocket of his waistcoat. He pulled out his wallet and tossed it to Marsh.

"There's a bit of cash in there. You'll need it."

The gesture caught Marsh off guard. "Thank you."

Will had tears in his eyes. "Pip, I . . . I've made so many terrible choices in my life. If . . . If you could find a way to prevent them . . ."

"We've all made mistakes. Me worst of all," said Marsh. He put a hand on Will's shoulder. "It'll be different next time. I promise."

"Well," said Will. He drew a long, shuddery breath. He held it for a moment before launching into a poor rendition of Enochian.

Even Marsh could tell Will wasn't so proficient as the children had been. He was far, far out of practice. But it didn't matter. The Eidolons roamed free in the world; Will caught their attention instantly.

Darkness seeped through the walls. The room reverberated with a crushing sense of unbridled malice. The floor canted slightly to the left. Marsh glanced at his watch. It had stopped.

He recognized the discordant syllables of his own name. The same syllables the children had begun to chant each time they'd seen him.

The Eidolons saw him. Studied him. Looked in him, through him, from within the very particles of his body.

Gretel winked. "See you soon."

Will panicked: "Wait! STOP!"

She plugged in her battery. The darkness pounced.

And Marsh—

Liv huddled in the garden shed, perched on the edge of her husband's cot as the wind howled outside.

She had turned back when she glimpsed the inky sky to the north. It didn't look like any storm she'd ever seen. It wasn't natural, and that scared her just as much as John had. Her anger at Raybould, her disgust with his lies and secrets, hadn't subsided. Still, she wished she hadn't returned to an empty house. There was nobody to hold her, nobody to keep the fear at bay.

But she'd turned her back on him when he called to her. Because she'd been petty, wanted to hurt him as much as his lies hurt her. And now she was alone with only terror for company as the darkness spread.

She buried her face in his pillow and wept. It smelled like the man she'd loved long ago.

Klaus stood before the corner window of his flat, watching as impenetrable darkness descended upon Aylesbury. Madeleine trembled beside him, wrapped only in a robe. He shifted the paintbrushes to one hand then wrapped his free arm around her. It wasn't romantic; he shared her fear.

The wind picked up. A ripple, a gust, a gale. It shredded the greengrocer's awning. An icy draft wormed its way past the window sash.

He shivered. Madeleine hugged him.

He should have taken her into his bedroom while he'd had the chance. But it had been so comforting, so normal, simply being around a woman who wasn't his sister.

God damn you, Gretel.

But he refused to give her his dying thoughts. He pushed her out of his mind.

He tightened his hold of Madeleine, pressed his face into her chestnut hair. "Thank you," he whispered.

The Eidolons swarmed into Marsh, infused him, dissected him particle by particle. They peeled the thin veneer of time away from his body like the fragile and worthless skin of an onion. He was a hole, a paradox, an impossible thing within which "past" and "present" held no meaning.

He had hurled himself into the crawlspaces of the universe, and his feeble existence had no meaning beyond the whims of the Eidolons.

Gwendolyn knew something was wrong the moment William rushed from the house with that damnable Marsh. But she hadn't realized just how terribly wrong things could go until she stepped into the garden and gazed up at a darkening sky. For that was as wrong as wrong could be.

But William was out there, somewhere, trying to stop this. She knew that as fully as she knew anything. And that gave her hope. She refused to panic.

She retreated into the house when the wind became a gale that tore at the hem of her dress. The Twins huddled together on a settee. Gwendolyn treated them with the most confident smile she could muster.

No, she wouldn't give in to fear. But it would be easier with William at her side.

Come back soon, my love.

Aubrey jerked awake. The newspaper slipped from his fingers to land on the rug beside his chair. He'd drowsed off again. He hadn't been able to concentrate since William's death. The doctors called it nervous fatigue.

Viola called his name. Her voice echoed through the great house. It wasn't like her to raise her voice.

Aubrey ran upstairs. He was panting heavily by the time he found her. She was in the largest of the guest bedrooms, standing before the window, carpet samples scattered on the floor behind her. She'd gone pale.

Viola pointed across the estate, toward the glade upstream of the manor. Or where the glade would have been, had it not been embedded in a roiling black fog.

Aubrey watched darkness spread across Bestwood. He wished, not for the first time, he'd leveled the glade and sold it to developers.

—And Marsh hit the floor with a *thump*.

"STOP!" Will's dying outburst echoed in his ears.

Marsh staggered to his feet, head spinning. He doubled over and swallowed down the urge to retch. The floor lurched at random, as though an Eidolon hovered nearby.

Somewhere close, somebody bellowed, "Oy! What are you smiling at, lassie?"

The voice was vaguely familiar, but Marsh couldn't place it.

He found his footing on the third try. The darkness had receded, but now the room was empty.

No. It was a different room.

This room had a window.

Where am I?

A window covered with blackout curtains.

The kind they'd used during the war.

When am I?

It started coming back to him: Gretel. The Soviets. The Eidolons. John.

A muffled scream sliced through Marsh's train of thought. A few moments later, he distinctly heard Will say, "My God. They've given you a name."

A rivulet of sweat trickled down Marsh's ribs.

"Son of a bitch," he whispered.

More voices. And footsteps. Coming down the corridor.

Can't fix anything if I get shot for a Jerry spy.

Marsh pushed the blackout curtains aside, praying the window wasn't painted shut. It wasn't. He eased it open, threw one leg over the ledge, then the other. He ducked under the sash and dropped into a hedge beneath the window. He pulled the window shut and crouched under the ledge.

The sun had set. The only light came from a faint orange glow in the western sky and the window behind him. The streetlamps were dark. Deep shadows stretched across St. James' Park.

Marsh recognized the view. He'd seen it countless times.

The blackout.

It was 1940.

Again.

epilogue

12 May 1940
Milkweed Headquarters, London, England

"Get up." Marsh took the girl by the elbow as Lorimer and Stephenson draped Will's arms over their shoulders and carried him out of the room.

What a fiasco. Will had lost a finger, and for what? They hadn't learned a damn thing about what the Jerries were doing at von Westarp's farm.

She paused, staring into the room where earlier Marsh had adjusted the blackout curtains. They had slipped aside again. Though it felt like the negotiation had gone on for days, it had lasted only long enough for the sun to set. Light spilled through the window onto Horse Guards Parade, and that was a violation of the blackout regulations.

Marsh pulled the prisoner aside and fixed the curtains. He took her elbow again.

"Ah," she said, smiling.

Marsh frowned. "What?"

"It worked."